The King's Bastard

ROWENA CORY DANIELLS

The King's Bastard

BOOK ONE OF THE CHRONICLES
OF KING ROLEN'S KIN

SOLARIS

First published 2010 by Solaris
an imprint of Rebellion Publishing Ltd,
Riverside House, Osney Mead,
Oxford, OX1 0ES, UK

www.solarisbooks.com

ISBN: 978 1 907519 00 0

10 9 8 7 6 5 4 3 2

A CIP catalogue record for this book is available from the
British Library.

Designed & typeset by Rebellion Publishing
Printed in the UK

I have been working on *The Chronicles of King Rolen's Kin* for a long time and many people have helped along the way. I must thank Chris McMahon and Lyn Uhlmann for their feedback, when we used to be the Thursday Critiquers. And I must thank the ROR writing group, Marianne de Pierres, Maxine McArthur, Tansy Rayner Roberts, Margo Lanagan, Trent Jamieson, Richard Harland and Dirk Flinthart for their support and advice. May we have many more ROR weekends of good wine, good food and in-depth writing craft discussion!

I'd like to thank my agent, John Jarrold, for taking a chance on an unknown author from Australia. And I'd like to thank my editor, Jonathan Oliver, for making me look a lot more intelligent and well informed than I really am. And a big thank you to Jennifer Fallon, Trudi Canavan and Karen Miller for their support of a fellow Aussie fantasy author.

And last of all my six children and my husband, for putting up with a mother and a wife who is always writing.

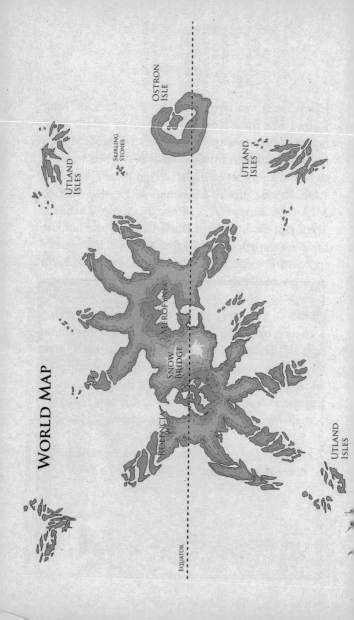

ROLENCIA

NEARLY THREE HUNDRED YEARS AGO, WARLORD ROLENCE MARCHED OVER FOENIX PASS AND CONQUERED THE RICH VALLEY, DEFEATING THE BICKERING CHIEFTAINS. HE NAMED HIS NEW KINGDOM ROLENCIA AND DECLARED HIMSELF KING ROLENCE THE FIRST, CLAIMING THE VALLEY FOR HIS CHILDREN AND HIS CHILDREN'S CHILDREN.

BUT HOLDING A KINGDOM IS HARDER THAN CONQUER-ING IT. NO SOONER HAD KING ROLENCE MADE HIS CLAIM, THAN KING SEFON THE SECOND OF MEROFYN SET SAIL TO PUT DOWN THIS UPSTART WARLORD. BEFORE THE WAR-LORDS OF HIS OWN SPARS COULD GET IDEAS ABOVE THEIR STATION.

MEANWHILE THE MERCHANTS OF OSTRON ISLE TRADED WITH BOTH KINGDOMS, GROWING RICHER, WHILE THE UTLAND RAIDERS PREYED ON EVERYONE, INCLUDING EACH OTHER.

☐ SEA/LAKES

▨ ARABLE LAND

▨ FOOT HILLS

▨ MOUNTAINS

DETAIL OF ROLENCIA

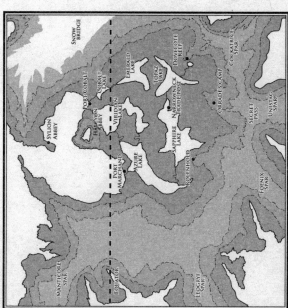

DISTANCE FROM ROLENHOLD TO DOVECOTE APPROX 50 MILES AS THE CROW FLIES

Chapter One

Rolencia, near Midwinter's Day

BYREN WENT FIRST, hoping to spot the Affinity beast's tracks so he could judge its size and the danger to his men. Despite the clumsy snow shoes, he ploughed on. Cold air stung his nostrils and the drifts lay deep with a crust of crisp ice crystals, glinting in the rays of the setting sun. Ah, how he loved Rolencia!

When he reached the rim of a small, treeless hollow, he searched for signs of the beast. No tracks in the smooth white snow. And they hadn't had a fall since dusk, last night.

'Slow down, Byren. Lence isn't with us this time,' Orrade called, short of breath despite the reserves of strength in his wiry frame.

Byren grinned ruefully. For as long as he could remember, he'd pushed himself to challenge Lence, but his twin had remained at the castle to welcome the

Merofynian ambassador. Byren did not envy Lence. As kingsheir, his twin had to marry to consolidate Rolencia's alliance with Merofynia. While Byren...

Orrade joined him, sucking in deep breaths.

To give the others time to catch up, Byren studied the bluffs and ridges of the Dividing Mountains which formed a barrier between the rich Rolencian valley kingdom and the savage spars. Familiar peaks told him they weren't far from the border of Dovecote estate. Why, if he climbed a tree and looked east, he could probably spot the nearest warning tower looming over the snow-shrouded forest and fields.

What was Elina doing right now? Last spring he'd caught her in the cold-cellar and demanded a kiss. She'd promptly clipped him over the head with a frozen ham, almost knocking him out. Moaning convincingly, he'd let her put fresh mountain ice on the bruise. Her contrite sympathy was better than any kiss. He smiled to himself. Back in Rolencia's war-torn past she would have made a fine warrior's wife.

'Say, Orrie, when our work's done here do you want to go down to Dovecote and visit your father?'

'Visit Elina, you mean.'

Byren chuckled and went to move, but Orrade stopped him. His friend's sharp, dark eyes surveyed the hollow, and his black brows drew together to form a single line of worry.

'What?'

'Don't know.' Orrade spoke slowly. 'Something's not right.'

Byren studied the trees lining the rim. Mostly evergreens, their skirts were mantled with snow and could easily hide the beast they sought. The size of a large wolf, with the markings of a leopard, lincis were rarely sighted this close to habitation. All Affinity beasts were dangerous but a lone predator was not a great threat for a party of armed men like his. And it was a lincis the villagers had reported, not a manticore pride or a fearsome leogryf. 'Could it be the beastie?'

'Don't know... nearly midwinter so the walls between the Seen and Unseen are at their weakest.' Orrade shrugged. Byren reached for his bow, but Orrade gave himself a shake and grimaced. 'No sign of the beast and I don't have Affinity, yet –'

'Byren Kingson?' The village's Affinity warder caught up with them, red-faced and insistent.

'Monk Hedgerow,' Byren greeted him, then had to wait while the man bent double, gasping. He had seen the monk ordering the villagers about, insisting on the best of the harvest for himself. No wonder he'd grown so plump in just one summer. Halcyon's monks were renowned for their fighting skills but this one would be useless if the warlord of Cockatrice Spar sent raiders over the pass, or if they met up with the beast. Byren began to regret not bringing the village's healer as well. She had looked lean and eager, despite having seen sixty winters. Consideration for the nun's age had stopped him; that and the thought of them bickering. Rivalry between the monks of Halcyon and nuns of Sylion went as deep as the rift between summer and winter.

'So where did they see this lincis, Hedgerow?' Byren prompted.

'Not far from here,' the monk said, and frowned. 'Why haven't you strung your bows?'

Orrade raised his eyebrows, and Byren shrugged. 'There's been no sign of tracks. It could be hours before we sight the beast, if at all.'

When the monk looked blank, Orrade added, 'If we leave the bows strung, the strings will lose tension. They'd be useless when we needed them.'

The monk seemed unconvinced, but gave an ingratiating bow. 'Kingson, I ask a boon. I shouldn't be serving a rural village whose only claim to fame is discovering a tin mine by accident. I'm a scholar, not a dirt grubber. You will be seeing the mystics master this midwinter. Can you mention my name to him? I've written five times asking to be transferred back to the abbey but my messages must be going astray.'

Byren was careful not to catch Orrade's eye. If the monks back at Halcyon Abbey found Hedgerow as annoying as they did, it was not surprising his requests had been ignored.

'I can mention your name, but that's not why I'm here, you know.' No, he'd been diverted from his true purpose by the report of the lincis sighting. Originally, he had been sent to escort the Royal Ingeniator to see if it was possible to link the village to the canal network so they could transport their tin. After three hundred years of rule, his family had linked the great lakes of Rolencia with a clever network of canals that made trade so much easier. Despite its longer pedigree and its claim to a higher culture, Merofynia had nothing to compare with Rolencia's canals.

'Just remember me to Master Catillum, that's all I ask, kingson. Please?' The monk fixed slightly protuberant eyes on Byren until he nodded.

Satisfied, Hedgerow set off down the slope only to stumble over his snow shoes, sliding down into the base of the hollow amid a rush of loose snow.

'Freezing Sylion!' The monk screeched.

'That should scare off the lincis,' Orrade muttered.

'Well, we wanted to either scare it or kill it. Come on.' Byren ploughed down after the monk, who was dusting snow off his goatskin cloak. Orrade followed, muttering under his breath.

'What's wrong?' young Chandler yelled from the rim of the hollow as the others joined him.

'Keep your voice down,' Byren warned. 'You don't want to scare off the little beastie.'

They laughed, all bravado. Byren smiled grimly. Five years ago he'd been just like them, an untried warrior of fifteen, desperate to prove his worth. Today he led a hunting party of half a dozen armed men, more than enough to tackle a lincis. The last thing he wanted was to return to the castle bearing someone's dead brother or son. But five of his warriors were the inexperienced younger sons of rich merchants and Rolencian lords, eager to distinguish themselves. Even though Byren's task was only to escort the Royal Ingeniator, they'd volunteered hoping for a run-in with warlord raiders or Affinity beasts. When the Affinity warder revealed the reported sighting of a lincis, Byren had thought it the perfect chance to give the youths some experience without too much risk. But, with the racket Monk Hedgerow was making, they'd be disappointed.

Byren and Orrade reached the monk in the hollow. 'So which way is it?' Byren asked Hedgerow.

The monk lifted his hands to his face, sniffed, and drew back, his lips twisting with revulsion. He flicked the snow away convulsively and began tapping on his eyelids, ears, mouth and chest while muttering under his breath.

'What now?' Orrade asked, scooping up a handful of the white, powdery snow. He sniffed, frowned, then thrust the snow towards the monk. 'I don't smell anything. What's wrong with it?'

Hedgerow stumbled back a step, tripped and fell into a drift so deep that only his legs protruded, thrashing about.

Byren was tempted to leave him there.

Orrade read his expression and grinned, then flung the snow away, dusted off his palms reached into the drift to grab one of the monk's arms. 'Come on.'

Together they hauled Hedgerow to his feet.

'It's a new seep. Affinity seep!' the monk whimpered.

Byren's amusement died. A seep would attract all manner of Affinity beasts. God-touched, they ranged from the bizarre to the deadly. 'Where –'

'Everywhere. The hollow's full of it!' Hedgerow gestured widely, then winced and ducked as if assaulted by screeching birds. His began to shiver. 'Probably triggered by digging the tin mine. You can't t–take from the land without paying Halcyon her due. I warned them but they wouldn't listen. Blame Sylion's nun. It's all *her* fault, now it's t–too late...' His teeth chattered and he slumped.

Byren shook him, waited for the monk to focus on his face, and said, 'you're an Affinity warder. You've been trained to contain –'

'This is seeping up from Halcyon herself. I need help. It's too powerful!' Hedgerow glanced around frantically. 'Besides, I don't have any sorbt stones. We'll have to go back and send –'

'We can't leave it uncontained. It'll contaminate the land,' Byren decided. He feared Affinity as much as the next man, but he knew his duty. After nothing for twenty years, this was the third Affinity seep reported since spring. And he'd led his men right into it. Sylion take this useless monk. 'Untamed Affinity will attract the beasts. It probably drew the lincis –'

'I tell you, I can't do this alone. I'm not very good. I barely passed my tests,' Hedgerow confessed in desperation. 'You don't know what you're asking.'

'I'm asking you to do your job. The villagers have been housing and feeding you just in case something like this happened,' Byren snapped, sickened. 'At least get your wards out, say your chants and contain it until we can locate the stones.'

They would have to send to Halcyon Abbey and that would take several days. The monk's mouth dropped open to reveal uneven bottom teeth. He blinked once.

Byren stepped back. 'Get to work.'

Hedgerow turned and ran. He made for a lightning blasted tree, fleeing Byren and his men, who stood watching from the rim.

Before anyone could move, the lincis, all muscle and dappled silver fur, charged from behind the dead tree, leapt for the monk and brought him down. Man and beast rolled, ploughing through the snow towards Byren and Orrade.

The five untried youths just stood and stared.

Only Winterfall plucked his bow from his back and began to string it.

Too close for the bow, Byren drew his spear. Aware of Orrade following suit at his side, he lunged, aiming to drive the point in behind the beast's neck. But the lincis was all sinuous movement and the spear skidded across its back, into its flank.

The lincis screamed at Byren, sounding more cat than wolf. Bright red blood soaked through its beautiful fur and its writhing wrenched the spear from Byren's hands, leaving him unarmed.

Without hesitation, Orrade stepped between him and the beast, lowering his own spear to make himself more of a target. 'Over here, beastie.'

'Save the kingson!' Winterfall yelled, letting his arrow fly and beckoning the youths, who recovered and ran down into the hollow towards the beast, shouting a challenge. The arrow overshot the beast. Always a danger when shooting downhill.

The lincis screamed again, whirling to face its new attackers. Too eager, young Chandler was out in front. The beast reared up on its hind legs, standing taller than him. Chandler fumbled his spear, trying to bring it up. The lincis swiped at him, sending him flying into a drift. Two fifteen-year-olds froze as it turned on them.

'Don't run!' Byren yelled.

But they did, with the lincis only a body length behind them.

Byren cursed, plucked the spear from Orrade's hand and threw it in one move. The spear took the lincis in the back, just off centre. The beast staggered.

Winterfall darted in, spearing it through the side. It rolled away, taking his weapon with it.

'Now!' Orrade yelled. Retrieving Byren's fallen spear, he led the attack. Heartened, the youths darted in, containing the wounded beast but careful to keep out of range of its thrashing claws.

Byren ran around the far side to drag Chandler to safety. The lad struggled to stand, holding his arm to his chest, face pale with shock and pain. Broken collar bone, Byren guessed.

Chandler managed a sickly smile and jerked his head towards the beast. 'Another Affinity kill, kingson. We've made Rolencia that much safer!'

'True. But next time attack as a team. With your bows, you could have picked it off from up on the rim.'

Chandler nodded, tears of pain making his eyes glitter.

Byren squeezed his good shoulder. 'You should have seen me the first time I faced a leogryf. Nearly pissed myself!'

Chandler laughed.

Byren frowned. Why had the beast leapt on Hedgerow? With eight armed men it didn't stand a chance – shouldn't have, if the youths hadn't panicked, Byren amended.

The lincis screamed in defiance, but it was weakening. As his warriors closed in Byren almost felt sorry for it.

'It's over,' he told Chandler. 'Come on. We'd better see if Hedgerow will live to complain another day.' He helped the youth down the slope then knelt to check on the monk, who lay in the churned snow covered in blood.

'I told you it was too much.' Hedgerow struggled

to speak between ragged breaths. 'No one listens to me. Now we'll have to send for another Affinity warder. The abbey will have to send a pair of stones to absorb the Affinity. Until then only a trained warder must come near the seep. Warn the village.'

'I will. But first we'll get you back safe,' Byren told him. 'Can you stand?'

'I don't know.'

Sliding his arm under the small man, Byren tried to help him up. Hedgerow gasped and passed out. Suspecting broken ribs, Byren let him slump on the snow.

'The nun's a good healer, I hear,' Orrade said, as he returned.

Byren nodded grimly. She'd need to be.

Straightening up, he looked around. His men had cut the beast's throat and were retrieving their weapons, preparing to string the body from two spears strapped together to support its weight.

'Eh, leave the lincis. You'll need to make a stretcher for Hedgerow.' Byren took off his own cloak and tossed it to Winterfall, who caught it and began devising a stretcher. Byren joined him but did not interfere. As he suspected, being the eldest son of a lord whose estate was in the foothills of the Dividing Range, Winterfall was used to dealing with injured men who'd seen the worst of beasts or raiders.

Judging him capable, Byren advised, 'Strap Chandler's arm to his chest. It'll make it easier for him to walk.'

Winterfall nodded.

Orrade caught Byren's eye with a look of sympathy.

Suddenly angry with himself, Byren turned away, moving towards the lightning-blasted tree. This should never have happened. At least Chandler would live, as for the monk... Byren leant against the dead tree. He'd let his dislike of the man colour his judgement. Perhaps the seep was too powerful for Hedgerow to contain. Perhaps he was not a lazy coward after all.

Byren's fingers brushed across parallel gouges in the trunk's satiny bark. He fixed on them, his memory nudging him, until recognition hit him with an odd little kick of satisfaction. The gouges were lincis territory markers. So that was why the beast had attacked.

Fiercely territorial, lincis marked their region by clawing tree trunks and leaving a spray of special urine which solidified, forming flame-coloured stones called lincuriums. The stones that formed in the depths of icy winter were renowned for their beauty. Occasionally a hunter would find some and make his fortune selling them to a renegade Power-worker.

Byren wanted the stones, hopefully a matching pair to set on rings for his parents. The thought of his mother's surprised delight made him smile. As a king's daughter from Merofynia, she had given up much to marry his father for the sake of peace. For their twenty-first wedding anniversary this spring cusp, they planned a grand Jubilee. He'd wanted to give them a special gift. Even better, lincurium were so rare that there was no chance Lence could get his hands on anything to equal the stones!

'You all right, Byren?' Orrade asked.

'Never better.' Byren straightened up, containing his excitement.

'We're ready, Byren Kingson,' Winterfall reported.

'Good.' He glanced to the sky then went down to join his men. 'Nearly dark, but there'll be no clouds tonight. If you leave now and walk by starlight you'll reach the village come midnight. Orrie and I will be right behind you. We'll bring the lincis in. Tell the headcouple no one is to come this way until the seep's been contained. They'll have to send for at least one pair of sorbt stones and another warder. The healer can advise them.'

Winterfall nodded. 'Chandler can manage on his own. With four to carry the stretcher and one to spell them we'll make good time. Are you sure you want to bring the lincis now? We can come back for it.'

'If we leave the body scavengers might get it and I've a hankering for a lincis fur coat,' Byren said, deciding he might just have one made up for Lence. It was the sort of finery that would appeal to his twin.

Winterfall nodded, then turned to the others. 'Right. If you want a hot meal and a warm bed tonight, get your backs into it.'

As they lifted the stretcher Hedgerow groaned and Byren wondered how long before he began haranguing them. Chandler picked up his spear to use as a staff. Winterfall took the rest of the spears, leaving two for Byren and Orrade to string the lincis from.

Orrade said nothing until they were out of hearing beyond the rim, then he swung around to face Byren.

'A hankering for a lincis coat?' He snorted, thin face animated. 'What are you up to?'

Byren grinned. 'This way.'

Orrade followed him back up the slope to the lightning-blasted tree. Byren pointed to the scratch marks.

Orrade frowned. 'Could it be...'

'It is. Lincis bury their territory markers so that only their own kind can sense them,' Byren whispered. 'Then they mark the surrounding trees like this. That's why the beastie attacked.'

Orrade nodded slowly. 'I don't see why you didn't say something when you first spotted the signs. We had the others to back us up then.'

'Because I don't want Lence to hear about it.'

Orrade said nothing.

Byren grinned.

'No good will come of baiting Lence, Byren.'

He laughed, leant his bow against the far side of the tree and dropped to his knees in the snow.

Orrade leant against the trunk, arms folded across his chest. 'Do you really intend to bring the lincis back with us? It'll be a struggle. Not that I'm complaining, mind you.'

Byren didn't answer, intent on digging. He used his hunting knife, the blade as long as his forearm, to break the crust and loosen the snow. Then he gripped the fingertips of his right glove in his teeth and tore it off, plunging his hand into the snow to feel for the hard, round lincurium.

'Any luck?' Orrade asked.

The cold burnt his fingers but he persevered, searching partly by touch, partly by sight in the rapidly fading light.

'Ha!' He pulled up three stones, one large and two smaller. Turning his hand over, he brushed snow off their glistening red-gold surface. Byren wanted nothing more than to light a fire and hold them to the flame to see if these were the finest winter-crystallines.

Orrade whistled softly, dropping to his haunches. 'Three lincurium. What a haul!'

'I'll get the two smaller ones set on matching rings for my parents. As for the larger...' Byren visualised it set on a simple chain. It would make an exquisite pendant. Exactly the right gift for his brother's betrothed. What would she be like, this daughter of the cunning Merofynian king, who had usurped his mother's brother? As cunning as her father, no doubt. As his old nurse would say, *the apple never falls far from the tree.*

Poor Lence, forced to marry –

'Byren,' Orrade warned softly.

A low growl sounded behind him. It was so deep it seemed to vibrate through Byren's body, setting his teeth on edge. He looked over his shoulder, catching sight of a juvenile lincis. It stood over the body of its mother. Not much smaller than her, it was probably due to strike out on its own come spring.

Kneeling in the snow like this, Byren felt vulnerable but he was not afraid. Two full-grown men could frighten off a lone, inexperienced lincis. If only he had collected the spears before heading back to the tree. The lincis was between him and the weapons.

Orrade came to his full height. Moving smoothly so as not to startle the beast, he slid his bow from his back and bent to string it.

Shoving the stones into his belt pouch, Byren went to rise, turning to face the lincis at the same time. One snow shoe twisted, obstructing the other. Heart thudding, he struggled to free the snow shoe, snapping the thongs that held his right boot in place. Standing at last, he glanced up to check on the beast.

About two body lengths down the slope, the lincis confronted them, hackles raised. Oh, but it was a beauty. The silvery fur made it hard to see against the twilit snow. Lence would have killed it for its coat alone, but Byren was content with the stones.

Unfortunately the lincis was not. A low, warning rumble came from deep in its chest, making its muzzle pull back from its teeth.

Byren swore softly. Too late to put the lincurium back, too late to climb a tree, too late to do anything but bluff.

With the speed and economy of long practice, Orrade stepped in front of Byren, reaching behind his shoulder for an arrow. His arm hit one of the dead tree's low-hanging branches, triggering a fall of snow and a terrible screech as if the dead tree itself was protesting. Before Byren could yell a warning, a large branch split from the trunk. Byren watched it swing for Orrade, gathering momentum as it fell, striking the back of his head below his right ear with a sickening crunch. His friend toppled into the snow, pinned under the branch between Byren and the beast.

The lincis sprang back startled by the noise, but it grew bold when it smelt the fresh blood from Orrade's head wound.

Byren's mouth went dry with fear.

Instinct told him if he lowered his guard to collect his bow and string it the lincis would attack Orrade, so he raised his hunting knife, eyeing the beast. The knife was an in-close weapon. No one in their right mind would tackle a lincis with only a hunting knife but all he wanted to do was scare it.

He leaped over Orrade and the fallen branch, roaring.

It might have been enough but, as he landed, his right boot, with no snow shoe to cushion it, went through the crust. Combined weight and momentum drove his leg down into thigh-deep snow, toppling him sideways. Hard to look menacing, when his head was level with the beast's. At least he was between it and his unconscious friend.

Desperate, he shoved his right hand out to lever himself up, only his hand went through the fractured crust plunging his arm deep into the snow. His right cheek stung as it slammed into the ice crystals. Rearing up, he twisted about trying to get purchase.

Meanwhile, the lincis padded back and forth a little more than a body length from him, broad paws barely denting the snow's crust, as it prepared to attack.

Stupid! In a heartbeat the lincis would be on him, going for his throat and then Orrade would freeze to death, if the seep didn't attract some other beast to make a meal of him.

Taking the knife blade between his teeth, Byren lurched back, trying to scramble out of the hole he'd dug with his thrashing.

The beast yelped.

Byren looked up, startled, then stopped struggling to gape. The knife dropped from his mouth.

An old woman, draped in straggling furs, clipped the lincis over the nose with the end of her staff as if it was a greedy piglet. 'Pah. Be gone!'

Though it could have crushed her old bones with one blow, it whimpered and slunk off, tail between its legs.

'Thank the goddess!' Byren muttered.

Thwack.

The old woman's staff connected with his head. 'Thank me, not Halcyon. She gets more than enough credit!'

Byren grunted. With tears of pain stinging his eyes, he blinked and tried to focus on the old woman. Though she looked, and smelt, like she came from the savage Utland Isles, she'd spoken Rolencian with the accent of Merofynia and, besides, she was old enough to be his grandmother, so he owed her the veneration due her many winters. 'Forgive my –'

'Hisst. None of your mother's courtly airs, Byren Rolen Kingson, or should I say Byren Myrella Queenson?' Her clever black eyes fixed on him. 'Mark my words.' She dropped the staff and her body straightened, eyes rolling in her head until only the whites showed.

Byren sucked in his breath, teeth protesting at the sudden cold. He might not have Affinity, but he knew it when he saw it. She was a renegade Power-worker, outlawed by his father's royal decree. If discovered, banishment or death were her only choices.

The old woman lifted one arm to point at him, hand twisted with the bone-ache. He was pinned in the snow, helpless as a hare in a snare.

'Seven minutes younger than kingsheir, yet destined to be king. Blood, I see, your twin's blood on your hands –'

'No!' Byren shouted.

His cry broke her trance and she focused on him, eyes brilliantly black despite great age. Wheezing with the effort, she leant down to scoop up her staff, muttering. 'Pah. The boy thinks he knows better!'

Byren stiffened. He was no boy. He'd killed his first warrior at fifteen and he'd been leading raids against upstart warlords since he was seventeen.

Thwack.

The staff connected with his head.

'Hey!' he protested.

'Silence, and listen. *Boy* you are, and *boy* you'll be until you learn to lead your people along the right path. But what is right? Right by might? Right by law? Right by tradition? Or is right a matter of perception?'

He stared, unable to make sense of her babble. As if he couldn't tell right from wrong!

He shook himself. *First things first. Check on Orrade.*

Byren leant back, grabbed the fallen branch and, with a determined wrench, hauled himself out of the snow pit, then shoved the branch off his friend. Kneeling, he rolled Orrade over, hardly registering the broken bow. His friend was unconscious, barely breathing. Blood from his head wound stained the snow, appearing almost black in the gathering gloom, and a pale fluid leaked from his eyes and nostrils.

Byren's stomach clenched. He'd seen enough men die from head wounds to know the signs. That pale fluid was bad.

'Always the same. Won't listen, can't see,' the old seer muttered. 'Waste of breath. I'll be off then. No, don't thank me...' Still mumbling, she turned her back on him.

'Wait,' he cried. Those with Affinity could sometimes heal. 'What about Orrie? Can you help him?'

She tilted her head like a curious bird. 'Your own father has outlawed renegade Power-workers. Why ask me?'

Byren brushed this aside. 'He's dying. I can't let him die.'

Her wrinkled face creased with a mixture of malicious spite and delight.

'Please,' he whispered.

That surprised her.

She hunkered down in the snow next to him, placing one grimy, clawed hand on Orrade's forehead. Byren watched anxiously as she concentrated, seeming to turn her focus inward, for several heart beats.

'He'll linger for a day or two then die,' she announced.

'But you can prevent that?'

She studied him. 'He won't be the same –'

'Doesn't matter. Uh...' Byren reconsidered. Affinity was tricky and those with it, doubly so. 'Do you mean he won't have his wits? Orrade would hate that. He'd rather die.'

'Oh, he'll still be your friend. But there'll be consequences if I use Affinity to –'

'Sylion take the consequences. I can't let him die.'

'What will you give me?' she countered.

He stared at her, shocked.

Her eyes narrowed. 'Do you expect me to help you out of the goodness of my heart?'

He nodded. 'I would.'

She laughed, then shook her head. 'You have a long way to go before you're ready to rule Rolencia. But perhaps –'

'So you'll do it?' he asked, concentrating on what was important. 'You'll save him?'

'I'll try. Good spot for a healing, plenty of raw power.' She replaced her hand on Orrade's forehead and her eyes glazed over. Sweat appeared on her top lip, popping up between the sparse silver hairs. Byren could see the effort required for healing, but he felt nothing as time stretched. It went on long enough for him to get a cramp in his foot. He massaged it surreptitiously.

'There.' She grunted with relief, sitting back on her heels to catch her breath. 'He'll pull through. But you'll need to get him somewhere warm to recover, and he'll never be the same.'

'Thank you, thank you!' Byren grabbed her shoulders, planting a smacking kiss on her papery cheek.

She stared at him, stunned, then smiled like a young girl.

He laughed and turned back to Orrade. 'Orrie, can y'hear me? Orrie?'

No answer. But his friend was breathing easier and Byren was sure his cheeks were a better colour already. He swung back to thank the old woman. 'You've done it, he's –'

She'd gone.

Chapter Two

BYREN SAT UP on his heels, searching the hollow. No sign of the seer. In fact, with all the churned-up snow it was impossible to tell that she'd even been there. The dark must be playing tricks on his eyes but her disappearance had made things easier for him. If she had been an ordinary old woman, he would have been bound by the travellers' code to offer her shelter. Since she was a renegade Power-worker, he should have urged her to leave Rolencia.

He grinned. His instinctive fear of renegade Affinity had faded when she proved to be such a terrible seer. As if he'd ever turn on Lence!

She should have stuck to healing. Still smiling, he glanced down at Orrade. His friend was still out cold.

Too cold.

It would be ironic if Orrade caught a chest affliction and died despite the seer's help. Already the first bright stars winked above them in an oystershell sky, heralding a fine, extremely cold night. Byren checked Orrade's head wound, binding it with a strip of cloth. The wound had stopped bleeding, but there was too much fresh blood to stay here and, besides, the seep would draw Affinity beasts down from the Dividing Mountains.

Hastily, he rigged a strap for his broken snow shoe. If only the branch had struck Orrade a hand's breadth lower. Then it would have connected with his broad shoulders and done no more than knock him off his feet and maybe wind him. Bad luck.

Sylion's luck. But then it was nearly midwinter and that cold, cruel god had a firm grip on Rolencia.

He collected the spear, then took off his bow and arrow quiver, hefting Orrade onto his back. Now all he had to do was walk until he reached the village. He turned towards the rim where he could still see the passage of Winterfall's party on the silvery snow. Just as he set off, the deep ululating cry of an ulfr pack on the hunt echoed down from the bluffs behind the village. The direction suggested the pack were between him and safety.

'Freezing Sylion!' He adjusted Orrade's weight. The blood and the seep would attract the Affinity beasts. Ulfrs were related to timber wolves, though larger and more cunning than their mundane cousins.

Guilt lanced him, sharp as a blade. He shouldn't have delayed for the lincurium. Orrade must not suffer because of his stupid rivalry with Lence.

With its walls, the village would not need to fear the pack, and he trusted Winterfall had the sense not to send anyone out to help him until the seep was contained and the area made safe. This meant he was on his own, which made climbing a tree useless. He didn't want to be staked out by the pack. The further he went from the seep, the better. Affinity beasts hunted ordinary animals for food, but raw Affinity would draw them. Hopefully Affinity lust would win out over hunger. He had heard reports of the beasts rolling in a seep in a state of ecstasy, an image he found hard to visualise.

But which way should he go? If he travelled east he would be on Dovecote land. He cast his mind back to steamy summers when he and Orrade roamed the estate. He seemed to remember a fortified farmhouse near the foothills. If he walked all night he would get there by dawn.

Byren turned east.

Used to skating the winter canals, his long legs ate up the ground. Despite the cold he was soon sweating, and Orrade seemed to grow heavier with every step. His weapons became a burden but he could not discard them.

Later, when he heard the ulfr pack calling again, he glanced up to the stars and judged he had been walking for two hours. The echoes off the bluffs tended to confuse the source of sounds, but he could not fool himself.

The pack was following him. Their silver-grey winter coats would make them hard to spot, but he did not need to see them. He could tell by the extreme hush of the snow-shrouded forest that its winter inhabitants had gone to ground. The pack was near.

'Halcyon help me!' he muttered, calling on the goddess of healing and growing things. He would not reach the fortified farmhouse. He needed somewhere defensible. If he could just reach the ridge that marked Dovecote land.

Adjusting Orrade, he set off again.

Half an hour later, he felt the land rise under him and looked up. About two bow shots away he could see starry sky through the trunks.

Now to choose a spot and start a fire... pity he didn't have a male and female firestone. Once placed in contact with each other the stones produced a blaze which sustained itself until they were separated. But only the very wealthy could afford them and they were treasured family heirlooms.

No time for *if only*.

Byren plunged on. By the time he reached the edge of the ridge, the night was filled with the luminescence of stars. He gently lowered Orrade and tried to catch his breath as he surveyed their sanctuary.

Halcyon had favoured him, for he'd reached the ridge where it fell away into a steep ravine, too steep for the ulfrs to attack from that direction. This left him with a half-circle to defend. The wind had scoured the edge of the ridge, stripping it of all but slivers of snow caught in the crevices. Luckily there was no wind tonight to howl down the ravine and tear their fire to shreds, leeching the heat from their bodies.

He propped Orrade in a seated position against a knee-high boulder near the cliff edge, and laid the two spears across his knees so that it looked like he was dozing, with the spears at the ready. Then he strung the bow and left it leaning against the rock as well. It was the best he could do. He would have to leave his friend defenceless for a few moments while he collected fire wood. Byren prayed the ulfr pack didn't find Orrade before he got back and hopefully, if they did, his ploy would keep them at bay.

Despite his weariness, he set off at a run. In the depths of winter there was plenty of fallen dead wood and drifts of leaves which had been blown into hollows during autumn's storms. The trick was to find them under the snow. But he had spent many a day with the hunt-master and knew what to look for. He made three trips, starting a fire after the first. On the last one he selected a sturdy branch his own height and swung it menacingly because the pack were approaching, slinking from tree to tree. First one beast then another howled. Even safe by his own hearth, the sound would have been enough to make Byren's hackles rise. Out here, it made his stomach cramp with fear.

Byren returned to their camp, walking backwards so that he did not turn his back on the pack. He knew when he was getting nearer the camp because the leaping flames of their fire lit up the trunks of the winter-bare trees that grew along the ridge. When he reached Orrade, he found his friend still unconscious, but he must have moved because he had slumped dangerously close to the edge. Worse, he'd knocked the bow over the lip.

'Sylion's luck!' Byren muttered. Why hadn't he anticipated that? A surge of anger warmed him.

No point in berating himself.

Byren pulled Orrade away from the edge. Wrapping his friend's cloak more securely around him, he wedged Orrade's back against the boulder so he wouldn't roll towards the cliff. He didn't stir.

'Orrie?'

No answer, but the seer had promised he would live. It was up to Byren to make sure he had the chance.

'Melt some snow, heat some food,' he told himself. Somehow, he had to stay awake all night after trudging through the snow all day. As long as the fire held out they would be safe.

He hoped.

Byren glanced up. Stars filled the dark bowl above him with an effervescence of light. He would be able to tell the time by the progress of the wanderers, oddly coloured stars which travelled in erratic loops across the heavens.

Turning to face the night he checked on their enemies. Now and then he caught glimpses of fire-bright eyes reflecting back at him and knew the ulfrs waited, silent and grim for the first chink in their defences. Taking the large branch, he split the end and wedged his hunting knife's hilt in the gap, securing it. Tying off the cord, he used his teeth to be sure the knot was tight. The makeshift spear was not a thing of beauty but it was better than a hunting knife alone. It would be strongest driven straight on. The cord binding it to the branch would work loose with too many slashing strikes. Now he had three spears and all he had to do was keep watch.

He glanced at Orrade. 'Trust you to snore your way through the night, leaving all the watches for me.'

There was no answering snort or smart reply. Byren felt a stab of fear and guilt. If Orrade died old Lord Dovecote would be devastated and Elina would be heartbroken. His own heart sank for he had intended, once Lence's betrothal was announced, to tell Elina how he felt. The proud tilt of her chin came to him, making his body clench. How he wanted her.

He gripped the spear shaft and vowed he'd bring Orrade home safe and then he'd ask her. Have to get her a betrothal gift, something special. Perhaps he could give her the lincurium pendant. No, the wife of the kingson could not outshine the wife of the kingsheir. He had to give Lence's betrothed the pendant.

If he got through tonight – no, *when* he got through tonight, he would make his way to the fortified farmhouse, borrow a sled and take Orrade to Dovecote Keep.

Byren added another branch to the fire and imagined their arrival, the family rushing out to help carry Orrade inside, Lord Dovecote old and frail now, Elina concerned for her brother, grateful to him and Garzik... Byren winced. Fourteen-year-old Garzik adored his big brother. Garzik had been begging to go on raids with them for the last year.

They were all depending on Byren.

He stirred up the fire and watched the night.

Much later, the crack of a branch collapsing into the fire startled him. Byren woke with a jerk and sat up, dismayed to find the fire had burned dangerously low. Worse, a medium-sized ulfr was only three body lengths from him, creeping in low on its belly.

He leapt to his feet, snatched a brand from the fire and yelled to startle it. The beast spun on its haunches, retreating to the forest of bare trees.

A single large ulfr with a thick winter coat watched him unblinking from the tree line. It was bold enough not to retreat. He snatched a rock and hurled it. The ulfr sprang nimbly to one side, opened its jaws in a silent laugh then melted into the shadows. A moment later he heard it howl and the others answer.

He suspected he had just seen the pack leader. Like wolves, a male and female pair led each ulfr pack, dominating the others with their cunning and strength.

Byren felt shaky and sick as the surge of fear drained away, leaving him exhausted. He hadn't even realised he'd fallen asleep. Weariness still dulled his mind.

Concentrate.

Build up the fire.

'That you, Byren?'

Silently, he gave thanks to Halcyon and darted around the blaze to kneel next to Orrade. 'How d'you feel?'

'Wonderful!' he said, but his eyes were firmly closed and he frowned fiercely.

Byren grinned. 'No, really. How do you feel? You've been out for ages.'

'Head's thumping fit to burst. But I'll live.'

'Just as well. Elina would never forgive me if anything happened to you.'

Orrade chuckled, then moaned as even this hurt him. 'Where are we?' He pried open one eye then closed it again, the effort too much. 'What happened and how'd we get away from the lincis?'

For some reason Byren didn't want to mention the old seer. 'Drove it off, but a falling branch clipped the back of your head. You're lucky your skull's thick.' Best to keep him talking. 'We're trapped, Orrie. An ulfr pack have pinned us on the edge of a cliff.'

'Build a fire.'

Byren blinked. Orrade's face was in the shadow of Byren's body, but ruddy fire light gleamed on his friend's hands where they clutched the cloak to his chest.

Fear settled in the pit of Byren's belly. The old seer had said Orrade would never be the same. Had she meant he'd be blind?

Like a three-day-old kitten, Orrade forced his eyes open and peered around. 'No stars to aid us tonight, just when we could have done with –'

'Orrie, the stars are bright enough to cast shadows and, if I move, you'll feel the fire's heat on your face.'

Those sightless eyes travelled to his face, following the sound of his voice. It was uncanny, but he was still blind.

'Byren?'

He heard the fear in Orrade's voice, the unspoken *don't leave me*.

'I am going to get you out of this, then I am going to take you home. You hear me, Orrie?'

His friend said nothing.

'You hear me?' he repeated. 'I am not going to fail you.'

'I know,' Orrade whispered.

Byren licked dry lips then glanced back to the tree line where the ulfr pack watched and waited. He had made a promise, but he didn't know how he was going to save his friend.

Orrade shifted on the hard rock. 'Could you have found a more uncomfortable bed?'

Byren grinned. Thank Halcyon, there was nothing wrong with his friend's wits. They spoke of this and that. It was easier to stay awake with Orrade conscious. Even so the night dragged.

Not long after midnight, when Byren reached for more wood, he found their supply dangerously low. He tried not to stare into the flames and destroy his night vision while he rebuilt the fire, but he had to look at what he was doing.

'Byren?' Orrade whispered, waking from a doze.

'Who else?' he countered.

Orrade grinned weakly. 'How goes it?'

'Just building up the fire.'

'How's the wood holding out?'

Byren glanced to the depleted pile.

'That bad, eh?' Though Orrade could not see him, he seemed able to read Byren's silences. He lifted onto his elbow, then levered himself to a sitting position with obvious effort. Only the boulder at his back seemed to hold him up.

Byren rubbed his jaw, feeling the prickle of unshaven skin. 'I could venture out to gather more –'

'That would be madness.'

He was right.

'Then I'll bring the fire in closer.' Byren began adjusting the wood.

'You stand a better chance on your own,' Orrade said. 'Leave me.'

Byren didn't even bother to reply. He stretched what was left of their fuel in an arc and set it all alight. With the fire burning in a semi circle the wood would run out faster, but it meant he had a smaller area to defend. And, when the fire did burn out, the hot coals might slow the ulfrs.

Shading his eyes, Byren stared into the tree line. The leader was watching him again, waiting. The beast seemed to know he could afford to wait. Byren wished his bow was not at the bottom of the ravine.

'What do you see?' Orrade asked.

'Mangy, winter-starved ulfrs,' Byren lied. Taking the three spears across his knees, he crouched next to Orrade.

Time stretched.

'If I were truly brave I would roll off the edge and you could save yourself,' Orrade muttered, rising to his knees and crawling around the boulder, feeling with his hands for the lip of the ravine.

'Don't say that. Don't!' Byren jerked him back, holding him so tight he could feel Orrade's muscles trembling.

His friend protested and pulled away. The hollows under his high cheekbones starkly defined his grim face.

Byren felt frustrated, helpless. 'We're going to get out of this, Orrie.'

His friend nodded once, but it was clear he wasn't convinced.

For a long while they were silent and the fire burned on, while the wandering stars crawled with deliberate slowness across their allotted paths.

Eventually, Byren shifted, easing his muscles, preparing for the worst. The ulfrs had begun to close in, their eyes glowing beyond the fire's semi circle.

He lifted one of the good spears and picked his first target, the male that had nearly crept up on him before. The distance was too great for an average man to throw but Byren was not an average man. Silently, he thanked King Rolence the First, who had bequeathed his descendants with unusual height.

The ulfr watched him, watched his eyes, not the spear.

When Byren went to throw it crouched, presenting a smaller target. Sylion take it, the beasts were too clever.

Byren swallowed.

The massive pack leader padded out from the tree line, lifted its head to reveal white fur on its chest and gave voice to that dreaded howl. Fear prickled across Byren's skin.

The rest of the ulfrs echoed their leader.

In the moment that the first, smaller male was distracted, Byren threw his spear with all his strength and training. It took the beast high in the shoulder. The impact threw the ulfr off its feet as its howl became a whine of pain. The others ducked and whined as if in sympathy, slinking back to the trees.

'You got one!' Orrade struggled to his knees, adjusting the cloak.

'They'll attack again,' Byren warned. He crouched and felt for Orrade's shoulder, thrusting the makeshift spear into his hands. 'If any of them get past me, deal with them.'

'How? I won't know where they are until their jaws close on me!' Orrade's voice dropped and he tugged on Byren's arm drawing him closer still. 'I'm going to die but I don't care as long as you live. I want you to know that I love you. I've always loved you!' He smiled ruefully as if he could see Byren's startled expression. 'And you've only ever had eyes for my sister!'

'But... the girls we've shared –'

'Meant nothing.' Orrade reached into his vest and pulled out a chain. On the end swung the symbol of the archer. 'I have foresworn women just like Palos.' Palos was a semi-mythical warlord whose feats with the bow had not been matched since. He'd almost united Rolencia in a time before King Rolence. His exploits were legendary.

But it was the more recent return of Palos that people remembered. During the rule of Byren's grandfather, a group calling themselves the Servants of Palos had sought to overthrow King Byren the Fourth. Their treachery had weakened Rolencia, inviting invasion from Merofynia and ultimately to the deaths of Byren's grandfather and uncle. At barely eighteen Byren's father had become king and defeated the Merofynians. In the first years of his reign he hunted down the remaining Servants of Palos, executing every last one, no matter who they were.

'You can't be a Servant of Palos,' Byren protested. 'You're loyal to –'

'Of course I am. This has nothing to do with the Servants of Palos.'

'Then why wear that hated symbol?'

'Don't you see? Palos was a great warrior. His followers loved and respected him, even though he wàs a lover of men.' Orrade sat forwards, one hand reaching for Byren, who pulled back. 'Byren?'

He did not know what to say. Casting a quick glance over his shoulder, he made sure the ulfrs were not creeping up on them.

Orrade's hand dropped, his face bleak. 'You despise me.'

Byren stared. Orrade looked no different, but he was, and every moment they'd ever shared flashed through Byren's head, tainting their friendship. He fixed on the most recent thing. 'Why did you offer to come with me to hunt the lincis?'

'To keep you safe. The king's forest is a dangerous place, especially this close to midwinter.' Orrade shook his head. 'Then you went and saved me!'

And suddenly it didn't matter. He was still Orrade.

Byren frowned at the chain and its damning symbol, resting on Orrade's vest. 'You should take that bloody thing off and throw it away.'

'Pretend to be something I'm not?' Orrade countered, temper rising.

'If your father knew he would disown you!'

'I know. He never speaks my brother's name,' Orrade admitted.

When Lord Dovecote discovered his eldest son was a Servant of Palos, he had turned him over to the harsh justice of young King Rolen. 'But it doesn't matter now. I'm going to die and I cannot die with a lie on my lips.' His unseeing eyes searched for Byren. 'I –'

The heavy pad of fast approaching paws made Byren look up. An ulfr, large as a small pony, charged their position.

'Down.' He shoved Orrade flat, aimed and threw his last good spear in one movement. The beast staggered, skidding on its side in the snow. But another came in from the other direction.

Byren plucked the makeshift spear from Orrade's hands, wedged the end with his foot and took the impact of the beast's leap on the spear point, guiding it over them, out into the ravine. The ulfr's weight and momentum tore the spear from his hands, taking the weapon with it as it fell. The beast's whine of pain still hung on the air as Byren spun to face the rest of the pack, empty-handed but for his eating knife.

Across the remains of the flickering flames the pack leader gave voice to another howl. To Byren it sounded like an exultation of victory.

'Save yourself. I'll divert them,' Orrade urged, lurching to his feet. He shoved Byren to his knees and, blind and defenceless, stumbled through what was left of the fire, heading towards the ulfrs with a cry of challenge on his lips.

'No!' Byren sprang upright and charged after him, knowing he would be too late. Even as he ran an ulfr leapt for Orrade.

Thunk.

An arrow took it high in the ribs. The beast whined but still collided with Orrade, knocking him down.

Thunk... thunk. More arrows followed.

Stunned. Byren stared as arrows blossomed in grey-furred thighs and bellies. Beasts fell whimpering and yelping. Their leader stared at Byren and uttered a strange whine, and the rest turned tail, slinking into the trees, leaving at least six dead and the wounded trying to crawl after them.

'Orrade?' Byren ran to him, leaping over a dead ulfr.

Orrade was trying to roll out from under the body of the one that had brought him down. Byren dragged him clear.

'You still here, Byren? Thought I told you to run,' Orrade muttered. 'What happened?'

'I don't know. Halcyon sent help.'

'Byren? Orrade?' Garzik called, as he darted through the trunks, a hunting bow strung and notched with an arrow. Behind him came half a dozen warriors wearing the Dovecote crest, the feather and the sword. Unlike most of the lords, the thirty-year peace had not made Orrade's father disband his estate's defences.

'Garza!' Byren laughed. 'What're you doing here!'

Garzik grinned. Seeing no more targets he returned the arrow to the quiver and released the bowstring, slinging the bow over his shoulder. 'Hunting an ulfr pack that's been troubling our farms on the foothills.'

'The howls led us to you, Byren Kingson,' the old Dovecote captain explained as he approached.

'With not a moment to spare, Blackwing!' Byren confessed.

Garzik grinned. He was obviously Orrade's brother, with the same thin frame and wiry strength but, at fourteen, his cheeks were still rounded and showed no sign of sprouting a beard. 'Now, will you take me raiding with you, Byren?'

The captain caught Byren's eye, with an almost imperceptible shake of his head.

'Ask again this time next year,' Byren temporised.

Garzik went to argue, but the Dovecote captain overrode him, pointing to the estate's only remaining Affinity warder, old Wispowill, who was standing over a dead ulfr and making the signs. 'Go help the monk. He has to settle the ulfrs' Affinity, now that it's been released on their deaths. Then dispatch the wounded ulfrs, and retrieve the arrows.'

As Garzik went off, Captain Blackwing gestured to half a dozen warriors, boys like Garzik or men in their fifties and sixties. 'Look what I'm left with, babes or grandfathers. All the able young men have been lured away to the ports where trade with Merofynia and Ostron Isle has made the lucky ones rich as lords. What are you two doing here, Byren?'

'Long story. The ulfr pack got between us and the rest of my men.' That reminded Byren. 'Winterfall and the others are up at the village with the new tin mine. They expected us back tonight. If you take your men up that way the villagers will help you hunt out the pack and you can tell Winterfall we're safe. But beware the new seep.'

'Seep? That explains the ulfr pack. Wispowill can deal with a seep...' He broke off with a frown, as he spotted two fourteen-year-olds struggling with an ulfr carcass. 'Here, that's not the way to go about it!'

Byren watched him march off. They'd keep the skins, but the carcasses would be left for forest creatures to scavenge. No self-respecting person ate Affinity-touched meat.

While the others set to work skinning the beasts, Byren knelt next to Orrade. His hand slipped under his friend's vest to close over the symbol of Palos.

Orrade's hand caught his arm. 'Why…'

'I'm hiding it.' With a tug, Byren broke the chain, shoving the pendant into his pouch. 'You'll be stripped and cleaned for the healer.'

'How'd Orrie hurt his head?' Garzik said as he returned and dropped to his knees beside Byren. 'Was it raiders or beasts?'

'Nothing so exciting, a falling branch!' Orrade told him.

His brother's face fell.

Byren laughed. 'Help me get him home, Garza. But first, did you bring any food?'

'Of course –'

'Good,' Orrade muttered. 'I could do with a hot dinner.'

Byren grinned and stood up, hauling Orrade to his feet. His friend went to move, tripping over a dead ulfr. Garzik caught him, laughing. Then the laughter died on his lips, as Orrade's sightless eyes sought the source of his voice.

'Halcyon save us!' The boy turned to Byren. 'Orrie's blind!'

Hearing this, the Dovecote captain came over, his gaze going straight to Byren who lifted his hands helplessly.

'It was the blow to my head.' Orrade touched the lump behind his right ear gingerly. Below the hasty bandage, matted blood made his long black hair a tangled mess. 'When I came round I had a pounding headache and I couldn't see.'

Byren sought Blackwing's eyes, hoping the experienced campaigner could offer him some hope, but there was only sympathy in his gaze. Byren felt sick to his stomach.

Garzik's face went white. 'What will Father say?'

'He'll say he's glad his son's not dead!' Captain Blackwing told them. 'Then he'll call for his healer. Prepare some hot food, Garza.'

While the lad built a cooking fire, Blackwing took Byren aside. He glanced to the Dovecote brothers, who were crouched by the fire adding chunks of salted meat and spices to the pot. 'I can send a couple of men back with you –'

'You'll need every man you have until you get to the village. Garza and I can manage, we're heading away from danger.'

'Hmmm.' Blackwing considered this. 'We're not far from the Ridgetop Farm. They can loan you a horse and sled –'

'I can skate. I'm not useless.' Orrade raised his voice. 'If Byren leads me, I can skate.'

'Of course you can,' Byren said. He and Blackwing exchanged looks. 'Can we borrow skates from you?'

The canals followed the lie of the land, weaving through the valleys. In midwinter, they formed frozen roads between the major settlements.

'Certainly.' Blackwing studied Orrade, who had to feel around to find wood to feed the fire. The captain lowered his voice to a whisper. 'Are you sure you can manage, kingson?'

'We'll tie him between us.' Byren said. 'He'll be fine.'

And he was, for a while. They travelled overland, reaching Topaz Lake in the hour before dawn, and strapped on their skates. Fortunately for Byren, they were basic skates – a bladed sole, with straps – so he could tie them around his large boots. From Topaz they followed the shoreline, skating northeast to reach the canals, and wended their way south to Dovecote stronghold.

They were skating three across when Orrade lost his balance. He sprawled on his belly, taking them with him. They laughed and lay there panting on the ice which reflected the brilliant stars. Then Byren realised Orrade was the only one not laughing.

'You all right, Orrie?' he asked, scrambling over to him.

'Sorry.' His friend struggled to sit up. 'It's my head... thumping fit to burst.'

'Can you keep going?' Byren asked.

'Of course I can. I'd do anything for a warm bath and bed,' Orrade said, but his smile was strained.

Byren hauled him upright and they skated on.

The second time Orrade fell, skidding full length on the ice, Byren slewed his skates side-on and came to a stop before he was jerked off his feet. Garzik did likewise, looking to Byren.

'We can build a sled and pull him,' Byren answered his unspoken question.

When they bent to help Orrade, he reared up on his knees like a startled deer. 'Quick, off the canal. They're almost upon us!'

The panic in his voice made Byren spin around. He saw no one on the lake, but a bend obscured his view along the shore.

'Hide!' Orrade lunged, his movements taking him towards the bank by chance.

'What –' Garzik began.

'Help him,' Byren urged.

They guided Orrade to the bank, but that wasn't enough. He began to climb it. 'We have to get out of sight, over the lip and lie in the snow.'

'Why?' Garzik muttered.

Then Byren heard the unmistakable, almost silent scissoring sound of many skate blades on ice. He ploughed up the slope, dragging Orrade with him. They rolled over the lip of the bank, lying flat on the snow with Garzik between them.

Peering over the lip, Byren watched a band of thirty silent, armed warriors surge around the bend. They were travelling so fast that they went past in a matter of heartbeats, which was lucky because the frantic scramble up the slope had left tracks that led right to where Byren and the others hid.

'Raiders, but which warlord sent them?' Garzik muttered in the silence left by their passage. 'Rejulas of Cockatrice Spar is closest, yet they did not wear cockatrice cloaks or carry his symbol.'

'True, and why would he send a raiding party over the pass into Rolencia's valley when he could attack the easier prey in the high villages?' Byren wondered aloud. There were other reasons why Rejulas would not attack which he could not share with his friends just yet. 'Why travel at night in total silence when a raid is meant to be noisy and frightening?'

'Because this is no ordinary raid?' Garzik guessed. 'I wonder where they were going?'

'Or coming from. This close to dawn they should

be headed back over the Divide.' Byren whispered slowly. 'Orrie. What do you…'

He broke off. Garzik lifted onto his elbows as they both stared at Orrade's ominously still body.

'Orrie?' Byren rolled his friend onto his back and tore off his glove to check Orrade's pulse. It beat steadily under the pad of his fingers. 'Out cold again.'

'He saved our lives. They would have killed us quick as look at us,' Garzik whispered. 'How did he know they were coming?'

How indeed?

'Must have felt the vibration when he hit the ice,' Byren guessed.

Garzik nodded slowly, accepting this.

But Byren was not so sure. He feared Orrade's prescience was a by-product of the old seer's healing. Had his friend lost his sight only to gain Affinity sight?

Never trust untamed Affinity, the old saying came back to taunt him.

'Come on, Garza, I'll carry him on my back. He can't spend another night in the cold.' If they skated all day they'd reach Dovecote stronghold by early evening.

But Byren didn't need to carry him. Orrade recovered as Byren hauled him down the slope. Though groggy, he was able to skate, so they went on.

All day, as they passed gaps in the snow-shrouded evergreens, they caught glimpses of the distant warning tower, tallest of Dovecote's old stronghold towers. Built on the outcrop of a defensible ridge, Dovecote Keep protected the lands within a day's hard ride as well as the pass to Cockatrice Spar.

Anticipating the old lord and Elina's reaction, Byren was feeling the strain by the time they reached Doveton. Little more than a village, it was built at the base of the ridge next to a small lake which was linked by canals to the major lakes. Everyone had retired for the night. The Old Dove did not approve of drunkenness and loose morals so their one tavern was already closed. There was no locked gate to stop Byren entering the single main street. Unlike the fortified farmhouses this village did not have high walls and gates. The people expected to have enough warning to take shelter in Dovecote Keep.

'Doveton looks deserted. Half the houses have no lights in the windows,' Byren observed, slinging his borrowed skates over his shoulders.

'That's because most of the young people have gone to Rolenton and Port Marchand to make their fortunes,' Garzik said.

'And to get away from father's dour rule,' Orrade muttered. Now nearly eighty, the Old Dove had been a contemporary of King Byren the Fourth. He'd outlived two wives and four sons. All his hopes rested on his heir, Orrade. Byren felt the weight of this.

'Come on,' Orrade muttered. 'Might as well get this over with.'

Garzik looked to Byren but there was nothing he could say so they trudged up the slope towards the lights of New Dovecote. Old Dovecote had been built and added to over the three hundred years since King Rolence united the valley people. It was dark and draughty and the plumbing was terrible.

Since the peace with Merofynia the great lords

had all built themselves modern residences and Lord Dovecote was no exception. New Dovecote sprawled on the ridge below the old stronghold. With its large windows, parquetry floors, gracious rooms and hot running water from cisterns on each floor, it was considered as fine as any Merofynian palace.

The original dovecote, which the estate had been named after, had been moved into the new great hall. Its ornate cage boasted doves bred for their beauty. Their frothy tails and plumes made them works of art. From New Dovecote's great hall double doors overlooked a terrace. On a fine day you could see Rolenhold. In pride of place two great royal foenix bronzes stood guard, one to each side of the doors. They'd been gifted to Lord Dovecote by King Byren the Fourth, in gratitude for his support quelling the spar warlords' uprising fifty years ago.

New Dovecote was not defensible but the old lord had maintained his original stronghold so that the family, their retainers and the townsfolk could all retreat to it if threatened.

Usually Byren would have gone around the back to the courtyard and entered through the kitchen. This place had been a second home to him while he was growing up. Tonight he headed straight for the double doors, too exhausted to delay. As they stepped onto the terrace he noticed the glow of a lamp in the window of Elina's ground-floor study. On second thoughts, he did not want to rouse the servants to answer the main doors. The commotion would drag the frail old lord out of bed and might trigger another brain spasm. Last spring the Old

Dove had suffered a spasm which left one side of his face and his left arm useless. Elina could let them in and she would know how to handle her father.

'Wait here.' Byren went over to the window and peered in. There she was, poring over the papers spread across her cedar desk, imported from Ostron Isle. Either she was checking the estate's accounts, or she was writing the history of the last Merofynian War. Byren had no trouble admitting Elina's scholarship surpassed his.

Her midnight hair and moon-pale skin gleamed in the lamplight. She was beautiful, with her wide cheekbones and tilted black eyes, but it was her expression of intense concentration that made Byren smile. He pulled off his glove and tapped his nails on the nearest square pane.

Elina looked up, frowning, then smiled and pushed back her chair, running over to unlatch the window.

Byren stepped back as it swung open, then he stepped in towards her as a rush of warm air caressed his face.

'Byren? What are you doing here? I did not expect to see you until the midwinter ceremony.'

He smiled despite himself, then sobered. 'I've bad news, Lina. Orrie's been hurt.'

She glanced past him to her brothers standing on the terrace. The taller leaned on the shorter. 'He's walking. Can't be too bad. Come around to the stable yard door.'

Without giving Byren a chance to explain, she swung the window shut, latched it and ran off taking the lamp with her.

Byren returned to the others. 'Elina's going to let

us in the stable yard door. Don't want to give your father a shock.'

Orrade and Garzik nodded. They went along the terrace which wrapped around the building. At the rear, modern stables had been built to house the Old Dove's prize horses. A much-used door opened from the house to the stable yards and it swung open now as Elina appeared with a lamp turned down low.

'Come in, quickly. I'll clean Orrie up and see if we need to wake the healer. Better come up to my chamber.'

She ushered them in, leading the way through the storage rooms and into the kitchen where half a dozen kitchen children, no older than ten, slept in a huddle in front of the ovens.

Lifting one finger to her lips she beckoned Byren and her brothers.

One child raised his head, a sleepy query on his lips.

'It's nothing, Rifkin, go back to sleep,' she told him.

Without waiting to see if Byren and the others followed, she slipped out of the kitchen and into the corridor which led to the public rooms.

This end of the building housed the library and music room, both Merofynian affectations. The family's bed chambers were on the floor above and servants slept in the attics. Elina headed straight for the private family stairs.

They had just reached the halfway landing when they met with the Old Dove coming down in his night shirt with a single candle.

'F-father,' Elina greeted him.

Chapter Three

THE FIERCE OLD lord raised his candle, straining to identify them with his failing sight.

'I see my wild boy's hurt himself.' Lord Dovecote spoke slowly to conquer the slight slurring caused by the brain spasm which had slowed him down, though no one could say he had lost his wits. 'What have you been up to, Orrie? And you, Byren. I suppose you and Lence are to blame for this. As for you, Garza, I seem to recall sending you off under Captain Blackwing's care. What're you doing back already? No ulfr pelts?'

'We found the pack attacking Byren and Orrade,' Garzik explained. 'If we hadn't –'

'Stories later,' Elina announced firmly, reminding Byren of the Old Dove. She glided up the stairs to take her father's arm. 'Orrade's bumped his head, father. I'm just going to clean –'

'I'm blind,' Orrade announced in a flat voice.

The good side of the old lord's face drooped to match the paralysed side.

'What?' Elina whispered, then rallied. 'I'll send for the healer, she –'

'There's nothing she can do, Elina. I'm blind,' Orrade snapped.

Elina ran down the two steps to search his eyes for any sign of response and, finding none, sent a stricken look to Byren. His heart contracted.

Her gaze returned to her brother. 'Oh, Orrie...'

'Blind?' Lord Dovecote echoed, coming down the steps.

Orrade looked towards the sound of his father's voice. 'I took a blow to the head. I've been like this since I woke up.'

Lord Dovecote's step faltered and he almost stumbled. Byren grabbed his arm and felt him tremble with shock. Garzik ran to take his father's other arm. For once the fierce old man did not brush them off.

'We can have Willowtea take a look. Can't we, father? She's an excellent healer,' Elina insisted, her tone bracing. 'Come, Orrie, let me clean you up.'

Orrade held out his hand. 'You'll have to lead me.'

Elina caught Orrade's hand in her own and led him up the steps. Byren followed slowly. Lord Dovecote gripped his arm as he mount the steps, his age suddenly showing.

'I'm sorry, grandfather.' the term was an honorific. 'He nearly died. I just wanted to get him home.'

Lord Dovecote squeezed his arm. 'Garzik, go fetch the nun. We'll be in your brother's room.'

He nodded and ran off.

'So Willowtea's still dispensing infusions?' Byren asked.

The old lord nodded. An estate the size of Dovecote could have had a healer from both abbeys, just as they could have had two Affinity warders, but their healing monk had died of old age two years ago and Lord Dovecote hadn't asked for a replacement. Byren suspected he was comfortable with nun Willowtea, who was almost as old as him, and couldn't be bothered with an ambitious young monk.

Elina bustled about the chamber, lighting lamps, sending Byren to fetch hot water from the spigot at the end of the hall. When he returned, she had settled Orrade in the chair by the fire and unwound Byren's hasty bandage

The sight of the ugly wound made Elina wince, but she began to sponge the blood from around it, picking long strands of matted hair out of the way.

She had cleaned the area by the time the healer arrived. Byren watched the old nun check the wound, then test Orrade's sight by holding a candle in front of him, trying to detect movement or response to light.

One of Sylion's nuns, the healer had been with the family since the lord brought home his first wife. Willowtea had helped with the births of their four children, seen them through their childhood illnesses, then laid out their crushed bodies when three of the sons were returned from the battlefield. The eldest, who had been executed as a Servant of Palos, had been buried in an unmarked grave. When the old lord's second wife had died giving birth to

Garzik, Willowtea had laid out her body. And now, after examining Orrade, there were tears in her eyes as she put the candle down, turning to them.

'You have Affinity, Willowtea, is there anything you can do?' Lord Dovecote asked.

'I can hasten healing, my lord, but I cannot change what will be,' Willowtea whispered. 'We will have to wait and see. He's been in contact with something odd –'

'Untamed Affinity,' Byren explained quickly. He didn't want to admit he'd pleaded with a renegade Power-worker to save Orrade's life. He would be tainted by association. 'There's a fresh seep up near the new tin mine.'

'That's the third in less than a year,' Elina whispered. 'The last time so many new seeps occurred was the summer the Servants of Palos tried to assassinate King Byren the Fourth.'

There was a moment's charged silence.

'Aye, seeps sprouted like sores on a diseased body that summer,' Willowtea whispered, then gave herself a shake and turned to Byren. 'So you stumbled into one?'

'While hunting a lincis. The seep was what attracted the ulfr pack down from the Divide.' Byren swung to face the old lord. 'That's where Captain Blackwing is, in the foothills, hunting down the pack.'

'Now is not the time for tales of hunting,' Elina announced. 'We need to get a clean bandage on Orrie and put him to bed.'

'What about some food? I'm starving,' Orrade insisted. 'I'm blind, not dead you know.'

Elina gave an unsteady laugh and glanced to the healer, who nodded.

'Garzik and I will raid the pantry,' Byren offered, hungry despite everything.

Twenty minutes later, he and Garzik came back upstairs with a plate of cold meat, cheese and a slice of fresh-baked apple pie for Orrade.

They found Elina sitting with him, a shawl around her shoulders. 'Father and Willowtea have gone to bed. I said I'd wait up with him.'

Byren put the tray on the chest next to Orrade's bed. 'Cold food but fresh.'

'I'm not complaining.' Orrade's fingers sought the plate. Byren had to stop himself from offering to help. No one spoke as Orrade found a slice of lamb roast and lifted it to his mouth.

'I'll sleep in here tonight,' Garzik announced. 'Orrie won't want his sister waiting on him.'

Elina smiled, then leant over the bed to brush her lips on Orrade's forehead. 'I'll be in first thing tomorrow.'

He nodded, feeling for the right end of the knife to cut the cheese. Byren found it painful to watch. He should have thought ahead and chopped it up. Not that Orrade would thank him for that.

'Sleep well, Orrie.' Byren opened the door for Elina and walked out into the hall with her. 'Where are the upstairs servants?'

'The old ones are asleep in the attics.' Elina's dark eyes twinkled, reflecting the candlelight. 'They snore so badly we do without their services in our bed chambers. As for the young ones...' Colour crept up her cheeks. 'Father has been laying down the law, saying who can marry who, that sort of thing. Why would they stay when they know they can work for wealthy merchant families who won't interfere with their lives and pay them twice as much?'

'It's the same everywhere,' Byren agreed. Though they didn't have those problems at Rolenhold because of his mother's tact. He opened the door to Elina's bedchamber. She slipped inside. It was cold and dark. He didn't want to leave her alone like this. 'I'll make up the fire for you.'

'Thank you.' She went to light the candle on the mantelpiece.

Her gasp surprised him and he looked up in time to see her suck her knuckle.

Springing to his feet, Byren caught her hand, turning it to the light. 'You're hurt?'

'It's nothing. A hot wax burn. Oh, Byren!' She bit back a sob.

He reached out to console her but she surprised him, running to the door, closing it so that no one would hear her cry. Resting her forehead on the door, she sobbed silently.

Byren couldn't stand it. He came up behind her, taking her shoulders in his hands, feeling her slender frame shake. She turned in his arms. Murmuring her name, he brushed the tears from her cheeks with the pads of his thumbs. He kissed her forehead, her closed lids, her wet cheeks.

And suddenly she was kissing him.

He didn't know how it happened but her skin felt so hot and her lips tasted salty. She strained against him, desperate for comfort.

From a great distance, one small part of his mind said, *Stop. This is not right. She doesn't want you. She wants to blot out the pain.*

He wanted to ignore it, but... gulping a breath, he lifted his head, forcing himself to pull back. She came after him.

He stepped aside and pulled the door open.

She stared at him, unable to understand, lips swollen with his kisses, eye lashes matted with tears.

He knew if he stayed one moment longer he was lost and he didn't want to make love with her in pain and desperation. Unable to speak, he stepped out into the hall, swinging the door closed behind him.

In the cold dark he dragged in ragged breaths, then felt his way along to the door of the chamber he and Lence always shared when they came to stay. Only a patch of starlight lit the nearest bed. He stumbled to it and threw himself on the covers. He could still smell her on his skin. His body ached for her. He'd never sleep.

HE WOKE THE next morning wondering why he felt terrible.

Then it all came back to him and, still dressed in the clothes of last night, he splashed water on his face then stepped into the familiar corridor where he had spent so many happy times as a child. His boots squeaked on the polished floor. The stained-glass window at the far end sent streamers of coloured light up the hallway. Lovely. But in case of attack they'd have to retreat to the stronghold where he, Lence and Orrade had played at being warriors with Elina running after them wanting to join in. How they used to tease her.

He smiled. They had all dreamed of being great heroes. Not much chance of that now, not with the alliance plans his father had set in motion.

Yet... those grim, silent raiders troubled him. The spar warlords swore allegiance to King Rolen, but they were always looking for a weakness to exploit. He'd have to mention the raiders to his father and find out where they'd struck.

A soft step made him turn. Seeing Elina, his heart lurched and his body clenched.

Elina blushed, the memory of last night obviously uppermost in her mind, too.

'Oh, Byren, you're awake. You look like you slept in your clothes.'

'I did.'

She blushed and glanced down into her apron, which she had folded up to carrying something. A tendril of long black hair had worked loose from her plait and it moved with each quick breath as if it had a life of its own. It fascinated Byren. He longed to lift it aside and take up where they had left off last night. He dare not move.

The silence stretched.

Then her apron gave a whimper and she laughed, opening its folds to show him three liver-coloured retrievers. They looked no more than two weeks old. The puppies squirmed over each other, eager and bright-eyed.

'Regal's had her pups so I'm bringing them for Orrade to see. I mean...' Her face crumpled, chin trembling as she closed her eyes, fighting tears.

Byren wanted to take her in his arms. He knew how she would feel and longed to explore the heat of her lips. With a start, he realised he wanted to do nothing more than hold her forever and protect her, yet he could not save her from the love she felt for her brother. Compelled to ease her pain, he opened his mouth but could think of nothing useful to say. So he remained silent, impotent.

She gave a muffled sound that was half sob, half laughter. 'Silly pups. They wriggle so, they'd take a tumble.'

'And fine pups they are, too,' he said, watching her face.

She smiled through her tears. 'Here, take the spotty one. He's the worst wriggler.'

Byren took the pup and she transferred the apron ends to one hand, using the other hand to wipe her face. She looked up at him, lashes damp with tears. 'Can you tell I've been crying? Not that Orrade will be able to see. Oh, Byren. I can't bear it. Father is devastated. I feared he'd have another brain spasm, when he found us on the stairs.'

Now was not the time to tell her how he felt and ask her to marry him.

She drew in a deep, shaky breath. 'I'm ready.'

They headed towards Orrade's chamber.

'Has the healer seen Orrie this morning?' he asked.

Elina nodded.

'What did she say?'

'The same, wait and see. I've been praying to Halcyon all night.' Her voice dropped as they approached the door. 'He's being so brave about it. I can't stand it.'

Byren grinned. 'That's Orrie for you.'

He opened the door, and Elina sailed in with a determined smile. 'Guess what I have, Orrie.'

Orrade lifted his head. He was sitting up in bed, a much neater bandage around his head. Someone had washed and combed his waist-length black hair, then braided it in one long plait which looked thinner than usual. Byren remembered Elina had clipped it at the back to clean the wound properly.

'And what do you have, Elina?' he asked.

'Go on, guess.'

Orrade rolled his sightless eyes towards his father and brother, who were on the far side of the bed. Unless you watched closely it was hard to tell that he was blind.

'Lord Dovecote.' Byren greeted him formally, out of respect. 'It is good to see you.'

'Byren Kingson.' The old lord acknowledged Byren with a half-bow. When Byren turned fifteen and became a man, the friendly cuff over the ear had become a formal greeting. He still missed it. But that was the Old Dove for you. Having fought beside Byren's grandfather and then his father in the last war against Merofynia, he had been ruthless in battle. The servants still whispered about how he had stood impassive while his eldest son was executed, because of his association with the Servants of Palos.

Cold disquiet gripped Byren. Sylion take Orrade and his ideals.

'I think I was too tired to explain properly last night. We owe our lives to Garzik and Captain Blackwing,' Byren said.

'It's all right. I told father about our last-minute rescue,' Orrade explained. He reached for his brother, who caught his hand in both of his and squeezed.

Lord Dovecote nodded. 'My son has told me how you refused to leave him, Byren. I am indebted to you.'

Byren said nothing, embarrassed.

As if sensing his discomfort, Elina turned to her brother. 'So, you can't guess what I have here, Orrie? Hold out your hands.'

'Why? Are you going to give me something loathsome?'

She laughed.

Byren's spotted pup wriggled, then whimpered.

Orrade turned his way. 'Don't tell me Regal's had her pups?'

Elina laughed again, then climbed onto the bed beside him, dumping two puppies in his lap. She beckoned Byren to bring the third.

He stepped up to the bed, placing the pup in Orrade's outstretched hands. His friend brought the wriggling lump of warm fur to his cheek and rubbed his chin on the puppy's back. His sightless eyes filled with tears.

Elina looked around, desperately searching for something to distract him. Her gaze fell to the pouch at Byren's waist. 'I see a glint of silver. What gift have you bought me this time?'

He looked down to discover the puppy's squirming must have worked the pouch's tie loose.

Before he could stop Elina, her hand darted to his waist pouch and she pulled out the chain. The symbol of Palos swung in an arc for all to see.

'An archer?' Elina frowned.

'Hush, girl,' her father snapped, springing to his feet.

One look at Lord Dovecote's face told Byren he knew this was no innocent representation of a bowman.

'Give me that... that vile thing!' her father ordered.

Lips parting in surprise, Elina walked around the bed to hand her father the chain with its damning pendant. Byren stood there helpless.

'What is it? What's wrong?' Orrade asked.

'Your father has found the Palos pendant. My pendant,' Byren said, then heard what he'd said and regretted it. But he could not take it back.

'Byren!' Orrade protested.

'Palos?' Elina repeated. 'But –'

'Don't do this, Byren,' Orrade pleaded.

'Servant of Palos?' Garzik whispered. 'Betrayer of Rolencia? Impossible, why would Byren betray his own –'

'Quiet!' Lord Dovecote's voice cracked like a whip. Everyone fell silent.

Except Byren. He had to make Lord Dovecote understand. 'It is a pendant of Palos but it has nothing to do with the traitors, who tried to –'

'You've foresworn women. You've chosen to join *their* ranks. Do you deny it?' Lord Dovecote demanded.

Byren did not look at Orrade, did not give him a chance to damn himself. 'Palos was a great leader. He nearly united –'

'Silence!' Lord Dovecote bellowed, then grimaced as if it pained him even to look at Byren. His words slurred badly. 'Your grandfather was my dearest friend. In memory of the man whose name you bear I will not reveal this to your father. But I won't have a filthy lover of men in my house!'

'It's not true.' Elina ran around the bed to Byren, catching his hands in hers. 'This must be a mistake. Tell me it's not true?'

But Byren could not, not without implicating Orrade.

Elina shook her head in disbelief.

Lord Dovecote started to stride around the bed. 'Get away from him, Elina. He's not fit to eat at our table.'

'Then banish me, not him.' Orrade's voice vibrated with anger. 'Because that is my pendant.'

'No, Orrie,' Byren whispered.

'Ha!' Lord Dovecote's eyes widened with shock and pain, then narrowed as he looked from Byren to his son. 'So that is how it is.'

Elina glanced from her brother to Byren. 'So that's why you...'

She dropped Byren's hand as if burnt, drawing back until her thighs hit the bed where she sat down abruptly.

'No, you have it wrong, father,' Orrade insisted. 'Byren was trying to protect me –'

Lord Dovecote's scornful laugh cut him off. 'Why would he do that unless he was your lover?'

He strode to the door, checked the hall and, seeing no servants, pulled on the bellrope, jerking it angrily. No one spoke as they waited for the servants to come. The old lord thrust the damning pendant into his vest, muttering under his breath, 'I must be cursed. First my eldest son, now this one!'

Orrade swung his legs off the bed, to stand in his night-shirt and bare feet. With his head wrapped in the bandage he looked vulnerable but determined. 'I can't let you suffer for me, Byren. I swear, father –'

'Silence. You are foresworn. Your word is worthless!'

Several worried servants bustled into the room.

Lord Dovecote straightened to his full height, silver hair bright against his pale, partly paralysed face. 'Before the gods and these servants I disinherit Orrade Dovecoteson. I disown you. I disown you, I disown you. Now leave my estate and never set foot on it again.'

The servants stood there stunned, a plump middle-aged woman with a damp apron, an old man with a candle trimmer, two girls of thirteen carrying clean washing and two boys of fourteen, who must have been out chopping wood for they were sweating profusely.

'I'll go, and gladly.' Orrade stood stiff and regal, looking like a younger version of his father.

The puppies whimpered. When one nearly fell off the bed Byren went to save it, but Elina scooped it up from under his hands.

'Don't touch it. Don't touch any of them.' She gathered all the puppies in her arms. Face damp with tears, eyes glazed with shock, she turned on him. 'Don't come near me. I never want to see you again!'

'Housekeeper, escort my daughter to her room. She's had a shock.'

'Father!' Garzik protested, as Elina marched out with the three women.

'Come, son and heir.' Lord Dovecote beckoned him.

Garzik glanced to Orrade and Byren.

'Now!' Lord Dovecote's voice cracked dangerously.

Garzik looked to Byren, who did not want to trigger another brain spasm in the old lord so he gave a slight nod.

When Garzik joined his father, the old man steered him towards the door then turned to the wood choppers. 'See that these two are out of the house and off Dovecote land by dusk.'

The two boys nodded mutely and Lord Dovecote marched out with Garzik, who cast one desperate look over his shoulder then was gone.

Orrade sagged. 'Byren, can you ever forgive me?'

He was too stunned to speak, even to think.

The silence stretched.

'Master Orrade?' one of the wood choppers finally ventured, out of his depth.

'Don't worry. I can find my own way off the estate.' Orrade waved a hand in their direction. 'Go, all of you.'

They fled.

Orrade sank onto the bed. 'Byren, I swear before Halcyon and Sylion, if I could undo this, I would.'

'Can't be helped,' Byren muttered, mouth dry. Then anger flashed through him. 'Why did you have to wear that bloody pendant?'

'If you hated it so much, why didn't you get rid of it?' Orrade countered.

Why hadn't he? Byren snorted. 'I forgot I still had it.'

Orrade grinned ruefully. 'You always were too easy-going.'

They said nothing. The great house was oddly silent, as if all the servants were creeping about and speaking only in whispers.

'Suddenly I am a man without home or allegiance,' Orrade said, his voice gradually gathering strength. 'But I can still hold to my ideal, a world where a man who follows Palos is respected for his intrinsic worth, not despised for his –'

'Eh, Orrie. I don't think Rolencia's ready for you or your ideals,' Byren muttered. He did a mental calculation. 'It's been nearly thirty years since the last Servant of Palos was executed, but their betrayal is still fresh in the minds of my father's generation –'

'Their betrayal? What of all the times the warlords betrayed Rolencia? What of King Byren the Wicked who locked his nephew in Eagle Tower? Little Lence was the rightful heir, but he never lived to rule!'

'You're right, our history is a litany of betrayals but –'

'The Servants of Palos are particularly hated because they are lovers of men. I know. I'm sorry, Byren.'

He shrugged, forgetting Orrade couldn't see. 'What's done can't be undone. I guess we should pack and go.'

'Go where? You can go back to Rolenhold. Father will keep his word and Elina and Garzik will not reveal the reason I was disinherited. You can be sure I will never betray you, so you will not lose your inheritance because of me.'

While Orrade spoke, the ramifications hit Byren. What would his father say if he knew...

Byren fought a wave of nausea as he imagined King Rolen's reaction. At eighteen, his father had seen his own father betrayed and nearly lose the kingdom, all because of the Servants of Palos. His father would be devastated and Lence...

His twin would never believe it. Byren felt relieved as he thought this through. Lence would vouch for him and help convince their father. The three of them had gone wenching together enough times for Lence to know it was a lie.

But hopefully it wouldn't come to that. No one need ever know, not Fyn, his younger brother who had been gifted to Halcyon Abbey, not his mother or sister. His mouth went dry. But what if the servants suspected Orrade's real feelings? He knew how quickly rumour could spread. Before long, lies would seem like truth to those who did not know him. He groaned because it wasn't even remotely true.

Why did Orrade have to carry that accursed pendant?

Someone knocked on the door.

'Yes?' Orrade called.

The door opened to reveal the kitchen boy, who placed Byren's travelling pack on the floor. 'Cook's packing some food for you right now.' He looked up miserably. 'What's going on, Master Orrade? They say you're leaving.'

'And so I am. Don't worry, Rifkin. Just bring the food as soon as it is ready.'

A picture of dejection, the boy nodded and ran off.

Orrade shuddered. 'Where will I go? If only I could see, I could offer to serve in your father's honour guard, but who wants a blind warrior?'

Byren grasped Orrade's shoulder. 'You're coming back with me. You may be blind but you still have your wits, Orrie. And there's not a man who can match you word for word.'

Orrade's mouth twisted in a bitter parody of a smile. 'You're suggesting I turn a pretty rhyme for my supper?'

'No. I'm suggesting you come back as my advisor, just as Captain Temor advises father.'

But Orrade was off on another track. 'You took the blame for me, Byren, and I can't take it back. I tried but...'

'Doesn't matter,' Byren said. But it did, for if the rumour spread his reputation would be destroyed.

At least he was sure Lence would vouch for him.

Byren grinned. The old seer couldn't have been more wrong about his twin.

Chapter Four

A FLASH OF annoyance warmed Fyn. The monks who should have been loading the sleds had wandered off. He lowered the bale and glanced back up the winding path to the abbey high upon Mount Halcyon. Almost dusk, no one else in sight.

The sleds stood on frozen Viridian Lake, waiting to be loaded so the monks could set off tomorrow. As a final-year acolyte it was not his place to tell first year monks what to do, but...

Jeering male laughter made Fyn stiffen. The sound carried from the next inlet along the lake's shore. He made his way carefully along the snowy bank, towards the outcropping that hid the inlet. Climbing onto the ledge, he crawled along until he could stretch out and look down onto the scene below, his head almost level with the monks'.

There were four of them, their different coloured robes revealing their affiliation with different abbey masters, but these four had always been fast friends, united by their similar natures. The monks had cornered a flock of grucranes. These large, cumbersome Affinity beasts survived Rolencia's cold winters by cohabiting with people. In exchange for a warm roost at night near the chimney pots of homes, they kept watch over the buildings. One of the flock was always awake, a stone clutched in its claw. If it fell asleep, the stone would fall and wake the others, so the birds made excellent sentries. Many a household had been saved from thievery or fire, always a constant threat with wooden homes, by the raucous cry of the sentry grucrane.

This particular flock slept on the abbey's chimney vents and spent their days on the lake, swimming and fishing in summer, fossicking along the shore in winter. Now they were confronted by Monk Galestorm and his three friends. The flock's leader had shepherded the birds into a hollow in the shoreline, effectively trapping them because, unless the heavy, ungainly birds took to the air, the only way out was closed off by Galestorm and his friends. Used to nothing but kindness from the monks, the birds milled about in confusion.

While his three companions watched, Galestorm shoved a stick at the Affinity beasts, then made an opening, only to dart in and block it off before the grucranes could escape.

Indignation filled Fyn. He wanted to jump down and defend the grucranes, but there were four monks and only one of him. It would be madness to risk a beating over a bird, even an Affinity-touched bird.

Galestorm misjudged the distance, or else really intended to harm the grucrane, for his next jab took it in the chest. It gave a raucous squawk of protest.

'Hey!' Fyn yelled, swinging his weight over the ledge and jumping down to the frozen lake below. A snow bank absorbed the impact of his landing.

'Fyn Rolen Kingson, what're you doing here?' Galestorm strode towards Fyn, swinging the stick so that it cut the air with a sickening swish.

Fyn's heart thundered and he glanced over his shoulder, but the rocks behind him were too steep to climb. He faced Galestorm. 'Leave the grucranes alone.'

'And what are you going to do about it, coward?' Cruel laughter followed Galestorm's taunt.

Fyn shrank inside. The moment Galestorm was distracted, the lead bird took off, flapping madly to gain height, then circling protectively as the others spiralled above him, heading towards the abbey.

'Did you hear?' Galestorm asked his ready audience. 'The kingson faints at the sight of blood –'

'Watch out. The birds are getting away,' Onetree yelled.

Galestorm spun around, swore, then tossed the stick aside. He pulled out his slingshot, grabbed a stone from his pouch and let fly into the mass of grucranes. One bird gave a forlorn cry, falling to the lake with a solid thump.

Fyn could not believe his eyes. 'You idiot!'

Galestorm faced him, his top lip lifting in a sneer.

Fyn tried to go to the aid of the injured bird but Galestorm stepped into his path, reaching for him. Without thinking, Fyn evaded the grab, caught

Galestorm's arm and flipped him off his feet. The air left Galestorm's lungs with a satisfying *whump* as he hit the ice, then skidded across the lake on his back.

The other three monks protested.

Fyn ignored them, hurrying over to the bird. It was trying to rise with an injured leg, wings flapping unevenly. Taking off his cloak, Fyn threw the woolen mantle over the bird, then gathered it in his arms. The Affinity beast was trembling badly and he pressed it against his chest to reassure it. Nothing infuriated Fyn more than wanton cruelty.

Shouts from Galestorm and his companions told him they were coming up fast behind him. He could not protect himself, let alone the bird. What had possessed him to interfere? They would kill the bird and beat him black and blue.

Still, he turned to face his tormentors.

'What's going on here?' a deep voice called.

Fyn looked beyond them to see Oakstand, the weapons master, approaching with Sandbank, a third-year healer.

'Why aren't the sleds being loaded?' the weapons master demanded. Oakstand was short, with a deep chest and a scar that puckered one side of his forehead, creeping up into his hair which grew white along the scar's length. It must have been striking once but now the rest of his hair was iron-grey. For a man who knew how to disarm and kill an armed opponent in three swift moves, he was amazingly patient with the boys.

'I've got an injured bird.' Fyn indicated the bundle in his arms. One long clawed leg projected from it in an ungainly manner. The bird had calmed down.

'A grucrane?' Healer Sandbank asked. 'Give it to me. I'll take it back to the abbey.'

Fyn handed the bundle over. 'Careful, something's wrong with its wing and I think one of its legs broke when it hit the ice.'

'So the kingson is a healer now?' Galestorm asked.

The weapons master frowned. 'Enough, Galestorm. I want the sleds packed and ready to leave at first light. Fyn, get back to the abbey.'

For a heartbeat Fyn considered revealing how the bird had been hurt, but it was his word against four monks and they could cause trouble for him later, so he hurried off. Behind him, Fyn could hear the weapons master ordering Galestorm and the others about and knew they would regret failing in their duties.

Monk Sandbank was already three body lengths ahead of him, following the winding trail up the slope to Halcyon Abbey. As Fyn watched, the healer rounded a curve, disappearing behind snow-cloaked evergreens.

Taking to his heels, Fyn ran up the slope, rounded the corner and looked up. No sign of the healer, who must have been hurrying to pass the next bend so quickly. Head down, Fyn concentrated on where he put his feet, not wanting to slip on the icy snow. Already the chill of the night was settling in and he was without a cloak. He rounded the next bend and nearly ploughed into a snowdrift.

That was strange. He didn't remember stepping off the path.

Fyn spun around only to find himself eye to eye with an old woman wearing moth-eaten furs. Her lips pulled back in a gap-toothed leer that might have been a smile.

Startled, he took a step back, overbalancing into the snowdrift. The snow broke the impact of his fall but he was still a little winded. Gasping, he lay stretched out on his back. When he went to get up the old woman prodded him in the chest with her staff, effectively pinning him there.

'You struck a monk.'

'He tried to kill a grucrane.'

'What's that bird to you?'

What indeed? Fyn shook his head, not even sure why he had bothered to answer her the first time. She was obviously mad, god-touched in her own way.

'No idea, just like the other one.' She shook her head and laughed to herself. It wasn't a pleasant sound, ending in a raw hacking cough.

After the fit had passed, while she was labouring to regain her breath, Fyn gestured up the rise behind him. 'If you are ill, seek out the healing monks. They have a hot potion for a cough like that.'

She glanced up behind him. The light was fading rapidly and he could hardly see her face for the glow of the nacreous sky behind her. Here, under the pines, it was already twilight.

Alert black eyes fixed on him. 'Most surely they do, Fyn Kingson, but not for the likes of me. No, not them pure and mighty servants of Halcyon!'

He did not know what to say to that.

'Not much longer.' She hawked and spat to one side, wiping her mouth on the back of her hand.

Obviously weary and ill, her eyes met his and held. 'Now, mark my words, Fyn Kingson.'

Her body jerked and her head tilted back until he could see the lines of dirt under her chin.

Fyn drew away in revulsion as an aura of power gathered around her frail form, making her seem larger. Even with his weak Affinity, Fyn could tell this was the untamed power of a Renegade.

'A seer!' He tried to scramble back, but the snowdrift held him. He should have been terrified. He should have denounced her to the mystics master, who would have ordered her immediate execution.

But he was fascinated, despite himself.

One clawed hand lifted to point at him, though from the angle of her head she could not see him. She was relying on Unseen sight.

'Unwanted youngest son, god-touched, nameless boy. I see you fleeing for your life. I see a day when the Goddess Halcyon's name is said only in whispers –'

Fyn laughed. He could not help it. The goddess was revered throughout Rolencia, served by seven hundred faithful monks in the abbey alone, all trained by the weapons master, sheltered behind defensive walls, built into the very mountain itself. Nothing could...

'Pah!' She shuddered and spat again, frowning down at him now that her vision had passed. 'None so blind as they who will not see! Very well, I wash my hands of you.'

She put her back to him, hobbling off between the snow-coated pines, their white skirts joining with the deep snowdrifts.

'Don't go that way. You're not following the path,' Fyn called after her.

She laughed softly and kept going. 'Follow me own path, boy, always have.'

He rolled over onto his stomach and came to his feet, determined to set her right, at the very least warn her off approaching the abbey, but when he turned around, she was gone.

'You there?' he called, brushing snow from his breeches.

'Is that you, Fyn?' the weapons master asked. The glow of his lantern gave the snow a golden cast as he weaved between the snow-shrouded pines. 'What are you doing off the path, lad? Don't you know it's not safe to be out alone so close to midwinter?'

At midwinter the cruel god, Sylion, reluctantly relinquished his hold on Rolencia, giving the kingdom over to the goddess's care. With a major change of power the barriers between the Seen and the Unseen world were dangerously weak. And to think, he'd been too surprised to use any of the wards to protect himself from renegade Affinity.

Fyn blinked, the after image of the master's light dancing in his sight. With the arrival of the lantern came full dark.

'Well?' the weapons master demanded. 'The others have all returned to the abbey.'

'I wasn't watching my feet, Master Oakstand,' Fyn said, knowing he sounded foolish. 'I...' He was about to mention the old woman, but was surprised to find that he could not speak of her. When he tried his tongue grew thick and clumsy in his mouth.

He swallowed and the sensation passed, but he suspected it would return.

'Eh, well, come on then.' The burly master led him through the snow and Fyn found he was only a few steps off the path.

They trudged up the hill in silence for a bit, then the weapons master slowed, his heavy eyebrows drawing together.

Fyn waited expectantly. Their lantern failed to illuminate the great looming towers of the pine trees that stood silhouetted against the froth of sparkling stars. Twilight seemed to have passed abruptly, something to do with the seer, Fyn guessed. He wondered if she was out there even now, watching them. He should denounce her but he couldn't, not when she seemed so frail and sick, not when she had a ring of dirt under her neck. He had never visualised a renegade Power-worker like that. Evil, perhaps... but not vulnerable.

Fyn glanced to the weapons master. Oakstand's scar from the last great battle with Merofynia reminded him that his mother had been betrothed to his father as part of the peace. Strange to think of Queen Myrella as a child, leaving her home in Merofynia to come and live in Rolencia, and his father waiting seven years for her to grow up. For the first time, Fyn wondered if the eight-year-old Myrella had felt as homesick as he had, when his parents sent him to the abbey at six years of age. It was not as if either of them had had any choice.

'They'll run the race for Halcyon's Fate on Midwinter's Day,' the weapons master said abruptly.

Fyn had to collect his thoughts. He nodded. 'The Proving.'

'Wanted to get this said before the race, Fyn. You're small, but winning's not about brute force, it's about strategy. You've got a good head on your shoulders.'

Fyn could see where this was going, and his stomach churned. His father expected that Fyn would eventually become weapons master, leader of the elite band of warrior monks, able to support Lence, when he became king. But...

The weapons master grinned. 'I'm offering you a place in the ranks of my elite warrior monks. Who knows. I've got plenty of fine warriors, but it's thinkers I need to train as leaders.'

Fyn's heart raced. This was everything his father had hoped for him and for the future of Rolencia. But... 'I can't do it.'

'What?' The weapons master looked stunned.

Fyn felt equally surprised. 'I'm sorry. I'd be the joke of the abbey.' Heat raced up his cheeks. All he wanted to do was run to Master Wintertide and ask his advice. 'Surely you've heard what they're calling me. Coward, snivelling –'

'Hold up. Is this about that time with Hawkwing?'

Fyn nodded miserably. 'I fainted when his finger was cut off.'

Oakstand laughed. 'The moment I turn my back to take a leak, you acolytes chop each other up. Teach you to be more careful next time!' He sobered, sharp eyes on Fyn. 'Now, as I remember it, you held his finger in place until the healers came while everyone else panicked.'

'He still lost most of his finger and I fainted.' Fyn felt the master wasn't taking this seriously. He'd suffered enough jibes since then to make his life miserable.

'True, but you fainted after the healers took him away.' The weapons master grinned. 'So what if he lost his finger? What's a man without a few scars?'

Fyn shook his head miserably. 'It's just –'

'Enough, lad.' Master Oakstand placed a hand on Fyn's shoulder and began to stride up the rise towards the gates, which were just around the next bend. 'You don't have to give me your answer right now. Think on it. Three of the last ten abbots came from my branch. Come on. Let's get inside before we freeze our balls off.'

Fyn had to lengthen his stride to keep up with the master. Oakstand was right, the role of weapons master was a step towards becoming abbot. Halcyon's fighting monks had earned their reputation through years of conflict. But that was in the brutal past. They were living in a new, more civilised age of study and prosperity.

As Fyn walked through the abbey's huge gates, he was relieved he did not have to accept the weapons master's offer immediately. It shamed him to admit he couldn't bear to see a bird suffer, let alone a person.

He'd never be a great warrior.

WHILE BYREN MADE camp, building a snow-cave on the bank of the canal, he kept one eye on Orrade. Working fast from long practice, he made the cave just large enough to crouch in, just large enough for two men and their travelling packs to stretch out. Once it was complete, they climbed inside and Byren heated some food on their small travelling brazier, tossing in salted meat and finely chopped vegetables, all prepared by the Dovecote cook. Halcyon bless her. This was their second night out and Orrade had been strangely silent all afternoon. Every now and then he grimaced with pain, and there wasn't a thing Byren could do.

'Hungry, Orrie?'

'Think I'll just turn in,' he muttered, rolling up in the blanket, huddling with his head in his hands.

'Head hurting?' Byren asked softly.

'Something awful,' Orrade admitted. So it must have been bad.

Byren wondered if this meant his friend was about to have another Affinity-induced vision and if Orrade had sensed the change in himself yet. 'How did you know the raiders were coming?'

'You asked me that before,' Orrade muttered. He rolled onto his back, eyes hidden under his forearm. 'I don't even remember warning you. Must have felt their approach through the ice like you said. Sorry, can't think now, Byren.'

Feeling useless, Byren stirred the food, cooking by the light of a single lamp. What would he do if Orrade became worse? The seer had said he would live, but men had been known to die from head wounds several days after getting up and walking around. At least they'd camped on the canal, so he could rig a stretcher and drag his friend. Get him straight to the castle healers.

That made Byren realise he would have to explain

why Orrade hadn't stayed at Dovecote estate with their healer. He would have to tell his parents Orrade had been disinherited. Old Lord Dovecote wouldn't want him to reveal the real reason, which meant thinking up a lie. Byren wasn't good at lying.

Soon dinner was ready. The meat had already been cooked and, as for the carrots, he didn't mind if they were a bit crunchy, so long as they were hot.

'Sure you don't want any?' He tried to tempt Orrade, who shook his head. At least he was still aware. That was good.

Byren forced himself to eat, leaving plenty in case Orrade was hungry later, then turned in. On a major canal during midwinter, this close to Rolenton there was not much chance of a predator attacking their snow-cave, so he did not bother to keep watch. He had made sure their snow-cave was hidden in a fold in the canal bank. Unless someone was looking specifically for them, it would be hard to find. Still, he slept lightly, a warrior's sleep.

Several hours later he rolled awake, on alert. Though he could not see the stars he guessed it was near midnight. A dull blue luminescence came through the arc of the snow-cave roof, a pale imitation of the stars' brilliance.

What had woken him?

There it was again, the softest squeak of snow being moved. He stared at the snow-cave entrance which he'd packed shut to retain their body heat. Snow shifted and fell in. Something, or someone, was trying to get in.

Byren left his blanket roll and crept around until

he was beside the closed opening, drawing his borrowed hunting knife. A hand poked through, followed by a head and shoulders. Byren grabbed the intruder and hauled him onto his back, knife at his throat.

'Arrgh!' Garzik gasped. 'It's me, only me.'

'Garza?' He released him. 'What are you doing here?'

The boy brushed off snow and crouched on his heels, warming his hands over the coals in the brazier. 'Looking for dinner. I had to run off without food or cook would have told father.'

'Garza?' Orrade surfaced, turning towards their voices. 'You ran away from Dovecote?'

'Don't sound so disapproving. Father disowned you.'

'Why are you here?' Byren tried again.

'I've come to serve on the king's honour guard,' Garzik announced.

Byren snorted. 'You have to earn the right to serve on the honour guard. A boy of fourteen is no –'

'Nearly fifteen. Besides, I've killed a wyvern –'

'Freshwater,' Orrade qualified.

'True,' Garzik admitted. 'But I saved you both from the ulfr pack, killed two –'

'It's not all about killing,' Orrade told him.

Garzik silently appealed to Byren.

'Well, you're here now,' he said, replacing the pot on the brazier. 'Let's get you fed. We can decide tomorrow if you go back.'

'I'm not going back.'

'Father will disown you,' Orrade warned. 'He'll make Elina his heir.' He grinned ruefully. 'He should. She'd do a better job than either of us.'

Garzik rolled his eyes.

'Don't roll your eyes at me,' Orrade snapped.

Byren dropped the ladle in the pot. 'What did you say?'

Orrade gestured to Garzik. 'I might be disowned but I am still his older brother and I –'

'By Halcyon, you can see!' Byren fumbled in his pack for the lamp and lit it.

Orrade winced at the light, turning away, then realised what he had done. 'I can see and my head's stopped hurting.' He sat up, blinking slowly as though testing his sight. 'There's some grey spots floating across my vision but I swear, I can see!'

Garzik threw himself on Orrade, hugging him fiercely. Byren watched, his own joy tempered because he feared Orrade's sight wasn't permanently restored. He didn't like the sound of grey patches moving over his vision.

'Now everything's all right.' Garzik sat back on his heels. 'We can both swear loyalty to King Rolen and next time you teach spar raiders a lesson, I'll come too!'

Byren grimaced. If only life were that simple. He was going home with the threat of his supposed association with the Servants of Palos hanging over him. All it would take was a slip of Garzik's tongue to land him in trouble. How would his father react? He wasn't called *King Rolen the Implacable* for nothing.

He should send Garzik back to Dovecote estate.

Garzik grinned at Orrade. 'Now that you can see, you can perform some deed of bravery and win a title and estate of your own!'

'Don't you care that I'm like Palos?' Orrade demanded.

Garzik laughed. 'You're still my brother.'

Orrade smiled, and shook his head in wonder, making Byren realise he couldn't send the lad back, even if he would go.

Garzik glanced his way. 'And Byren is still the finest warrior I have ever seen.'

Orrade snorted. 'And you've seen so many. But Garza, it's not true. Byren only claimed to own the pendant to try and save me from father's wrath.'

Garzik turned awed eyes to Byren. 'You did that for Orrie?'

He shrugged this aside. 'Come and eat. Truth be told, I didn't even think, just reacted.' No, if he'd given it any thought he would never have put himself in this position. Shouldn't have had to. Orrade and his stupid pendant.

Byren summoned a smile as he passed the boy a bowl of reheated dinner. 'Here, have this. We should be at the castle by lunchtime tomorrow.'

'Good.' Garzik accepted the bowl. 'Piro will get such a surprise.'

'No more picking on her,' Orrade told him, watching his brother fondly as he gulped down the strew. 'Piro Kingsdaughter is nearly a woman now, and won't want to play silly childish games.'

'Since when?' Garzik challenged.

'Speaking of my family.' Byren cleared his throat. Time to deal with unpleasant truths. 'I'll have to tell mother and father that you've been disinherited, Orrie. It would be wrong to let you eat at their table without letting them know.'

Orrade nodded. 'I've been thinking. They don't

need to know the details. I'll tell them it's between father and I. That's true enough. I'll offer King Rolen my sword. I've always liked Captain Temor.'

Byren nodded. Temor had served his father since the Merofynian war and trained them all when they were boys. He would probably accept Orrade, but it would be a big drop from Dovecote heir to one of the king's honour guard.

PIRO SHIFTED FROM foot to foot, trying to contain her impatience. She was terribly disappointed, and the scent of glues and stiffeners used to create the milliner's elaborate head-dresses made her feel dizzy. Maybe, if she inhaled deeply several times in a row, she'd look sickly enough for her mother to cut the shopping short. Could she manage a believable faint?

She thought she could fool the milliner but not her mother. Queen Myrella knew how good she was at play acting. If only the milliner had sent a message to say that the hercinia feathers hadn't arrived yet, then she wouldn't have come shopping. She hated being polite and having to mind her manners. But it had seemed worth it to see feathers that glowed in the dark.

Because the hercinia birds were so rare they had almost died out and her father had banned the use of their feathers for all but royalty. Not that Piro wanted a head-dress adorned with hercinia feathers, no, she just wanted to see them for herself to discover if they were as brilliant as the feathers of her own pet foenix. Privately she doubted that any bird, Affinity or otherwise, could be as handsome.

While the milliner fitted her mother's new head-dress for the midwinter ceremony, Piro gazed out the window into Rolenton Square. She could just see the base of the shop's sign.

A familiar profile, carried on broad shoulders, strode by.

Piro gasped. 'Byren!'

'Byren?' her mother echoed. 'Surely he hasn't brought the Royal Ingeniator back already?'

'It is Byren!' Piro dashed towards the door, throwing it wide open. Sure enough. There he was, unmistakable because he was so much taller than everyone else. And he was with Garzik as well as Orrade, so he must have gone on to Dovecote estate. They all wore packs on their backs, slung with skates.

'Byren!' With a yell she set off after him. Heads turned.

He spun around, saw her racing across the cobbles and gave that crooked grin that made one dimple appear in his cheek.

She laughed, throwing herself at him. He caught her around the waist, lifting her into the air and swinging her around. She loved it.

Effortlessly, he set her down. 'Uh. You're getting too big for this, Piro!'

'I don't even come up to your shoulder!' She laughed.

'I meant too old.'

She ignored that. The longer she could put off growing up, the better. Being a grown woman meant always behaving with decorum and a thousand restrictions that would drive her mad. No, she'd fight every step of the way. Why limit herself, when she'd rather be out riding with Byren than sitting in her mother's solarium balancing the castle's books or cross-checking the kingdom's laws? 'What are you doing back already, Byren?' She nodded to Orrade and grinned at Garzik. 'So your father finally let you out without a nursemaid, Garza? Where's Elina? What happened to your head, Orrie?'

The three of them exchanged looks and Orrade fingered the bandage.

'A branch fell on me,' Orrade said. 'Elina's not well. She may not come to the midwinter ceremony.'

'Oh, no.' Piro didn't try to hide her disappointment. 'What's wrong with her?'

Orrade opened his mouth but nothing came out.

'Piro?' Byren frowned at her. 'What are you doing running around Rolenton like a seamstress's apprentice on half-day? Mother wouldn't approve. Where is she by the way? Have you snuck away again?'

'Not this time,' Piro admitted then saw his expression. 'Oh, don't be angry with me, Byren. It's such a pain being expected to behave like a –'

He looked past her. 'Tell that to Mother. Here she comes!'

Piro winced but the queen only had eyes for her son, as she swept towards them.

'Byren, it is you!' Queen Myrella grabbed his vest and pulled his face down to hers, planting a kiss on each cheek. Then she stepped back beaming. Only a single stray curl revealed how she must have thrown off her head-dress to dart after Piro. She smiled at the two Dovecote brothers. 'Orrade. And Garzik, how you've grown! I trust your father is well.'

'Well enough,' Orrade answered stiffly.

The queen touched his bandage briefly. 'What happened to you, Orrie? Are you all right?'

'A small head wound. It's nothing.'

'That must have given your father a fright. Where is he?'

'What are you doing, Mother, strolling around Rolenton without the honour guard?' Byren chided. 'You're setting a bad example for Piro. No wonder she's half-wild!'

The townspeople, who watched them at a respectful distance, smiled as the queen laughed like a carefree girl. It wasn't as if they needed a guard in their own home town.

'Lence took the guard to get an ale while we did our shopping,' the queen explained.

'Oh, I'm so glad to see you, Byren,' Piro announced. 'You can take me down to the wharfs to watch the sled ships.'

'You're just glad to see me because you hate shopping,' he teased, then grew serious. 'Mother, have you heard from Winterfall or the Royal Ingeniator?'

'No. Is something wrong?'

'We found a new seep, but don't worry. They're sending for sorbt stones and the Affinity warders will control it.'

'Queen Myrella,' Orrade began. 'There's something you should know. I've –'

'Queen Myrella!' An old woman threw off her hood, shuffling out of the crowd to confront them.

Even though her voice was little more than a rasp, it carried on the cold, still air. 'Queen Myrella, true heir to Merofynia, heed my words!'

Byren swore under his breath. Piro glanced to him. Why was he worried? An old woman couldn't hurt them, could she?

'Be off with you!' He went to drive her away.

'Byren,' the queen protested. Piro knew their mother always listened to the poorest of their kingdom. That's why the people of Rolencia loved her, even though she was the daughter of a Merofynian king.

But when the queen took a good look at the old woman, her face went slack with shock. Was this someone from her mother's past, Piro wondered, a Merofynian palace servant, who had come down in the world?

Byren gestured. 'Be off with you, old –'

The woman silenced him with a single piercing look. The laughter died on Piro's lips as the woman dropped her staff and stiffened, her eyes rolling back in her head.

Since Piro became a woman at autumn cusp unwanted Affinity had been growing in her, so she had no trouble recognising it at work now. Tension made the very air taste strange and Piro's vision blurred. She blinked repeatedly until she realised she was seeing the shift caused by Unseen power acting on the Seen world.

Piro went very still, like a deer startled by a predator. A seer with renegade Affinity – her secret would be revealed and she would be sent away like

Fyn!

'You live a lie, Queen Myrella, queen of lies!' The old woman shrieked.

Discovering she was not the object of the old seer's prediction, Piro relaxed fractionally. Her mother took a step back, colliding with Byren who steadied her.

'Your lies will be the downfall of Rolencia and the death of those you love. You think you're safe but one rotten apple turns the rest!' Blind-to-the-seen-world eyes turned to Piro. She felt sure this seer would recognise her growing Affinity and denounce her.

'Like mother, like daughter!' the old woman wheezed. 'Do not make the same mistake –'

'Filthy untamed Affinity!' Lence swore, thrusting through the crowd. A dozen young honour guards wearing the symbol of the royal house of Rolencia followed him. Rich red foenixes, their scales picked out in gold thread, gleamed against the black background of the surcoats.

'Be silent, Utland Power-worker!' Lence ordered.

The old woman's trance left her and she cast him one swift glance before fixing Piro with urgent jet-black eyes, stumbling towards her. 'Piro Myrella Queensdaughter, don't deny your –'

Piro smelt death on the old woman. It turned her stomach and she pulled back instinctively.

'Here, leave m'sister alone!' With one shove Lence sent the Power-worker flying across the swept cobbles.

She hit the wall of the Three Swans Inn and collapsed in a snowdrift, her head at an odd angle.

Piro stared, stunned. The old seer was dead.

Now she could never reveal Piro's secret. A surge of relief filled her, followed swiftly by guilt as she turned on Lence. 'You killed her!'

He lifted his large hands, looking down at them as if surprised by what he had done. Like Byren he was a head taller than most men, but he had a deep barrel chest and the arms of a blacksmith.

Lence grimaced and wiped his hand on his thigh. Revulsion twisted his handsome lips. 'She shouldn't have brought her filthy untamed Affinity into Rolencia!'

Dismay swamped Piro. Would Lence dismiss her as quickly if he knew about her Affinity? 'But she was just an old woman. She wasn't even a very good seer!'

It was true. Piro was nothing like her mother.

'Hush, Piro,' the queen whispered. She looked ill. 'Lence did the right thing. We cannot have –'

'But she should have been arrested and given the choice of banishment or death,' Piro insisted. 'That's the law. You're always making me memorise the law.'

'Enough, Piro. It's for the best,' Byren urged. His attention was on their mother, who was visibly wavering as if her legs might give way. He slid an arm around her shoulder. 'Come sit down, mother.'

Orrade took her other arm.

'Uh, Orrie, Garza. Didn't see you there,' Lence muttered, then looked about eagerly. 'Where's Elina?'

'She's sick,' Garzik whispered, still staring at the seer.

Like him, Queen Myrella stared at the old woman's body, which lay abandoned like an empty husk.

Piro shuddered. She had never seen violent death.

Surely the seer knew the laws of Rolencia? What had been so important that she risked death to warn them? Piro tried to remember what had been said to her mother, something about living a lie because she was the true heir to Merofynia and this would cause Rolencia to fall and her loved ones to die.

Impossible. Rolencia was strong, so strong that when her mother's younger brother, King Sefon, died seven summers ago, her parents had decided not to get involved in Merofynia's civil war, not because they couldn't have ridden into Merofynia and taken the throne, but because they didn't want to waste the blood of young Rolencians on foreign soil.

Piro licked dry lips. How could avoiding war cause death?

She shuddered, glad the old seer hadn't had a chance to betray her Affinity. Perversely, though, Piro wished she could have heard the rest of the old woman's prophecy, if only to discover how mistaken she was. Rotten fruit, what next?

Lence turned to one of the honour guard. 'Fetch the Affinity warders and get rid of the body.'

They would burn the old woman then scatter her ashes over water, saying the words to dispel her power. It was the only way to be sure that no taint of her untamed Affinity lingered.

'You.' Byren beckoned another of the honour guard. He still supported their mother, who looked lost and distracted. 'I need you to borrow a carriage to take my mother and sister back to the castle.'

A clattering of hooves made them turn. Astride his sturdy roan, King Rolen bore down on them, the crowd parting hurriedly.

'Father!' Now Piro knew everything would be all right.

Taking in the situation, King Rolen swung his leg over the horse and dropped to the ground with a grunt, the landing jarring all his old wounds. Piro winced for him. Her father had been growing stiffer recently. But he still radiated the energy that had saved their kingdom from invasion thirty years ago.

'Myrella, are you all right?' he demanded, enfolding the queen's small frame in his arms. Byren stepped back while their mother assured the king that she was fine. Their father looked to Lence. 'What happened?'

'Mother and Piro were assaulted by a renegade Power-worker,' Lence spoke up. 'I dealt with her.' He gestured to the body, which the honour guard had yet to remove.

King Rolen's heavy brow gathered in a frown. Piro knew that look. Now there would be trouble. Ever since his own father and elder brother had been killed by renegade Power-workers on the battlefield, her father had set out to eradicate everyone with untamed Affinity from Rolencia.

'Right.' King Rolen began roaring orders.

Piro marvelled. Within a matter of moments, a carriage had been found and she and her mother were bustled into it. As they tucked the blankets around their legs and adjusted the heated bricks, she overheard her father telling Byren, 'It's just as well you're back early. We've had a complaint about a rogue leogryf that's taken to preying on the villagers up near the pass to Foenix Spar. You and Lence can handle it.'

Piro peered out the carriage window. She had never seen a live leogryf.

'Can I go too?' Garzik demanded. Then remembered his manners and dropped to one knee, placing a hand over his heart. 'I mean, I offer my service –'

Her father laughed, hauling him to his feet. 'Of course you can. We need every able-bodied man, even if he is not much more than a boy!'

Garzik looked as if he was torn between being pleased or slightly affronted.

King Rolen turned to Orrade. 'What happened to your head, lad?'

'Took a fall. King Rolen, I –'

'How's the old Dove, feisty as ever?'

Orrade nodded and went to speak, but the king turned away to deal with his honour guard and the disposal of the seer's body.

The carriage gave a jolt and began to rattle over the cobbles so Piro saw no more.

'It's not fair,' she muttered. There was Garzik, only a year and a bit older than her and he was allowed to go hunting with Lence and Byren, but she never would. She sighed. Right now she was heading for the safety and boredom of the castle while Byren and Lence went off on the king's business. The high point of her day was seeing a feather that glowed in the dark and even then she'd been let down. 'Why can't I go with Byren and Lence?'

Her mother's distracted gaze drifted across the carriage as if she was seeing something beyond its panelled walls.

'Why can't I go?' Piro insisted. 'I would love to see

a leogryf. I'd be no trouble.'

The queen blinked.

Piro frowned. What was wrong with her mother? By now she should be lecturing her on the proper behaviour for a kingsdaughter.

It was that renegade Power-worker.

Startled and dismayed, Piro slid off her seat, dropping to her knees on the floor of the carriage and taking her mother's hands in hers to offer comfort. 'Don't worry, Mother, that... that...'

But she could not do it. She could not form the words to speak of the old seer.

The queen's luminous, obsidian eyes focused on Piro. A sense of imminence filled Piro and her heart quickened.

'That...' her mother stumbled then, as she forged on, Piro felt a shiver of relief. 'That seer!'

'Yes!' Piro nodded. 'She pretended to be a seer but she had no idea. Everything she said was wrong.'

Distress tightened her mother's features. The queen's lips worked and her chin trembled as if she was holding back tears or fury.

'What is it?' Piro whispered, empathy making her skin prickle. She felt as if her mother was about to reveal something vitally important.

The queen pressed her fingers to her mouth, took a shuddering breath then shook her head. She tucked a strand of hair behind Piro's ear. 'It's nothing.'

But it wasn't. Piro pulled back to sit on her seat. Something the old seer had said had disturbed her mother deeply.

Surely nothing could threaten Rolencia, not while

her father held the kingdom together. At nearly fifty he was getting old, but in Lence and Byren he had strong warriors to defend Rolencia from beasts, spar warlords and Utland raiders.

It was probably the part about loved ones dying that worried her mother. After all, anyone could fall from a horse and break their neck like poor Uncle Sefon had, or catch a cold that went to the chest. And Lence and Byren were always facing danger. If their ongoing joke about who was due to save the other's life could be believed, they could have died a dozen times these last five years.

An image came to Piro, a body in the snow. In her mind's eye she dropped to her knees turning the body over, fearing the worst. But it was not Byren or Lence. It was Fyn.

She almost retched.

Stop it, she told herself. Fyn is safe with Halcyon's monks. It would break her heart if anything happened to any of her brothers but, despite the time he had spent at the abbey, she was closest to Fyn.

That image had to be the product of her over active imagination. She was not a seer – her growing Affinity had shown no sign of developing in that direction. Thank the goddess!

Suddenly afraid she'd betrayed herself, Piro focused on her mother. The queen stared distractedly out the window as the carriage climbed the steep road that repeatedly turned back on itself before reaching the gates of Rolenhold. Good, her mother hadn't noticed.

As if sensing her scrutiny, the queen met her eyes. 'Why do you look so worried, Piro?' she asked. 'Is something wrong?'

'What? No.' Piro looked down, adjusting the blanket over her knees. If she admitted her unwanted Affinity her parents would have to gift her to Sylion abbey. She'd be shut up with hundreds of other women, forced to worship the cold god of winter when she loved the sun and laughter. 'Nothing's wrong. Nothing at all.'

That seer was mistaken, Piro told herself. *She must have been wrong about everything else because she was wrong about me being like Mother!*

'We're home.' The queen sounded relieved.

Piro looked up at the castle's steep walls. Its domes and towers gleamed in the winter sun but instead of feeling a sense of homecoming, she fought a sense of entrapment. Piro put it down to wanting to hunt the leogryf, rather than sit and study.

Why couldn't her life be simple, like Byren's?

Chapter Five

BYREN RODE INTO Rolenhold's stable courtyard on a borrowed horse. With everyone about to leave to hunt the leogryf, he had to grab his father and explain Orrade's disinheritance. He stood in the stirrups. Where was King Rolen?

There, speaking with Captain Temor and Lence on the far side of the courtyard. Good.

'Come on, Orrie. Now's the best time.' Byren swung his leg over the mare and dropped to the cobbles. Orrade and Garzik followed suit. They were right behind him as he approached his father.

A group of new arrivals rode in between them, six or seven men on horseback, followed by a wagon-load of servants and belongings. They were led by a handsome man whose grim, rigid features seemed vaguely familiar. He rode one-handed, the other arm caught in a sling. His warriors wore the vivid blue surcoat of the Cobalt estate, with the coat of arms emblazoned on their chests. In the lower corner was the original Cobalt House symbol, the silver dalfino, a winged, warm-blooded fish. In the upper corner was the inverted crown, added when King Byren the Fourth's bastard married into Cobalt House.

'You, sir.' The injured man fixed on Byren, who stood a head taller than everyone else. He spoke Rolencian with a slight accent and his voice carried despite the din in the courtyard. 'Direct me to the king.'

'Who wants me?' King Rolen turned.

Orrade leant close to Byren to mutter in his ear. 'Who is that? I feel I should know him.'

The man dismounted gracefully, handing his reins to Byren, who accepted them without protest. Dressed in his stained travelling clothes Byren could easily be mistaken for one of his father's men-at-arms. Lence sent him a rueful look, one corner of his mouth lifting. Byren grinned and beckoned a stunned stable boy, who ran over and took the reins, apologising profusely. All around them the new arrivals were dismounting and handing over their reins as the stable lads took the horses away.

The general hubbub died down and everyone gathered to hear what the stranger had to say.

'King Rolen.' Even with one arm in a sling, the man managed to give an elaborate bow, reminding Byren of the Ostronite ambassador. That helped him place the accent. One thing was certain, the mannered style of clothes the stranger affected would not catch on at court. You'd never see Byren wearing a coat with shoulder pads, a nipped-in waist and lace at the cuffs and throat.

'My king.' The injured man straightened up, standing almost as tall as King Rolen. That was when Byren saw the resemblance. 'I have come to swear fealty and to demand justice.'

'Justice?' the king repeated with a frown, then it cleared. 'Why, you're young Illien, Spurnan's boy!'

His cousin, Illien? Byren stiffened. Illien's father, Spurnan, was King Byren the Fourth's bastard son by a travelling minstrel he'd bedded when he was only sixteen. The boy had been fostered out to Lord Cobalt, who'd married him to his daughter. After the old lord died, King Byren's bastard had inherited the Cobalt title and estates. Had he been legitimate, Spurnan would have been king, not Rolen, which would have made Illien kingsheir, not Lence. It had never meant anything to Byren when he was a boy. He'd adored Illien because, in those days, his cousin was everything a warrior should have been.

Now Byren studied Illien's face, trying to find the youth he used to admire in this elegant foppish man. He'd been seven and Illien twenty-two, when the old Lord Cobalt had sent Illien to Ostron Isle. There'd been an argument, something the adults never mentioned in front of the seven-year-old twins. As far as Byren knew Illien and his father had not reconciled.

'Weren't you living on Ostron Isle these thirteen years?' King Rolen asked, although their ambassador to Ostron Isle would have kept him informed.

'Yes,' Illien said, unabashed by the reference to the argument with his father. 'I've been serving my family's interests on Ostron Isle but, just this last summer, I swallowed my pride and contacted father because I was marrying into one of the great Ostronite merchant families and I wanted his blessing. Five days ago, I came home so that he could meet my bride when...' His voice wavered and he shook his head, face flushing with deep emotion, unable to go on.

Byren's throat tightened in sympathy.

'Raiders, my king,' a grizzled warrior in Cobalt-blue explained, one hand going to the injured man's shoulder. 'Old Lord Cobalt came to meet my master's ship when –'

'Raiders attacked us!' Illien ground out.

'Utland raiders dared to sail into the Lesser Sea?' King Rolen demanded. 'They haven't done that for twenty years!'

'Is that how you were injured, lad?' Captain Temor nodded to the sling.

'Yes, captain. And I am Lord Cobalt now.' He gave the slightest of bows, a dip of the head as befitted a lord addressing an old and respected man-at-arms. 'My father is dead.'

'Spurnan's dead?' King Rolen muttered. He stared hard into the middle distance, then shook himself. 'That leaves only the Old Dove.'

Garrade of Dovecote and Spurnan of Cobalt had stood by Byren's father, when he had come into the kingship. He'd only been eighteen and it had looked like Merofynia would crush Rolencia, which was still reeling from the attempt by the Servants of Palos to usurp the throne in Spurnan's name. The bastard had sworn he was not involved and his subsequent support of Rolen had proven his loyalty.

'This is bad news, indeed,' King Rolen said.

'Worse still, my bride...' Illien of Cobalt could not go on.

'Dead?' King Rolen whispered.

Cobalt nodded.

The thought of Elina in the hands of Utland raiders made Byren's heart thunder. He ached for action.

Lence stepped forwards. 'I'll lead a punitive attack on the Utlanders.'

The men around him cheered and Byren's heart lifted as Lence turned to Illien to assure him that his bride and father would be avenged. King Rolen smiled with pride and waited for the cheering to die down.

Byren had heard the stories of how his father spent the first seven years of his reign ensuring the safety of the kingdom by leading punitive raids against the savage Utlanders. There were four large clusters of islands and many small scattered ones.

'But which Utlanders?' Byren asked, turning to the new Lord Cobalt. 'Which Utlanders attacked Port Cobalt, Illien?'

Cobalt frowned at him.

'You remember Byren,' King Rolen said. 'He and Lence used to give you no peace.'

A smile lightened Cobalt's expression but only briefly. 'Which Utlanders?' He ran a hand through his long black curls. 'I don't know. It was dark, the fires, the screaming...' He fixed on Byren. 'I didn't stop to ask their names and affiliations, I was fighting for my life!'

'Of course.' Lence glared at Byren.

Byren nodded. 'But there are many Utland isles, we could attack innocent –'

'It doesn't matter which Utland isle sent the raiders,' King Rolen decided. 'All that matters is that we teach them the Greater and Lesser Seas are out of bounds.'

Lence nodded. 'If we set off now –'

'You'll miss the midwinter ceremony and insult Halcyon,' Captain Temor interrupted gently.

Their father nodded. 'Better to go after spring cusp when the seas are not so dangerous. That gives me time to call for ships and captains, get the support of the warlords. If we sail out in strength we can deal these Utlanders such a blow they'll crawl back to their hovels and not come out for another twenty years!'

Everyone cheered.

But Byren couldn't put his heart into it. From what he'd heard it was hard enough to claw a living from the Utlands at the best of times. If Lence's ships burnt innocent Utlanders' homes and food stores they would starve before their crops could be harvested the next autumn.

At the same time, if the Utland raiders had united under a charismatic leader they could cripple Rolencia's sea trade, the very trade that had bought them so much prosperity these last two decades.

'...go with Lence and Byren?' his father was saying to Cobalt. Captain Temor had moved off, leaving the king alone with his sons and nephew. 'Of course you're welcome to hunt the leogryf, Illien, but –'

'The arm? I cannot fire a bow or throw a spear. Still, I would be honoured.' Cobalt glanced to Lence. 'That's if you can think an injured man won't slow you down?'

Lence straightened. 'You'll always be welcome, Illien.'

A smiled tugged at Cobalt's mouth but his eyes remained shadowed. He stepped aside to give directions to his men-at-arms.

'Fancy seeing Illien again,' Lence muttered. 'Say, Byren, d'you remember the time he let us sit astride his stallion?'

Byren grinned. 'We were only six. Our feet couldn't reach the stirrups.'

'What, you rode Black Thunder?' their father demanded, then chuckled. 'Eh, I'm glad I didn't know. It's good to have him back, though I wish it could have been under better circumstances. At least Illien and his father made up their differences before he died.'

That reminded Byren. 'Father, there's something I must –'

'My father has disinherited me, King Rolen,' Orrade interrupted.

'What?' The king looked startled, then inclined to laugh. 'Always said the Old Dove's temper would get the better of him one day. I felt the hard edge of his tongue often enough when I was a lad. Don't worry, Orrie, he'll come 'round. Spurnan did.'

'What did you do that was so bad, Orrie, forget to give Halcyon her due last Feast Day?' Lence teased.

Orrade shook his head. 'It's not –'

'Not something to be laughed at,' Cobalt said, rejoining them. He acknowledged Orrade with a nod. 'If I had not been such a hot-headed youth, my father and I would have reconciled years ago. I should have admitted I was wrong but I was too proud.' He broke off, frowning at Orrade. 'Swallow your pride, lad.'

Orrade shook his head. 'It's not that simple.'

Lence frowned. 'Why did he disinherit you, Orrie?'

'That is between my father and I, kingsheir.' Orrade retreated into formality.

Byren watched his twin stiffen. Young Garzik went to say something in Orrade's defence, but Byren elbowed him.

'King Rolen, I've come to offer my sword in your service,' Orrade said, dropping to one knee and drawing his sword, a serviceable one he'd taken from the estate's armoury, not the blade which had been wielded by lords of Dovecote for over three hundred years. He offered the weapon, blade across his open palms. 'Please accept –'

But the king was already shaking his head. 'Your father will change his mind, wait and see.'

Orrade remained on his knees. 'Not this time, King Rolen. I am without land or allegiance. Please accept me.'

As Byren watched his father wrestle with this, he saw the larger ramifications. King Rolen did not want to offend the old lord, who had been his staunchest ally.

The silence stretched uncomfortably.

'A man has to live or die by his word of honour,' Cobalt said softly. 'I know what it's like. Go to your father, apologise and –'

'Impossible,' Orrade cut him off, eyes on King Rolen.

Cobalt looked grim. Lence glanced from him to the king.

'Orrade nearly died trying to save me,' Byren spoke up. 'I would trust him with my life.'

'Then have him in your honour guard,' Lence snapped.

'That's it!' King Rolen muttered, relieved. 'You twins are old enough to form your own honour guards. Let Orrade serve the kingsheir.'

He strode off leaving Orrade on his knees.

'I'm sorry.' Lence stood over Orrade, whose lowered, bandaged head hid his expression. 'But a king must trust his men implicitly. Mend the break with your father and all will be well, Orrie.'

He turned and walked off, with their cousin falling into step beside him. Cobalt's voice carried back to Byren. 'Your father's right. What are you now? Twenty? A kingsheir should have his own honour guard –'

'We ride in half an hour!' the hunt-master shouted. Immediately, the level of noise in the stables doubled.

On his knees, Orrade shuffled until he faced Byren. 'I offer my fealty, Byren Kingson.'

Byren was both embarrassed and annoyed. His first impulse was to tell Orrade to get up, but he understood that to preserve his dignity, his friend had to complete the ritual of service given and received. 'I accept your fealty, Orrade Dovecotesheir. Now, get on your feet. We ride in –'

'Not Dovecotesheir,' Orrade corrected as he sheathed his sword, rising to confront Byren, his face flushed and his eyes glassy. 'I have no name other than my given name.'

Byren realised he had unwittingly rubbed salt in Orrade's wounded pride. 'Then I'll give you another. Orrade Byrensman.'

Orrade's eyes glittered with unshed tears. His mouth opened but Byren did not want to hear what he was about to say.

'Can I join your honour guard too, Byren?' Garzik shoved between them. 'Can we have our own surcoats with our own symbol like King Rolen's honour guard? Can we –'

Byren laughed. 'Enough, Garza, run to the kitchen, fetch food for us.'

Eager as a puppy, he darted off, dodging the castle youths, the hunt-master's apprentices and the castle's Affinity warders, who were checking their supplies. Naturally both Sylion and Halcyon's warders insisted on accompanying them, neither wanted the other to gain an advantage. It was annoying because young Nun Springdawn would insist on having her own snow-cave and Monk Autumnwind was growing frail.

'Thank you, Byren,' Orrade whispered, recalling him to the present.

Byren shrugged. 'I'm sorry about Lence, Orrie. For him everything is black and white, always has been.'

'True, but this time he's right,' Orrade admitted. 'If you can't take a man at his word, he's worthless.'

He went to move away, but Byren caught his arm. 'Actions speak louder than words. Spurnan proved that when he supported father against the very men who would have put him on the throne.'

But nothing could lessen the bleak gleam in his friend's tilted black eyes.

Byren glanced at Lence, who was checking his saddle girth, with Cobalt at his side. Between them, half a dozen youthful warriors, sons of the great lords and merchants, clamoured to join the kingsheir's honour guard. Byren knew a moment's jealousy. He should be there with Lence, sharing in this moment as they planned their honour guards.

Worse, the warriors they'd fought alongside these last five years were obviously eager to swear allegiance to serve Lence, while all he had was a disinherited son and a boy who'd run away from his domineering father.

Byren stiffened. He didn't mind being the spare heir – let Lence marry for political reasons – but he hated being second best.

'Eh, Illien?' King Rolen passed Byren as he strode towards Cobalt and Lence. The youths parted respectfully and Cobalt turned to face the king.

'We've got half an hour, come see Myrella. She'll be delighted...' Rolen broke off as his bad knee gave under him, causing him to lurch to one side.

Only Cobalt's quick thinking saved him from falling. 'What is it, Uncle?'

Byren tensed. Illien's father had never been formally recognised, hence the inverted crown on his coat of arms, so his son had no right to call the king 'Uncle'.

'Sylion take this knee. It's never been right since my horse rolled on it,' King Rolen muttered, completely disregarding Illien's breach of protocol.

'The healers –'

'Have done what they can, but it stiffens up.'

'Valens?' Cobalt beckoned a perfumed servant who, now that Byren had a better look, had to be fifty if he was a day. Surely that glossy black hair was not natural? 'My manservant has wonderful hands. He can massage away the stiffness. Let me make a gift of him to you, Uncle.'

Valens bobbed down on one knee, head bowed. Byren saw his father blink in surprise. Having a personal manservant was an Ostronite custom.

'But how will you manage, Illien?' Rolen asked, glancing to Cobalt's bandaged arm.

He shrugged this aside. 'Please, let me do this for you. At least let him try.'

Valens lifted his head. 'If I cannot get the stiffness out of your knee in ten days you may chop off my hands!'

'Extravagant Ostronites!' Orrade muttered in Byren's ear.

'Uncle?' Cobalt pressed.

'Very well.' Rolen laughed.

'I'm honoured.' Cobalt bowed. 'King Rolen, I must speak with you on another matter. I bring grave news from the elector.'

Byren frowned as his father led Cobalt away. What could the Elector of Ostron Isle have to say? If it was important Byren would hear about it at the next war table meeting. He had enough on his mind without borrowing trouble.

BYREN LAY ABSOLUTELY still, breathing slow and deep, wary of giving his position away. They were lucky the village's hunters had been tracking the leogryf and were able to lead them straight to its lair. The beast was old and canny, and knew the mountains well, but it was the leogryf's age that was its downfall. Although its wings were broader than the greatest of eagles', it could no longer lift its weight, so its lair was not atop a lonely pinnacle, but deep in a cave off a narrow goat track high on the Dividing Mountains. The beast had been spotted dragging its kill to feed in the privacy of the cave.

Shifting on the snow-covered rocks, Byren tried to keep his muscles limber. Who knew how long they would have to wait? Strange how he could feel bored and frightened at the same time. Not that he would ever admit to fear in front of Lence.

He licked dry lips.

Though old and weaker than it once was, the leogryf stood as tall as Byren's chest and, with one slash of its paw, could still disembowel a grown man or break his leg.

It was too dangerous to get in close. Byren had argued that they should trap the beast and dispatch it quickly, but Lence had got the idea in his head that he had to kill it from close quarters. Both the hunt-master and the Affinity warder had tried to talk him out of this and failed.

Byren adjusted his white fur coat, which blended perfectly with the deep snow. Focusing across the path to where his twin hid, Byren could just make out the gleam of Lence's eyes in the shadow of the rock crevice and a flash of white teeth as he smiled. In a way he was glad they were facing the leogryf alone together. Nothing had been right between them since Orrade had refused to reveal why he was disinherited. Cobalt was always at his twin's side, where Byren should have been.

The track zig-zagged up behind Lence to the cave entrance, which was the only way in. Eventually the leogryf would come back to its lair.

There was no breeze so they could not get downwind of the beast, but luckily its sense of smell was fading. To help disguise their own scents, Byren and Lence had scrubbed their bodies, aired their furs and rubbed dried heather on their skin.

The rest of the hunting party were waiting further down the track watching the three different approaches, ready to warn them when the beast was spotted and drive it back this way if it tried to retreat.

Not long now. The big muscles of Byren's legs trembled with tension. Waiting was always the worst. He had chosen to crouch on the extreme edge of the track. Behind him was a sheer drop into the ravine. Lence couldn't have done it. His head swam just looking at a drop like that, but heights had never troubled Byren.

Just then, a distinctive bird's cry floated on the cold, still air. Byren tensed and caught Lence's eyes across the path. The lookout's signal. Lence nodded. The leogryf approached.

Soundlessly, Byren strung his bow and selected an arrow, determined not to let the beast slink away wounded. It was better to kill it outright. If Lence's spear missed its mark, his arrow wouldn't.

Heart beating like a great drum, he rolled his shoulders to ease the tension and fixed his gaze on the path. Like him, Lence would be preparing to meet the beast. But Lence's weapon of choice was the spear. There was no glory in killing from a distance.

Winter coat white against the snow, the leogryf's fur almost cloaked its presence as it padded up the path, wings folded along its back, forming a shield. The angle was bad for a shot, too great a chance of missing the spot where the shoulder met the neck. Still, Byren could have attempted it, an arrow striking there would pierce the beast's lungs or heart, but he held back so that Lence could make his move.

His brother would wait until the beast moved between them, then leap in to drive the spear in behind the foreleg, under the wing nodule. If the angle was right the spear would sever the spine, crippling the leogryf. Then Lence could finish it quickly and, tonight, the hunting party would celebrate his bravery around the feasting fire.

Byren held his breath as the leogryf hesitated. Massive head down, it sniffed the snow suspiciously. Unable to make out their scents, it kept coming, moving into full view.

Byren bit back a whistle of appreciation. They'd known from the size of the paw prints and the length of the stride that the beast was big, but knowing and seeing were two different things. Rearing on its hind legs this leogryf would be twice as tall as a grown man. Though hollow-boned, it would weigh more than him.

Barely breathing, Byren waited as the beast prowled up the path. The moment its head passed them, Lence sprang from behind the rock, took aim and threw. But the leogryf reared back and Lence's spear missed, skittering across the snow not far from Byren.

The beast spun to confront Lence, tattered wings lifting, revealing its back and providing a target for Byren. He could have put an arrow into the base of the leogryf's neck, but Lence had a second spear and Byren was not about to spoil his brother's chance of making the kill.

Lence aimed and threw. This spear took the leogryf in the shoulder. It screamed in fury, staggering, then snarled and dropped to all fours, muscles bunching to leap.

Byren sprang to his feet, aimed and let the arrow fly, but the beast chose that instant to spring. His arrow lodged in the muscle of a rear leg. Again, it gave that uncanny scream.

The leogryf collided with Lence, its momentum carrying him to the ground.

Lence did not stand a chance.

Byren plucked another arrow, notched and drew.

Thwang.

The string broke.

He'd waxed it only this morning, but there were no guarantees in life. Dropping the bow, he reached for his hunting knife. It was razor-sharp and as long as his forearm. He knew the others would be making their way up the track but they would not be in time to save Lence.

Desperate, Byren leapt onto the rock he'd been crouching behind and flung himself onto the leogryf's broad back. The half-raised wings collapsed under the impact.

The leogryf released Lence and reared, trying to throw Byren. His thighs flexed, clamping around the beast's flanks. The leogryf writhed, wings struggling to beat, thick mane nearly blinding him. It was worse than breaking a horse.

Byren buried his face in the leogryf's neck and held on with one arm, while reaching past the thick mane. He plunged the knife into the point where the leogryf's shoulder met the neck.

The beast screamed again and rolled, tearing the knife hilt from Byren's hands and crushing the air from his chest. It sprang to its feet, rounding on him.

He lay sprawled in the snow, facing certain death, unable to lift his head, unable even to catch his breath. He must not die like this!

Yet he could not move.

The beast took one step, then another, then fell to its knees and collapsed. Hardly able to believe his life had been spared, Byren scrambled to his haunches.

'Lence?' he croaked, gulping great lungfull's of cold mountain air. His legs shook so badly he had to crawl, praying all the while to Halcyon for his twin's life, praying the beast had not managed to get its rear legs into his brother's belly and disembowel him, or torn out his throat.

Chapter Six

LENCE LAY ON his stomach. He must have turned and tried to run. The thick fur of his winter coat was shredded from his shoulders to his buttocks. Only the many layers of cloth underneath had saved his back from being lacerated. Byren's knees ploughed through the fine white snow as he dropped beside him. 'Lence, speak to me.'

His brother stirred and Byren rolled him over. Lence seemed unhurt, thrusting Byren's helping hands away.

'I'm all right, just winded. Saw nothing but stars for a bit.' Lence grimaced and shrugged his massive shoulders. 'M'back feels like the beastie danced on it.'

Byren grinned with relief. 'I guess he did.'

Lence came to his feet easily enough, his gaze going to the fallen leogryf. 'So what happened?'

Byren pointed to the wound as they approached the beast. 'I was lucky. My hunting knife found its heart.' He stepped around the body, onto the far side near the drop but, before he could retrieve his knife, he saw an impossible sight.

A second leogryf stood poised on the high rock behind Lence, about to attack. Just as Lence spun to see what had startled him, the beast leapt.

'Down, Byren!' Lence threw himself across the fallen leogryf, shoving Byren out of the path of the attacking beast. They both went down, sprawling in the snow. Byren's legs swung off the ledge. He felt the weight of his thick-soled winter boots drag him over and scrabbled for purchase on the slippery snow-covered rocks. Lence grabbed his arm. Byren clutched him. For a terrible moment he felt Lence begin to slide towards him, then Lence wedged his legs between two rocks and saved them. Relieved beyond measure, Byren swung his weight onto the ledge.

Even as this was going on Byren was aware of the leogryf sailing over them. He rolled closer to Lence and looked up to see the beast's paws scrambling as it hung suspended in mid-air, wings battling to prevent its fall. Then it dropped. Its feral scream of fury echoed up the ravine walls.

Byren wriggled around to peer down over the ledge's lip. He was in time to see the beast battling valiantly to prevent its fall, but its ragged wings were in even worse condition than the larger one. Unable to gain height, it was rapidly tiring. A vicious gust of wind drove it into the cliff face, stunning it. Then it tumbled out of control towards the jagged rocks below.

Byren felt the impact in the pit of his stomach. That could so easily have been him.

'Who would have thought there'd be a second one?' Lence muttered.

'It was the female,' Byren said as he made the connection. 'Leogryfs mate for life. The male must have been bringing back its kills to share. We were lucky this time.'

Lence sat up on his heels, careful not to look towards the ledge's edge. 'You saved my life. Again!'

'Then you saved mine. That makes us even.' Byren grinned.

'No. Not even. There was that time when –'

'Doesn't count. You would have saved yourself.'

Lence rolled to his feet, backing away from the drop. 'I owe you.'

Byren would have argued but the others arrived. They came shouting and marvelling over the fallen leogryf. Seeing both brothers alive and well they cheered.

Monk Autumnwind approached the beast to say the chants over it. The Affinity that had been released when it died had to be settled. It was best to be sure with matters of power. Before he could start, Nun Springdawn hurried over to join him. Her manner made it clear she thought it her business to make sure he went about this correctly.

Byren hid a smile and turned to find the hunt-master inspecting the beast. He checked where the hunting knife was wedged then shook his head and laughed. Retrieving it, he wiped it clean and strode over to Byren. As if it was an honoured sword, he presented it to him, hilt first across his forearm. Byren took it and slid the knife into its sheath.

Garzik bounded over to Byren demanding to know exactly what had happened.

'Watch what you're doing.' Lence grabbed the youngster's arm, pulling him away from the edge. He caught Byren's eye with a shake of his head. Were they ever so heedless? 'Come over here, Garza.'

Byren and Lence returned to the place where the others crowded around the leogryf. They were perched on rocks or struggling to get a glimpse of it, impeding each other on the narrow path.

'Byren killed it with a single blow of a hunting knife,' the hunt-master announced.

They cheered. Orrade clapped him on the back saying something but his words were drowned out as the others all shouted at once, demanding to know how he'd managed it.

Lence raised his arms. 'He leapt on its back to save m'life.'

They cheered again.

'That's right,' Byren agreed. 'Then the beastie's mate would have killed me but for Lence's quick thinking!'

'We heard the second one's scream,' the hunt-master said, shaking his head. 'I missed it. I –'

'I should have suspected,' Autumnwind muttered, rising and dusting snow off his hands.

'Yes. Leogryfs mate for life,' Springdawn said, as if this was obvious.

'Don't worry,' Byren spoke quickly. 'The villagers missed it too.'

While the others discussed this, the hunt-master turned to Byren. 'I've never seen a leogryf slain with a hunting knife. King Rolen the Third was the last man to kill one with a spear!'

Byren shrugged. 'It was that or end up in the beast's belly.'

'Trust Byren. He always has to go one better.' Lence slung an arm around Byren's shoulders, but his voice held a tinge of bitterness, reminding Byren that his twin had wanted the honour.

As the men cheered he turned to Lence, worried. His brother's black eyes gleamed with laughter and rueful admiration.

Relief eased the knot in Byren's belly. Today had proven the old seer wrong. Nothing would come between him and his twin. Nothing could. He caught Cobalt watching them and grinned. His older cousin returned the smile with a shake of his head which Byren took to mean that he and his twin were lucky to be alive. And didn't he know it.

One of the hunt-master's apprentices returned Lence's spears and they set about tying the beast across them to carry it back to the village.

'Now we know what your symbol should be,' Garzik told Byren, his eyes glowing.

'What symbol?'

'Your honour guard's,' Garzik explained. 'A foenix facing a leogryf!'

Byren laughed. The men lifted him off his feet, onto their shoulders. Their cheers drowned all thought. Blood rushed through his veins. He'd faced death and come out the other side. Throwing back his head, he felt a great shout of laughter roaring up through him and let it out.

Life sung in his veins.

'Byren Leogryfslayer!' the men chanted. 'Byren Leogryfbane!'

At that moment he looked over to Lence, willing him to share this. Cobalt leant close to his twin, to make a comment. For a heartbeat his brother's eyes glittered strangely. Then the men spun Byren around so that he lost sight of Lence. He demanded to be let down and they released him, still shouting and laughing. Disoriented and disconcerted, he staggered a little.

'One blow, straight to the heart!' Garzik crowed. 'With only a hunting knife!'

'A lucky strike,' Byren protested. The men laughed and refused to believe him. Though he tried to contain the grin, he felt his lips pull back. After all, it was an achievement. Then Byren remembered his twin's odd expression. If Lence's spear had been thrown true it would have been him they lauded as the leogryf slayer. 'Enough of that.'

But his protests fell on deaf ears. The rest of them, the sons of the kingdom's first families and the hunt-master's apprentices, congratulated him.

'We'll take the leogryf back to the village to celebrate tonight,' the hunt-master announced. The Affinity warders would lead the village in making atonement to Halcyon, for they had killed one of her creatures. 'Then tomorrow, we head down to Rolenhold. Don't want to miss the midwinter feast!'

The men agreed.

Soon they were trudging back to the high mountain village, where the others told the story of how Byren had killed the leogryf with nothing but his hunting knife. The villagers were in awe of him and very relieved to be free of the beast. When they learnt that the male's mate had been hidden in the lair, they were horrified and apologetic. Byren assured them no harm was done and it too, was dead. They insisted on honouring the hunters with a feast and set about preparing it.

All the while Lence's smile got tighter and tighter. No one but Byren seemed to notice and there was nothing he could do, for to turn down the villagers' feast would have been churlish. He had saved his brother's life and Lence had returned the favour. This should have been enough to settle his fears, but Byren was aware of a small kernel of worry growing within him, planted by the old seer.

It wasn't as if he'd meant to steal Lence's glory. He could hardly have let the beast kill him. Halcyon forbid it, that would make him the kingsheir!

When the others went out to the feasting fire Byren remained in the village council hall to think. The building had been dug into the mountain side for protection from the winter's cold so one wall and half the roof were made of natural stone. With a chimney at each end and a series of narrow shuttered windows tucked under the steep roof, it could house all the adults of the village. Right now it held the hunting party's belongings. He rolled his bow in oiled cloth and tucked it away with his pack. You had to look after your weapons. It might mean the difference between life and death. It nearly had today when the bow string broke.

It was strange. As twins he and Lence were very similar, yet so different. Sometimes Byren felt closer to

Fyn. Almost midwinter. Fyn would be coming to the castle for the ceremonies and celebrations. It would be good to see his serious younger brother again and Fyn's arrival was sure to make Piro's face light up.

Just then, the hunters broke into a drinking song and Byren glanced through the open door to see the others sitting around the feasting fire, eyes alight with laughter, cheeks reddened by the flames. Lence was in the midst of them, drinking and laughing loudest of all.

Time to join them and slip quietly into the background. Byren checked the edge on his hunting knife and slid it into its sheath. In the early days of father's reign it was customary to go armed at all times, but his father had forbidden the wearing of even ceremonial swords in the castle during celebrations. Too many duels between hot-headed warriors had resulted in deaths and blood feuds.

Byren turned to go outside.

The village's head couple stood in the doorway.

'Byren Rolen Kingson,' the old man said, giving a jerky bob of his head. His wife followed suit. 'We've come about Unistag Spar. My wife's cousin lives over the Divide on Foenix Spar and –'

'Unistag raiders have attacked her village three times this winter, took their store of winter grain and all the marriageable girls,' the wife interrupted indignantly. 'And I want to know what King Rolen's going to do about it.'

The husband sent Byren an apologetic look. Strictly speaking, this wasn't King Rolen's responsibility. The spars were ruled by petty princelings, warlords, who held power by hereditary right, enforced with the sword.

Byren knew what his father would say. In fact, it wasn't his place to take this to his father. He glanced past them to the campfire and Lence.

The old man took in the direction of his gaze. 'We came to you because you killed the leogryf.'

Byren was beginning to wish he hadn't.

'And it's no good saying my cousin should go to the Foenix warlord for help,' the old woman said, as if in answer to something Byren had said. 'Because there's no point their warlord protesting to the Unistag warlord. The warlord of Unistag is so frail he won't see spring. His heirs are fighting over who will wear his helm. Meanwhile their warriors, greedy for grain and glory, are raiding Foenix Spar.'

Byren nodded. Rolencia's spies had reported this. 'Look, I'll mention it to the king, but I can't promise anything.'

They nodded.

He grinned. 'You could always suggest your cousin move over the Divide into Rolencia. Nowhere's safer!' Even Merofynia had been rocked by civil war when his mother's younger brother died and more recently the Merofynian spars' warlords had fought a series of bitter battles.

'See,' the old woman said. 'The kingson agrees with me.'

Thanking him, the old man backed out, drawing his wife with him. Byren headed towards the feasting fire. The change of warlord on Unistag Spar could mean trouble for Rolencia. A young, ambitious man would set out to impress his followers and that could mean raids on the Rolencian valley people as well as other spars.

He felt a surge of purpose solidify. It looked like he'd be busy this spring. If Lence led the fleet against the Utland raiders, Byren would have to contain the spars. The warlord of Unistag Spar wasn't the only warlord testing King Rolen's strength. That reminded him, he must tell his father about the raiders he'd seen skating across the valley.

Before approaching the feasting fire, Byren slipped around the far end of the hall to relieve himself, his hot stream cutting a channel in the snow.

'You and Lence used to try to write your names in the snow but you'd always run out,' Cobalt said as he joined him, unlacing his breeches one-handed.

Byren laughed as he laced up. 'And we only had to write five letters!'

'Well, you were just lads of six or seven at the time.' Cobalt finished, managing to refasten his breeches despite his injured arm.

'Eh, Illien?' Byren felt he had started on the wrong foot with him because of the trouble with Orrade. 'I'm sorry to hear about your father and your –'

'Yes.' Cobalt cut him off. In the brilliant starlight his face creased into a grim smile. 'I used to dream of the day I'd return with a shipload of Ostronite treasure to lay at my father's feet. But when I did, it killed him.' He saw Byren did not understand. 'I was bringing my bride and a king's ransom of jewels home to Cobalt estate. In thirteen years I'd done well and married well and I was proud of it. I wanted to show my father that he had misjudged me so I converted my assets to jewels, portable wealth. But the raiders must have had a spy on Ostron Isle, because they knew. They demanded the jewel chest.'

Byren frowned. Raiders attacked the spars and the merchant ships. If they captured someone important they'd usually hold them to ransom, not murder them. The old lord had been unlucky. And, as for Cobalt's wife... raiders were always stealing girls and young women. Life was hard on the Utlands, women were precious. 'You were unlucky, Illien, that's all.'

'I believe we make our own luck,' he said. 'As you did today. You did well tackling that leogryf, Byren. Your bravery has inspired –'

'What else could I do? I couldn't let the beastie make a meal of Lence.'

Cobalt studied him. It was hard to read his expression in the starlight. He lifted his good hand to rest on Byren's shoulder, had to raise his chin only slightly to meet Byren's eyes, reminding him that the blood of King Rolence the First ran true in both of them. 'Lence is lucky to have you.'

Byren shrugged this aside. Singing from the feast fire carried on the still, cold air. The scent of roasting mutton made his mouth water and his stomach rumble.

'Some say it's a pity only seven minutes stands between you and the throne,' Cobalt remarked softly.

Byren stepped back so that Cobalt's arm dropped between them. 'I don't want –'

'Like I said. Lence is lucky to have you,' Cobalt cut him off and Byren thought he must have misinterpreted the comment. This was confirmed when Cobalt continued. 'Especially with the unrest in Merofynia. When he marries Isolt –'

'He told you about that?' The official announcement would be made Midwinter's Day.

'No, King Rolen told me.'

'Father?'

'I spoke briefly with him before we rode out, remember. I carried a message from the Elector of Ostron Isle.'

'You're that close to the elector?'

'My bride is... was his niece.'

'Ah, I'm sorry.' Byren realised he knew nothing about his cousin.

The level of good-natured revelry from the feasting fire rose another notch as two merchant sons raced to drain their tankards to the encouragement of the men. Most of them would be too drunk to stagger to bed tonight. Byren winced. He had a suspicion Rolenhold's court would appear uncouth to his cousin after Ostron Isle.

'The elector wanted your father to know that Warlord Palatyne has become overlord of all the Merofynian spars and King Merofyn has recognised his authority.'

'He never!' Byren insisted, then digested this in silence. After the last poisoning attempt the Merofynian king had never really recovered. The warlords, sensing weakness, had tried to snatch Merofynia. His father's spies had reported that Palatyne was the most powerful of them but... 'So this Palatyne succeeded in defeating the other warlords?'

'And he has half the lords of Merofynia on his side.' Cobalt hesitated, then went on as if deciding Byren was ready to hear this. 'If your brother marries Isolt he'll have to watch Overlord Palatyne. Or maybe he'll send you to Merofynia to keep Palatyne and the rest of the lords in line.'

'But King Merofyn –'

'Is old and frail. He's a spent force. The people are fed up with his taxes and his religious oppression. Meanwhile, Palatyne swaggers around Port Mero, king in all but name.'

Byren said nothing. This did not bode well for his twin.

Cobalt slid his good arm around Byren's shoulders and turned him towards the feasting fire. 'So, Lence is lucky he has you.'

As they approached the others Garzik saw them coming and darted over to Byren, drawing two youths with him.

'Woodend and Highfield want to join your honour guard, Byren,' Garzik beamed.

Both boys – sons of merchants – nodded eagerly and dropped to their knees, offering their swords before he could say anything. He wouldn't have been human if he wasn't pleased to have won their admiration. Byren grinned and the two youths promptly placed their hands over their hearts and began to swear the oath.

'A Fealty Ceremony?' Cobalt muttered. He strode around to where Lence now stood. 'I insist mine is the honour to be first to formally join Lence Kingsheir's guard!'

Sinking gracefully to one knee, he lifted his good arm to place his injured hand on his heart. The other castle youths, young lords like Cobalt and elder sons, jostled to be next. Lence accepted their fealty with obvious satisfaction.

Younger sons and merchant sons hurried to Byren's side of the fire. With a sinking heart, he realised the castle's defenders were choosing sides in a battle he did not want to fight. But he accepted the fealty oaths with good grace, for he could do no less. The feasting continued and, while the others drank and laughed, Byren thought on what he'd learnt from Cobalt.

Much later, as they bedded down in the Council Hall, the village women presented him with their prettiest maiden. She beamed, pleased with the honour of sharing his bed. Her eyes had been painted to make them look huge and glass beads had been threaded through her waist-length hair. They tinkled as she bowed and the men – those who weren't already snoring – made appreciative noises, joking about his prowess.

Byren knew she would have been chosen because she could not conceive tonight so he need not fear creating another bastard. Many a time he and Lence had enjoyed a village's gratitude for chasing off spar warriors or Affinity beasts, but tonight he realised he could not bed this girl, not when he could still feel Elina weeping in his arms, heartbroken over Orrade's blindness.

Fool! He should have sent word that Garzik was safe with them when they returned to the castle, and that Orrade's sight had returned. He should have put Elina's mind at rest but they'd left to hunt the leogryf in such a rush...

'What's wrong, Byren? Have you forgotten how to do it?' Lence teased.

He glanced up, startled. The women of the council had left and the girl waited expectantly, a smile lighting her eyes.

No. He could not bed her, not here in the hall where the dark was their only privacy, not ever, not when it was Elina he wanted.

He lifted his hands, wondering how to do this without hurting her feelings. She blinked in dismay, the smile slipping from her face as she read his expression.

Byren caught her hand, bowing over it, using his best court manners to ease the rejection. 'I'm sorry. But my heart is already taken.'

'What about your prong?' some wit shouted.

Heat stole up Byren's face as he released the girl's hand.

Her face crumpled and she fled. Silence fell as the door slammed shut behind her.

'You've disgraced her,' Lence hissed, taking a step closer. 'What's wrong with you, Byren?'

'Enough, Lence,' Cobalt intervened. He cast Byren a curious glance, then led Lence away.

Byren hesitated. He wanted to call his twin back and explain but he couldn't. He was not formally betrothed to Elina and with the way things were between him and her father, he might never be.

So he turned away, grabbed his bed roll and retreated to the far fireplace where he lay down with his back to the others and stared at the flames. After a moment he heard Orrade and Garzik loyally join him and the others bedding down. The last lamps were doused, then the hall became quiet except for snores and sleepy mumbles.

Chapter Seven

TENSION CRAWLED ACROSS Piro's shoulders, as she wished herself invisible. Here she was, trapped between her parents and Sylion's mystics mistress whose tapping cane grew ever closer as she approached. The abbess kept pace with the old mystic so they would arrive together to formally greet her parents. Piro had tried to avoid this meeting, claiming she needed to feed her foenix, but her mother had insisted that it was time to put away her childhood things.

I must not give myself away. I must not...

She halted the litany running over and over in her mind for fear it might attract the attention of the mystics mistress. Neither of the castle's Affinity warders had noticed the change in her since autumn cusp. But, although the mystics mistress was blind, she was said to be even more powerful than Halcyon's mystics master. Piro feared her many years of experience.

Think of something else.

Fyn! Yesterday Fyn arrived with the abbot and the monks but she hadn't had a chance to speak with her brother yet so he didn't know about the sudden blossoming of her Affinity with the gods.

There she was, thinking of it again.

If the mystics mistress wasn't specifically looking for it, could she sense the change in Piro from a distance? Piro didn't know.

There was so much she didn't know about having Affinity.

'And have you been doing any more paintings, Piro Kingsdaughter?' the abbess asked kindly, once the formal greetings finished. She always treated Piro as if she was seven, not almost a woman at thirteen. The abbess was plump and pink-cheeked with sharp, brilliant eyes, and looked as if she should be a successful shrewd sweets merchant, not the spiritual leader of an abbey that served the cruel, hard god of snow and ice.

'Such skill with a brush in one so young is a gift from the gods.'

Piro flushed. She must not look at the mystics mistress. But she felt as if her deception was branded across her forehead.

'Pirola,' her mother admonished. The queen always used her full name when she was annoyed.

Piro opened her mouth to speak but her father stepped in.

'We discovered a renegade Power-worker in Rolenton just a few days ago.'

'We heard,' the abbess said. 'A terrible business. My sympathy, Queen Myrella, it must have been –'

'Lence dealt with her,' King Rolen said. 'Our Affinity warders made sure her body was disposed of safely.'

Piro hid a smile. There had been a fierce argument between Springdawn and Autumnwind over who would lay the old woman's spirit to rest, with Springdawn winning because she held supremacy over all things to do with winter and women. Piro had been crossing the courtyard between Sylion's oratory and Halcyon's chantry when she overheard them going at it like cats and dogs.

'Tell me, mystics mistress.' The queen lifted one hand. 'Are the predictions of seers always hard to understand?'

This had been worrying Piro too. She'd even considered asking Springdawn when the nun returned from the hunt but had discarded the idea because she did not want to be lectured for hours on end. The nun was a terrible bore and Piro had been delighted when her tutoring finished the day she turned twelve.

The mystics mistress shook her head. 'There are very few seers and they are generally avoided, as they will speak only the truth.'

Piro glanced to her mother who had gone pale.

'I don't think she was a true seer,' Piro said quickly.

'Why's that, child?' the mystics mistress asked, turning her blind but oddly penetrating eyes on Piro.

Because I have Affinity and she said I was like my mother.

Piro swallowed. 'Because she claimed mother's loved ones would die since we did not make war on Merofynia and take the throne when King Sefon died. But I don't see how refusing to make war could lead to –'

King Rolen laughed. 'There will be no war with Merofynia. The seer was mistaken.'

'That is quite possible,' the mystics mistress agreed. 'The greatest scholars of both Sylion and Halcyon Abbeys have been studying past prophecies and have come to the conclusion that the future is a many-branched tree, while the past is a single trunk. So you see the seers' visions often go down paths that may not happen.'

Her father chuckled. 'Then what good are seers?'

'They warn us of what might be, if we are not vigilant,' the mystics mistress explained patiently.

'A wise king knows he must be ever vigilant.' Rolen patted the queen's arm. 'As Myrella and I are. Plans have been made to ensure –'

A shout from the back of the great hall cut him off and the growing commotion silenced the chatter on the king's dais. Everyone peered through the forest of columns, their embossed foenix pattern picked out in gold leaf, red carnelian stones and black marble. Several of the king's old honour guard, men who had served him in those terrible early days, reached for their absent sword hilts out of habit. The ambassador from Merofynia looked around uneasily. His little page took a step closer, eyes wide.

Piro experienced a vivid flash of memory, as she saw the seer fly through the air to strike the wall and her crumpled body sliding to rest on the snow bank. Piro's heart raced and her palms grew damp with fear. Was this new threat something the seer had tried to warn them about?

But when she strained to hear, the voices sounded surprised rather than angry. Then she heard her brothers' names and relief settled her stomach.

'The twins are back!' Queen Myrella exclaimed. 'Just in time for the festivities tomorrow.'

Everyone turned to see Lence and Byren march down the centre of Rolenhold's great hall. The warlords and their honour guards stepped aside. These warriors were decked out in all their finery, fur cloaks and spar surcoats, but none were as fine as her brothers even in their rough hunting clothes.

'You must be very proud of your sons, Queen Myrella,' the abbess said, wistfully.

As her mother made some reply, Piro's heart swelled. A head taller than nearly everyone else, Lence and Byren radiated good health and vigour. No wonder the young women looked on them with desire and the older ones with appreciation.

It was mid-afternoon and the great hall was packed, but everyone pulled back and a hush fell over the crowd as the hunt-master's apprentices dragged in the body of an enormous leogryf.

Then, as if released from a spell, people began chattering excitedly. King Rolen strode down the two steps from the dais, embracing Lence, then Byren. He took his time, inspecting the beast as he walked around its great length.

'Queen Myrella?' The Merofynian ambassador offered his arm.

Piro watched as her mother graciously accepted and stepped down from the dais. That was the difference between Rolencia and Merofynia, the difference between her mother and her father. The king was a sturdy, bluff man who said what he thought. The queen was a dainty, polished woman who spoke three languages and had tried to raise her daughter to be the mirror image of herself. The problem was that Piro might look like another version of her mother, but in her heart she took after her father.

Picking up her skirts, she jumped down from the dais and darted between the excited nobles, pushing through to join Byren. Standing so close to the beast made her realise how massive it was. 'It's huge!'

Byren grinned. 'From nose to tail tip it's twice as long as I am tall!'

'And those teeth!' She marvelled as one of the men prised the jaws open. Everyone gasped in amazement.

'...driving his hunting knife in here,' the hunt-master was saying. He showed her father and the gathered nobles where the blow had been struck. 'Byren went straight to the heart, killed it with one blow!'

'You killed it?' Piro turned to her brother.

'It attacked Lence. I didn't think, I just –'

But they didn't let him finish. King Rolen strode up to Byren, clasping both his shoulders. 'Truly, I am blessed with sons any king would envy!'

The hunters and King Rolen's honour guard cheered, the deep hearty sound echoing off the ceiling above like waves on the shore.

Piro laughed and hugged Byren, glancing to their mother, eager to share the moment. Queen Myrella had gone very still, as she stared at someone behind

Byren. Piro glanced over her shoulder, identifying a well-dressed stranger with his arm in a sling.

She tugged on her mother's sleeve. 'Is that Cousin Illien?'

'Cousin... yes, your father has acknowledged the blood tie,' she whispered.

Piro turned to have another look. Why, he had the same square jaw as Lence. He even carried himself like her eldest brother. Anyone could tell he was their kin. With one arm in a sling, and his elegant coat, he cut a fine figure. It was sad to think he'd lost his father and bride to the Utlander raiders.

King Rolen raised his arms, calling for silence. 'Well done, second son. It is a feat worthy of our ancestor, King Rolence the First!'

Piro hid a fond smile as Byren's face went a shade darker and he glanced about as if wishing he could slip away.

'A drink to celebrate. Bring the Rolencian red laid down the year I married Myrella!' King Rolen called. Servants scuttled off to fetch bottles and goblets. Midwinter feast was a time for drinking around the fire and telling tales of great deeds – a great deal of drinking and boasting.

Piro loved the tales of bravery and honour. If only she had lived in those times, when kingsdaughters had to ride to war to save their people!

She felt a tug on her arm and turned. She expected it to be her mother about to tell her it was not proper for her to sit around the feasting fire and listen to tales that could turn bawdy, but it was Fyn.

This close to him she was surprised by how much

he had grown. He was almost a head taller than her now. At nearly seventeen he would soon leave the ranks of the acolytes and become a monk. In fact, one of the Proving trials was to be held tomorrow.

Eyes pleading, Fyn glanced to the nearest door.

There was no need for words. They slipped away, Fyn leading her out the west passage towards Eagle Tower. The air was much cooler in this section of the Hold and the sound of the revelry soon faded, cut off by the thick stone walls.

'What is it?' Piro asked, her breath misting in the cold.

'Not here.' Fyn jerked his head upwards, indicating the tower where they could be private.

BYREN SIPPED HIS red wine, savouring the rich taste, while waiting for a chance to speak with his father. Finally the hunt-master and Lence moved off to refill their drinks, and he was alone with the king for a moment. He looked for his mother but she was entertaining the Merofynian ambassador. A pity, he would have liked the queen to hear this too.

'Has the warlord of Unistag sent anyone, father?' he asked. The warlords were supposed to renew their allegiance to the Rolencian King each midwinter and, if the warlord couldn't come, his delegate should.

'No,' King Rolen muttered. 'Not unless his delegate arrives before tomorrow evening –'

'Don't expect anyone. His heirs are fighting over who will take his place. My guess is, they couldn't agree who should represent him, because if they did it would be agreeing on his successor.'

'And where did you hear this?' Lence demanded, coming up behind him with Cobalt and Captain Temor.

Byren repressed an irrational surge of guilt. 'The villagers.' He was not about to reveal that they'd come to him, and not Lence, as the king's representative. 'They were complaining about Unistag raids on Foenix Spar driving people over the Divide.'

King Rolen nodded. 'Looks like we'll need to teach the Unistags a lesson this spring.'

'Sooner, before they can come over the pass and raid our villages,' Lence agreed with relish, having caught the last part of the conversation. 'I claim the honour of leading the fleet to the Utlands.'

'That reminds me,' Byren said, on another track entirely. 'I saw a band of thirty raiders in the valley. Have you had reports of an attack?'

His father shook his head. 'None. Are you sure they were from over the Divide and not from one of our lords' estates?'

'They wore no lord's emblem and they moved with deadly purpose.'

'But how can you be sure they were warlord's men?' Cobalt asked.

Byren hesitated. He'd been fighting spar warriors for five years now and his gut feeling told him they were not Rolencian. But, if they were spar warriors, why would they come down into the valley? Most raids occurred just over the pass on the high villages and mostly when they were desperate to feed their people. There had to be a better way...

'They were raiders, I just know,' Byren muttered. 'Father, I've been thinking. What if we built granaries –'

'Halcyon Abbey has a great granary,' Lence reminded him.

'Yes. But I meant to share with the spars.'

'What?' Cobalt mocked gently. 'Give away Rolencia's bounty? That would only make the people of the spars lazy. Why work when they could come a-begging?'

Lence and King Rolen laughed.

Byren felt his face flame. 'I'm trying to think of a way to stop the raids, Illien.'

'Teach them a lesson!' his father snapped. 'That's what m'father did and his before him. It's all they understand.'

'Not much better than Utlanders!' Lence added.

He and King Rolen laughed and refilled their wine goblets.

'The queen seems very close to the Merofynian ambassador,' Cobalt remarked in the lull that followed. 'Does she miss her home?'

Lence scowled. 'Rolencia is mother's home.'

Byren glanced to their mother. She was listening to the old ambassador. Probably talking about Lence's planned wedding, which would be announced on Midwinter's Day.

'My wife knew the ambassador when she was a child in Merofynia. He was a friend of her father's,' King Rolen said.

'That explains it then, Uncle,' Cobalt said. 'You are a lucky man, Queen Myrella is still a lovely as ever.'

Byren's father glanced to the queen, smiling fondly. 'We'll have been married twenty-one years this spring cusp and it will be three hundred years since King Rolence claimed the valley, uniting it under his banner. Yes, I am a lucky man. You must stand on the royal dais at the Jubilee, Nephew.'

'I would be honoured, Uncle.'

Obviously pleased to see their cousin acknowledged and formally welcomed back into the family, Lence slung an arm around Illien's shoulder. 'A toast to Rolencia!'

As they refilled their cups Byren experienced a stab of intense emotion. It took a moment for him to realise it was jealousy and he dismissed it as unworthy.

'Ever killed a saltwater wyvern, Illien?' Lence asked.

'No, but the Elector of Ostron Isle has a pet one. It's all the fashion.'

'Eh, Ostron Isle! What'll they come up with next?' King Rolen rolled his eyes.

Lence launched into the tale of his first wyvern kill and Byren excused himself. He had to write to Elina, to let her know that Garzik was safe and Orrade had recovered his sight. Retreating to his chamber, he spent a long time over the ink well. He longed to beg Elina's forgiveness and make everything right between them, but he couldn't find the right words. So in the end he stuck to the facts, sealed the note and sent for a courier to take it to Dovecote.

PIRO FOLLOWED FYN up the steep steps to Eagle Tower. The stairs had been built curving around the inner wall so that defenders could back up, shielding their bodies if the castle walls were ever breached. Not that they would be. Rolenhold had never been taken.

She concentrated on keeping up with Fyn's longer legs. Why couldn't she have been born tall and strong like her namesake? On top of the tower Fyn paced to the battlements and Piro joined him, glad of a chance to catch her breath. Silently, he looked down across the snow-covered Rolencian valley with its network of iced-over canals and streams linking the lakes, right across to Mount Halcyon and the abbey.

Now that he had her attention Fyn seemed to be having trouble getting started.

'That leogryf... no wonder father is proud of Byren,' Piro said. 'And he will be even prouder when you are welcomed into the weapons master's branch of the brotherhood. Why, one day you may be weapons master yourself!'

He glanced at her, then looked away, uncomfortable.

Her heart sank. 'What is it?'

'The weapons master already offered me a place in his ranks, but I turned him down.'

She stared at him, horrified. If King Rolen knew, he would be furious.

Fyn grimaced. 'I couldn't kill on order.'

She searched his face. Lence and Byren had no trouble leading raiding parties. 'I don't –'

Fyn sighed. 'I hate to see anyone hurt, even animals. I could never be a warrior.'

'Oh,' Piro whispered. She had never given much thought to the warriors her brothers killed or injured. Lence and Byren had always seemed so powerful, larger than life, like her father. Now, after seeing the leogryf and hearing how Byren killed it to save Lence's life, she grew fearful for them. 'But sometimes you have to kill or be killed.'

'I know. If anyone hurt you or mother I'd protect you,' Fyn muttered grimly. His obsidian eyes fixed on Piro and she caught a glimpse of the man he might become. It made her shiver. His voice softened and he was a worried youth again. 'But how could I kill men who are simply serving their warlord?'

Piro worried her bottom lip with her teeth. Fyn had always been kinder than the twins. It had never occurred to her that this could make his life harder. 'I don't know what to say. Father expects you to become weapons master so you can support Lence when he is king.'

'I know!' He was clearly frustrated and worried. 'I've been thinking and I see only one way out of this. When the masters make their selection from this year's acolytes, the mystics master must choose me.'

'It would be a great honour to be chosen for a mystic,' Piro said slowly. 'Not as useful to father or Lence, but –'

'So you see, tomorrow I must be first across the lake, first to find Halcyon's Fate, but only someone with great Affinity can find it and I'm… I barely registered when they tested me. I don't know what I'll do.' Desperation lent an edge to his voice.

Impulsively, Piro clutched his arm. 'You'll do it, Fyn, I know you will!'

He gave her a smile that said he appreciated her faith in him, even if it was misplaced.

Piro saw that she had to help him. For the first time since she'd developed Affinity she was glad she had it.

'Don't worry.' She squeezed his arm. 'Everything will turn out right tomorrow. Trust me.'

'Thanks, Piro.' He patted her hand as if she was too young to understand.

She bristled. She would be fourteen on Midsummer's Day.

'We'd better get back,' Fyn announced.

Still fuming, she followed him down to the great hall. The leogryf had been hauled away to be stuffed and mounted, and would join the other animals in the trophy chamber where it would be honoured as one of Halcyon's beasts.

Meanwhile King Rolen was holding the usual midwinter hearing. Four times a year he opened his hall to give ordinary Rolencians a chance to have their grievances heard and settled. Usually it was farmers disputing over fields or merchants arguing over shoddy goods.

Lence sat beside their father, being trained to follow in his footsteps. Byren stood behind their mother's chair, one arm resting on the high back. Funny, she hadn't seen it before but that was the way they were. Despite what he'd said about the leogryf, she knew her father favoured Lence and her mother adored Byren. As for her and Fyn, they were only spare heirs. And sometimes Piro suspected her mother thought she was more trouble than she was worth.

'I'd better get back to the monks,' Fyn whispered. 'Don't tell anyone.'

'Of course not.'

He headed towards the ranks of the monks but Piro hesitated. She knew she should join her mother and listen to the hearing. As a kingsdaughter she had to learn the intricacies of Rolencian law. Her mother knew it better than her father. But it was so boring. She had never understood how people could get irate over a few gold coins, or a field of corn. Maybe she would just slip quietly away.

'Pirola Rolen Kingsdaughter,' her mother called. Everyone turned. Piro wished she could sink through the floor. 'Come sit beside me. Listen and learn.'

She dared not disobey.

Piro took her seat at her mother's side. In the cleared space before the dais an old man and a youth of about fifteen were confronted by one of Halcyon's monks, who wore the umber robe of a village Affinity warder.

'By King Rolen's decree it is against the law to hide Untamed Affinity,' the warder announced. Piro stiffened. 'And isn't it written that everyone with Affinity must serve the church or risk becoming a channel for evil?'

The crowd nodded.

'And yet this man,' he pointed to the old farmer, 'this man has tried to deny the abbey his son!'

As people muttered under their breath, Piro swallowed and glanced down, noting how her mother's hands had tightened on the chair, until her knuckles showed white.

King Rolen cleared his throat. 'Is this true, Farmer Overhill?'

The old man dropped to his knees. 'I swear, King Rolen, Queen Myrella, my son's Affinity did not show until this year. I did not know.'

'Mystics master?'

A thin man of no more than forty stepped out of the ranks of monks, surprising Piro. The old master must have died since she saw him at winter cusp. Piro had noticed this mystic before because of his malformed arm which was hidden inside his robe. His shaved head gleamed with intricate tattoos revealing that he had attained the highest level of knowledge. To have been chosen as mystics master at so young an age, he had to be very gifted and dedicated. Piro was glad his attention wasn't focused on her.

'Affinity usually shows up by the age of six but it can remain dormant until puberty or some crisis triggers it. The boy should be in training,' the mystics master said. He caught the abbot's eye.

The old abbot spoke up. 'He can come back with us when we leave.'

The farmer lifted his hands pleadingly. 'If I send my only surviving child to the abbey, who will run my farm? I am too old to do the heavy work!'

'Send the son to the abbey!' yelled someone. 'We don't want untamed Affinity open to evil in our village.'

'Punish Overhill. He wasn't going to tell anyone about his son's Affinity. They've been hiding it!' yelled another. 'Banish him!'

Several voices echoed this eagerly.

Farmer Overhill moaned. His son tried to comfort him, but the men-at-arms held them apart.

Piro felt sorry for the farmer. She wanted to jump down there and order the men-at-arms off them. She glanced to her father.

'You know the law,' King Rolen said. 'Everyone with Affinity must serve the gods or risk becoming channels for evil. Unlike Merofynia, we won't allow renegade Power-workers to wander around stirring up trouble!'

People muttered under their breath in agreement. Rolencians had a low opinion of Merofynian customs, especially with regard to Affinity. Piro noticed her mother's tight lips. Her parents loved each other, but the role of Power-workers was the one thing they could not agree on.

Her mother leant closer to the king. 'If you banish the farmer you will have to reallocate his lands. The people from his village are far too eager to gain from his misfortune. If they had been more helpful he would not have been so desperate to keep his son with him.'

'Yet the son must go the abbey or be banished along with his father,' King Rolen whispered. 'I cannot ignore the law for anyone, not even you, my love.'

'Confiscate the farm!' the warlord of Leogryf Spar yelled. 'I would. No mercy for those who would hide Affinity.'

His sentiments were echoed by others.

King Rolen held up his hand for silence. Piro knew her father walked a narrow path. If he was too cruel, his own people would grow to hate him, yet if he was too lenient, his warlords would grow bold and raid Rolencia's rich valley. Word of the Utland raid on Port Cobalt had reached the spar warlords, which made King Rolen look weak. Ruling Rolencia was one long battle to keep the lawless elements under control.

'What do you think, kingsheir?' King Rolen asked.

'The law must be obeyed,' Lence said. 'Unless he serves the gods, the boy's choices are banishment or death. The old man is lucky you do not punish him for trying to hide his son's Affinity.'

King Rolen nodded. Piro felt sick to her stomach.

Muttering made her glance to the faces of Farmer Overhill's fellow villagers. She noticed the greedy gleam in their eyes. Her mother was right, they were too eager.

'But you can't send the boy to the abbey. There is no one to work the old man's farm. He'll starve!' she protested, only just remembering to keep her voice low.

'Quiet, Piro,' Lence snapped. 'The son has to go to the abbey. Without laws we are no better than the savages of the Utland Isles.'

From the corner of her eye, Piro noticed Byren shifting his weight. Abruptly, he leant forwards between their parents' chairs. 'Why not ask the abbot to send the gardening monks to help out on the farm during planting and harvesting? They could take most of the produce back to the abbey, and leave the old man enough to live on.'

Lence snorted. 'The old man won't last more than a couple of winters. What happens to the farm then?'

'At least he will have the winters in his own home,' Byren said. 'As to the farm, it is the son's inheritance. Let ownership go to the abbey once the old man is dead. When winters are hard the monks feed the needy. This way all Rolencia benefits, not just some greedy villagers.'

'Well said, Byren.' Queen Myrella placed her hand on the king's. 'Rolen?'

He nodded, stood and cleared his throat. 'Hear my judgement...'

Piro stopped listening. Though the judgement was fair, she felt hollow. People were so quick to turn on those with Affinity. It was fear that provoked it, fear of the Unseen and fear of how untamed Affinity left the god-touched person open to evil.

As she watched Farmer Overhill and his son being led away – the youth to the monks, the old man to his none-too-friendly fellow villagers – Piro vowed to hide her growing Affinity.

At least it was good for one thing, she could help Fyn find the Fate tomorrow.

Chapter Eight

LATER THAT EVENING Byren could hear the familiar drinking song echoing up the stairwell from the great hall. By rights he should go down there and join the table where his brother sat, surrounded by the young men of Rolencia, but he hesitated. Had he sensed a growing antagonism in Lence or was he imagining it because of the seer's prediction?

This was ridiculous. He wished he had never met the old seer.

Had he acted differently since that day? Going over things, he was sure he hadn't. And he wouldn't!

Byren strode down the stairs.

Lence was in the midst of Rolenhold's young men, arm wrestling as they cheered him on. He sat at a table in front of the huge fireplace. Over this hung King Rolence the First's shield and sword, a symbol of his ancestors' long tradition of service to protect the kingdom, and the royal banner of

Rolencia. Byren felt a surge of pride in his family's achievements.

'Ho, Byren,' his father called. 'Come take your turn. The best arm wrestler from Rolenhold is going to challenge the best of the warlords' men.'

He glanced to the other tables and saw that the warlords' honour guards had already selected a champion. He was a grizzled warrior from Manticore Spar, not as tall as Lence but broad through the chest. By the old burn scars on his brawny arms, Byren guessed he was a blacksmith when not leading raiding parties. The man grinned and yelled a challenge, revealing a gap where three teeth were missing.

Byren searched the eager faces of the warlords. Only four of the five were present. If Rolencia was the hub of a half wheel, then Manticore Spar was the first spoke on the wheel whose people were considered little better than Utlanders. Living on the farthest of the spars, they were fiercely independent, and they had to be, as they were constantly preyed upon by Utland raiders.

The next spoke on the wheel was Leogryf Spar. Their current warlord was a steady man who could be relied to keep his word and, so far, he had always supported King Rolen.

The third was Foenix Spar. Over the last three hundred years, their warlords had generally been loyal to Rolencia. Just as well, since they guarded the pass over the Divide that led to Rolenhold itself.

The fourth spoke was Unistag Spar and their warlord was dying with no clear successor.

Last of all was Cockatrice Spar. Another crucial spar, their warlord held the lands which bordered closest to Merofynia. If he turned traitor, Merofynia's invading army could cross Cockatrice Pass and march deep into Rolencia's soft underbelly before the king could muster his defences.

Of the five current warlords the loyalty of only two was guaranteed. The Unistag warlord's failure to appear and renew his loyalty would be noted.

There was a shout as Lence defeated his challenger.

'Come, Byren,' King Rolen beckoned. 'It's down to you and Lence now.'

Garzik and several of the youths started chanting his name. 'Byren Leogryfslayer. Byren...'

'Lence Kingsheir. Lence Kingsheir!' Cobalt started up a chant and Lence's supporters joined in.

Though Lence was heavier through the chest than Byren, their arm wrestling ability was about the same. And Lence had beaten everyone else so he would be tired. Byren caught Lence's grimace as he flexed his arm. The last thing he wanted was to upstage his brother again. On impulse he decided to refuse.

There, it wasn't so hard to prove the old seer wrong.

'Sorry,' Byren muttered, massaging his shoulder. 'Pulled something when that leogryf rolled on me.'

'Right.' King Rolen clapped his hands together. 'Then Lence must uphold our honour. Come on.'

The grizzled blacksmith and his supporters marched over, heckling and jeering as the man took his seat opposite Lence.

The hunt-master joined Byren. 'You didn't mention that injury when we were on the Dividing Mountains. I would have put some arnica on it.'

Byren opened his mouth to lie but the hunt-master, who had known him and Lence since they were boys, had already read his face.

'Better put some on,' he advised in a low voice. 'Lence won't thank you for going easy on him.'

Byren nodded. He hadn't thought of that. By trying to avoid the seer's foretelling, he had almost made things worse. His head spun.

The men were chanting now – 'Rolenhold! Rolenhold!' – as Lence and the blacksmith battled, massive fists locked, forearms flexed so that the muscles stood out like cords under their skin.

The blacksmith's face grew darker as he strained. It was obvious he would not let Lence win to curry favour.

'Manticore! Manticore!' the spar warriors bellowed.

Byren found his hands had curled into fists as he willed Lence to win. His brother hated losing.

The blacksmith's massive biceps jerked with strain, veins stood out on forearm and at his temples. His arm trembled.

With a sudden grunt, he lost the battle.

Lence slammed the blacksmith's fist onto the table top. Rolenhold cheered. His followers swung Lence up onto their shoulders.

Byren stepped back to let them pass as they made a victory march around the great hall. Lence raised his arm in a fist. Byren grinned.

'Remember the arnica,' the hunt-master said, before he walked off.

Yes. Arnica. With a start Byren realised he was going to lie to his twin to keep the peace. How had it come to this?

Across the great hall he noticed the abbot, with several of his masters and the castle's Halcyon Affinity warder. Without intending it, he found himself weaving through the tables towards their quiet corner.

He had to know if a seer's prediction could be avoided.

The masters and the abbot all rose as he approached. He gave them a bow, acknowledging their age and learning. 'I have a question regarding Affinity.'

'Slaying beasts like the leogryf releases the Affinity that animates their physical bodies, returning it to the Unseen world. But don't worry. It cannot affect you unless you have Affinity and we know you don't,' Autumnwind, the castle Affinity warder, assured him. 'And the correct atonement to Halcyon was made so you have not slighted her.'

'Eh, it's not that,' Byren admitted.

'Ask.' The mystics master gestured, looking interested.

Byren took a moment to frame his question. He could hardly blurt out that the seer said he'd kill his twin to claim the throne. 'Have you heard about the renegade seer who confronted us in Rolenton Square?'

They nodded.

Byren cleared his throat. 'She said some things about my mother that have upset her. Can a seer's prediction be avoided?'

The Affinity warder glanced to the mystics master.

'Seers see possible paths and often only nexus points of great importance. We must put clues together to make sense of what they have seen,' the master said, a rueful smile tugging at his lips. 'I'm sorry I can't be more helpful.'

Byren waved this aside. 'Does that mean we can't avoid –'

'Not at all. The future is a road with many destinations, not all of them will eventuate. Tell the queen I am happy to consult with her, if she needs me.'

'I will.' Relieved, Byren bowed and went to back off but another thought occurred to him. 'Farmer Overhill says his son's Affinity came on him at fifteen. How can Affinity suddenly appear in someone who has shown no sign of it?'

'We are still discovering the ways of Affinity, kingson,' the castle Affinity warder admitted.

'But we know this much,' the mystics master said. 'If it doesn't show by the time a child is six years of age, it may surface at times of life-changing events, the birth of a child or escape from certain death.'

'Could a healer with Affinity accidentally trigger Affinity?' Byren asked, getting to his real question at last.

The Affinity warder glanced to the master.

'According to the abbey records this hasn't happened for a hundred and twenty years,' he said. Eyes that were far too keen fixed on Byren. 'Why do you ask?'

'Just curious.' Byren quickly thanked them and backed off, his worst fears confirmed. He would have to watch over Orrade and make sure no one realised his friend now had Affinity. If they were lucky it would never show again. He could only hope that he had not done Orrade a disservice, insisting that the seer heal him.

And as far as he and Lence were concerned, Byren did not have to worry for he would never kill his twin. Maybe Lence was a little annoyed because the glory of the leogryf kill should have been his. That was only natural, but they'd shared too much to let something like this come between them. It was time for a peace offering. As Byren crossed the hall he noticed Orrade. His friend lifted a tankard and beckoned him. All the young men who had sworn fealty to Byren were with him. How would they feel if his supposed connection with Palos came out? Byren hated the thought of letting them down so he shook his head. Orrade stiffened imperceptibly, then turned his back on Byren.

BYREN FINISHED DRILLING the hole through the base of the second leogryf incisor. The tooth was as long as his index finger and a dull ivory colour, part of a matching pair. After threading the two incisors on each side of a row of smaller teeth he tied the ends of the leather thong, then headed out intending to present it to Lence. The trophy necklace had taken him most of the morning to complete. His real betrothal gift wouldn't be ready for a while yet. He'd gone down to Rolenhold first thing this morning to see the silversmith, who promised to have both the matching rings and the lincurium pendant ready soon.

Striding down the castle corridor, Byren dodged busy servants scurrying past with buckets of steaming water drawn from the hot-water cistern at the end of the hall. Others bustled by with freshly pressed clothes and polished boots. The smell of polish, crisped cotton and lavender-scented wool filled the air. The abbot would stage the race for Halcyon's Fate at midday and everyone wanted to see it. Byren had to find his twin before they left for the township, because after that their day would be taken up with ceremony and feasting.

He went looking for Lence. In the great hall he headed for the knot of drinkers by the fireplace, identifying his father and Captain Temor. Who was that with them?

Illien of Cobalt. He'd recognise those padded shoulders anywhere. There was nothing wrong with Cobalt's shoulders so why pad them? He supposed his cousin hadn't had time to get Rolencian-style clothes made up yet.

'...because it's never happened here, Captain Temor, that doesn't mean it can't happen in Merofynia,' Cobalt was saying. 'Palatyne's a canny man, as befits the warlord of Amfina Spar, the two-headed snake. He let the rest of Merofynia's warlords tear each other to pieces like a pack of wild dogs so that when he stepped in they had nothing left to throw against his men. That's how he became overlord of the spars. And, by keeping them under control, he's earned King Merofyn's gratitude. But the ordinary people of Merofynia are sick of this upstart overlord strutting around, taking what he wants. They were fed up with King Merofyn anyway, with his greedy taxes and his religious fervour. Now that he stares death in the face, he's turned to the gods, calling on those with untamed Affinity to find a way to bargain with death itself. Why, they say there are more renegade Power-workers in Port Mero than bakers!'

'Filthy Untamed Affinity,' King Rolen muttered. 'Execution or banishment is all they deserve.'

'Very true,' Cobalt agreed. 'I was telling Lence Kingsheir only yesterday how the people of Merofynia look back on the rule of Queen Myrella's father with great longing. I swear, Uncle, if you were to march into Port Mero right now the people would cheer you as a saviour!'

'More the fool me. What of the lords and their men, Cobalt? You can bet they won't lay down their arms and welcome me into their Great Halls!' King Rolen laughed. 'Besides, soon we'll have Lence betrothed to King Merofyn's daughter. All Rolencia wants from Merofynia is peace and a chance to grow prosperous.'

'Yes, Merofyn's daughter,' Cobalt muttered looking worried.

'What have you heard about Isolt?' Captain Temor asked.

Cobalt gave a delicate shrug. 'You know what they say, what's suckled at the breast cannot be forgotten. For all that she's a pretty thing, she is her father's child.'

'Cunning and cold?' Rolen pressed.

Cobalt shrugged. '"Be careful what you whisper on your pillow. It will find its way back to your wife's father and brothers."'

Temor nodded. 'Wives taken to cement alliances always owe their loyalty to their family, not their husband.'

'Ha! My Myrella has proven the exception to that rule.' King Rolen grinned. 'Don't worry, Illien. I'm sure Lence will make the most of Isolt. She's only fifteen, young enough to mould.'

'We can hope so,' Cobalt agreed, and for the first time Byren wondered if his father had made the right decision. An uncomfortable feeling settled in the pit of his stomach. All his life, his father had been a legendary figure who had saved Rolencia from invasion at only eighteen years of age. But what if the king had misjudged the balance of power this time? There had been times recently when Byren hadn't agreed with his father's decisions. The Utland raid was one example. It struck him that for many years now his father had trusted his old honour guard as advisors, men who were certainly loyal but they had never lived outside Rolencia. Was his father...

'Byren, I didn't see you there,' Cobalt greeted him, his dark rippling curls travelling across his back as he turned. Small jewels had been woven through the hair at his temples and they winked as they caught the light.

Why didn't he tie his hair back like a warrior? Byren repressed that thought as unworthy, while Cobalt's sword arm was still in a sling.

'Would you like a wine, cousin?' Cobalt asked.

'No, thank you. Have you seen Lence?' Byren addressed the question to the group as a whole.

'He went to Eagle Tower to clear his head,' Temor said.

'Tell him not to be late,' King Rolen advised, then caught Cobalt's eye. 'You know Lence, always chasing something pretty in a skirt.'

'And very good at catching them, from what I hear.' Cobalt winked.

King Rolen gave a great belly laugh. 'More luck to him!'

Cobalt topped up the king's glass, then Temor's. Again, he offered Byren the decanter. 'A cup of Rolencia's finest for you, Cousin?'

Byren shook his head and weaved through the forest of brilliantly decorated columns. Did Illien think their castle garish compared to Ostron Isle? It was Rolencia's custom to cover every surface with intricate carving, picked out in paint and gilding, enhanced with semi-precious stones. He left the great hall, passing under the arched doorway, its delicate floral carving highlighted by gold leaf on a pale blue background. Normally he wouldn't notice it, today he paused to study it and decided it was beautiful, what ever Illien thought.

As a small boy he'd adored Illien Cobaltson. Now he'd looked for, but did not find, the friendship he'd hoped would eventuate with Cobalt the man, and he did not understand why. Taking the passage, then crossing the courtyard, Byren headed for Eagle Tower.

'Byren?' Orrade called, catching up with him at the base of stairs that led up to the tower's first-floor door. Orrade glanced about, then stepped around the far side of the stairs so that they could speak privately.

'Why did you turn down the village girl?'

'Elina –'

'That's never stopped you in the past.'

Byren shrugged. 'It's different now.' For a heartbeat he tried to find the words to explain. It was true he and Orrade and Lence had gone wenching many times in the past. But it was different then, then he hadn't felt so deeply for Elina, then he hadn't known that Orrade preferred men to women... another thought struck him. 'You didn't think that I... that you –'

'No, not at all.' Orrade flushed and Byren suspected he had.

He was reminded of how he had snubbed his friend last night. If the true reason for Orrade's disinheritance was revealed, the men of Byren's honour guard would turn on him. And then Byren would be forced to deny him or lose the respect of his men.

'Listen, Orrie –'

'No, you listen. I've been thinking things through. Your honour guard don't understand why you turned the girl down. And you can't tell them about Elina because you can't offer her marriage now because of me. I've ruined things for you.' Orrade touched his chest where the damning symbol of Palos had lain hidden. He lifted troubled but determined eyes to Byren. 'I was wrong to join your honour guard. I don't want to be a liability. Release me from my oath so I can leave Rolencia.'

Stunned, Byren did not know what to say. Without Orrade he need not fear discovery...

Orrade must have read his face because he nodded once and turned on his heel and strode off.

Byren ran after him, catching up half way across the courtyard to grab his arm. 'Don't do this, Orrie. Stay.' He searched for a good reason. 'Think of Garzik. Who will watch over him?'

'Freezing Sylion!' Orrade flicked free of his hand, and cast a meaningful glance to the men-at-arms on the wall-walk who could see them below in the courtyard. 'I'm trying to protect you. I've lost position and family, I don't want that to happen to you!'

'Stay.'

Orrade searched his face. 'Why?'

Byren had no answer.

'Do you want me to stay, Byren? Tell me straight, because I'll go if you want me to.' Orrade's voice shook with repressed emotion. 'I couldn't stay knowing that you despise me.'

In a flash Byren understood. 'This is about last night when I snubbed you. Eh, Orrie. I'm a coward. I looked at you and my honour guard and I thought what if they knew about us. They'd –'

'There is no "us", Byren. I've loved you since we were fourteen. I've stood at your back and fought for my life, knowing you'd protect me, knowing that you trusted me not to turn and run.'

It was true.

Byren grasped his shoulder. 'I couldn't ask for a truer friend.'

Orrade blinked tears from his eyes and clasped Byren's hand where it rested on his shoulder. He had to clear his throat to speak. 'That's why I'm offering to go. I'd rather live as a beggar than dishonour you.'

'It would dishonour me if you left,' Byren said, and discovered he meant it.

Orrade met his eyes, face naked. What Byren read there made him look away. He was not worthy of such devotion.

Orrade cleared his throat, gave a small, jerky nod and walked off, leaving Byren alone in the courtyard.

He turned to face the steps to Eagle Tower. He had only a few moments to find Lence and give him the gift before the race for Halcyon's Fate started.

He took the tower's shallow steps two at a time, enjoying driving his powerful body.

'What's the rush?' Lence grinned. 'I could hear you thundering up the stairs like a wild boar.'

Byren laughed. The air was sharp and cold. It felt good on his face. He went to the battlement, leaned on the stone next to Lence and took a deep breath. It struck him that they hadn't been alone together for more than a moment or two since he came back with Orrade and Garzik. He put this aside and studied the snow-laden rich valley and Mount Halcyon itself, hub of the crescent.

Byren inhaled. He could smell beef seasoned with rosemary roasting for the feast tonight. Life was good. 'I have something for you.'

'Oh?' Lence turned to him.

Byren glanced down at his hand and hesitated. Once the kingsheir's betrothal was announced his twin would be swamped with exquisite and expensive gifts from the nobles, merchants and warlords, gifts that would make his token seem very meagre.

'It's just something I made.' Byren opened his hand to reveal the plaited leather thong, strung with the leogryf's teeth. As he looked down, he realised it was a boy's gift.

Lence stared at the trophy necklace.

'You keep it,' he said slowly. 'You earned it. After all, I can hardly give a string of leogryf teeth to the

Merofynian kingsdaughter. It would confirm her worst fears. Illien says they already think us little better than spar warriors.'

Heat raced up Byren's cheeks.

'I see you wasted no time finding a reason to go to Dovecote,' Lence muttered.

'Orrie was injured.'

'He looks fine now. Was Elina pleased to see you?'

Byren's stomach clenched with pain. Elina... she had disturbed his sleep every night since he had been thrown out of Dovecote estate. In his dreams he would go to her and she would scorn him, telling him to go off with Orrade instead.

'Didn't waste any time, did you?' Lence asked.

'What?'

'My betrothal hasn't even been announced and you're already trying to charm your way into Elina's bed.'

'You fancy her!'

Lence nodded. 'And what's more, I've tasted her sweet fruit.'

'No, you never!'

'Autumn cusp, in the hay after the Harvest Feast.'

Byren blinked, shocked. Knowing Lence, it was no idle boast. Girls were always eager to lift their skirts for the kingsheir. But Elina? The most Byren had achieved was that kiss in the cold-cellar while she treated the bruise she'd given him, and he hadn't dared more because...

'Lord Dovecote would be furious if –'

'Fifteen's marriageable age and she'll be seventeen come spring cusp. Why hasn't he let her make an alliance? He's greedy, keeping her for himself to run his household. Besides, Elina's old enough to know her own mind.'

That was true, but... Byren remembered holding her as she wept in his arms. 'She deserves better than a fling in the hay, Lence.'

'Well, that's all I can offer, remember!' Lence snapped. 'I'm to be married to the Merofynian kingsdaughter. So, go ahead, woo her, marry her if she'll have you. But one day she will be my mistress. Most men are happy for their wives to swive the king!'

Byren took a step back, startled by his vehemence, startled that Lence would think like this. Of course he'd heard of the goings-on in the Merofynian court and the Elector of Ostron Isle was known to demand sexual favours for patronage. 'Cobalt's been putting ideas in your head.'

'Illien's seen the world,' Lence told him. 'All we've ever seen is Rolencia. Illien knows what's really going on in the Merofynian court.'

Did he? Byren didn't know who to ask. And if he had known who, it would have to be someone with Rolencia's best interests at heart. What if marriage to Isolt did not bring peace? What if it embroiled them in a civil war? As he went to speak the first horn sounded, calling the acolytes to the Proving.

Lence glanced out to the east where the town and lake were bustling with activity. 'The race will start soon. Are you coming?'

Byren caught Lence's arm. 'Elina turned me down. Don't let her come between us.'

'Oh, I won't.' Lence flicked his arm free and gave

Byren a smile that made his twin look like someone else. 'I'll have her one day.'

Then Lence brushed the grit from the stone balustrade off his palms and left the tower top. Byren stood for a moment, stunned. How had things gone so wrong?

He and Lence had always competed for girls and glory but it had never turned nasty until now.

Grimly, Byren tucked the leogryf necklace inside his vest. It might be a handmade gift like the ones they had given each other as children, but a gift won at great risk was not a trifle.

Byren fingered the foenix spurs he wore around his neck. Three years ago, he and Lence had gone to capture a foenix and bring it back for the castle menagerie. It had died defending its nest. Lence would have smashed the eggs. Byren had brought them home for Piro. Now that he thought back over the years, he could see many small things that proved he and Lence saw the world differently. His twin had made no secret that he'd fancied Elina, but then he fancied a lot of women. It would be ironic if he lost his twin's trust over Elina when he had no chance to win her himself.

Worse, what if Cobalt's assessment of the balance of power was right?

Byren was overwhelmed with the need to see Fyn. Not that Fyn knew what was going on in the Merofynian court, but he would let Byren talk about his worries and Fyn had a way of cutting through to what was important.

Chapter Nine

FYN WRESTLED WITH the clasp on his shoulder guard, fingers clumsy with cold. Here he was, heart thundering ready to burst, and the race hadn't even started.

The cold leather strap slid through his fingers a second time. 'Freezing Sylion!'

The tent flap opened and Byren strode in. 'Eh, you're running late. I'm in luck!'

'Can't get this buckle done up,' Fyn muttered. He'd hung back behind the other acolytes, hoping Piro would come to wish him luck, only she hadn't. Neither had his father or mother, not that he'd expected them with their official duties. But Piro...

'Here, let me.' Byren, pulled the buckle tight, then cinched it securely. 'How's that?'

Fyn swung his arm. The padded leather shoulder protectors were tight, but still loose enough to give him full range of movement. 'Good.'

During the race across the lake acolytes would do their best to knock each other down. They were supposed to strike only between the knee and shoulder, hence the protectors. But in past years legs had been broken, shoulders dislocated and skulls fractured.

'Thanks, Byren.' Fyn picked up his quarterstaff. The ash rod was as tall as him and as deadly as a sword in the hands of a skilled opponent. For today's challenge both ends had been wrapped in padding. Still, a blow from the staff would knock the air from his lungs if Fyn wasn't quick enough, or maybe even crack a rib, and then he'd have no chance of finding the Fate. Mustn't let that happen. He glanced up at his brother who was watching him with a thoughtful expression. 'What?'

'Nothing. I can see you've got a lot on your mind.' Byren gave him a rueful grin. 'Beat the others across the lake and catch the eye of the weapons master. Who knows, maybe one day you'll be weapons master of Halcyon Abbey!'

Fyn nodded, not surprised that Byren expected this of him. But he intended to be first across the lake to get his hands on the Fate. Hopefully, when he looked into its satiny surface, the mists would clear and he would see a vision. If he did, his place with the mystics was ensured.

Byren came to his feet. At twenty he was a little more than three years older than Fyn, but he was a head taller and bigger boned. Fyn knew he would never grow as big as the twins. He was the runt of the litter, which was why his father had been only too happy to gift him to the abbey.

Fyn fought a wave of self-doubt and worthlessness. He'd been fighting it all his life.

'Halcyon's luck be with you, little Fynnish.' Byren used his childhood nickname, then hesitated. His hand rose to touch the sigil Fyn wore around his neck. Made of silver, it was embossed with the royal foenix. When he became a monk, Fyn would renounce his place in the succession and return his foenix emblem. He wasn't sure how he felt about that. Monks were supposed to sever all ties with the material world, but he was still tied to Rolenhold.

Byren tucked Fyn's sigil inside his chest protector. 'I've always thought it unfair that you were gifted to the abbey. Lence and I have had all the fun while you've been studying dry old histories since you were six!'

Fyn wasn't about to admit that he found the dry old histories fascinating, besides Byren's idea of fun was leading raids against the warlords or tracking Affinity beasts.

'It's not so bad. Master Wintertide says we all serve Rolencia in our own way,' Fyn muttered, his mind on the task ahead. He hung his skates over his shoulder. Now that the race was about to start his mouth felt dry and his stomach tense. Other years he had laughed along with the townsfolk when the acolytes knocked each other flying, skidding across the ice like court jesters. 'I just hope I don't make an idiot of myself.'

'Make the other acolytes eat ice!' Byren gave Fyn a friendly thump on the arm. 'Now go out there and do father proud. I'll be cheering you on!'

Fyn looked up at his brother. Of all his family, only Byren had bothered to come to wish him luck. He opened his mouth to thank him, but his brother gave him a bone-crushing hug and headed for the tent flap.

Just before he got there he thumped the heel of his hand to his forehead and turned back. 'Freezing Sylion! I almost forgot. Come straight to the bell tower when you get back. Father has a big announcement to make.'

'What is it?'

'Can't say.' Byren winked, black eyes gleaming roguishly as he slipped out of the tent. He wasn't as handsome as Lence, but his slightly crooked grin was somehow more charming. No wonder the girls whispered like a flock of excited birds when he walked past.

Fyn wondered what his father was planning, then put it out of his head. King Rolen had made it clear his third son's future was not with the royal family. And that was what today was all about, proving himself to the mystics master.

Turning the staff over and over, Fyn changed hands and passed it behind his body without breaking momentum. The quarterstaff spun so fast it was a blur. He was good with weapons. He should be, he'd practised long and hard. But his heart wasn't in weapons training, that was why Lonepine always beat him. One day his friend would be weapons master, not him.

Time to go.

Fyn took a deep breath, smelling the pine resin from the cones that burned in the tent's brass stove and the linament the other acolytes had used on old bruises. He stepped outside into the brilliant, but distant white sunlight of Midwinter's Day. The tent flags hung limp in the still, frosty air. Last night's snowfall had been shovelled aside into waist-high drifts revealing the cobbled streets of Rolenton wharfside.

He caught himself looking around for Piro, unable to believe she had forgotten. Only she knew how important this was to him. He was surprised and hurt, and just a little worried. Piro was nothing if not loyal. Why hadn't she come to wish him luck?

He hoped she was all right.

Fyn smiled to himself. Piro could take care of herself. She could always use one of the tricks he'd taught her and, if that didn't work, knowing Piro she'd talk her way out of trouble. Besides, who would dare hurt King Rolen's only daughter?

The upper wharves were nearly deserted. Down on the lakeside wharf most of the acolytes and monks waited. Dressed in the Goddess Halcyon's earthy colours, browns, olive-greens and burnt orange, they looked like scattered autumn leaves. Only the abbot wore the red of Halcyon's fiery heart, with a circular torque inset with lapis lazuli, a sign of his office.

The abbess of Sylion and her nuns were clustered at the other end. In their robes of blue, aqua and grey they looked like a patch of shifting shadow on snow, a reflection of the cruel god of winter. The abbess stood out, dressed in pure white, wearing a torque inset with blood-red cornelian stones. Later tonight, at the midwinter feast, she would symbolically hand over Rolencia to the abbot. The days would soon grow longer and Sylion would relinquish his grasp on their valley kingdom.

As for the people of Rolenton, their excited chatter filled the air. They crowded the houses and warehouses bordering the lake's shores. Many had ridden out to the lake's snowy banks to find a good vantage point. Determined to enjoy the event, they had set themselves up with blankets, steaming honeyed mead and hot food. From where he stood, Fyn could smell roasting cinnamon apples and sweet potatoes sprinkled with cheese and chilli. His stomach rumbled. He'd been too nervous to eat this morning.

'Ho, Fyn! What's keeping you?' Lonepine swung his staff at Fyn's head, just missing. 'Ready to eat ice?'

'You'll be the one eating ice!' Fyn made a mock swing. Lonepine blocked. The two of them strained, strength against strength. Lonepine was the same height as Fyn, but heavier. Fyn was just about to break the stalemate with a trick stumble when the weapons master strode past.

'Save it for the race, lads!' Oakstand gestured to the wharf below. 'The others are already lining up. Don't keep the abbot waiting.'

They broke apart.

'We'll see who eats ice.' Lonepine's warm brown eyes gleamed a challenge. He had a square head and ears that tended to stick out, making him look more like a butcher's apprentice than a monk. 'Come on!'

As Fyn turned towards Sapphire Lake, Lonepine thrust the tip of his staff between Fyn's legs, toppling him into a snowdrift. With a laugh Lonepine took off down the steps, jumping the last four.

Spitting snow from his mouth, Fyn blinked, only to discover he was sprawled in someone's shadow. Piro?

'You all right, Fyn?' Feldspar asked. He looked deadly serious as always but Fyn could hear the nerves his friend was trying to hide.

Rolling to his feet, Fyn brushed crushed snow from his knees and looked up. If he made it across the lake ahead of Lonepine, this tall, skinny youth was his greatest rival. Like Lonepine, Feldspar had already chosen his monk's name and it proclaimed his goal. The stone, feldspar, was a tool of the mystics. Competition for a place in the mystics was tough. Some years none of the acolytes were chosen. It didn't help that Feldspar was one of Fyn's best friends.

'Halcyon's luck be with you,' Feldspar said earnestly.

'And you,' Fyn said, meaning it, no matter what it cost him.

They hurried down the steps to the wharf, then onto the lake's icy surface where the others had already strapped on their skates. The acolytes were quiet and tense as they checked the straps of their protectors, and wiped sweaty palms on their leggings.

Fyn did up his skates then stood balanced on the narrow blades. Across the frozen lake lay his goal, Ruin Isle. Named for its stone statues which dated from before the abbey's written history, the island would be sacrosanct for the duration of the race, forbidden to all but the acolytes, for somewhere in those ruins the mystics master had hidden Halcyon's Fate.

And Fyn had to find it.

He transferred the staff from one hand to the other. Glancing over his shoulder, his gaze was drawn up beyond the town's snow-covered roofs, to his father's castle. Rolenhold stood high on a great pinnacle of rock. Behind it were the mist-shrouded peaks of the Dividing Mountains. In the three hundred years since King Rolence the First built the stronghold's original tower, the castle had been added to and reinforced. It had never been taken.

Fyn's heart swelled. This was his home and he would do his father proud.

He searched for the royal banner, finding the brilliant red foenix on black background draped from the merchant guildhall bell tower. He could just make out his mother seated with a blanket over her knees on the fourth-storey balcony. His father was sharing hot, spiced wine with his brothers, nobles, great merchants and warlords.

He could not see his sister beside his mother. In fact, Fyn could not see his sister anywhere. A kernel of worry formed in his belly.

'They're bringing the horn.' Lonepine nudged Fyn. 'Not long now!'

To win the highest accolade they had to not only find the Fate but make it back across the lake to blow that horn. Other acolytes would form teams to help each other, networks of trust that they would rely on later when they were monks, trying to make their way up in the hierarchy. A rush of energy filled Fyn for he could only trust two of his companions, which put their team at an immediate disadvantage.

Shifting his weight from skate to skate to keep warm, he studied the dais where the abbot stood. They had the horn but there seemed to be a delay. If only it would start.

'Spread out and form one line along the lake's edge,' the acolytes master ordered.

Twenty-two acolytes shuffled along, holding their quarterstaffs at the ready. Fyn faced the lake, sucking in great gulps of icy air which stung his nostrils and made his eyes water. Dimly, he heard the abbot wish them Halcyon's luck. Then the mystics master blew the horn.

A great cheer went up from the people of Rolenton. The rush of sound filled Fyn's head, sweeping him up, sweeping him along with the others.

Out of the wharf's shadow, blindingly bright sunshine reflected off the ice. The acolytes bunched together, all making for the island. A few tried to sprint away. Many followed Lonepine's example and concentrated on swinging their staffs, sending their fellows to the ice before making a break for it.

Like some multi-legged beast the whole mass travelled across the ice, some breaking free of the pack, only to be tackled by followers. Fyn ducked a blow, sending Foxtail down with a strike behind the knee.

Darting away from the main group, he tried to put some distance between himself and the others. Someone clipped him between the shoulder blades, knocking him down head first onto the ice. His face stung with cold.

Eat ice!

Scrambling to his skates, he skidded sideways. Riverford came after him. Fyn avoided Riverford's strike, but lost the chance to counter, his momentum swinging him around. Fighting with quarterstaffs on the ice was difficult. The skates had a mind of their own.

Fyn took a glancing blow and twisted desperately, trying to get his staff between them.

Feldspar shouldered Riverford aside, sending him sprawling. Fyn caught his friend's arm, steadying him. 'Thanks.'

'Come on, you two, quit playing around!' Lonepine sped past.

The three of them took off towards Ruin Isle. Fyn's thigh muscles flexed, driving him forwards with each gliding stride. His eyes watered, stinging from the cold wind. Fyn concentrated on building up speed as they overtook and passed a half a dozen acolytes who had stopped to fight amongst themselves. He cast one swift glance behind him. The race had broken up into several small battles.

Only one other group remained between them and the island. These acolytes put their heads together and turned, preparing to defend their ground as one of them took off his skates and strode up the beach to search the island.

Fyn's heart sank.

'Looks like Hawkwing has organised his friends to back him up,' Lonepine shouted.

Neither Fyn nor Feldspar bothered to answer, saving their breath.

Hawkwing's five supporters waited, spinning their staffs. Fyn slewed his skates side-on to slow down. He caught Lonepine's eye and glanced to the acolytes on the far left. Lonepine nodded. He would tackle them.

Fyn held Feldspar's eye, letting him know he would handle the two on the right. That left the one in the middle for Feldspar.

Fyn skated in, feinting with a high blow, changing it at the last instant. Ducking under the acolyte's strike, Fyn knocked his first opponent's legs out from under him and followed up with a blow that took the second's breath away.

Fyn straightened up in time to see Feldspar put down his attacker, but one of Lonepine's acolytes had gotten away from him. Foxtail was as cunning as his namesake. He rounded on Feldspar, who wasn't expecting an attack from that quarter.

Foxtail aimed a blow at Feldspar's shoulder which bounced off, onto his head. It sent him reeling and the tall youth went down like a felled tree.

Furious, Lonepine barged into Foxtail, knocking him off his feet. The downed acolyte skidded across the ice on his back like a stranded summer beetle.

Fyn darted between the other acolytes who were struggling to rise, and leant down to grab Feldspar's arm. 'Are you all right?'

Feldspar managed a sickly grin. 'Why are there two of you?'

'I'll go after Hawkwing!' Lonepine announced and took off.

'Come on.' Fyn helped Feldspar upright, tugging him along as he headed for the island.

Hawkwing's supporters didn't come after them, electing to deal with the next group of acolytes, fast approaching.

Feldspar shook off Fyn's helping hand within a

few heart beats and they reached the island's snowy shore together. Lonepine's boot prints showed where he had taken off his skates to run up the beach.

Fyn unstrapped his skates and slung them over his shoulder, then he hurried to catch up. 'Which way?'

Feldspar was already climbing the snowy slope, his expression focused inwards as he tried to sense the Fate's location. Feldspar had excellent Affinity.

'Strange,' he whispered, 'I can't seem to –'

The crack of wood striking wood interrupted him. Fyn ran over a rise into a grove of winter-bare trees. Through the mottled silver trunks he saw Hawkwing and Lonepine circling each other in a clearing.

'I'll take care of Hawkwing. You two go on,' Lonepine ordered.

'Ha. You'll be eating snow before me!' Hawkwing sneered and leapt to the attack.

As they fought furiously, Fyn turned to Feldspar. 'You lead.'

'I don't know what's wrong. I can't sense a thing,' the tall acolyte confessed. He frowned, trying to discover the Fate. Meanwhile, in the clearing below a flurry of blows fell with dull thuds and grunts of effort.

'If you can't sense it, we'd better separate,' Fyn decided. This gave him a chance to find the Fate for himself. 'I'll take this side of the ruins. You take the other.'

Fyn nodded and ran off to his right, avoiding Hawkwing and Lonepine, who had stopped to catch their breaths. They leant on their staffs, panting in a way that would have been funny if they hadn't been so serious.

Stepping out of the trees into another clearing, Fyn shaded his eyes against the glare of the sun reflecting off the snow. Individual ice crystals gleamed like diamonds.

A grey stone obelisk stood before him. Topped by a cap of white crusty snow, it signalled the entrance to the ruins. Slowing down, he looked around for physical clues as to where the mystics master might have hidden Halcyon's Fate. His own Affinity was weak and if Feldspar couldn't sense the Fate, then Fyn would have to stumble over it before he felt its subtle tug. But he was a good tracker, so he looked for signs the master might have left last night. He was out of luck however. A light snowfall had hidden everything.

Fyn searched all the places he could think of, the forks of tree trunks, the mouths of statues, anywhere that might conceal a small, semiprecious stone on a silver chain.

Upwind of each statue, snow mounded into a heap while on the downwind side the wind had carved out hollows. It was both beautiful and eerie. Each statue depicted one of the god-touched beasts. He searched the statue of a leogryf, wings outspread, frozen in mid-attack, then a foenix with its head reared back, about to strike with its razor-sharp beak. Next he came to a wyvern. The sea dragon was poised to leap, again wings outspread. Then there was a cockatrice. Taller than a man with razor-sharp leg spurs, it had the tail of a serpent and could spit poison. The unistag had lost its horn. With the body of a horse and the head of a stag it was a graceful beast. Only the manticore was undamaged. Once its lion's body would have been painted blood-red. The paint had long since worn off but its tail of hard chitin still arched above its back, ready to strike. That barb carried deadly poison and could pierce armour.

Each statue was carved from white marble and each was mantled with fine snow, but none hid the Fate.

One small part of Fyn's mind whispered. *Feldspar lied about not sensing the Fate. He wants to find it before you do.*

But he knew Feldspar too well. If Fyn hadn't been so desperate to become a mystic, he would have been pleased to see his friend chosen.

Trudging through the knee-high snow, Fyn moved between a row of pillars, entering the roofless, ruined temple which stood in the centre of the island. Feldspar was already there, his saffron thigh-length robe bright against the snow. The thin acolyte's plait, which grew from the crown of his head, swung over his shoulder as he spun to face Fyn. He'd lost his cap and his shaven skull gleamed in the sunlight. A band of tattoos circled his head like a crown, each symbol represented a subject or a skill mastered.

'Did you find the Fate?' Feldspar demanded.

'No. You?'

'I can't sense it at all. I don't know what's wrong.'

They could hear the shouts of other acolytes now, beginning their search. Frustration filled Fyn.

'Keep looking,' he urged.

Feldspar nodded and plunged off to continue the search. Fyn headed towards the right side of the island with renewed urgency. The others must not beat him to Halcyon's Fate.

Ploughing through the snow, he was glad he knew this part of the island well. He'd come here with Piro last Midsummer to paint and practise the abbey's martial arts.

Suddenly, he felt a pull. His heart lifted and he concentrated on the sensation, eyes almost closed.

The Fate acted on his Affinity, drawing him towards a grove of trees, now bare and stark. At its centre was a fallen statue, an amfina. The snake-lizard was artistically writhing back on itself, both heads rearing to attack. It rested at an angle on a block of stone, forming a little cave.

Fyn's breath caught in his throat and his skin prickled. The Fate was hidden here somewhere.

As he ran towards it, Fyn remembered how Piro had hidden under the statue to surprise him at midsummer. Then it had been covered in Evening Glowvine. A memory came back to him, the white flowers' rich honey-cinnamon scent. Glancing into the hollow under the statue, he saw nothing but snowy shadows today. He concentrated on the twin-headed amfina with its vestigial legs and wings. Both mouths were open, ready to attack. Fine-powdered snow filled both sets of jaws. The jaws!

Fyn climbed onto the statue's mid-back and dipped his fingers in the snow that filled the primary head's jaw. Half-numb with cold, he felt something small and hard. With a surge of triumph, he pulled it out.

Halcyon's Fate swung on its chain, silver links gleaming in the sunshine, but his eyes were on the

Fate itself. He had never seen it this close before. The stone was really a perfect spiral shell made of opalised stone, all colours and none.

Fyn jumped down, boots sinking into the snow. Holding the Fate up to the sunlight, his heart soared. This was his vindication.

It meant he deserved to join the mystics despite his weak Affinity, for Halcyon would not have drawn him here if she did not approve of him.

He had to tell Feldspar and Lonepine.

But as he turned to go something caught his eye. What was that under the statue? Startled, Fyn plunged his hand in and felt a wool-covered shoulder. Grabbing the white cloak, he pulled the spy out.

Quick as a cat they spun around. A hood fell back to reveal hair dark as a raven's wing, moon-pale skin and furious black eyes set in a pretty, all too familiar face.

'Piro? What are you doing here?'

Chapter Ten

SHE STAMPED HER foot. 'Now you've gone and spoiled it, Fyn!'

'You're not supposed to be here!' He was horrified.

'You weren't supposed to find me.'

He ignored that. 'This island is sacred for the duration of today's Proving. Piro, if the abbot knew ... not even royal blood could save you!'

'Then don't tell him!' She brushed crusted snow off her knees, pretending indifference, but her hands trembled.

He wanted to shake her. 'Why, Piro?'

She nodded to the Fate, spinning on its chain. 'Only yesterday you were telling me how much you needed to become a mystic. Well, now you can.'

'Yes.' He dismissed that, more concerned for her safety. 'But you shouldn't be here. This race was designed to Prove the winner's Affinity so the island has been purified and...' He stopped dead. He'd felt a tug on his Affinity and had thought it was the Fate drawing him to it, but...

Piro looked away, a guilty flush creeping up her pale cheeks.

Closing his eyes he focused his Unseen senses and reached out and felt a rush of resistance from her. If she hadn't had any Affinity he would have felt nothing.

Realisation hit him with such force that his head swam. It was Piro's Affinity he'd sensed. Not only had his sister found the Fate and hidden it from Feldspar's Affinity, she had drawn him to it. 'You have more Affinity than I do. You've been hiding it!'

She shrugged this aside, eyes fixed earnestly on him. 'I found the Fate for you, so you could be a mystic!'

'Oh, Piro!' How could he be angry with her when she'd risked so much for him? He felt so much older. At thirteen she didn't understand the consequences. 'Don't you see? I didn't earn it, so I can't take it. It wouldn't be right.' He glanced to the amfina statue wishing it could have been otherwise. Though he did not deserve the Fate, he desperately wanted to join the mystics. For a heartbeat, he toyed with the idea of lying but he couldn't live with himself if he did. He sighed. 'I'll have to put it back.' A thought struck him. 'Did you move it? Where did the mystics master hide it?'

'Don't.' She caught his arm. 'You're spoiling everything. I was only trying to help.'

'And we'll have to tell our parents about your Affinity.' Fyn's mind ran on ahead. Their mother would be devastated. She had already given up one child to the gods' service. 'No wonder you haven't told anyone.'

Piro nodded miserably. 'You saw them at the hearing yesterday. The law must be obeyed. If the warlords thought Rolencia's royal family believed themselves above the law, they'd revolt. Merofynia would attack. If I tell our parents they'll have to send me to the abbess. And I'd hate that, always doing the right thing, never saying what I really thought, shut away from summer, always serving winter. I couldn't live like that, Fyn.'

'You can't keep your Affinity hidden. It –'

'I have so far, from both the castle Affinity warders and from both the abbey mystics. I've been as close to them as I am to you right now. Can you feel anything now?'

He focused and tried to sense her again. She registered on his senses with an absence which was odd. 'No... at least. You don't feel neutral. The only reason they haven't noticed is because it takes effort to sense Affinity. I felt something before when I tested you and my Affinity's weak. You'll give yourself away somehow and there'll be a terrible reckoning.'

'But why would they suspect? I've already been tested. No one guessed mine was dormant then. Oh Fyn, it's so strange. Mine came on me suddenly and it's getting stronger. Things like the Fate have been calling me. They have a sort of hum that's just on the edge of hearing. Don't you sense it?'

Fyn shook his head. Piro was more of a mystic than him, yet he had been sent to the abbey, forced to give up family and position in the world. Where was the justice in that?

'Don't tell mother and father, Fyn,' Piro whispered. 'Please?'

'We must. It'll be worse if we hide it like Farmer Overhill. No one will believe our parents didn't know. Even father's old honour guard will be angry with him.' Exasperation and fondness fought for supremacy. 'Abbey life is not so bad, Piro.'

'That's not what you said last time we talked. At least now I can slip away and...' Her eyes widened in horror. 'Why, if I was sent to the abbey I'd have to give up my foenix –'

'Oh, Piro. You are such a baby!' He felt like shaking her.

She glared at him and opened her mouth to speak, then stopped.

They both heard the steady thumps of someone running through the snow.

'Please Fyn, promise not to tell?' Piro pleaded, glancing over her shoulder.

'All right, but only if you –'

She darted back into the nook under the statue, her white cloak blending with the shadowed snow.

Fyn spun around to see Feldspar enter the clearing. Desperate to hide Piro's presence, Fyn went around the statue to meet him.

'You found it!' Feldspar reached him, gaze drawn to the Fate in his hands. 'I confess I didn't think you had it in you. You must present it to the mystics master.'

And have his mind searched? Fyn shuddered. He could not hide anything from Master Catillum. He would betray Piro for sure. A solution came to him and he thrust the Fate towards Feldspar. 'You take it. I don't have enough Affinity to be a mystic.'

'Then how did you find it?'

'Lucky chance.'

'Not chance, fate!' Feldspar studied the spinning opal with obvious longing, but he made no move to touch it. 'I admit, I had hoped I'd be the one. But if not, then I'm glad it's you. Have you looked in it yet? The vision is your reward.'

Torn by conflicting emotions, Fyn stared into the opal's strange surface. As it spun on the end of the chain the spiral shell turned, glinting in the light: green, blue, the occasional flash of red. What was his Fate? What should he do?

Bright colours glimmered. A noble feast. A girl with tilted, liquid eyes and no eyebrows, a sweet-faced girl, whose expression was schooled to betray nothing, but underneath it he could sense her fear and a deep sadness.

Stranger still, he felt as if he knew her.

'Fyn?' Feldspar nudged him. 'What did you see?'

'A girl.'

Feldspar groaned. 'Some mystic you'll make. Monks are supposed to be celibate.'

Shame flared hot in Fyn. He shoved the pendant into his friend's hands. 'You're right. I'm a fraud. You take it.'

Feldspar had to take it or drop it. He held up the sacred Fate, staring into the opal's iridescent surface. 'I can't. I –'

'You found it, Feldspar? I always said you'd be mystics master one day!' Lonepine joined them, grinning with delight. Then he mimed a blow to Fyn's head. 'I left Hawkwing with a headache that'll stop him enjoying tonight's feast. Now we must get back to sound the horn!'

Feldspar met Fyn's gaze, torn between honour and desire. His eyes held a question.

'I want you to present it to the master,' Fyn told him firmly. He had to protect Piro, no matter what it cost him.

'Only if that is what you truly want,' Feldspar whispered.

'Of course we do!' Lonepine rolled his eyes. 'What's holding you back? Come on!'

Lonepine headed off towards the island's shore.

'I'd rather I'd found it myself,' Feldspar whispered.

Fyn understood exactly how he felt. This time Piro had gone too far.

'Byren?' Queen Myrella beckoned.

He left Garzik and Orrade to join the queen. Her companions, women of the noble and great merchant families of Rolencia, moved away politely.

'Mother?' Byren knelt next to his mother's chair so that their conversation would be private. There were dark circles under the queen's beautiful black eyes and hollows under her cheekbones. With a start Byren wondered if his mother was sickening for something. Concerned, he placed his hand over hers, small and cold. 'How can I help?'

She smiled and glanced down, covering his hand and squeezing his fingers. But when she looked up her mouth was tight with worry again. 'Do you know where Piro is? She told me she was coming down early with Seela, but she wasn't here when I arrived. I just know Piro is up to something. '

He'd been wondering where his sister was. 'You know how she hates royal duties. She's probably off playing with her foenix. She's only a child.'

'In a year and a half she'll be fifteen. I was betrothed to your father at eight and married at fifteen. Besides, this is Fyn's chance to prove himself. She'd never fail him.'

His mother was right. Byren was torn between annoyance with Piro's thoughtlessness and fear for her safety. 'You want me to look for her?'

The tightness across his mother's forehead and around her eyes relaxed. 'Do you mind?'

He patted her hand. 'Of course not.'

But when he went to rise, she held onto his fingers. 'Search the guildhall below. She knows what we have planned so she should be here by now. She's probably hiding downstairs, sulking because I snapped at her this morning.'

He nodded, yet his mother still did not release his hand. He waited. She seemed to have trouble framing her thoughts.

'What is it, Mother?'

'When this is over, do something for me?'

He smiled. 'Anything.'

'Go hunting with your brother.'

'That's no hardship.' He laughed, secretly amazed that his mother should be aware of a rift he was only just discovering. 'What –'

'It is hard to be the king-in-waiting,' the queen whispered. 'It looks like your father will live another twenty or thirty years, with Halcyon's blessing. Having no real power but many boring duties, Lence watches you. You have a way with people. Everyone likes you and he can't help wondering if you will end up king instead of him.'

Byren snorted. 'But I'd only inherit if Lence died. Surely you're not suggesting...'

His mother frowned, watching him intently.

He felt the beginnings of a headache and tried to remember what he'd been saying. 'Freezing Sylion. I don't want to be kingsheir!'

The headache passed and his mother looked relieved. 'No, Byren, you don't. But maybe the people would prefer you to Lence, and that worries him.'

Frustration welled up in Byren. 'I don't see what I can –'

'Take a step back. Don't put yourself forward so much. Let Lence shine.'

He was already doing that, not that his mother knew.

'If I hadn't killed the leogryf, Lence would be dead and I'd be kingsheir,' he muttered, struck by the injustice of it all.

Garzik hurried over to them. 'Some acolytes are heading back from Ruin Isle!' He peered across the lake. 'I swear... yes, one of them is Fyn!'

Queen Myrella released Byren's hand and gave him a gentle push. 'Go. And think on what I've said.'

He slipped away from the royal balcony, annoyed and more than a little worried. But first, he had to find his sister.

After making a quick search of the guildhall, without success, he heard a carriage draw up. After pimping and preening, the Merofynian ambassador had arrived with his retinue.

Byren had run out of time to find Piro. He only hoped she was safe back at Rolenhold with her foenix, even if that meant she was deliberately misbehaving. He made for the stairs to the bell tower. Their father would just have to make the announcement without Piro, not that it mattered. It was Lence's big moment.

But halfway up the steps, he met his twin, headed down.

'Hey, you're going the wrong way. The balcony's up there!' Byren protested.

Lence grinned. He'd been drinking with his honour guard and Byren could smell the fine Rolencian wine on his breath. As usual, his spirits had improved for being just a little bit drunk.

'But I'm headed for the back stairs, Byren. That's where I'm meeting the prettiest little serving maid you ever saw.'

Byren frowned. There wasn't time for dalliance. Their parents would make the announcement as soon as the Merofynian ambassador joined them. Even now, he was being greeted by merchants on the front steps. They would probably delay him for a few minutes as they invited him to dinner with the intention of setting up trade deals with Merofynia. 'But –'

Lence shook off his hand. 'They've lined me up with the Merofynian king's daughter, Byren. She's probably got buck teeth and bad breath. I think I deserve a bit of fun!' He took off down the steps. 'Don't worry, I won't miss the announcement of my own betrothal. I'll arrange to meet this maid later, but first I'll collect a kiss.'

'What of Elina?'

'What the eyes don't see the heart doesn't grieve!' He called over his shoulder.

Byren hesitated. Lence wouldn't want his company, but if the maid was as pretty as he said, he might get distracted and keep their father waiting. King Rolen's temper was legendary. Better follow and keep an eye on him.

Just as he started down, Byren heard the thump of a body hitting the wall and the scrape of a sword being drawn. His heart missed a beat and his hand went to his belt, reaching for his missing sword hilt.

Cursing, Byren took the stairs four at a time, barrelling into the dark little foyer at the base. There was no sign of the serving maid, only three swordsmen, none of whom could be called pretty.

Despite his slightly inebriated state, Lence had disarmed one man. Now he swung this attacker around, using his body as a shield to protect himself from the remaining two. The man's cockatrice cloak impeded his struggles. Byren drew his ceremonial dagger and threw. Though it wasn't designed for throwing, it took the nearest attacker in the back. He fell to his knees with a cry. The other spun around, sword lifting.

Byren had nothing, not even a cloak to wrap around his arm as a shield.

Lence shoved his man forwards. He collided with Byren's attacker, knocking them both off balance while the cloak remained in Lence's hands. Seizing this chance, Byren kicked the attacker's sword arm and the weapon flew from his fingers. Byren drove his fist into the man's jaw. The swordsman staggered back, knocking his companion to the ground.

The man scrambled for the sword and sprang to his feet. Lence backed into the corner. The men advanced on him.

PIRO HUDDLED, SHIVERING in her hiding place while she waited for Fyn and his friends' voices to fade as they moved off. Fyn was right, she should not have come here. If she was discovered, the abbot could order her execution. Not that she thought he would, but she couldn't be certain, for no kingsdaughter had ever insulted the goddess of Halcyon before.

She felt sick to her stomach.

This was worse than the time she'd climbed onto Byren's hunter and been thrown.

If she was caught on Ruin Isle today she would disgrace her family. If only she'd thought before she acted, instead of looking forward to pleasing Fyn. That had proved a disaster. Now he was furious with her.

Hot tears stung her eyes. Blinking them away fiercely, she hugged her knees and waited until she heard the horn which meant the acolytes were safely back in Rolenton. Then she crawled out.

Slinging her skates over her shoulder, Piro rubbed her arms and legs to get her circulation back. She had meant to help Fyn become a mystic. Now which branch of the monks would he join?

He wasn't like most men.

Last midsummer, Fyn had taken her into a deserted stable where the straw was thick on the ground, and had shown her how to escape if someone tried to grab her, how to throw her attacker and where to kick to do the most damage.

It had been a wonderful midsummer. They'd rowed out to Ruin Isle so he could teach her how to use his bow. She had barely been strong enough to draw it but was soon hitting the target. Fyn had never once told her she couldn't do something because she was small and female. And she hadn't ridiculed him when he asked if he could use her paints. She still had the watercolour he had done of Rolenhold with Lake Sapphire reflecting the castle's golden onion domes like a mirror. No, Fyn wasn't like the others.

And now, because of her, he wouldn't be a mystic.

Tears burned her eyes. Wiping her face on her sleeve, she turned towards Rolenton. She had to find Fyn and apologise. She wouldn't be happy until everything was right between them.

Reaching the island's shore, she strapped on her skates and looked across the lake to Rolenton. Just then the bell tower's song rang out. Piro cursed roundly, using words the stable boys used when they thought she wasn't listening.

She'd forgotten her parents' big announcement!

BYREN LOOKED ABOUT for a weapon, anything to divert the attacker from his twin. Nothing.

The door to the stairwell swung open and Fyn stood there, saffron robe gleaming in the dimness.

His eyes widened as he took in the situation.

Seeing one of Halcyon's renowned warrior monks, the swordsmen collected their wounded companion and backed out the far door, blades raised defiantly.

Lence cursed. 'They're getting away!'

'Let them,' Byren snapped. 'In case you hadn't noticed, they're the ones with swords!'

Fyn stepped inside and let his door swing shut behind him. 'What's going on? Are you all right?'

'I'm fine,' Byren said. 'What about you, Lence?'

He rubbed his head. 'I can't believe that pretty little serving maid set me up.'

'I can't believe someone made an attempt on your life in our own home town,' Byren whispered.

'Who?' Fyn asked.

'One of the warlords.' Lence lifted the cloak for Byren to see. It hung from his fingers supple and rich, feathers as fine as fur. Cockatrice cloak. Too expensive for any but a nobleman or a wealthy merchant, or...

'A warrior from Cockatrice Spar?' Fyn guessed.

'Too easy,' Byren muttered. 'And there's no reason for that warlord to turn on us.'

'Agreed.' Lence rubbed his jaw. 'Besides, he'd never be fool enough to send his own men.'

'Are you saying someone set him up? Another of the warlords?' Fyn muttered. 'But they are all here to renew their oaths of allegiance.'

'Not all of them,' Lence countered. 'The Unistag warlord is missing.'

'His successors can't decide –' Byren began to explain.

'They could have heard a rumour about the betrothal,' Lence said, thinking aloud.

Fyn looked confused.

'We've been keeping the warlords in line with Lence as bait, a possible alliance with one of their daughters, you see. Now that he's getting married...' Byren shrugged.

'Married?' Fyn mouthed, glancing to Lence.

'Don't you dare congratulate me!' he warned.

Byren grinned. 'We'd be in trouble if the warlords ever stopped fighting amongst themselves long enough to unite against us!'

Fyn's eyes widened. 'But father is their king.'

Lence sent him a withering look. 'What do they teach you at the abbey?'

Fyn flinched.

'The spars make poor farmland. The warlords are constantly looking to expand their territory and Rolencia is the richest prize. They're always sniffing around, looking for weakness in each other or us,' Byren explained. 'Killing King Rolen's heir would make one of them look strong to the other warlords. It might be enough to unite them against us.'

'Why now?' Fyn asked.

'The balance of power is about to change,' Byren said, 'Lence is to be betrothed to the Merofynian kingsdaughter.'

'Buck teeth for sure,' Lence muttered, shaking his head.

Byren grinned, glad Lence was back to normal, even if it had taken an assassination attempt to cheer him up.

'I don't understand,' Fyn protested. 'Why does Lence have to marry a girl from the Merofynian royal family? We haven't had trouble from them since before mother and father –'

'No. But...' Byren glanced to Lence. He was being no help. 'But when mother's younger brother, King Sefon, died in mysterious circumstances –'

'He fell off his horse while hunting,' Fyn corrected.

'They found him with a broken neck in the forest and his horse walked back to the stables,' Byren countered. 'That was just over seven years ago. His death made mother the rightful heir to Merofynia. While Merofynia was having its war of succession, father could have invaded and claimed the crown in her name. We didn't and mother's cousin became king. King Merofyn the Sixth has no love for Rolencia but he does have a daughter. Marriage between second cousins, Lence and the kingsdaughter, will cement a shaky peace.'

'But why –'

'Enough history. You saved my life again, Byren.' Lence faced him, a grin on his lips, but a penetrating look in his eyes. 'Two minutes later and you'd be kingsheir right now.'

'No thanks needed.' Byren laughed, relieved. 'Besides, if I was kingsheir I'd have to marry your bucktoothed kingsdaughter!'

'That reminds me.' Lence grimaced. 'Duty calls. Come on.'

As they climbed the stairs to the bell tower, Byren rolled up the cockatrice cloak. It was one of the more common ones, a mix of brown, red and gold feathers, but still expensive. It meant whoever had sent the assassins had deep pockets.

He was aware of Fyn following quietly. Sometimes Fyn seemed so knowing, and other times he failed to understand the real world. That's what came of being reared by a pack of prayer-chanting monks.

Lence stopped on the top step. He glanced to the rolled-up cloak in Byren's hands. 'We'll have to tell them about the assassination attempt –'

'But we don't want the Merofynian ambassador knowing about our troubles with the warlords,' Byren anticipated. 'I'll hide the cloak to show father later.'

Lence nodded and went ahead.

After this close call, Byren wished he'd found Piro. In all probability, she was safe back at the castle playing with her foenix, but this escalation of violence would be one more thing to make their parents' eyes gleam with worry.

No wonder he'd never wanted to rule Rolencia!

STILL SHAKY FROM walking in on the assassination attempt, Fyn followed his brothers into the chamber on the fifth floor of the bell tower, where their parents waited. Through the open doors, he could see the balcony and the roof tops of the grand merchant houses which framed Rolenton Square.

'There you are. What kept you?' his mother greeted them as she hurried over. 'Just look at you, Lence. Anyone would think you'd been fighting!'

As she folded Lence's ermine-edged cloak neatly over his shoulders, Lence rolled his eyes. Byren winked at Fyn, who did not understand how they could be so cool-headed. His heart still hammered.

'You do your father proud,' Queen Myrella said, arranging Lence's kingsheir emblem in the centre of his chest.

Lence brushed her hands away. 'Leave be, mother. I'm not six years old.'

She ignored him and stepped back, a fond smile on her face as she turned to Fyn and Byren. 'Let me look at my three boys.'

Lence and Byren were dressed in rich red and black, the royal colours, their cuffs trimmed with gold embroidery. Their vests were decorated with red garnets and black onyxes. Fyn wore only the simple saffron robe of an acolyte.

'They're fine, Myrella,' King Rolen assured her, linking his arm through hers. 'The ambassador will be here any moment. Where's Piro?'

The queen cast Byren a quick look. He gave an almost imperceptible shake of his head which Fyn caught. He held his tongue. Only he knew where Piro was, and he hoped she stayed safely hidden until all the acolytes left Ruin Isle.

'Oh, Rolen. I forgot to tell you. She had a sore throat so I told her to stay in bed,' his mother lied straight-faced, which surprised Fyn. Or perhaps Piro had pretended to have a sore throat. He wouldn't put it past her. She was such a minx.

Then he heard boots on the stairs. 'Here comes the Merofynian ambassador. '

He stepped aside as the elderly man entered, followed by several servants, among them a page boy who carried a small, gilt chest. They were all dressed in the height of Merofynian court fashion.

Their sleeves were so long they would have dragged on the ground if they had not been pinned up with jewelled broaches. Fyn frowned. Were those real foenix feathers in their velvet hats? His father would not approve. King Rolen had tried to breed foenixes in captivity to restore their numbers.

'Ah, Lord Benvenute,' his mother greeted the ambassador. 'I see you brought the miniature of Isolt Kingsdaughter.'

'Welcome.' The king clapped the ambassador's shoulder and the man winced. 'Let's get this started.'

Then King Rolen took the queen's arm and they stepped out onto the balcony to enthusiastic cheering. It made Fyn's heart lift. The people of Rolencia were loyal, even if the warlords weren't.

Normally Lence would have gone next, but the ambassador followed before any of the kingsons. As the Merofynian king's representative, he ranked above them.

Standing out on the balcony in the crisp winter air, Fyn was suddenly aware of their vulnerability. Several good bowmen on the roof opposite could have wiped out the Rolencian royal family in a couple of heart beats.

Where was Piro? Was she safe?

His father held up his arms signalling for silence and the cheering died away. The king turned to the queen, lifting her hand, kissing it. They shared a private smile. It pleased Fyn to see them happy.

Rolen turned to the crowd. 'Rolencia has known many years of peace and prosperity since I was lucky enough to make Myrella Merofyn Kingsdaughter my queen.'

The crowd cheered again. From the level of noise they'd already been imbibing heavily. Hot honeyed mead for the farmers and best Rolencian red for the merchants and nobles. It was a festival, after all.

'Today we celebrate for a special reason,' King Rolen said, and the people grew quiet. 'Today, Lence Kingsheir will take Isolt Merofyn Kingsdaughter for his betrothed!'

The roar of approval deafened Fyn.

The ambassador turned to his page who opened the chest. From its azure velvet bed he took out a gold locket and opened it, holding it up for the crowd to see.

'Isolt Merofyn Kingsdaughter,' Ambassador Benvenute said. The crowd cheered again, though no one could have seen the miniature portrait when Fyn, who was only a body length away, could not see her face.

Fyn glanced to Lence. His brother looked grim. He'd made it clear how he felt about having to marry a girl he had never met. No doubt the artist had flattered King Merofyn's daughter. But even if she were beautiful, she was the daughter of a man who, if what Byren said was true, had come to the throne by murdering their mother's younger brother and defeating all other contenders. If the daughter was as ruthless as her father, poor Lence would never have an easy night's sleep!

'I am here in Isolt's place, to give her betrothal vows,' Benvenute said. He placed the locket in Lence's hand. The words of betrothal were said, and when the ceremony ended, Lence slipped the miniature over his head. It settled just above the foenix emblem. For the first time, Fyn saw those symbols as chains of servitude. His brothers had no more choice as to how they served Rolencia than he did. That reminded him, he still had to prove himself to the mystics master. But how? His stomach churned.

Piro! A wave of mingled frustration and admiration swept him. He had promised he would not reveal her secret. But how long could she hide it? And was it even safe to do so? He didn't want his sister becoming a channel for evil. The first thing he had been taught on entering the abbey was how to say the warding chant to clear his mind and tap on the vulnerable points of his body so that his Affinity could not be used by a renegade Power-worker. They sang the chant every night before falling asleep and every morning upon waking, so that it was drilled into their minds.

His father signalled for silence and the cheering died down.

'When you drink your toast tonight,' King Rolen raised his voice, 'drink to another thirty years of peace between Rolencia and Merofynia!'

At his signal the bells began their song of celebration. And Fyn slipped away to find Piro.

Brave, but silly girl.

Chapter Eleven

PIRO FROWNED AS the celebration bells rang on and on. Too late to join her family for the announcement now. Her mother would be furious. Resentment roiled in her belly. No one had told her what the announcement was about, yet she was still expected to be there.

She climbed onto the wharf and headed across Rolenton. Avoiding the bell tower square and the inevitable confrontation with her mother, Piro begged a ride in the back of a cart with half a dozen minstrels who had never seen King Rolen's daughter. The entertainers had been hired to perform for tonight's feast and, as she listened to their happy chatter, Piro wished her life was as simple. Maybe she should run away with them. Her mother had trained her well. A Merofynian noblewoman was expected to be able to run an estate employing a thousand people, do the accounts, know the law, speak three languages, play a musical instrument, paint a reasonable likeness and recite the great sagas. She could live a minstrel's life.

But she was only fooling herself. She could never leave her family.

With a sigh, she planned an apology for her mother as well as one for Fyn. It seemed she was always apologising.

BYREN HAD NOTICED Fyn slip away and wondered why he was in such a hurry, but he still had to find Piro, so he jogged down the stairs and set out across the square.

Monks and acolytes mingled freely with townspeople and the warlords' noisy honour guards. With all the farm folk who had come in to Rolenton for the festivities, the square was packed and Byren despaired of ever finding Piro. If she was back at the castle he'd be wasting his time. Best to check the foenix's pen first.

Byren was about to return to the square's stables and get his horse when he heard raised voices coming from the end of the lane beside the Three Swans. His belly tightened, responding to their menacing tone. A muffled voice protested. His father had heavy penalties for thievery but it was impossible to stamp it out.

Byren didn't know who might be down the end of that lane but whoever it was, was the king's subject and it was his duty to protect them. He turned down the lane thinking the sight of his Rolencian royal colours should be enough to frighten off the thieves. If not, he'd knock a few heads together.

'Let me past.' Fyn sounded as if he was trying to be reasonable.

Fyn? Byren broke into a run. Covering the last two body lengths, he peered around the lane's bend in time to find Fyn confronted by four monks. They did not look much older than him and they had him backed up against the far wall. Last year's acolytes, Byren guessed. Curious, he hung back in the shadow of a staircase. The stench from a fresh pile of tavern refuse was bad despite the cold. Byren concentrated on breathing through his mouth.

'...and I won't take the blame for the grucranes leaving!' the ringleader announced.

'I haven't said anything,' Fyn protested.

'You were seen walking up the path to the abbey with the weapons master. What were you talking about?'

'The Proving.'

'Proving? You and your friends shone in the Proving today.' The ringleader shoved a finger in Fyn's chest. 'But don't think you three will outshine us. Beartooth –'

'My friends have nothing to do with this, Galestorm.' Fyn's voice shook with repressed anger. 'This is between you and me, and you know it, so leave Lonepine and Feldspar out of it.'

'But it is so much fun baiting that skinny streak and seeing him squirm. It's sure to drive Lonepine to throw the first punch!' Galestorm sneered with triumphant cruelty. 'Then we can chastise him, for an acolyte must obey a monk. And you three won't be monks until spring cusp, so we plan to make your lives miserable until then. And after that, well, accidents can happen. Even a monk can trip on the stairs.'

Byren went cold. Fyn had never told him abbey life was this dangerous. Every instinct told him to go to Fyn's aid, but he held back. He didn't want to shame Fyn by stepping in before he could help himself. Besides, his brother had to go back to the abbey and, when he did, Byren wouldn't be there to help him.

'Now, take off your clothes and climb into that pile of rubbish,' Galestorm ordered.

Fyn folded his arms.

'Are you disobeying a direct order, acolyte?' Galestorm gloated.

'It's not a fair order and you know it!' Fyn countered.

Galestorm looked to his three friends. 'Did you hear me give this acolyte an unfair order?'

They shook their heads.

'Right.' Galestorm rubbed his hands together eagerly. 'Strip him and toss him into the rubbish.'

Fyn writhed and twisted, avoiding them. Before anyone expected it, he caught one of his attackers with a throw that sent him into the rubbish heap. Byren felt like cheering. But there were three more and they had all been trained by the weapons master so they knew the moves and counter moves, same as Fyn did.

The outcome was inevitable.

Byren waded in. They were too absorbed attacking Fyn to notice him coming up behind them. He could have ordered them to back off and they would have. But he wanted to get his hands on them. Seizing Beartooth by the shoulders, Byren jerked him off balance, then shoved him on top of his friend. Suddenly Galestorm was alone, facing Fyn and

Byren. The monk recognised him, looked worried for a heartbeat, then tried to brazen it out.

'So your big brother does your fighting, Fyn Kingson?' he sneered.

This was exactly what Byren had feared.

Fyn was so angry his hands shook.

'He was doing fine on his own,' Byren said. 'I just thought I'd even the odds. Two of King Rolen's kin should be able to stand up to four of Halcyon's monks!'

The other three had scrambled to their feet now and looked to Galestorm for guidance. Unlike hotheaded Galestorm, they were clearly not eager to tackle both the kingsons.

'Come on, Fyn.' Byren slung an arm around his brother's shoulders and deliberately turned his back on the others.

His neck tingled as they walked off. Were these monks cowardly enough, not to mention foolish enough, to attack them? But Galestorm and his companions must have thought better of it for Byren and Fyn made it safely out of the Three Swans' lane.

Fyn turned to face Byren, shrugging off his arm. 'Thank you for helping me, but –'

'Now they'll come after you when I'm not around, I know,' he muttered. 'Not much I can do about that, I'm afraid. Don't get caught alone. Stay with your friends. That Lonepine looks like he could handle himself.'

'Feldspar might be the mystical type but he can handle himself too,' Fyn insisted.

Byren studied Fyn.

'What is it?' Fyn asked.

'I got the impression that this is not the first time Galestorm and his bullies have picked on you. Why didn't you say something? And why do they dare to bully a kingson?'

Fyn sighed. 'At the abbey I am just Fyn. We're supposed to leave our past lives behind, especially once we take our monk's vows. The abbey has great ideals but reality is different. In a place where all are equal in the goddess's sight, the masters vie for power. The abbot is chosen from their ranks and to be abbot is to rule all of Halcyon's abbeys and oversee the distribution of the goddess's wealth. He is only one step less powerful than father.'

Byren rubbed his chin, he hadn't considered it that way. 'But you're still a kingson. Why do they dare –'

'That's the problem. Galestorm knows my birth will help me rise to become the master of whatever branch I enter and he resents me for it. Besides, I caught him tormenting a grucrane and now they've flown off, leaving our abbey without its sentries.'

'They'll come back. Where else will they sleep these cold winter nights?' Byren rubbed his brother's shaven head. Fyn had lost his cap in the scuffle, revealing his crown of tattoos. Soon they would shave off the thin plait that grew from the top of his head and begin the first of his monk tattoos, above and between his acolyte tattoos. On that day he would become the lowest of the monks. Byren summoned a smile. 'I'm the lucky one. I don't envy you or Lence. Now come up to Rolenhold and share a drink with me. An acolyte who's nearly a monk can still enjoy a fine Rolencian red, can't he?'

Fyn grinned. 'I can and I will. But first there's something I must do.'

'Yes. You'd better warn your friend to watch out for Galestorm.'

Fyn hesitated for an instant. 'Exactly. See you later, Byren.'

As he watched his younger brother forge through the crowded square Byren wondered what Fyn was really up to, then dismissed it. He had to get back to the castle and find Piro. And when he found her, he was going to give her a piece of his mind. It was time she grew up!

PIRO CLIMBED DOWN from the minstrels' cart with a word of thanks, then slipped away through the servants' courtyard. She was not looking forward to apologising to Fyn or her mother. Then she remembered she hadn't fed her foenix yet, so she went to the kitchens.

Three summers ago Byren and Lence had tried to trap a foenix which had been ravaging the high farms on the Dividing Mountains. The birds were very rare now and their father wanted to capture a pair for the royal menagerie , but this foenix had turned vicious to protect its nest. Byren had brought the two eggs back to Rolenhold and Piro had kept them warm, turning them every day, but only one had hatched. Now her foenix was as big as a large chicken, though his legs were longer in proportion to his body. He had yet to develop the crest and beak sharp as a dagger, but he did have the brilliant red feathers as fine as fur, and the gleaming red chest scales. Because foenixes liked heat she kept him in the menagerie which was glassed over, and warmed by hot vents from the pools far below the castle. King Byren the Fourth had built it before the wars distracted him from collecting Affinity beasts. According to the old stories he'd liked animals better than people. Piro had never known her father's father but she often felt a sneaking sympathy for him.

'How's my pretty boy?' Piro whispered. She admired the foenix as he ate kitchen scraps from her hand, then rubbed his throat on her fingers. He blinked his emerald eyes and made a soft interrogative sound in his throat. Piro was sure he understood everything she said and, unlike her mother, he never scolded her or tried to change her.

'There you are!' Seela, her old nurse, pounced on her. 'The queen wants you, and be quick about it.'

Seela bustled Piro up the stairs, warning her to mind her tongue as they hurried along to her mother's solarium. It had been decorated with a recurring flower, vine and animal motif. These wound in and around each other in complex patterns. Picked out in paint and semi-precious stones, every surface glistened, catching the light. The chamber ran the length of the west wall, which was illuminated by deep-set diamond paned windows, so it was pleasant even in midwinter. But Piro hated it because it felt like a prison to her. Its walls were the invisible walls of royal expectation, fine lace, female giggles and lessons in law and account keeping.

Piro found her mother surrounded by the ladies

of the court. They were laying out clothes and jewellery for tonight's midwinter feast, gossiping and laughing, twittering like birds.

Piro dutifully bent one knee. 'You wanted me, queen mother?'

Myrella dismissed her women. While they collected their combs and shawls, Piro shifted impatiently from foot to foot, her toes damp in her riding boots.

People said she looked like Queen Myrella, but they were nothing alike. Her mother had been a dutiful daughter to one king, then the equally dutiful wife of another. Piro couldn't get through the day without treading on someone's toes.

She was a little taller than the queen but just as fine-boned. Her mother had been considered a beauty in her day. At nearly thirty-six the queen's fine skin was barely lined, and her black hair, hidden under a fashionable head-dress, held hardly any grey. All her life Piro had been disappointing her mother. If the queen was a potter and Piro was her pot, then the queen was constantly pinching and prodding her into a shape that was not natural.

Piro mentally rehearsed her apology. As soon as the last woman left, she launched into her speech. 'I am so sorry, mother. What with all the excitement and Fyn's friend finding Halcyon's Fate, I –'

'Forgot? I thought as much, but you're no longer a careless child. At your age I was planning my wedding! How do you think Lence felt, when you didn't bother to turn up for his betrothal?'

'Betrothal?'

'To King Merofyn's daughter.'

Piro was stunned. 'I... I did not know. You should have told me.'

'Delicate negotiations have been going on for two years. Hardly the sort of thing a careless child needs to know!'

Piro was stung.

Her mother smoothed down the central panel of her heavily embroidered velvet gown and frowned as she looked Piro up and down. 'That dress won't do. Off with it.'

'I don't see why I have to get changed. The feast is not until this evening.'

Before her mother could speak, the door opened and her old nurse came back.

'Not ready yet, Piro? They're waiting for you in the trophy chamber,' Seela said. 'I caught a glimpse of him. Such a good-looking man. Clever too, they say.'

'Who are you talking about?' Piro fought a sinking feeling.

The old woman cast her mother a sharp look. Seela had been the queen's nurse and tutor when she was a child, having come with her from Merofynia. After the marriage Seela had stayed on to help rear the royal children. 'You haven't told her, Myrella?'

In a flash, Piro realised what this meeting was all about. Just as Lence must marry to strengthen Rolencia's alliances, so must she. 'Who have I been betrothed to?'

'A fine young warlord,' her mother spoke soothingly. Seela stepped behind Piro to undo the laces of her gown. 'This is just a first meeting. Either of you may decide not to take it any further.'

But they both knew Piro could not decline without offending the warlord. He was some upstart princeling from beyond the Divide, the petty ruler of a barren spar of land that stretched out into the sea. Piro snorted. A mere barbarian warlord, not even a kingson!

Not that there was a king's son the right age for her. Ostron Isle was ruled by an elector, chosen from one of the great merchant families who held court feasting and bickering over trade agreements. And the last Merofynian kingson had been her mother's younger brother. Poor little Sefon, her mother always called him. Queen Myrella hadn't seen her brother since he was a toddler and she was eight years old. After his death, the throne had passed to King Merofyn the Sixth who was older than Piro's father. From what she'd overheard, he was a nasty piece. His own wife had killed herself to escape him. Piro was relieved her parents weren't trying to betrothe her to King Merofyn.

Even so, the thought of political marriage made her burn with resentment. She had always known she would have to marry to further Rolencia's alliances, but until today that had been in the distant future.

'I don't want to m –' Her voice was muffled as Seela pulled the gown over her head. Piro blinked, '– marry. I'm not ready.'

'Those boots will have to come off,' her mother said. 'Sit by the fire while I find your gold-beaded slippers.'

'The ones that match the red and gold velvet gown, Myrella?' Seela asked.

'Yes. And she can wear the gold head-dress.' The queen adjusted her own head-dress. It was the married woman's style with a little hood that sat forwards over her face and fine gold net which confined her hair.

Being unmarried, Piro's head-dress was a small cap which would sit on the crown of her head, held in place with a few pins, the fine mesh falling to her shoulders, beaded with mandarin garnets.

'I don't want to –'

'Take those boots off!' her mother called over her shoulder. She picked the gown up by the shoulders and shook it to get the wrinkles out. Several little sacks of lavender fell on the floor.

Piro sat on the chest in front of the fire wearing only her woolen chemise. She tugged at the laces of her riding boots. They were made of soft suede, bleached white to match her gown, and weren't designed for snow. Even her woolen stockings were damp.

Seela put the boots and stockings aside then rubbed lavender-scented oil into Piro's cold toes, chaffing them to get the blood flowing. It felt good, even better when Seela slid silk stockings onto her feet.

'Silk?' Piro muttered.

'Fix those stockings in place,' Seela said. 'There's a good girl.'

'I'm not a good girl.' Piro rolled the ends of the stockings over her garters to hold them up just above her knees. 'I don't want to marry some hairy, half-savage warlord!'

Piro was very aware of her mother and Seela exchanging glances.

'And I will tell father so!' Piro announced.

Her mother's mouth settled into that familiar thin line of annoyance. 'Arms up.'

Piro held up her arms and wriggled as the gown settled over her shoulders. Seela pulled the lacing tight.

'Red suits you,' her mother said.

Piro frowned. Just then Seela surprised her with a dab of expensive Ostronite myrrh. The perfume wafted up around her face, sweet and fruity, exotic as Ostron Isle itself.

Queen Myrella turned Piro around to look in the mirror. Taking a hairbrush, she unravelled Piro's plaits. Once her hair was loose, it fell in wavy ripples to her waist, black as sable. 'You have lovely hair.'

'It doesn't matter what I look like,' Piro said. 'I'm not... Ouch!'

Seela had jabbed her scalp as she stood on a foot stool to pin Piro's cap in place. 'Sorry.'

She draped a net of fine gold mesh over Piro's shoulders. It gleamed in contrast with her hair. Piro tugged her royal emblem out of the dress's bodice. Her small, silver foenix pendant glowed against the rich velvet.

'You look just like a kingsdaughter should!' Seela beamed.

Piro fumed.

'Something's missing,' the queen murmured. 'I know. Fetch the ruby choker from my jewellery box, Seela.'

The old woman scurried over to the dresser where several jewellery boxes had been left open. She began sifting through one.

Piro watched proceedings mutinously.

Queen Myrella stepped closer to Piro, her face next to Piro's in the mirror.

'Do you think I wanted to leave my home when I was betrothed to your father?' she whispered. 'I was only eight years old. I never saw my mother and my baby brother again. My father visited once, when I was wed at fifteen. But I never complained. I married King Rolen to stop the constant warring between our kingdoms. Rolencia and Merofynia have been ancestral enemies forever. Hardly a summer went by without some skirmishing. Now we have had peace for nearly thirty years. I did my duty. Lence is doing his. You must do yours!'

The queen's brilliant black eyes met Piro's in the mirror. For a heartbeat Piro was too startled to speak. She had never considered that her mother might not have wanted to marry. 'But you love father.'

'Now I do,' her mother revealed. 'Ahh, Piro. Give this warlord a chance. Don't close your heart and mind against him.'

'Here it is,' Seela announced, placing the choker around Piro's throat.

It was heavy and gleamed against her skin. Her fingers stroked the gold filigree and cabochon star rubies. She stared at the person in the mirror. This grand kingsdaughter didn't look like the Piro who had begged a ride with a cart load of minstrels. She looked older, aloof and angry.

Piro hated not being in control of her life.

'She reminds me of you at the same age,' Seela whispered. 'So beautiful.'

Piro glared at her face in the mirror. She'd drawn both their portraits and she had no illusions. 'My chin is more pointed and my mouth is bigger. I'll never be a beauty like mother.'

Queen Myrella spun her around by the shoulders. 'Beauty's only a tool, and not a very good one. You're on your own after the first five minutes. Now, you go down to the trophy chamber and –'

'That's what I am, just a trophy!'

'Mind your tongue,' Seela snapped. 'Don't you shame your mother. She's a kingsdaughter in her own right with a better claim to the Merofynian throne than Merofyn the Sixth!'

Queen Myrella shook her head with a half-smile. 'Don't rake over the past, Seela. I am queen of Rolencia. One kingdom is enough for me. Now, off you go, Piro. And just this once, think before you speak!'

FYN MADE HIS way through Rolenhold's great hall, keeping watch for a green-grey robe and Galestorm's distinctive, thick neck. The hall was so packed it was hard to find anyone. All around him monks and acolytes celebrated as they relived the race to Ruin Isle.

He sighted a saffron robe surrounded by fellow acolytes and recognised Lonepine, who was re-enacting the battle with Hawkwing. Fyn smiled to himself, remembering how he'd have hung on every word only a year ago. Letting Lonepine enjoy his triumph, Fyn waited until the story came to an end, then caught his friend's eye.

'Come, join the fun, Fyn.' Lonepine would have pulled him into the centre of admiring youths.

'We need to talk,' Fyn mouthed.

Lonepine forged through the younger acolytes and joined Fyn saying, 'Feldspar is meeting with the mystics master. He's due back soon. His place will be ensured when we get back to the abbey.'

'That's what I wanted to tell you. We need to stick together. Galestorm thinks I told the weapons master how he injured the grucrane.' The only people he'd told had been Lonepine and Feldspar.

Lonepine's brows drew down and his hands curled into fists.

'No you don't,' Fyn said quickly. 'That's all he needs, a chance to teach you a lesson. Besides, I can look after myself.'

'When the odds are fair.' Lonepine held Fyn's eyes. 'And we both know Galestorm likes the odds to be in his favour.'

The older boys bullied the younger boys, the older acolytes bullied the young ones, and the monks bullied everyone they could. It was the way of the abbey. If you were lucky you found a safe niche and kept out of trouble. Fyn had always admired Wintertide because the boys master punished bullying. But his old master could not be everywhere.

'Well Galestorm didn't succeed this time and as long as we stick together he won't get another chance.'

Lonepine went to speak, but a young acolyte called him over to sort out an argument over which stroke he had used to fell Hawkwing.

'Be right there.' Lonepine laughed. 'Come on, Fyn. Have some fun.'

Fyn noticed Farmer Overhill's fifteen-year-old son watching from the edge of the group. He would have a hard time in the abbey, being thrown in with the small boys when he should have been in the year below Fyn. 'Say, Lonepine, keep an eye on the new boy.'

His friend glanced over his shoulder. 'Another stray?'

Fyn grinned. 'Just do it. I can't hang about, I'm seeing my brothers.'

'Then watch out for Galestorm.'

'You too, and warn Feldspar.'

Fyn crossed the busy hall, heading for the far door. Just as he stepped out into the connecting hall someone hailed him. He got the feeling they had been lying in wait for him. Catching the flash of a dark robe, he turned, his hands lifting defensively.

'Ahh, Fyn Kingson, I didn't mean to startle you.' History Master Hotpool beckoned him into the shadows. As a master, he wore a silver torque with one row of lapis lazuli. 'I hear the mystics master has offered your friend Feldspar a place. You must be pleased for him, but where does that leave you? This made me wonder why you hadn't come to ask me for a place.' Though he fixed Fyn with a fond, avuncular look, his eyes held a predatory gleam.

Fyn avoided his gaze. He had not gone to the history master because, though he had a genuine love of history, he did not like Hotpool. The master's smile did not reach his eyes and the monks who went into his service complained of favours they did not wish to give.

Fyn cleared his throat. 'Master Oakstand said he would offer me a place with the warrior monks, so I thought –'

'The weapons master?' Hotpool frowned. 'I would not have thought you were the type to favour brawn above brains, Fyn. Besides, I know you turned him down.' His eyes narrowed. 'Did you hope to pass over both and aim for a cleric's place? Four of the last ten abbots have been clerics. Is that your goal, to rule Halcyon's abbey since you can't rule Rolencia?'

'I am just a lowly acolyte,' Fyn said quickly, heart hammering with discomfort. 'I can only hope that in their wisdom, the masters select the right vocation for me.'

Before Hotpool could comment, he bowed and slipped away.

Knees shaking, Fyn cursed Piro. It was all her fault. If she hadn't interfered he might have found the Fate and then he would have been with the mystics master right now, safe from Master Hotpool and others like him.

Fyn headed for his brothers' chambers. Life was relatively simple for Piro, but she had certainly complicated his life.

Chapter Twelve

THE QUEEN AND Seela pushed Piro out the door of the solarium, into the long corridor, with admonishments still ringing in her ears. For one tempting moment, she considered running to the stables and hiding in the hay loft. Last winter she might have done it, but with the arrival of her Affinity had come the realisation that she would have to grow up and face the world eventually.

Still, her feet dragged as she made her way along to the trophy chamber. She understood why her father chose to meet the warlord there. The room housed tributes collected by the royal family of Rolencia over the last three hundred years. There were great metal shields, decorated with beasts as fierce as the barbarian warlords who had once carried them.

Niches in the walls housed porcelain urns of rare oils from Ostron Isle and vases encrusted with semi-precious stones. Also from Ostron Isle came cedarwood furniture, carved so skilfully it seemed alive. Over the fireplace hung the Mirror of Insight. In all the years Piro had peered into it, it had never done anything but reflect the room's trophies and her own curious face.

There was a stuffed wyvern, though not as large as the ones which roamed the Royal grounds of Merofynia. The taxidermist had done a wonderful job, standing it on its rear legs so that it was taller than a man, mouth open to reveal razor-edged teeth. Its gleaming sapphire eyes were real jewels which winked with reflected light. Its short upper arms were raised to claw and its wings were extended to display their delicate membrane. It stood to one side of the oriel window which looked out over Rolencia.

On the other side was a stuffed foenix. This bird had roamed the menagerie back in her grandfather's time. It was taller than Piro. A crest of brilliant red feathers added another head and a half to its height. It was not as fierce-looking as the wyvern, though its beak was hard as metal and its chest was covered in scales as hard as armour, plus it had dangerous spurs on its legs. Like the wyvern, its eyes were real stones, emeralds.

If they did not find a mate for Piro's foenix, he would end up like this one and then the only foenixes people would ever see would be stuffed ones.

Piro stopped outside the carved oak door of the trophy chamber, heart hammering. Two pillars rose up to an arch over the door. Their decoration was the royal foenix, gold on deep red, with onyx stone touches. Piro ran her fingers over the embossed surface, then, taking a deep breath, she felt for the door handle. Somehow, she must not antagonise her father.

Piro could have loved King Rolen, if he'd only let her. Throughout her childhood he had been a distant figure, striding in to take her older brothers hunting, while she had been lucky to get a pat on the head in passing. Now he was going to marry her off.

Anger rolled through her. How could she marry a strange barbarian warlord? Her mother's last words rang in her head. Still smarting from those comments – she was not a thoughtless child – Piro decided she would keep an open mind and give this warlord a chance, but if he proved impossible, she would have to refuse her father.

And that was a frightening thought.

She licked dry lips and went to turn the handle, but it turned under her hand as a servant opened the door, backing out. Sweetbreads and a bottle of Rolencia's famous red wine had been delivered on a trolley which stood in front of the oriel window. Her father and another man were standing in the window's curve. The light from the leaded panes was behind them, so she could not see their faces. The warlord was not as tall as her father, but then few men were. Only Lence and Byren were bigger.

Feeling at a disadvantage, she glided across the room, assuming the graceful walk her mother had taught her.

'You sent for me, royal Father?' Piro said, dropping her gaze and bowing from the waist, since this was a formal occasion.

When she looked up King Rolen beckoned her. 'Piro Rolen Kingsdaughter. I swear you are as beautiful as your mother was the day I married her.'

'I will not be old enough to marry until I turn fifteen,' Piro pointed out. 'And that is not until the midsummer after next.'

Her father ignored this, leading her around the food trolley. 'Meet the ruler of Cockatrice Spar. Warlord Rejulas... my daughter, Piro.'

She gave him the minimum dip of her head. After all, she was a kingsdaughter and Rejulas was a mere warlord.

Cockatrice Spar was not the largest of the ridges that fanned out from the Dividing Mountains, but it was the one nearest Merofynia. Border wars were always going on over the Disputed Isles, a cluster of islands off the coast from the spar. As a student of history, Piro understood her father was marrying her to this warlord to ensure the safety of Rolencia's borders. She would be expected to spy on her husband and report back to her father and brothers. It was necessary, but she still resented it.

Piro looked up and caught the warlord staring at her. He smiled as if he knew what she was thinking.

A jolt ran through her. This Lord Rejulas was an unusual man with a 'witchy' look around his narrow eyes and high cheek bones. There had to be a bit of Utland raider in him, back a generation or two. She guessed he was several years older than the twins, but not near thirty, for there was no silver in the hair at his temples. Rather than the much-admired black eyes, his were brown, and met hers thoughtfully.

So this was the warlord she was supposed to marry? She would be hard put to find a more striking man. But he dressed like the barbarian he was. He even wore a vest of wyvern scales. How many men had died so that he could show off that sun-on-sea rippling blue vest? His shirt leather was so soft the women of his tribe must have chewed their teeth down to stubs on it. He was in for a surprise if he thought she would chew his leather!

A gold clasp in the shape of a cockatrice, the tall bird with the serpent's tail, held his cloak at the shoulder. The cockatrice cloak was one of the rare pure black ones, the feathers so fine they were nearly fur. Most of his long black hair was plaited behind his head. The front half was drawn over to one side and hung in a long pony tail by his right ear. It was held at intervals by gold bands, one for every man he had killed in battle. His battletale, as it was called, was almost solid gold. If she was really lucky, he would get himself killed in a border skirmish. Small chance of that!

And, judging from the appraising look he gave her, he was intelligent. Good. She hated stupidity.

She met his gaze. He grinned, confidently. She disliked him on instinct but, before she could speak, her father indicated the board game which sat on a low table in the bay window.

'Why don't we play Duelling Kingdoms? You have probably played a version of this game, warlord Rejulas. The way we play it here at court is more complex. The rewards are greater but then so are the risks. Will you play?'

Was her father being subtly cryptic? Piro wondered, and glanced to Rejulas to see if he thought so.

'How can I refuse?' he replied, with a smile that said he would rise to the challenge.

'Would you like to be the Elector of Ostron, Piro?' her father asked. The ruler of Ostron Isle was in charge of the wild cards, Unknowables. The elector could not win, but neither could he lose, since the real battle was between the two kings. 'I'll take King Rolence the First's piece. And you can play King Merofyn the First, Rejulas.'

Piro's father smiled grimly as he sat down at the triangular table. She took her seat and studied the familiar board. Rolencia and Merofynia were two crescents, one opened to the north, the other to the south. They were linked at their closest ends by the Snow Bridge. In real life this was a series of high ridges where the air was so thin only the locals could live comfortably. The people of the Snow Bridge formed fiercely independent city states, which monitored the three passes between Rolencia and Merofynia, taking their cut of all land trade.

From the mountains that bordered the outer crescents, long spikes stretched into the sea. In real life these ridges were broken, with small islands scattered about them.

Piro picked up the piece she was to play. The carving of the Elector of Ostron was as tall as her shortest finger and engraved with lifelike detail. Tiny jewels were set in his turbaned crown. Judging from Lord Cobalt, this style of clothing was well out of date. The wild cards were stacked on Ostron Isle which lay to the east of Merofynia.

'Turn over the first Unknowable, Piro,' her father said.

When the game began, each king was evenly matched with the same number of trained warriors, plus five warlords and their warriors. The object of the game was to invade the other kingdom.

There were three ways to attack. One was over the Snow Bridge which linked the two kingdoms. Snow closed the passes from autumn to spring. The thin air and exertion could wipe out half the army, or the inhabitants of the Snow Bridge could open the gates of their city states and turn on the men, to loot the army.

The next way to invade was to sail around the warlords' spars and navigate the outlying islands where the ships were prey to storms, Utland Raiders and wyverns. All these obstacles had to be overcome to reach the two kingdoms' vulnerable crescent valleys.

The last and least used way, because it entailed bribing a warlord to betray his king, was to march across the spar nearest to the invading king's harbour. In Merofynia's case, Cockatrice Spar.

That made Piro wonder. If her brother was betrothed to the Merofynian kingsdaughter they did not need to ensure this warlord's loyalty, did they?

It struck Piro that the game assumed the two kings would always seek to conquer one another. What if they were both content to rule their own lands? He father certainly was.

'Ready, Piro?' her father prodded.

She stacked the cards neatly. As the Elector of Ostron Isle, she held the Unknowables, factors beyond the kings' control, storms that sunk ships, Utland Raiders that destroyed fleets, treacherous warlords who betrayed their king, or the elector himself might support one king against the other.

Piro picked up the top card and read aloud. 'The city states of the Snow Bridge refuse to open the passes to the king's army.'

It was a setback for the warlord. Her father smiled and his eyes gleamed. 'Your move, Rejulas.'

The warlord rubbed his chin thoughtfully.

'Piro, we will have our wine,' her father said.

She pulled the trolley closer and poured two elegant silver goblets of the gleaming, rich wine. Its celebrated colour appeared on the royal emblem. She loved the fruity smell, associating it with winter nights, festivals and story telling.

King Rolen accepted his wine and Rejulas did likewise.

'To Rolencia, may her borders always be free from threat,' her father gave the traditional toast.

'To Rolencia and Cockatrice Spar, brothers-at-arms,' Rejulas replied. At the same time he moved half of King Merofyn's army into the waiting fleet and embarked on the sea journey to Rolencia's vulnerable inner crescent.

King Rolen would have to counter. He savoured a mouthful of wine and studied the board.

'You don't drink, Piro Kingsdaughter?' Rejulas's smile was quizzical. He had an easy charm, as if he was used to getting his own way.

'I don't know yet if I have reason to celebrate,' she replied, watching for his reaction.

His eyes widened. Good.

'Piro, the sweetbreads,' her father suggested swiftly. He sent five ships to meet the Merofynian fleet. 'Your move, Rejulas. You will find I am most experienced at keeping what is mine!'

Piro cut a small loaf into thin slices. Its surface was crusted with honey-glazed almond slivers.

She could feel Rejulas watching her. She desperately wanted to know what manner of man he was. She felt an itch crawling across her skin, heralding the build-up of Affinity in her body. With every sense strained to interpret his actions, she held out the plate of sweetbread.

He took it from her. Dropping a dollop of cream on a slice, he offered it to her. It was neatly done, not something you would expect from a barbarian, and the smile that accompanied it was rueful, as if he was apologising for having misjudged her.

Piro accepted the bread with a cautious smile of her own. She took a bite, anticipating the sweetness of almonds and honey as the sweet bread melted on her tongue. Instead her mouth was filled with a vile taste. Burning fumes rushed up the back of her nose, threatening to choke her. She could not possibly swallow.

Piro grabbed a napkin as she sprang up from the table, sending the game of Duelling Kingdoms to the floor. Turning away she spat the food into the napkin but still the fumes lingered. A fit of coughing shook her. Tears streamed down her cheeks.

She could not get the taste from her tongue. Fearing she might throw up, she stumbled a few steps further. Both men stood. Rejulas reached out to steady her.

She sprang away from him, clutching her father's arm, and held on as she fought to catch her breath.

'Something go down the wrong way? Here, sup this.' King Rolen held his wine for her and she gulped to drown the taste. The wine was everything it should have been, smooth and redolent of plums.

'Th-thank you,' Piro managed. Feeling a little better, she wiped her eyes and glanced into the mirror over the fire place. She must look a fright. Her cheeks were hot and glistening with tears. Her cap was crooked. Her head and ears buzzed with excess Affinity. Even her vision wavered as the Unseen world tried to usurp the seen world.

'Your pardon, Father, Warlord Rejulas,' she said smoothly, if a trifle huskily. The queen would have approved of her control, Piro thought as she stepped closer to the mirror to straighten her head-dress.

'Next time don't rush your food,' King Rolen told her. 'Girls, eh, Rejulas? We will have to start the game again. Pick up the pieces, Piro.'

As she replaced the last pin and looked into the mirror to smooth her hair, the wyvern came to life. It went to tear off her father's head.

Spinning around, she drew breath to scream a warning. But her father was safely in his chair by the table and warlord Rejulas was about to resume his seat.

The implications made her head spin.

'Pick up the pieces, kingsdaughter,' her father ordered, growing impatient.

When Piro turned back to the mirror it reflected nothing more alarming than a table, two men and the stuffed wyvern.

What was going on? In her mind's eye she kept seeing her father struck down by the wyvern.

'Piro?' The king frowned at her.

She stared at him, horrified. He was going to die and he would never believe her if she tried to warn him!

She backed out of the room.

'Piro, come back here!' King Rolen roared.

She ran out the door.

In the corridor she hesitated, unsure where to go with so many people in the castle.

The door swung open behind her. Rejulas stepped out, obviously sent by her father to bring her back. When his hand closed over her arm she felt a wave of nausea.

'Let go!' As she twisted free, her fingers brushed the wyvern-skin vest. 'Barbarian!'

His breath drew in on a sharp hiss and caught her hand, twisting her wrist cruelly. 'The only difference between you and me, is that three hundred years ago your family clawed their way over the Divide and conquered the valley people, kingsdaughter!'

Piro fled.

BYREN THREW THE door open to their shared chamber to find Lence waiting for him. Seated on his mahogany desk, his brother swung one booted foot.

'So you went to find our little brother,' Lence said.

He had been searching for Piro but their old nurse had found her first. No need to tell Lence that.

'Just as well I did. Some monks were about to beat him. I asked him back here for a drink. He should be along soon.' Byren went to the desk and poured himself a honeyed mead. It was still steaming, the servant must have just left.

As he went to take a mouthful Lence caught his arm. 'You shouldn't have told Fyn so much after the assassination attempt. He hasn't been invited to take a chair at the war table, Byren.'

'He's our brother.'

The door swung open and Fyn walked in. Lence dropped Byren's arm.

'Ah, Fyn. Share a drink with us,' Byren greeted him, pouring another tankard. He lifted his own. 'To Lence's betrothed, may her teeth be straight and her smile pretty!'

Lence smiled grimly. 'Doesn't matter what she looks like. As long as she does her duty, I'll do mine. I'll let her know who's in charge right away.' He tilted back his head and gulped some mead.

Byren felt a stab of pity for Isolt.

Fyn sipped his mead, looking from Byren to Lence. He opened his mouth to speak, but thought better of it. Lence took out his dagger and began to clean his nails with the tip.

Byren put his tankard down. For the first time in his life he felt uncomfortable with Lence. Things left unsaid hung between them, threatening to erupt, but not with Fyn present. Byren didn't know which was worse, waiting for Lence to confront him, or waiting for Fyn to leave so Lence could.

Byren stretched and went over to the weapons display to select a knife, weighing it, feeling the balance. 'Lost my ceremonial dagger in the attack.

Sylion take them. Reckon they'll be picking the jewels out of it right now, counting themselves lucky. This knife feels well balanced. What do you think, Lence?'

His brother shrugged, casting Fyn a swift glance. 'The proof of the knife or the man is in their actions. Throw it and see.'

Byren stiffened, hearing a criticism of Orrade. Was his defence of Orrade the reason why Lence was withdrawing from him? Fyn also stiffened, responding to the undertones in Lence's voice, so Byren wasn't imagining it. He strode over to the target, stepping onto a line, scraped in the floor boards by years of eager youths.

'If you think one of the warlords sent the assassins, which one was it?' Fyn asked.

Byren threw his knife. It hit the target just above centre.

'Not bad.' Lence continued to swing one boot, while cleaning his nails with his dagger.

'Let's see you do better.' Byren walked over to retrieve his knife. The soft wood-panelled wall to one side of the fireplace showed many small pit marks where daggers had missed, reminding Byren of their boyhood. He longed for those happy days before betrothals and honour guards. 'Give us a look at your betrothed, Lence. Does she have buck teeth?'

'She's pretty enough, if the artist can be trusted.' Lence pulled the locket over his head and tossed it to Byren, the chain trailing behind like a bird's long tail.

Byren caught it. 'Mother and Father made a political match and they're happy.'

'True. But that's rare.' Lence drained his honeyed mead, wiping his mouth. He stood, turning the knife in his hand to throw. The way he moved held menace. 'My go.'

Placing the tip of his boot on the starting line, he tossed his knife expertly. It quivered in the target, just to the right of Byren's mark.

Lence retrieved his knife.

Byren flicked the locket open. The artist had painted Isolt Merofyn Kingsdaughter from a three-quarters view. She looked stiff and a little frightened. Black hair, milky skin, luminous black eyes. No eyebrows, hair pulled back under a sapphire-encrusted coronet, high lace at her throat. Byren didn't think much of the Merofynian fashions. Too mannered.

'Why would the warlords want to destabilise the balance of power?' Fyn asked. 'Surely they don't want Rolencia to be at war with Merofynia?'

Lence said nothing, sending Byren a loaded look.

Fyn shifted, trying to contain his frustration, as neither of them answered. Much as Byren wanted to trust Fyn, Lence was right, they did not have their parents' permission to discuss war table matters with him.

'Come here, Fyn, and take a look at Lence's betrothed.' Byren said.

Fyn joined him, glanced at the miniature and gasped.

'What?' Byren prodded.

'She's... she's got no eyebrows!' Fyn stammered.

Lence caught Byren's eye with a cryptic look. Fyn had sounded like he'd been about to say something else.

'So what?' Lence snapped. 'Ambassador Benvenute assures me that's the fashion in the Merofynian court.'

Byren frowned at the face in the locket. 'She might be pretty but she doesn't look happy.'

Lence shrugged. 'Who would be happy with King Merofyn for a father? I hear he's gone through four food tasters since his unistag horn was stolen. Maybe I'll win his gratitude by sending him another one, a pure white one, perfect for detecting poison. I know! The warlord of Unistag Spar hasn't renewed his vow of loyalty. He can prove it by trapping a unistag and sending me the horn!'

'If he's failed to renew his vow, it's father's forgiveness he must win,' Fyn pointed out. Lence grimaced.

'Yes, Rolencia must do something about that warlord,' Byren said quickly, to divert Lence's anger from Fyn.

Their younger brother turned the miniature over, studying the Merofynian kingsdaughter. 'That's not a good likeness of Isolt.'

Lence snorted. 'And how would you know?'

Fyn looked startled, then guilty. 'I... I looked into Halcyon's Fate by mistake and she was in my vision. She was at a feast but her eyes were sad.'

'You'll be a monk soon and girls will be the last thing on your mind.' Lence grinned. 'Or do the monks get around their vow of chastity?'

Fyn's face went bright red.

'Hey, Byren, let's get a girl for Fyn before he gives up the world. With his pretty face it shouldn't be too hard to find one who'll lift her skirts.' There was a hard edge to Lence's laughter that Byren didn't like or understand. Was Lence angry because he'd been forced to give up Elina? Byren wondered how he would feel if he had to watch Elina take another man for her lover, or, worse, her husband. With a jolt he realised that he hadn't given up hope. Not yet. Somehow he would win her trust, win her back.

Fyn went to turn away.

Lence caught his arm. 'So you think yourself too good for the rest of us, master monk?'

'Leave him alone, Lence. Fyn never asked to be a monk!' Byren snapped. 'More importantly, if Fyn saw a vision in Halcyon's Fate, then he should be the one the mystics master accepts, not his friend. Why don't you go to the mystics master, Fyn?'

Lence let Fyn go. 'Well?'

Fyn did not meet their eyes. 'It was an accident. Feldspar dropped the Fate. I picked it up and the vision came. Much as I'd like to be the one, Feldspar deserves his place with the mystics.'

Byren frowned. Fyn was lying about something.

Lence snorted. 'I don't know about you, but I'd rather be a warrior than a mystic!'

Fyn stared at Lence, the gulf between them obvious to Byren. Lence's top lip curled. Quickly, Byren retrieved the miniature from Fyn saying, 'here's your locket, Lence.'

It made him realise he had been doing this sort of thing for a while now, diverting Lence, smoothing things over. He couldn't remember when it had started, only that it had become second nature to him. He turned to Fyn. 'Your throw, pick a knife.'

Fyn stepped over to the weapon display and selected a knife.

'Yes, take your throw,' Lence urged. 'Let's see what you're made of.'

Byren's stomach knotted.

Fyn lifted his knife, but before he could take aim the door to the hall flew open and their father stalked in.

'I swear I'll throttle that girl when I catch her. Do you know what your sister's done now? Thrown away a year's negotiation with the warlord of Cockatrice Spar!' His gaze settled on Fyn. 'Do you know where she is?'

'I don't know, Father. I've been here, with Lence and Byren.'

'That's right,' Byren said.

'Well, don't just stand there. Go find her!' King Rolen roared. 'I'll be waiting at the war table. Curse her for a wyvern's whelp!'

'You two go,' Lence said. 'I must tell father about the assassination attempt.'

'What?' King Rolen muttered, then glanced swiftly to Fyn.

'Fyn came upon us in the middle of it. Because of him the swordsmen fled,' Byren explained. 'Three of them armed, and us with nothing but our ceremonial daggers, in Rolenton itself!'

'Bold and confident,' King Rolen muttered. He focused on Lence. 'Are you all right, lad?'

'Of course.' Lence laughed but it was not a happy sound.

Byren glanced to his father, who appeared not to notice the undertone of anger. Was he the only one who heard it?

'If Byren had been two minutes later he would have been kingsheir now,' Lence said.

King Rolen's worried eyes turned to Byren, who shrugged this aside. 'I was lucky to be in the right spot at the right time. Come on, Fyn. Don't forget to tell father about the cockatrice cloak, Lence.'

As he led Fyn outside Byren remembered that their father had been the younger son and he had only inherited the throne after his older brother died on the battle field. Byren shuddered. Hopefully Lence would live to a ripe old age and have many sons.

'Be glad you've been gifted to the abbey,' he told Fyn as they stopped outside the chamber door. 'Right, we'd better split up to find Piro.'

PIRO HAD RUN straight to her foenix only to have her old nurse catch her kneeling there. The only other surviving menagerie beast, the unistag, gave voice as if to warn her. Turning from the waist, Piro watched Seela approach with a sinking sensation.

'There you are!' Seela cried, wringing her hands. 'Your father is stalking around the castle bellowing for you. What have you done, child?'

'It was awful, Seela. I saw Father's death!'

Seela's face registered surprise, then went slack with shock and Piro realised she'd given herself away.

She sprang to her feet, clutching her old nurse's hands. 'You mustn't tell anyone. Please, don't —'

'Of course not. What do you take me for?' Seela demanded.

Stopped midstream, Piro gaped, then simply accepted her old nurse's assurance, focusing on the most important thing. 'I must warn Father. I can't let him be killed!'

'Warn him and he'll want to know how you know.'

Again, Piro stopped to think. 'I'll say it was a dream.'

'Unless you say it was a foretelling dream sent by the gods through your Affinity, he'll dismiss it.'

She was right. Piro's shoulders sagged and she searched her old nurse's face. 'What can I do, Seela?'

'It's time you knew, Pirola.'

'Knew what?'

Seela's sad dark eyes settled on her. 'Your mother's Affinity came on her at around the same age –'

'Mother? But –'

Seela nodded sadly. 'It was about a year before her wedding. We hid her growing Affinity, Myrella and I. We were doing fine until her father came for the wedding.'

'King Merofyn the Fifth?'

'Yes. After the marriage Myrella had a vision. She saw her father dying on the deck of his ship, killed by Utland pirates. She begged him not to sail back to Merofynia, to take the overland route, but she couldn't tell him why.

'If she had, the marriage would have been annulled and war would have resulted. So Myrella let her father set sail to his death. He never reached Merofynia and your mother has kept her Affinity hidden all this time.'

'You're saying I shouldn't warn Father, that I should let him walk into a trap?' Piro shook her head, backing up a step.

'What if it is a false vision? You have no way of knowing, not without consulting the abbey mystics. What if you have misinterpreted it?' Seela pressed.

Piro licked dry lips. Before today, her Affinity had helped her find lost possessions and guess which Unknowable card would turn up. It had never frightened her. Now it made her cold with fear.

She could still taste the evil fumes on the back of her throat and, when she closed her eyes, she could still see the wyvern about to tear her father's head from his shoulders. Her stomach clenched. She squeezed her eyes shut. Tears slid down her cheeks. Brushing them away angrily, she refused to believe that her Affinity made her a channel for evil. This must be a message from the gods.

The vile taste had to mean that Rejulas might appear sweet but he was not to be trusted. And the wyvern's attack meant that Merofynia threatened... but it couldn't, not when Lence had just been betrothed to Isolt.

Piro began to pace, aware of Seela watching her. Perhaps she was mistaken, and these messages were the cruel jests of evil powers. Was the goddess angry with her for profaning the Proving today?

Her head spun and she sank to sit on the lower fence rail of the unistag's pen. He came to her, leaning over the top rail to nuzzle her head, his velvety stag's muzzle soft on the back of her neck. She rubbed his throat, taking comfort in his warm coat. He was looking for Affinity, which she usually let him lick off her fingers but, after the vision, she was drained of power. A part of her wanted to run to the abbess right now and ask the mystics mistress if her visions could be trusted. If she did, the abbess would claim her for Sylion Abbey and she couldn't bear that.

'Your father is in a fury. You must find him and apologise,' Seela urged. 'Swallow your pride, kingsdaughter, and marry a barbarian warlord. Because...' She broke off suddenly.

Piro turned to her. 'Why must I marry the warlord, Seela? What do you know, that I don't?'

'I'm just an old woman whose nurslings have all grown up.' Seela looked stricken. 'And I can't keep them safe, now that they must play Duelling Kingdoms for real.'

Piro's skin went cold. 'Where's Father?'

'At the war table.'

The war table was housed in a room directly above the trophy chamber. The table was covered with a scale model of their kingdom, its seas and surrounding enemies.

'You must go back to your chamber and prepare an apology for your father,' Seela said. 'Stay out of sight.'

Piro nodded, intending to do no such thing. It was only as she was walking back to the family's wing that she remembered the old seer's words.

Like mother, like daughter. The seer had been right!

Piro rubbed her arms to settle the goose bumps. Just because the old seer had been right about one thing, that did not mean she was right about anything else. The mystics mistress had said the future held many possible paths... but Piro didn't know how to find the right path.

She would tell her mother about the dream and ask her advice. Silent on her indoor slippers, she ran up the servant steps to her mother's private chamber which was down the far end of the solarium. A tapestry hung over the door to the servants' stair to keep out draughts, but it did not stop the voices.

Piro slowed. That was her mother speaking, but who was the man with her? She crept to the tapestry and parted it a chink to see the new Lord Cobalt standing much too close to her mother, who had her back to him as she looked through the diamond panes of the narrow window.

'I was twenty-two and you were only a year older, Myrella. I adored you. I thought you were wasted on Rolen.'

'And I told you I had room in my heart for only one man.'

'That's not the way I remember it. You told me you loved me and –'

'That I would never betray my husband.' She sighed, turning to face him. Seeing how close he was, the queen brushed past him to pace over to the fireplace. Piro was struck by how small and fragile her mother looked next to Illien, who was almost as tall as her father.

The queen turned to face Cobalt. 'I did love you, Illien. I was lonely. To Rolen I was a means to an end, to you I was a person. But nothing ever happened so we have nothing to be ashamed of. And then your father sent you away.' She summoned a brave smile. 'I have thought of you many times over the years and hoped you were happy.'

He came closer, voice dropping. 'I thought of you, too. Myrella. I never forgot...'

She held a hand up between them in a gesture of refusal. 'What I said still stands, Illien. Rolen's known me since I was eight years old. It took twenty years of marriage and four children but he has learnt to trust me. He loves me and I love him for the good qualities he has.' Tears glittered in her eyes. She cleared her throat, adopting a more formal tone. 'I was so very sorry to hear about your father and bride. Had you been married long?'

'We were wed...' his voice cracked, 'the day before we set sail –'

'Oh, Illien!' She reached out to him.

He went to her, sinking to his knees so that he pressed his face to her chest as he wept. She stroked his dark hair, her voice soothing.

Piro let the tapestry fall back into place, stunned. Her mother had loved Illien? Still loved him? But he was the opposite of her father, cultured, elegant, clever... Piro winced.

Stunned, she retreated down the stairs, her stomach churning. Unbidden, Affinity swelled under her heart like a thousand anxious butterflies. She had thought herself safe from it after the vision. Affinity had to be used or it would surface when she least wanted it to.

There was only one thing to do.

Chapter Thirteen

FYN RAN STRAIGHT to the menagerie where the foenix lived. No sign of Piro. Though he rarely saw the bird it remembered him and gave a low interrogative chirrup of greeting. He stooped to scratch the foenix's scaled chest. As he stood up Byren arrived, his broad shoulders blocking the entrance.

'So you thought to look here too, Fyn? No luck?'

Fyn shook his head and rose. They strode out of the courtyard together and along the hall.

'Don't take Lence to heart,' Byren said. 'He's angry all the time now and it eats away at him.'

'I don't see what he's got to be angry about. He's kingsheir and father's favourite. Of all of us, he's most like father.'

Byren frowned for an instant, then dredged up a grin. 'Except Piro. She inherited his temper.' He shook his head. 'I don't know what's got into her this time.'

'Her heart's in the right place,' Fyn said, remembering how she'd risked the abbey's wrath to help him. 'But she doesn't think things through.'

They came to a point where two sets of stairs from different wings fed onto a hallway with many doors.

'I'll try the kitchen. Cook is probably hiding her again. If not, I'll ask Seela,' Byren said. 'You try the stable loft.'

Fyn nodded.

Illien came down the stairs from the family wing and crossed the hall to join them. 'Byren, what's going on?'

'You might as well know. It'll be all over the castle by dinner time. Piro's turned down the warlord father wanted her to marry. And now she's hiding,' Byren revealed.

Fyn put two and two together. He'd heard how the new Lord Cobalt had ridden in demanding justice on behalf of his father and bride.

'And this is little Fyn?' Cobalt asked with a smile. 'Not so little now. Last time I saw you, you were still in the nursery and Piro was a baby.'

'I'll always be little compared to Byren and Lence,' Fyn said. He felt he knew this man already. It had to be the family resemblance. He caught himself staring and remembered his manners. 'I'm sorry to hear about your loss.'

Grief's shadow darkened Cobalt's eyes, making the lines that bracketed his mouth severe. 'They will pay. Lence has sworn to help me avenge them.'

'We can't have Utland raiders attacking our people,' Byren said, though he seemed resigned rather than righteous. 'Meanwhile, we must find Piro.'

'I'll help. Where should I look?' Cobalt asked.

'We've already tried the menagerie,' Byren said. 'But she may circle back. She loves the Affinity beasties.'

They separated. With a nod to Cobalt and Byren, Fyn ran off.

The stables were deserted, the workers all madly preparing for the feast. Fyn climbed up to the loft, calling softly for Piro. She didn't answer but that didn't mean she wasn't there. He made a thorough search of the long loft with its sweet-smelling hay. No sign of his sister.

Before he could climb down, the stables filled with angry men saddling their horses.

Fyn listened at the top of the ladder. The men had the clipped accents of barbarians from beyond the Dividing Mountains and they occasionally threw in unknown words which made their speech hard to understand. When he heard their destination was Cockatrice Spar, he understood. Their warlord had been insulted and they were about to ride out of Rolenhold, even though it was nearly dusk on the shortest day of the year and their warlord had yet to renew his oath of allegiance at the feast tonight. No one in their right mind ventured abroad when the barriers between the Seen and the Unseen were at their weakest.

After the last horse was led out, Fyn climbed down the ladder to the floor below. The stable was warm and smelt of horses, earthy and familiar. He dusted hay off his leggings and saffron robe and headed out into the stable courtyard where two dozen of the warlord's honour guard adjusted their cinnamon-coloured cockatrice cloaks. They talked and laughed too loudly to show that they were not intimidated by King Rolen's men-at-arms, who stood on the ramparts, weapons in hand, watching them.

No one looked at Fyn. With all the visitors, servants, minstrels and men-at-arms crowded into Rolenhold, one more shaven-headed acolyte was unremarkable. A man in a wyvern-skin vest shoved past Fyn to speak with an old man nearby. Fyn just caught his words.

'...the ability to outfox every other warlord, that's all that makes King Rolen's blood royal. Well, we'll see who's the better fox!' he snarled. 'Keep your eyes open and report to me.'

The old man nodded. Fyn wasn't surprised to learn that Rejulas had a spy at Rolenhold. The warlord mounted up, and kicked his horse's flanks to get the beast moving. The mounts had more sense than their riders. It was late and cold, and getting colder, and the horses wanted to go back to the stables.

Warlord Rejulas led his honour guard through an archway into the main courtyard. The great gates had been winched open and, shrouded in a tense silence, he and his men rode out. They would be lucky if they got further than Rolenton tonight but, with the attempted assassination fresh in his mind, it was the gesture of defiance that worried Fyn. How would the other warlords react? No wonder his father was furious with Piro. Still, he couldn't help feeling sorry for her.

Fyn might have been angry enough to throttle his sister, but he didn't want anyone harming her. Everyone wanted something from him. Not Piro.

She was ready to risk the abbey's censure to help him. Now she was in trouble and he had to find her.

He headed for Eagle Tower, the last of Piro's favourite places. The long connecting corridors were dark, no torches had been lit yet. Shadows clung to the alcoves, hiding the brilliant colours of the carved friezes.

PIRO SLIPPED INTO the unistag's enclosure and held her hands out to him, calling him gently. When she was upset her Affinity built up until it crawled across her skin like ants, making her grind her teeth to prevent a cry. She focused the power on her hands and the unistag came willingly. He began to lick the Affinity from her fingers.

Within moments her tension eased. She stroked the unistag's velvet muzzle. What a handsome beast he was. With the body of a white horse and the head of a noble stag, his single horn gleamed like mother-of-pearl. Roan unistags had horns of red ivory, which were not as highly valued.

'Should you be in there with that Affinity beast?' a voice that was all too familiar asked softly.

Piro spun. The last person she wanted to confront right now was the new Lord Cobalt. She could still see him, face pressed to her mother's breast, being comforted.

The unistag shied away. Startled by her reaction, it trotted to the far end of the enclosure.

'Illien – I mean, Lord Cobalt. I'm quite safe, truly. I've known the unistag since I was little.' But only recently had she let him nuzzle her hands to relieve the build up of Affinity. Had the new Lord Cobalt noticed? Her back had been to him and besides, he had no Affinity, so she was safe.

She stepped out of the enclosure, letting Cobalt close the gate behind her while she went to the fountain which had been turned off for the winter and held her hands under the water spigot. It was warm, having been pumped up from one of Halcyon's hot pools deep under the castle.

'You must be Piro. You are so like your beautiful mother,' Cobalt said, coming up behind her.

Piro turned, deliberately flicking her hands dry. Beads of water scattered him, landing on the embroidered velvet of his fancy coat. He took a step back, attempting to brush the water off.

'Uh, sorry,' Piro lied.

Cobalt shot her a quick look. 'I hear your father is furious with you.'

She shrugged, pretending a nonchalance she did not feel. 'Someone is always furious with me.'

'They are trying to force you to marry a man you do not love. A pretty girl like you... the boys must be lining up to dance on feast days. I suppose you already have your heart set on –'

Piro laughed at the absurdity of it. 'I'm only thirteen!'

He recovered quickly. 'Most girls are planning their wedding at thirteen.'

'I'm not most girls.' She glared at him and he hesitated. She wished he would just go away. She didn't want to think that there was ever a time when the queen was lonely, when her father did not value her mother enough to make her feel loved.

Cobalt frowned, then smiled charmingly. 'I see you are an original thinker, as they say in Ostron Isle.'

She liked that description, but for some reason she didn't want to accept any compliments from him. All she wanted was to cut the conversation short and escape. 'I have to go now. I'm very sorry about the raiders.'

'The raiders... ah.' He came over and sat on the edge of the fountain, sinking his head into his hands. 'I still can't believe it's true. To have my father snatched from me when we had only just reconciled after thirteen years. To lose my bride...'

He could not go on. His shoulders shook.

Piro's stomach knotted and tears stung her eyes. She rubbed his back between his broad shoulders. His long curled hair felt like silk under her hand and black onyxes winked at her, entwined amidst his curls. Why would a man bother to make himself look so fine, unless he planned seduction?

How could she think such a thing as he sobbed over his murdered bride?

'...it was all my fault. My stupid pride,' he whispered, despair making his voice thick. 'If I hadn't carried a chest of jewels to impress my father the raiders wouldn't have been tempted.'

Prompted by the urge to relieve his pain, Piro's Affinity rose up through the core of her body, warming her, rolling down her arms into her fingers. Only last week she had eased the pain of one of the cooks who had burnt her hand by drawing off the sensation. No one had noticed then, so now she tried it with Cobalt, opening her senses, willing to share his pain to help ease it.

Nothing.

Blank.

She pulled back a step.

His head remained bowed. 'I'm sorry, child. A man may weep inside, but he must be strong for his men. Forgive my lapse. I... I was overcome.' Cobalt lifted his head. His eyes were red-rimmed, tortured, but she had sensed no emotion in him.

She took another step back. 'That's all right. Byren weeps every time he hears the Tale of the Bone Flute.'

Even while Piro spoke, she was trying to fathom this new Lord Cobalt. Either he truly felt nothing and it was all a sham, or he was so well walled she could not reach him, yet he had claimed to be in the throes of deep emotion and asked her forbearance.

'Why do you look at me like that, little Piro?'

She blinked. Oh, his black eyes were so sharp... they made her skin prickle with fear.

'I can't get over how like Lence you are,' she said to divert him, 'well, a mixture of father and Lence.'

He smiled. 'Blood will leave its mark. I am your kin, after all.'

'I have to go now, Mother's expecting me,' Piro lied, then she turned and walked away, when all her instincts told her to run.

BYREN HAD NO luck in the kitchen, so he headed back to the war table chamber to see if Fyn had found Piro. One of the younger men of his father's honour guard was on duty at the base of the stairs outside the trophy chamber. This was unusual. His father must be feeling the need for a show of strength. He stopped to exchange a word just as two servants approached, pushing a trolley laden with firewood. The noise was so bad he just nodded to the guard and went up the stairs, accompanied by the rattling of the wheels that echoed up the stairwell. Even so, he could hear raised voices from the war table room on the floor above. His father and Lence yelling at each other? Impossible.

Byren thrust the door open, surprising the king and his twin in the midst of a heated argument. Both turned to him.

He was so startled he simply stood there.

His father gestured impatiently. 'Shut the door.'

'Byren, you tell Father I'm right. The Merofynians despise their king and fear his bullying overlord,' Lence said. Byren recognised Cobalt's refrain. 'The country is ripe for an uprising. We should –'

'We've signed a peace accord, you're betrothed to King Merofyn's daughter,' Rolen interrupted. 'What kind of king would I be to dishonour my word?'

Lence made the same impatient gesture their father had used a moment before. 'But –'

'Peace means trade and prosperity, Lence,' their father insisted. 'War means death and –'

'To the victor go the spoils!'

'True,' King Rolen conceded. 'But there's no guarantee we'll be the victor. You've only ever led raids, in and out quickly, warrior against warrior. Sometimes it is enough to take their spar symbol for the warlord's men to retreat. But war...' He shook his head. 'War is brutal. At best, fields are ruined and people starve, and at worst, women and children are murdered. War turns ordinary men into monsters. Believe me, I've seen it!'

Lence snorted. 'You've grown old, father. Old and tired.'

'Lence!' Byren protested, shocked.

King Rolen blanched. His mouth settled in a grim line. 'When you've seen your brother and father writhing on the ground as they die in agony, when you've had to order the execution of a man who was your childhood friend, then you can tell me I'm a coward!'

'I never said you were a coward, Father,' Lence said, 'just old and tired. It's about time you stepped aside and let a young man –'

'Step aside?' King Rolen bellowed. 'You... you insolent wyvern! Get out of my sight!'

'But –'

'Lence,' Byren interrupted, stepping between them. Veins stood out on his father's forehead, the skin had become enflamed and his neck muscles corded. What if he had a brain spasm like the Old Dove? Byren grabbed his brother's arm. 'Come, help me find Piro.'

His twin snatched his arm free.

'This is not over,' Lence told their father, and stalked out.

Byren hesitated as the king went to follow, to have the last word, but his bad knee turned under him and Byren caught him as he fell, helping him to a chair. His father cursed fluently.

'Lence doesn't mean it,' Byren muttered.

'Yes, he does. He's young and impatient. I know what I was like at his age. I hated diplomacy. But, Byren, I'm done with war. We've had thirty years of good harvests, uninterrupted trade with both Merofynia and Ostron Isle. Nowadays the meanest crofter lives as well as a prosperous merchant did when I was a lad. I want peace and prosperity for my people. I'm not a –'

'I know, Father.' Byren straightened up. 'Should I send for one of the healers?'

'What? No. They've done their best.' Rolen rubbed his bad knee. 'I'll give Cobalt's manservant a chance to prove his boasts. Hopefully...'

Byren heard the unspoken words. Hopefully he could fix it, for King Rolen couldn't afford to look weak.

'I'd better go, catch up with Lence.'

FYN MET HIS brothers as he turned into the corridor that led to the war table stairwell. One of his father's honour guard stood silently at the landing at the base of the stairs, about a body length from them.

'I couldn't find Piro,' Fyn reported.

The twins barely nodded, radiating tension.

'Rejulas just marched out of Rolenhold with his warriors. Where's father?' Fyn asked. 'Does Mother know what's going on? Have you found Piro?'

'Piro's still hiding,' Lence said. 'Do you know where she is?'

Fyn shook his head. 'No. I told you I didn't.'

'If you won't help us, you might as well go back to your monks,' Lence snapped.

Fyn felt heat steal up his cheeks. The honour guard on duty studiously looked the other way. Fyn was about to protest when Lence shoved past him and walked off.

Fyn glanced at Byren, who shook his head in silent apology. Lence rounded the corner, the thump of his boots fading.

'He's not angry with you,' Byren whispered.

'With Piro. I understand. Can't Father say they've reconsidered Piro's betrothal?' Fyn lowered his voice even further. 'Cockatrice isn't the only spar.'

'No, but it is one of the most powerful. Father can't afford to let Rejulas ride off without renewing his allegiance. The warlord of Manticore Spar is only waiting for a sign of weakness to flout royal authority.'

Fyn nodded. This wasn't news to him.

Byren fixed on him. 'Can you find Piro and keep her out of sight until father calms down?'

'Of course,' Fyn said. 'What will you do?'

'I'll find Mother. She needs to know what's going on.'

Fyn nodded. He watched Byren jog after Lence then glanced up the corridor towards the stairs and the war table chamber. That was another sore point. Both he and Piro were considered too young to attend the war table. He'd been hoping that this time it would be different.

Fyn backtracked, crossed the courtyard and ran to the top of Eagle Tower. No sign of Piro. If he couldn't find her, then no one could. It looked like she had wisely decided to keep out of sight for a while.

Right now he wanted to know what was being discussed at the war table. He had a right to know. His mind made up, he left the tower.

* * *

PIRO HURRIED ALONG the castle corridors. She wanted to know why the alliance with warlord Rejulas was so important. As his wife, she would have inside knowledge of his plans. Why was this important to her father and brothers, when there was no threat from Merofynia? Picking up her skirts, she darted down the corridor to the base of the steps which led up to the room that housed the war table.

One of the honour guard stood there. Usually the stair was unguarded. It made her uneasy.

'Father sent for me,' she lied with a straight face. 'I think I'm in trouble.' That was true enough.

'Chin up.' He winked.

She felt a stab of guilt. All her life she had been teasing the honour guard with her tricks.

The soft soles of her good indoor slippers made almost no sound as she hurried up the steps to the next landing. Pausing to catch her breath, she crept to the door and strained to overhear her parents through the thick oak. Her heart beat uncomfortably fast.

Her mother spoke soothingly. But she could tell from her father's tone that he was furious. How was she going to explain her actions and warn him, without revealing her Affinity?

Hands grabbed her arm and covered her mouth, pulling her away from the door. She squirmed desperately as she was dragged away across the landing.

'Have you forgotten everything I taught you?' Fyn whispered.

In a flash she remembered and drove her elbow into his midriff. He grunted with pain, but did not release her, although his hand did slip from her mouth. 'Let me go. I want to know what's going on.'

'So do I, but if you make any more noise they'll hear you, as I did.'

She stopped struggling.

'Father is in a fury, Piro. Warlord Rejulas rode out of Rolenhold with his honour guard. The alliance is ruined. The other warlords are muttering amongst themselves, threatening to defy Rolencia. Father needs time to calm down,' Fyn warned softly. 'Come with me.'

He let her go and she spun to face him. 'Where to?'

Fyn signalled for silence, smiled and led her to another door. He held his finger to his lips again and she nodded impatiently. Then he opened the door to the twins' lesson room. She had never been inside, having resentfully stood at the door and wondered about the knowledge she, as a female, would never know.

Looking back now, she realised she probably had a broader and more useful education than the twins. Like them she had studied law and accounting, but her mother and Seela had also tutored her using books from Merofynia. Many were the times she had dressed up to play out roles from the history of both kingdoms.

The lesson chamber was not at all mysterious. It was cold and dim. The desks and chairs, abandoned five years ago when her brothers become men and outgrew their tutors, were covered in a thick layer of dust.

'I found this one day when Lence and Byren shut me in the cupboard,' Fyn whispered as he opened a door and stepped inside, beckoning her. Its shelves were full of inks, papers, old vellum scrolls and books. Fyn pulled some books off the shelf and pressed his ear to the wooden back of the cupboard. She did the same.

Now she could hear their voices quite clearly. She met Fyn's eyes, delighted.

'Enough of that,' her mother said. 'We must concentrate on mending this breach. We'll send someone after Rejulas to apologise and invite him to the spring cusp celebrations. Piro's been wild in the past but this is the last straw. It's time she grew up. She –'

'She spat out the food he gave her, acted like it was spoiled!' King Rolen said.

'Perhaps it was,' Byren suggested.

'It was not. I tasted it.' King Rolen roared. 'Then, when I asked her to pick up the Kingdoms pieces, she fled like an ulfr pack was after her. I sent Rejulas to bring her back, thinking he'd win her over, but she said something to him that made him march off.'

'It doesn't matter what little Piro said or did, Myrella's right,' Captain Temor said. 'One of the warlords sent hired killers after the kingsheir today. We can't hold the Jubilee celebrations without Unistag Spar renewing their loyalty, their absence would make Rolencia look weak. And we can't afford to lose Rejulas's support.'

A chair scraped on the boards as someone stood up. 'I'll go after him.' It was Lence.

Silence stretched and Piro could imagine them all exchanging glances.

'That could just work,' the queen said softly. 'Any warlord would be flattered to have the kingsheir apologise in person.'

'Take some of your father's honour guard,' Captain Temor said.

'No. I'll take my own,' Lence replied.

'You have them sworn already?' King Rolen asked stiffly.

'Seven, with more wanting to join. How many do you have, brother?'

'Not sure,' Byren muttered. 'But it's a good idea to invite Rejulas back for the Jubilee celebrations. He can spend some time with Piro. Let him be the one to break the betrothal when he discovers what a bad-tempered little wyvern she is!'

Piro could hear the smile in his voice.

'She bared her teeth at him already today,' King Rolen complained. 'I don't know what possessed the girl!'

'Don't be too hard on her, father,' Byren said. 'If she understood how serious things are, she wouldn't have offended Rejulas. Once Rolencia's warlords hear how Palatyne united all the Merofynian spars under him, they'll be dreaming of doing the same. I think it is time she and Fyn took their seats at the war table.'

At last! Piro held her breath.

Her mother sighed. 'Piro's too wilful. She never thinks before she acts. Maybe in a few years.'

'If I'm old enough to be betrothed,' Piro muttered under her breath, 'I'm old enough –'

'Hush,' Fyn hissed. 'Father's speaking.'

'...trust Fyn, but only so far. He's been at the abbey since he was six. His loyalty is divided.'

'I trust Fyn,' Queen Myrella protested. 'He's loyal to us.'

'Give me one good reason why I should trust him,' Lence snapped.

There was a strained silence. Piro closed her eyes, knowing how her mother must be torn, unable to reveal the Affinity which enabled her to glimpse into some people's hearts.

'Very well.' King Rolen sounded tired. 'If he can't be trusted, he can't have a seat at the war table.'

Fyn slipped out of the cupboard, his face ashen. Torn between hearing more and consoling him, Piro followed.

Fyn came to a stop on the far side of the room in the window embrasure. Frost rimmed each diamond pane of glass. He looked sick.

'Father and Lence didn't mean it, Fyn,' she whispered, her breath misting in the chilly air.

'Of course they did.' His voice shook with anger. 'Father was the one who gifted me to the abbey. What did he expect? At least they'll let you take your seat in a few years.'

'Not if I tell them about my Affinity.' Tears stung her eyes. 'Oh, Fyn. I looked into the Mirror of Insight and I saw the wyvern about to tear father's head off. I came to warn him about Rejulas.'

'Forget Rejulas. He's a just an upstart warlord, greedy for power. Merofynia is the real threat. I'm no mystic, Piro, but even I can interpret what you saw. The wyvern is the symbol of Merofynia. King Merofyn threatens Rolencia.'

'But Lence is betrothed to his daughter. Is King Merofyn so treacherous that he would betrothe his daughter, while preparing for war?' Piro whispered.

'Besides, who would want war, when we could have peace?'

'Oh, Piro.' Fyn shook his head. 'You are such an innocent.'

'I am not. Even I know that war brings death!'

'War brings wealth and power for the victor.'

'If you love war, why don't you serve the weapons master?' she snapped.

Fyn sank into the window seat and turned his face away from her.

'I'm sorry, Fyn,' she whispered. 'And I'm sorry about today and the Fate.'

'It was brave of you, Piro.' He gave her an odd look. 'Or didn't you stop to think about the risks?'

'I did. But I didn't intend to be caught.'

He shook his head ruefully. 'Feldspar deserved to find the Fate. His Affinity is stronger than mine. Even your Affinity is stronger than mine.'

Piro winced. She sat in the other half of the window seat and hugged her knees, wishing she could cheer him up.

'Maybe I should go to the abbess of Sylion, tell her I have Affinity and renounce the world,' she said, without conviction. 'At least I'd escape this plotting.'

Fyn snorted. 'You are an innocent. You can't escape plotting in an abbey. Being King Rolen's kin would make you a target in the mistresses' power plays. Besides, our parents won't want to let you go. You're too valuable a Kingdoms' piece. No, Piro. You were right and I was wrong. Tell no one for now.' He reached out and squeezed her hand. 'Will you promise me that?'

She worried her bottom lip with her teeth. 'Seela knows.'

He rolled his eyes. 'Why did you –'

'I wanted to warn Father. She stopped me. Don't worry, she won't tell.'

'Why not?' Fyn countered. 'She and Mother are thick as thieves.'

Piro debated with herself for a moment, then spoke. 'Have you ever wondered why you and I have it?'

'Affinity? Just bad luck –'

'No. We inherited it from Mother.'

He stared at her.

Piro nodded, almost laughing at his stunned expression. 'She's been hiding it all these years. Seela told me. Mother's Affinity came on her when she became a woman, like me. She didn't tell anyone because she had to marry Father to keep the peace.'

'Who would have thought?' Fyn shook his head slowly. 'Well, if she can hide it, then so can you.' He stood up. 'Pay attention and I'll teach you how to block out dangerous Affinity.'

She stood opposite him and mimicked his actions as he tapped his closed eyes, then his ears, then his mouth, then his heart, whispering all the time in a sing-song way.

'What're you saying?'

'Calling on Halcyon to protect me. I suppose the nuns call on Sylion but I don't think it matters what you say. The words and actions are just to help focus the will. Have you seen enough?'

She nodded.

'Then show me.'

She repeated the actions, humming in time to the tapping under her breath.

'Right. When you get really good at it you only have to think about it to set up the protective wards. And on no account let a renegade Power-worker touch your bare skin. It gives them access to –'

'As if I would!'

He grinned. 'Promise me you'll practise the wards every day.'

'I will, but Fyn, I won't see you again until spring cusp.'

He caught her hands in his. 'Don't worry. If there's any trouble Mother will help hide your Affinity.'

'She hates me!'

'Nonsense, Piro.'

'She does. I'm always doing the wrong thing. I'm a disappointment to her.' The immensity of it made Piro's eyes sting and she gulped back a sob. 'I've insulted Rejulas so the other warlords will defy father and –'

'Enough.' Fyn released her hands and clasped her shoulders, giving her a little shake. 'Everything's going to be all right. Lence will sweet-talk Rejulas and Byren will keep the warlords under control. Lence is betrothed to the Merofynian kingsdaughter which means we can look forward to another thirty years' peace. So your vision was wrong.'

'You think so?' She searched his face.

'Of course. Just keep out of Father's way until he's calmed down.'

Chapter Fourteen

BYREN WATCHED PIRO and Fyn slip into the great hall. Tonight Fyn did not join the monks, but came to the high table with the rest of the royal family, taking his seat at the end beside Piro.

King Rolen muttered under his breath.

Byren hid a grin. With the allegiance oaths about to begin their father could not reprimand Piro. Clever girl. By the time he'd had his dinner and drunk too much rich Rolencian wine, the edge would have gone off the king's temper.

Byren sipped his drink and began to relax. With Lence gone he did not have to watch everything he said and did. He was shocked how bad things had got between them. You'd think saving his brother's life twice in a matter of days would improve Lence's temper. But no.

What more could he do?

He wished he'd never met up with that old seer. But, if he was honest, he had to admit she'd made him aware of something that had been developing for a while, so he should really thank her because, now that he was aware of it, he had a chance to fix things with Lence.

Come to think of it, where was Lence? He should have returned from Rolenton by now. Byren's stomach tensed.

Though his twin was accompanied by his honour guard, he was still vulnerable to a lone archer... Knowing Lence, he would say there was no point in worrying and refuse to live his life shadowed by fear.

Byren told himself Lence was probably dismounting in the stables right now.

But who had sent the assassins? Not Rejulas, he had been expecting to marry into the royal house of Rolencia. Not Unistag Spar, they were too busy with internal power plays.

No, the assassins had to have been sent by the warlord from Manticore. Even now, the man strode up to the dais to make his bow. Middle-aged, but still vigorous, he wore his iron grey hair in two battletales, both laden with gold rings. Heavy black brows made him look angry. With his gleaming black armour and vivid red cloak, he looked arrogant, standing there in fabulously expensive manticore chitin chestplate. Even King Rolen did not own a suit of chitin armour.

Hand on heart, the warlord of Manticore Spar renewed his pledge of loyalty to King Rolen.

If this warlord made a move in the spring, Byren would have to lead a punitive war party over the Dividing Mountains against him. Odd, Corvel of

Manticore Spar was almost his father's age, had come to the warlordship at fifteen and held it for thirty years. He had at least four strapping sons to help him now, so he had nothing to prove. The spar's emblem, the blood-red-furred Affinity beast with the body of a lion and the tail of a scorpion, glinted in the light of many candles. Repugnance filled Byren. What kind of warrior would swear allegiance with one breath, while sending assassins in the next? Or perhaps he wronged Corvel.

Corvel of Manticore came to his feet but, before the next warlord could take his place, a youth of about seventeen shoved through the servants who were clustered near the kitchen entrance and ran into the centre of the hall.

'He lies!' the young warrior accused, his voice ringing in the arched vaults above. 'Even while Warlord Corvel was dining at the king's high table, his raiders attacked my village.'

There was a hushed intake of breath.

'Rubbish!' Corvel dismissed the accusation.

'You can prove this?' King Rolen asked the youth.

He nodded and pulled a torn spar symbol from inside his jerkin. Byren noted how the youth's hands trembled, but he did not think it was with fear.

With a flick the youth unrolled the emblem to reveal a red manticore on a field of black.

'That tattered thing?' Corvel sneered. 'That could have been taken during a raid any time these last thirty years. I admit I've sent raiding parties over the Divide before, but I'd be a bloody fool to let my warriors raid while King Rolen's guest.'

'You thought you'd be gone before the news came,' the youth insisted, voice rising. Tears glittered in his furious eyes. 'You didn't gamble on me skating day and night to get here. I want justice for my village, for my kin!'

'Justice,' voices echoed from the watchers, moved by the youth's conviction.

'I am falsely accused!' Corvel roared.

'It is possible,' the queen whispered. 'One of his own sons, ambitious to impress his men, might have gone raiding without asking Corvel's permission.'

'Father?' Byren leant past his mother, having to raise his voice to be heard above the talk of the crowd. 'What if he's telling the truth? Remember the raiders I saw skating across Rolencia's valley?'

'Proof is easy,' King Rolen muttered, then slammed his fist down on the table and the hall fell silent. 'I gather your villagers defended their homes, lad?'

'With their lives!' he bristled.

'Then we can identify the bodies of the raiders killed. That will prove who...' he ran down as the youth was shaking his head.

'They took their dead with them. Those of us who could run fled into the caves. While we were hiding, they took their dead and burned the village.'

Byren stiffened. Raiding was commonplace, but the warlords didn't destroy the villages they raided. They left enough intact for the people to rebuild, otherwise there would be no village to raid the next time.

'This is a new development,' Queen Myrella whispered.

'Captain Temor, take this youth aside,' King Rolen ordered. 'We'll hear his case after the loyalty pledges.'

As Temor escorted the youth to a private chamber, the words his mother had spoken echoed in Byren's mind and a kernel of worry solidified in his gut. Sending assassins into Rolenton had been a new development, too.

What was keeping his twin? Lence knew he was supposed to sit on their father's left while the warlords swore their fealty. What if he had become separated from his honour guard? What if spies had reported Lence's riding out? What if whoever sent the last assassins seized this chance to send more?

'What is it?' his mother whispered.

'It's Lence, I –'

'I know, he's late!'

'I should go down to Rolenton. He might be in trouble.'

'Yes... but if he's not, he won't thank you for coming after him.'

She was right. Byren couldn't just turn up and announce that he was there to take Lence home. At least he knew where they were. Temor had reported that Rejulas had taken over a private chamber at the Three Swans. But if Byren knew, others would know too. The more he thought about it, the more Lence's absence worried him.

'But it would be perfectly natural for you and your friends to celebrate Lence's betrothal tonight by going down to Rolenton's taverns,' his mother suggested softly.

'And meet up with Lence at the Three Swans.'

'Exactly!'

At that moment the last warlord finished his oath and the musicians began to play as great plates of food were carried up from the kitchen.

'Suddenly I'm not hungry,' Byren muttered. 'Wonder if the others feel like celebrating...'

LESS THAN AN hour later, Byren and half a dozen friends strode into the entrance of the Three Swans, calling for a private chamber, hot mead and food. Since the Three Swans was the second largest inn in Rolenton, it was their second stop. The delay had gnawed at Byren's composure, but he didn't want to arouse suspicion, not with Lence, not with Rejulas or any of the other warlords' spies.

'A private chamber,' Garzik insisted, enjoying himself. 'And be quick about it.'

The serving girl ran off, only to have the innkeeper bustle out, wiping her hands on her apron.

'Ah, Byren Kingson,' she greeted him. 'I don't have a chamber to spare. I've already had to turn out half a dozen merchants for warlord Rejulas and Lence Kingsheir –'

'Lence? My brother's here? Where is he?' Byren repeated. Pretending to be a trifle drunk he raised his voice. 'Lence?'

'Lensh?' Garzik echoed, not having to pretend.

'Hush, Garza,' Orrade warned. Only he knew the real reason for their roistering.

The innkeeper glanced to the second door of the private chambers. Garzik interpreted her look and weaved over before Orrade could stop him. Flinging the door, Garzik revealed a crowded private room. The solid oak door shuddered on its hinges. A sudden silence filled the room.

At a glance Byren saw that Lence and Cobalt were at a table with the warlord himself, while two dozen Cockatrice men cast dice with Lence's honour guard.

'There he izh!' Garzik announced. 'Hey, Byren. I found Lensh. Want to come drinking with us, Lensh?'

Lence muttered something under his breath and sprang to his feet, striding towards them.

The innkeeper wisely hurried off, leaving Byren to face his irate brother. There was nothing for it. He had to carry on now.

'Lence!' Byren swung a friendly arm around his shoulders, his new ceremonial knife digging into his ribs. He wouldn't be able to draw in a hurry. Pretending to lurch drunkenly, he shifted to give himself access to the weapon. If there was nothing wrong he would look a fool, but he didn't care as long as his twin got home safe.

'What are you doing here?' Lence demanded.

Byren glanced at his friends, who had wandered into the room and were laying bets on the outcome of the dice. Tankards were being passed around. Orrade tried to intercept Garzik before he took one, without success. Rejulas's men seemed to have overcome their enmity, though they were quick to raise a bet and mutter an oath. For all that it appeared a friendly scene, Byren could sense a lot of tension even from this quick jumble of impressions.

'What are you doing, Byren?' Lence repeated.

'Why, we're celebrating of course! Can't celebrate your betrothal without you.' Blinking owlishly, Byren fixed on Rejulas as he joined them. He went to pat Rejulas on the shoulder but missed and clutched at him to steady himself. Leaning closer, he spoke secretively. 'As for you, you made a lucky escape. Our sister's no angel, more like a cockatrice. All smiles one moment, spitting poison the next. But maybe that's the kind of woman you fancy, coming from Cockatrice Spar!' He went off into a peal of laughter.

Cobalt's eyes narrowed, but Rejulas obviously decided he was too drunk to take offence and laughed along with him.

Lence looked disgusted. Of them all, he should have known Byren would never jeopardise an alliance.

Byren sensed Cobalt watching him closely and was careful not to let his cousin catch his eye.

'So let's share a drink!' Byren linked an arm around Lence and Rejulas's shoulders and stumbled towards the small table, away from the dicers. A single lamp illuminated this end of the room. Three tankards and a scrap of scribbled paper lay on the table. 'What're you drinking?'

He swooped a hand down to grab the empty tankard and sniff it, while trying to see what was written on the back of a torn broadsheet, the sort that advertised minstrels. But before he could make sense of it, Cobalt swept the table clean as though the paper had only been rubbish and called for more hot mead.

Byren spun a tavern chair around and dropped his weight onto it, hearing it creak in protest. Even though he sprawled his forearms on the back of the chair, he made sure his knife was free of obstruction and his back was to the wall.

'Yes, a toast to your betrothal, Lence Kingsheir,' Rejulas said. 'Or would you prefer Rolencian red?'

'No more drinking,' Lence objected. 'Byren's had quite enough. I should get him back to Rolenhold.'

That was what Byren wanted, but it wouldn't look right if he agreed too easily.

'Can't go back yet, not without celebrating,' he objected. 'Just one tankard and then we'll go.' He fixed on Rejulas. 'So are you coming for the Jubilee? Going to give little Piro another chance? If you take my advice –'

'We don't need your advice, Byren,' Lence spoke up quickly. 'Rejulas has agreed to come back to the castle tonight and renew his vow of fealty. It was all a misunderstanding, caused by a thoughtless, spoilt brat.'

Piro was no spoilt brat, but Byren let this pass for now. He lurched out of the chair and extended his arm across the table towards Rejulas. 'Then let me be the first to –'

He deliberately overbalanced and fell under the table. Where was that scrap of paper? His hand closed over it, just as Lence reached under and hauled him upright. Cobalt was still watching him. Did their cousin see through this act?

Better get out quick.

Byren let Lence take his weight. Clutching his stomach to hide the paper tucked in his hand, he groaned. 'Don't feel so good, Lensh.'

'That's all I need!' Lence muttered.

'I'll take him home,' Orrade said quickly, joining them.

'Yes, take him home,' Cobalt urged. Byren could hear the unspoken, 'before he can do any more damage' and bristled, even though this was exactly what he wanted.

'I should go back to Rolenhold now, swear my fealty oath,' Rejulas said. He stood and signalled his men.

Lence called for the innkeeper.

Byren had to keep up with the pretence of being a nauseous drunk, while the rest of the party gathered and Lence borrowed a carriage to take him back to Rolenhold. Rejulas called for their horses, intending to follow with his men.

Lence helped Orrade lift Byren into the carriage, none too gently. He sprawled in a dark corner as Orrade sat opposite him.

'What possessed you, Byren?' Lence demanded from the doorway. 'You know how important Rejulas's support is. It's just as well I'd already won him over. Your stupid behaviour has gone a long way towards undoing the good I've done!'

Byren said nothing. Lence should have known better. Cobalt hardly knew him and even he'd been suspicious. Byren wanted to justify himself but if he revealed the ruse now it would only make Lence furious. Seething, Byren remained silent.

'Well?' Lence demanded.

Byren produced an effective snore.

Lence swore. 'Get him to bed, Orrie.'

He slammed the door and walked off.

Orrade said nothing until the carriage began to rattle over the cobbles.

'Well, what did it say?' Orrade prodded.

'What?' Byren muttered, still fuming. Usually it was he who helped Lence to bed after a night of too much drinking.

'The paper you grabbed from under their table.'

'Eh?' Byren sat up. 'Did anyone else notice?'

'I doubt it. You should have been a player, Byren.'

He grinned and pulled the crumpled paper out from inside his vest. By the silvery starlight coming through the window, he and Orrade tried to interpret the drawings. It seemed to be a scribbled map of Cockatrice Spar in relation to Rolenhold, with the major estates, roads and canals marked. It had been drawn with smudged charcoal and was hard to interpret, with arrows and splotches that may have represented fighting men on the march.

'They were discussing strategy,' Orrade said.

'Working on the best way to defend Rolencia,' Byren agreed. His twin had been safe all along, looking out for Rolencia's future. Perhaps tomorrow, when Lence cooled down, he'd reveal the subterfuge and they'd laugh over it.

He rubbed his knee which still ached from the impact after Lence had shoved him into the carriage. Then again... perhaps he would never reveal the ruse.

'You'll have to go straight to bed,' Orrade said. 'I'll return to the great hall, let you know how it goes.'

'Huh?' Byren had made himself look a fool in front of Lence, Cobalt and Rejulas, and was beginning to regret it.

'The call to arms. King Rolen will announce the punitive raid on the Utlanders tonight and call for support.'

He was right. The warlords and nobles would each swear to send a certain number of men and the merchants would supply ships and supplies, then they would drink to the raid's success. And he would be in bed, supposedly too drunk to attend. Not that he was comfortable with the idea of the raid.

'They don't even know which Utland raiders killed old Lord Cobalt,' Byren muttered. 'But they'll kill a few and burn some miserable little cottages to the ground to teach the Utlanders a lesson.'

'I agree, it's not fair. But unless Lence punishes them, the Utlanders will become a problem. Can you think of a better solution?'

Byren frowned. He couldn't. But it still felt wrong.

WHEN BYREN TOOK his seat at the war table first thing the next morning, Lence leant closer to whisper, 'No headache?'

Byren glanced away, annoyed, because Lence's waist length hair was loose on his shoulders, Ostron-style, instead of held in a warrior's plait.

'No. No headache.' He wasn't going to lie.

'You deserve one, if ever –'

Captain Temor cleared his throat then nodded to their father.

'Yesterday convinced me that we need to ensure each of the warlords' loyalty,' King Rolen said. 'Thanks to Lence, Rejulas has reconsidered. By the time he comes back for the Jubilee, Piro had better be ready to give her betrothal vows. As for the Manticore raiders... Corvel denied all responsibility, but he's sending some men over the Divide to rebuild the youth's village to prove his loyalty –'

'I still think the raid is suspicious,' Byren protested.

'You went off drinking instead of staying to hear the evidence, so no one cares what you think,' his father snapped.

Byren felt heat creep up his face. His mother caught his eye with a worried look but he had no intention of revealing his subterfuge now.

'Since Rejulas has sworn fealty and agreed to come back for the Jubilee, Piro will have another chance with him,' the queen said, filling in the silence. 'She's a good girl. She knows her duty.'

But would she do it? Byren wondered. And should she have to? For the first time he wondered how Isolt Merofyn Kingsdaughter felt about having to marry his twin.

'We have four of the five warlords behind us. They've sworn to send men with Lence when he goes to teach the Utlanders a lesson,' King Rolen said. 'Yet the warlord of Manticore Spar swears fealty with one breath while, for all I know, one of his sons sends raiders behind our backs. If Unistag does not elect a new warlord and swear loyalty before the Jubilee, Rolencia will look weak. We can't afford –'

'I agree.' As Lence sat forwards something glinted in his hair, dark semi-precious stones, onyxes. Byren blinked, surprised and dismayed. 'Since Byren nearly spoilt my efforts with Rejulas, I suggest he approach

Unistag. Let's see if he can bring in a warlord's loyalty!'

'It's not the same,' Byren protested. Lence's approach to Rejulas had been from a position of power in his home town, with the might of the castle behind him. He hadn't been asked to go marching into an enemy camp as an ambassador. 'If I go to Unistag Spar it will seem Rolencia is trying to interfere with the choice of warlord. It's not like I could enforce it anyway, not without a small army.'

'So now you need a small army?' Lence mocked. 'Your honour guard not enough?'

Byren bit back a sharp retort and caught his mother's troubled gaze across the table.

'Well, Byren?' his father prodded.

Byren sprang to his feet. 'Very well. The sooner I go, the better. I'll be back with the warlord of Unistag's loyalty before the Jubilee or I won't be back at all!'

Captain Temor came to his feet. 'With your permission, Rolen. I'd like to go with him. An older, wiser head could offer advice.'

His father hesitated, then nodded.

Byren marched out, torn between relief and mortification to have the captain of his father's honour guard accompany him.

'Wait, Byren,' Temor called.

He paused at the top of the stairs.

Temor joined him. 'I'll select a dozen men-at-arms, veterans who know what they're doing –'

'You're right, my honour guard are all too callow.' Byren faced the truth. 'How many should we take?'

'Around twenty-five. Another twenty will do us no good if the Unistags turn on us, and twenty-five is small enough to travel light and fast.'

Byren squeezed the older man's shoulder. 'I'm lucky to have you, Temor. I plan to ride across the foothills and hire mountain ponies at the tradepost.' Horses could not make it over the steep terrain of the Pass.

The captain nodded.

'We can leave first thing tomorrow.'

THAT EVENING, BYREN slipped into Halcyon's chantry to burn a candle and ask the goddess to watch over him and his men when they ventured into Unistag Spar. Since the god Sylion had symbolically handed over their world on Midwinter's Day, the goddess Halcyon was now the dominant force as they headed towards spring. Besides, you prayed to Sylion if you were going out on a raid like the one Lence would be leading against the Utlanders. Sylion dealt in death. Halcyon dealt in life and Byren hoped he wouldn't have to kill anyone to win the spar warlord's loyalty.

The chantry was cold and empty. Row upon row of glittering icons represented Halcyon's bounty, stylised goats heads, bulls, cocks and sheep, wheat, rye and barley, all painted in rich colours, decorated with gold leaf, lined the walls. Above the central dais a mural depicting King Rolence the First bestowing Mount Halcyon on his Affinity warder told the story of the founding of Halcyon Abbey.

From the marble pillars to the decorated ceiling above, Byren's steps echoed softly. Halcyon's Affinity warder was with his abbot, along with Springdawn and the abbess. All the representatives of the gods had been called together to discuss the number of Affinity seeps and work out a strategy for containing them. Three in under a year was a bad omen.

Byren had chosen to come to the chantry at this moment because he knew he would be alone. He didn't want to be caught by either Halcyon's Affinity warder or the healer. Both were elderly men who'd seen him grow from a babe in arms and were inclined to offer a great deal of well-meant advice.

The sacred lamp burnt under the central dome giving off its familiar, aromatic scent of vanilla and sandalwood, reminding Byren of endless ceremonies. The lamp was never extinguished and had been lit from the original flame, which was kept burning deep below Halcyon Abbey. Byren picked his way through the pews to the royal devotional box. It was only just deep enough for the chair which could seat a member of the royal family, with a single sconce to burn a devotional candle. He closed the cherrywood-carved screen and prepared to light his candle.

Soft footsteps made him stop. Had Lence followed him to apologise? He waited for the cherrywood screen to open. But no, Orrade knelt just on the other side of the screen and lit a candle, standing it in the large sconce there. As the flame flickered, a tendril of fine smoke rose in the still air, dreamless-sleep scented smoke. Orrade leant forwards to inhale it. The effect of the mild narcotic would bring him closer to Halcyon and help focus his thoughts.

Byren considered letting Orrade know he was

there, then decided to wait. He'd already heard how everyone cheered Lence and Cobalt, volunteering to go on the Utland raid. He felt excluded and he had only himself to blame.

'May Halcyon protect and watch over this venture to Unistag Spar,' Orrade whispered. 'May she care for Elina and my father, may she protect Garzik and stop him from doing anything rash. May she keep Byren safe from harm –'

'How touching,' Cobalt said, his voice too soft to echo.

Orrade went very still, then turned slowly. He would have risen but Cobalt had already reached him and placed one hand on his shoulder, holding him on his knees.

Orrade cleared his throat. 'I pray to Halcyon for success –'

'You pray for the kingson's safety,' Cobalt cut in. 'I know your secret.'

Orrade went very still. 'I don't know what you –'

Cobalt lifted the smaller man to his feet, swinging him around hard so that the carved screen creaked with the impact. Orrade was pressed against it only a hand's breadth from Byren. He went to move but they blocked the door and besides, Orrade could protect himself. Byren's name had been mentioned and he feared if he came out of the devotional box now it would confirm everything Cobalt suspected. Besides, he was shocked by Cobalt's sudden violence, which seemed so out of character.

'Don't play the innocent with me, Orrade. I've seen the way you look at him, or don't look at him,'

Cobalt whispered. 'Does he know why you were disinherited?'

'I don't know what –'

Cobalt silenced him with a kiss that was not gentle. He persisted until Orrade stopped struggling, then he pulled back with a soft laugh. 'Deny all you like, your body betrays you.'

Orrade said nothing. Shame for him heated Byren's cheeks. Now he could not venture out and look them in the eye.

'Good.' Cobalt all but purred. 'I want to know what Byren is planning. You will report to me. Don't deny me.' Cobalt jerked Orrade so that his head thumped against the wood. 'I could ruin you with one word –'

'And I could ruin you!'

'I don't think so.' Cobalt smiled. 'I am the injured party, my bride and father cruelly murdered.' When he said this Byren realised he was using his supposedly injured arm to prod Orrade in the chest. 'No one will believe a word against me. But you... you have refused to reveal why you fought with your father, and you are Byren's shadow. Why, you are closer to him than his own twin!'

Orrade did not try to argue.

Cobalt released him. 'Now we understand each other. Report to me and I'll keep your secret.' His voice dropped. 'I may even reward you.'

He stepped back, his soft indoor slippers silent on the marble tiles.

Freed, Orrade lifted one hand to his mouth, staggering slightly. He stared after Cobalt's retreating back.

'I'll leave Rolencia before I betray Byren,' he called after Cobalt.

The older man stopped and turned to face him, his features barely visible in the single lamp light. 'Go, and not only will I tell King Rolen why you were disinherited, but I'll tell him Byren is your lover –'

'That's not true!'

'Truth is highly overrated,' Cobalt told him. 'King Rolen nearly lost Rolencia because of the Servants of Palos. When I was growing up, they still whispered of how he stood stone-faced during the executions. Even my father, his own half-brother, was afraid of him. Do you think the king would hesitate to order Byren's execution if it meant saving Rolencia for his precious Lence?'

'The king would never believe –'

'Oh, I can be very convincing, Orrade. I'm sure I could persuade my uncle, especially when it is half true.'

Orrade dragged in a ragged breath. 'You bastard!'

'No, my father was the bastard. It was the only thing that stood between him and the throne!'

Orrade said nothing.

Cobalt laughed softly, turned and left. His mocking laughter hung on the air after he had gone.

Shaking with fury, Orrade paced back and forth across the chantry. Finally he dipped his fingers in the font which held water from Halcyon's sacred pool, splashing it on his face as if to wake himself.

Muttering a string of inventive curses, Orrade spun and stalked out of the chantry.

Byren waited a few moments then left the royal box. His first thought was to warn his father, but what could he tell King Rolen without implicating himself and Orrade? It was clear now that Illien of Cobalt was a manipulative, cunning man who could not be trusted, but any proof would mean revealing the true reason for Orrade's disinheritance. Though this had nothing to do with the Servants of Palos, their betrayal was still too raw and recent for his father to separate the two.

But there was still his mother.

Byren left the Chantry, heading straight for the queen's private chamber.

When Seela met him at the door her worried face creased into a fond smile of welcome. 'Ah, Byren, so good of you to drop by and visit your old nurse.'

He flushed, amused by her pointed teasing. 'Is Mother in?'

'Yes, but she's having one of her bad turns. I've put her to bed with some dreamless-sleep. Mayhap that will bring her some peace.'

'I hope so.'

'Was it something important? Do you want me to give her a message?'

He shook his head. When his mother had these turns she would rise late the following afternoon and be groggy for a day or two. There was nothing the healers could do for her. 'I don't want to worry mother. I'll see her when I get back from Unistag Spar.'

Seela nodded. 'Give your old nurse a hug and may Halcyon watch over you.'

He hugged her, surprised to discover her flesh was thin over her bones. She had always been the rock in the centre of his childhood, a haven of safety and understanding. Now she needed protecting.

'Goodbye, Seela.' He kissed her forehead.

She flushed with pleasure. 'What was that for?'

He smiled. 'No reason.'

As he went off to pack, he decided it was just as well he had not spoken with his mother. For some reason he could never keep anything from her. She would have wormed the reason for Orrade's disinheritance from him and it was not his secret to share.

He found himself at the door to his father's private chamber. Because of his mother's turns they had separate sleeping chambers. Maybe if he just put in a word or two to make his father more careful of Cobalt...

He knocked and swung the door open to find his father lying face down, naked on his bed, while Cobalt's manservant massaged the king's massive shoulders, scarred skin gleamed with Ostronite oil in the golden lamplight.

'Father?'

'Eh, Byren. What is it?' King Rolen asked, lifting his head and blinking as though waking from a dream.

Byren said the first thing that came into his head. He could hardly suggest the king watch out for Cobalt in front of Cobalt's servant. 'I came to see how the knee was, Father.'

'Enough for now, Valens,' King Rolen said, swinging his legs off the bed and tucking the towel around his waist. He stood beside the bed, one hand on the upright to steady himself as he tested the knee. A smile broke across his weathered features. 'Eh. I can bend it without pain.'

'The pain will come back, King Rolen,' Valens warned.

Byren hadn't been aware that his father's knee hurt with every step. He crossed the room. 'If it's your knee that's the problem, why massage your back?'

Valens flicked a disdainful glance to Byren. 'I must massage the knee, hip and back every day. The knee throws the back out –'

'And don't I know it!' the king muttered.

Valens nodded. He took several dark bottles from his case. Measuring a little from each he poured the liquid into a goblet of wine and stirred. 'And you must drink this every morning and night to bring down the swelling in the joint.'

King Rolen accepted the goblet, sniffed and took a sip. He looked relieved then drained the lot. 'Ah, that's better than any of the herbals my healers give me. I was afraid you'd ruined a good wine.'

'Never, King Rolen. We Ostronites know the value of Rolencian red!' With a bow, Valens continued to pack his tools away in a leather case.

'So, can I offer you a drink, Byren?' his father asked.

'No. I'm off to bed. I want a clear head for an early start tomorrow.' Byren hesitated but Valens showed no sign of leaving. He had begun polishing his father's boots. 'I'm glad your knee is feeling better.'

'My knee? My whole back feels better. It's never been the same since that riding accident.' His father slung an arm around Byren's shoulders. The king was nearly fifty now and he was a big man, deep through the chest with a bit of a belly on him, but Byren could feel the strength in his body and the vigour as he walked him to the door. 'I swear I feel twenty years younger!' Then he grew serious. 'While you're dealing with Unistag's warlord, I want you to listen to Temor's advice. He's had thirty years, dealing with spar leaders.'

'I will, Father. Good night.'

Byren headed back to his chamber relieved that his father was feeling better but frustrated with the meeting. If only he could reveal the truth about Cobalt's attempt to blackmail Orrade.

Orrade's sudden declaration of love had endangered them both. What was wrong with his friend? Orrade had certainly enjoyed women in the past.

Byren's hands itched to grab his friend and knock some sense into him. If only it was that simple!

Chapter Fifteen

FYN FOUND ROLENHOLD strangely empty without Byren. His brother had ridden out the day after midwinter with a Captain Temor, a dozen men-at-arms and his honour guard of twelve likely lads, Orrade and Garzik amongst them. Enough to deter treachery, but not enough to be a threat to a newly elected warlord, was how Byren had described it to him.

Several days ago his mother had taken one of her turns. Complaining of sleeping badly, she had retreated to her private solarium, which made his father worry. Lence went around like a bear with a sore tooth, while Piro hardly spoke and seemed preoccupied.

The four days of formal celebrations to welcome back the goddess Halcyon were finally over and, for once, Fyn was glad to return to the abbey.

'What will you do,' Piro whispered, 'now that you can't join the mystics?'

They stood to one side of the royal party, who were farewelling the abbot and the masters. It was early morning and the nuns of Sylion had already left Rolenhold, hitching the sails of their sled-boats to catch the breeze.

'Don't worry, I'll find a branch of the abbey to take me,' Fyn said. 'Maybe the clerics. Then, when I become abbot, I can send the weapons master to serve Lence.'

He expected her to laugh at this, but she nodded seriously. 'That way you wouldn't have to do the killing.'

No. He'd just send others to their death, he realised with a sickening lurch. How did leaders live with their decisions?

'Oh, Fyn. Last night I dreamed of Byren. He was running through the forest, running away from wyverns,' Piro whispered urgently. 'Do you think it was a vision?'

'That's silly. Wyverns live near water, not in the forest,' Fyn argued.

'They could have been freshwater wyverns.'

She looked so miserable he wanted to shake her.

'Byren will be fine. If you had a dream about a unistag confronting Byren, that might have been a vision. But not a wyvern.'

She managed a smile. 'You must be right. But, Fyn, I think my Affinity is getting stronger.'

Bitterness churned in him. He'd had to give up family and position because of his Affinity. He was the superfluous third son, when the king already had an heir in Lence, with Byren in reserve. Worse, his family didn't trust him. This midwinter at Rolenhold had convinced Fyn his place was with the abbey.

'Fyn?' Piro prodded. 'What's wrong?'

The weapons master blew the horn, signalling that it was time to go. Piro gave a little start of fright.

He hugged her. 'You'll be all right. Mother's been able to hide her Affinity all these years. You will too!'

Her tears felt wet on his cheeks as she kissed him. 'Oh, Fyn. I have such a bad feeling!'

He wanted to stay and reassure her but... 'Piro, I must go.' The abbey contingent was already marching, taking him with it.

'I know. Goodbye, Fyn,' she called, running a little way out the gates with him.

Then she fell behind as the masters marched the monks and acolytes down the steep road to Rolenton. They sang in time to their steps, the masters leading the chant. With the crisp morning air stinging his face and his fellow monks around him, Fyn felt a sense of belonging and realised, until today, he had not given up hope of returning home. Well, from now on the abbey would be his home. He had to forge a place there or be overwhelmed in the battle for position.

They were still high enough on Rolenhold's pinnacle for Fyn to look out across the fertile crescent valley of Rolencia. The Dividing Mountains curved away behind him, forming a half circle. In its hub was distant Mount Halcyon. The snowy-tipped peak stood like a beacon, glinting in the sun. In three days he would be there, safe in the abbey built into the side of the mountain.

As soon as they returned to the abbey, he would ask Master Wintertide's advice. As an acolyte, Fyn should have consulted the acolytes master, but he was a close friend of the history master. And that master had been watching him since they spoke on Midwinter's Day, smiling when their eyes caught. It worried Fyn more than he wanted to admit.

On Rolenton wharf they loaded up their sleds, strapped on their skates and prepared to set off across Sapphire Lake. Once across the lake they would travel the canal to Viridian Lake and Halcyon Abbey.

Because Fyn and Lonepine were the same height, they were usually paired together to pull a sled. Fyn helped his friend with his straps then turned so that Lonepine could buckle his.

'Don't bother,' Feldspar called, jumping down from the wharf to a snowdrift on the ice. 'I've been sent to find you, Fyn. Master Firefox wants you.'

'The acolytes master?' Surprised and a little worried, Fyn climbed back onto the wharf and wandered through the monks.

He found the acolytes master speaking with the history master and waited at a polite distance for them to finish. Farmer Overhill's son stood to one side, looking uncomfortable. Fyn felt sorry for him. It was bad enough joining the abbey as a six-year-old, but to be fifteen and to know as little as a six-year-old would be a nightmare.

The history master glanced once at Fyn, nodded in reply to something Master Firefox had said, then hurried away.

'There you are, Fyn Kingson,' Firefox greeted him, jovially. 'I can recall how troubled I was the year I had to find my place amid the priests, so I thought I'd put you out of your misery. This midsummer, when you give your vows, I will take you into my service. Training the minds of young acolytes is one of the most important tasks in the abbey.' He gave Fyn a friendly smile but his eyes were hard and meaningful. 'You could go far with me as your master. Few have the influence I wield.'

Firefox hinted that Master Wintertide's friendship would not further Fyn's career. But he had never expected that kind of return from friendship. Hiding his distaste, he gave the bow of an acolyte to a master.

'I thank you.' He didn't want to actually say no, the acolytes master could make his life miserable. 'I will think deeply on this.'

'You do that. Meanwhile, take this youth with you.' He nodded to the Overhill boy. 'Escort him to Master Wintertide when we reach the abbey.'

Fyn nodded. By ordering him to mind the new boy, Firefox was reminding him how little control he had over his own life.

Young Overhill shifted uneasily. Fyn took pity on him. 'What's your name?'

'Joff of Overhill, but... I suppose I'll have a new name at the abbey.'

'Not until you are ready to become a monk.' Fyn led him towards the waiting sleds. 'I haven't chosen my monk name yet. Come on. We'd better strap on the sled.'

'Ho, Fyn, what was that all about?' Lonepine asked when he returned.

'I'm to watch out for Joff,' Fyn explained.

'Good.' Lonepine grinned. 'We can take turns pulling the sled.'

'Will you take up Master Firefox's offer?' Joff asked Fyn.

'The master offered you a place? Why didn't you say?' Lonepine demanded.

Fyn shrugged. He didn't want to talk about it here, where anyone might overhear.

'It would be a wise move.' Lonepine winked. 'Then you won't have to compete with me to be weapons master!'

Fyn laughed and mock-punched him, but his heart was not in it.

PIRO WAITED IN her mother's private chamber down one end of the solarium. Listening for the distinctive *chink, chink* of her mother's walk, every second step punctuated by the heavy ring of keys she wore at her waist. Keys for chambers, keys for account cabinets, keys for chests and keys for cellars. She was hoping her mother had the key to her problems.

After taking off her head-dress and cloak, Piro sat in front of the fire to get warm. Her cheeks still stung from standing on the battlements in the cold breeze to see the last of the monks glide off across Sapphire lake.

Staring into the flames, Piro wound her cap's red satin ribbons through her fingers. Her eyes felt gritty from lack of sleep and loud sounds made her jump. The dream about Byren was only one of many nightmares. Since looking into the Mirror of Insight her dreams had been haunted. Every night as soon as she drifted off, she saw wyverns rampaging through the castle corridors, eating in the great hall, drinking and laughing while her people went in fear of them. She dreaded falling asleep.

Piro was desperate enough to turn to her mother. How did the queen hide her Affinity? How could she have let her own father ride to his death? The more Piro thought about it, the more she realised she did not know her mother, had never known her.

'What are you doing, sitting here all alone?' her old nurse asked, bustling in with an armful of freshly laundered linen. She began folding things, slipping lavender bags between the layers as she tucked them away in various chests.

'Where's mother?'

'With your father, entertaining the Merofynian ambassador. He'll be going back soon. When next we see him it will be the Jubilee and Isolt Kingsdaughter will be with him.' The old nurse frowned at Piro. 'You must be on your best behaviour next time you see Rejulas –'

'I can't face him, Seela. I don't know what to do. My Affinity is getting worse!' Piro gestured wildly, cap swinging by its ribbons. 'Rejulas handed me a slice of perfectly good sweet bread with cream but when I tried to eat it I nearly choked. Father later ate the whole loaf so there was nothing wrong with it. If the Affinity wasn't trying to tell me to beware Rejulas, what does it mean?'

'It means you can't trust what you see, hear or feel. Ahh, Piro!' Seela's face creased with sympathy. 'To be god-touched is not a pleasant thing. Your mother's had to live with it all these years, never knowing if the nightmares she has are visions or simply bad dreams. As for Rejulas, I know what you're like. You went into the trophy chamber all churned up with anger and resentment. No wonder you couldn't eat.'

'No. It wasn't me. It was a message from the gods. I'm sure of it.'

Seela rolled her eyes.

Piro put her hands on her hips, cap dangling. 'I'm going to ask mother.'

'No, don't trouble her.' Seela closed the chest and came over to Piro, taking the cap from her and smoothing the crumpled ribbons. 'I didn't tell her about your Affinity. Don't disappoint her.'

Piro's shoulder's slumped. 'I'm sorry if I'm a disappointment to her.'

'You misunderstand me. She'd be disappointed in herself. We'll keep this a secret, you and I.' Seela summoned a smile. 'From what your father says Rejulas is a brave, clever man.'

'I still don't trust him.'

'Words are cheap, deeds ring true. This is what I told your mother when she was fretting about coming here. She was only a little thing, eight years old. I told her, only by King Rolen's actions can we know if he is trustworthy. Give him a chance to prove himself. And she did and look what happened!' Seela took Piro's hand. 'The best thing you can do is close your heart and mind against the Affinity, just as your mother has done, and do your duty as a kingsdaughter.'

Piro sighed. Since this was also Fyn's advice, she nodded. 'All right, but I can't sleep for the nightmares.'

'We can banish those. A little sleeping draught will do the trick. Your mother has been taking it for years. Whenever it gets bad we say she's having one of her turns and she retreats to her private chamber so that I can dose her. I'll water down some dreamless-sleep for you this very night. You're worrying needlessly.' Seela patted Piro's arm. 'I know. Let's prepare a performance for the visiting nobles. We can get the costume chest out and do one of the midwinter pageants!'

Piro nodded slowly. Usually she enjoyed performing but now it all seemed so trivial.

Seeing her expression, Seela clucked her tongue. 'Dreamless-sleep will settle the nightmares. It works on your mother. You'll see.'

And Piro had to be satisfied with this as Seela bustled off. Alone again, she paced the chamber. It was all very well to say that Rejulas's action would tell her what kind of man he was, but what if she was already married to him when she discovered he could not be trusted? How would she escape him?

FYN ARRIVED AT the abbey as the sun was setting behind the Dividing Mountains. After pulling the sled for three days solid, his thighs and shoulders ached.

All he wanted to do was rest, but first he had to take Joff to the boys master. This happened to suit him, since he wanted to ask Master Wintertide's advice.

He dumped his travelling pack on his bunk and turned to .Joff, who was standing in the acolytes' dormitory looking out of place while the others unloaded their packs, checked the work roster then shuffled off to line up for the hot baths.

'Come on, Joff.' Fyn headed for the corridor, pointing out the rooms as they passed them. 'This wing of chambers houses the acolytes in order of rank, oldest at this end, the youngest down here.' He passed that door and entered the spiral central stairs, gesturing upwards. 'The hothouses are high above in the crater's mouth, set on the shores of Lake Halcyon. That's where we bring on the seedlings so the farmers can make an early start with their planting. Otherwise they'd never get two crops harvested each summer.'

Joff nodded as they headed down the steps. As a farmer's son, he would be familiar with monks delivering hothouse seedlings.

'Fyn?' Lonepine called over the acolytes' balcony. 'You're rostered to work in the gardens tonight.'

Fyn cursed under his breath.

'But we've only just got back,' Joff muttered. 'How could you be rostered to work? That's not fair.'

'Who said abbey life was fair?' Fyn muttered, then took pity on Joff's confusion. 'No. It's not fair. But that's the way it is. The acolytes master is warning me.'

'Why?'

'Because I haven't accepted his offer.'

'Why not?'

Fyn sighed. 'You ask a lot of questions.'

Joff shrugged. 'If I don't ask, how will I ever learn?'

Fyn grinned. During the sled ride he'd discovered he liked Joff.

'This way.' Fyn continued down the stairs to the next level. 'This is where the boys live. They're aged between six and twelve, so you'll be the oldest. But don't worry, Wintertide is the best of the masters.'

He jogged down the corridor towards his old teacher's chambers, pausing in the entrance. 'Master Wintertide?'

'He's not here,' a small boy said.

'Do you know how long he will be?'

The boy shook his head. 'Is there a message I can give the master?'

Fyn hesitated. When he had been Wintertide's servant, bigger boys had offered him bribes to spy for them. He'd refused no matter how much they tried to intimidate him. He had no idea how many masters this boy served.

'The abbot called all masters up to his chambers,' the boy volunteered.

Fyn suspected the masters and the abbot were discussing Provings so far. He suspected his presence was like turning up an Unknowable card in a Duelling Kingdom games. If he was put with the wrong master, the balance of power in the abbey hierarchy would be disrupted.

The first prayer bell rang.

Fyn grimaced. He could delay no longer. The gardens master was easy-going, but if Fyn reported for work late he would be insulted.

'I'll leave you here, Joff,' Fyn said. 'Master Wintertide will be back soon.'

He headed for the corridor and the spiral stair.

But before he got there an arm snaked out of the boys' bathing chamber, catching him by the collar of his robe. Jerked off his feet, Fyn was hauled into the bathing chamber, his heels dragging across the damp tiles. Galestorm's face, among others, whirled past him as he was spun around and around, then shoved across the room. The tiles were slick with steam and he fell painfully to his knees, skidding.

The bathing chamber was empty but smelt of soap and small boys. In front of him, Fyn saw a familiar wall mosaic illustrating Halcyon's blessings, stylised grain sheaves entwined with the beasts of the fields. It was reflected in a bathing pool. Steam rose off the water which had been pumped up from the hot springs below.

Fyn's stomach lurched as he came to his feet, turning to face his tormentors. He'd only just returned to the abbey and they were after him already.

Galestorm was with his usual followers, Onetree, Whisperingpine and Beartooth, and this time there was no Byren to come to Fyn's rescue.

'Not so brave, eh, kingson?' Galestorm asked, prowling towards him. 'See, I told you he was a coward. Are you going to beg?'

Fyn did not know what to say. Nothing would satisfy Galestorm.

'Just look at this place.' Galestorm gestured to the bath chamber, then clicked his tongue against the roof of his mouth. 'Filthy little boys. It needs cleaning. You can start in that corner.' He pointed to the far end of the chamber where grime had caught between the tiles. 'Clean it, with your tongue.'

Fyn stared at Galestorm.

'Are you disobeying a direct order, acolyte?'

Fyn swallowed. They weren't going to let him get out of this.

Galestorm stepped towards him. Desperate, Fyn darted forwards, elbowed Galestorm in the ribs, side-stepped Whisperingpine and shouldered past Onetree. He made for the door, only to be caught by Beartooth.

The big monk pulled Fyn's arms up behind his back and dragged him over to Galestorm, who rubbed his bruised ribs thoughtfully. 'You're going to be sorry you did that. But first I have some advice for you. I hear Master Firefox offered you a place?' When Fyn didn't answer, he nodded to Beartooth, who obligingly jerked Fyn's arms up behind his back.

Fyn bit back a cry. 'He did, but I refused.'

'Very wise,' Galestorm agreed. 'And you're going to keep refusing, because Onetree is going to be acolytes master, I'm going to be the history master, Whisperingpine is going to be clerics master, and Beartooth is going to be weapons master. But if you joined any of those branches that wouldn't be possible. So you go right on refusing.'

'I mean to.'

Galestorm smiled as if he didn't believe Fyn.

'Give him something to help him remember,' Galestorm said and walked out. Fyn ducked, trying to protect his vulnerable parts from the rain of blows.

A little while later, dripping wet and moving carefully, Fyn climbed the stairs. He ached all over and, he suspected, he would feel worse tomorrow.

Returning to the acolytes' bedchambers he changed into a dry smock and leggings, then went up to the hothouses. He was walking slowly as he made his way over to the gardens master, who took one look at him and led him to a quiet corner.

'You're late,' Sunseed said.

'I apologise, master.'

Sunseed studied him. 'They were careful not to leave any marks on your face.'

'How did...' Fyn began, then realised he had been tricked. 'I don't know what you mean.'

'Of course. And I'm not going to ask who did this. Take my advice. Stay with your friends and don't be caught alone. Do you want to go down to the healers?'

Fyn shook his head.

'Then follow me. We must check the starkiss buds. The mystics master thinks they will open tonight.'

Fyn's spirits lifted. Master Wintertide had never missed the blooming of the starkiss flowers and the beating had convinced him more then ever that he needed his old master's advice, for it wasn't possible to avoid being caught alone.

BYREN TOSSED AND turned, unable to sleep despite having pushed his men these past five days. Their camp, at the Upper Portal just over the border formed by Unistag Pass, was bitterly cold. The fire alternately cooked one side of him, while the other froze. He couldn't shake the feeling that Lence wanted him to fail on this mission and the thought made him sick at heart. If only he had never met the old seer, if only Cobalt hadn't returned to Rolencia to bring his views of foreign policy to Lence's ears. Of course, Lence would rather win power than marry power. Then, like a dog with a bone, Byren's mind would circle around to the other fear that ran under his every waking moment like a river running under the ice, waiting for spring to break free.

What could he do about Cobalt?

He couldn't confront Cobalt. There was a great deal of sympathy for him at court. And Byren had no right to reveal Orrade's secret. The dilemma was really Orrade's not his. It only became his problem if he was implicated. Frustration chewed away at the lining of his stomach. His instinct was to take action.

At last he rolled to his feet, wrapped his fur cloak tighter and went to check on the night watch. With his back to the fire, he closed his eyes for several heartbeats then opened them, sight adjusted for the night. The stars were bright enough to cast shadows now that he was out of the fire's range.

He sucked in a deep breath, but it left him unsatisfied. This pass was not as high as the Snow Bridge between Rolencia and Merofynia, but the air was thin. Even though Byren filled his lungs with each breath, he felt light-headed.

They were lucky, they hadn't run into any leogryfs, or centicores. And he hadn't seen any of the warlord's lookouts, but that didn't mean the lookouts hadn't seen his party. He had made no attempt to hide his arrival. This was an official visit, not a punitive raid. Here he was, at the Upper Portals, first camp over the pass and they still hadn't run into Unistag defenders. Odd.

He heard someone humming under his breath, recognising Garzik. Strange what men did to keep themselves awake. 'So, that's how you plan to warn our attackers of your presence?'

'Byren? Uh, sorry,' Garzik whispered, sounding shamefaced. 'I didn't think.'

'Not thinking can get you killed.' He didn't want to carry Garzik's dead body back to Dovecote estate. Not that the old Lord would let him in the front gate. Ah, Elina... somehow he had to make things right between them. For now he concentrated on the things he could control. 'Silence and vigilance. We are in the territory of a warlord who has not renewed his fealty oath.'

Garzik nodded and, with a touch on his shoulder, Byren moved on to the next man on night watch. Orrade's outline was hard to pick out against the rocks.

Creeping up as silently as possible, Byren whispered, 'No trouble?'

'Heard you coming,' Orrade muttered.

Byren could hear the grin in his friend's voice, and a reluctant smile tugged at his lips. He could never stay angry with Orrade.

'Couldn't you sleep, Byren?'

'I like doing extra night watches after marching all day.' He lowered his voice. 'Must keep an eye on your brother, Orrie. Garzik's a brave lad but he's got a lot to learn.'

Orrade sighed. 'I know. Were we ever that young?'

Byren laughed softly. He wished Orrade had never confessed how he felt.

Since they'd marched out of Rolenhold, Orrade had said nothing about his confrontation with Cobalt, even though Byren had made an effort to be alone with him on several occasions. Byren didn't know what to do. He couldn't believe Orrade would betray his plans to Cobalt, yet, considering the alternatives, he found it hard to think otherwise.

Taking a deep breath, he tried to broach the subject tangentially. 'It's a surprise to see Illien back, see him as Lord Cobalt.'

He felt Orrade stiffen.

'Do you know what he argued with his father over all those years ago?' Orrade asked.

'No.' Byren was surprised by the question. 'Lence and I were only seven at the time. The grown-ups never told us.'

'I think it would be worth knowing.'

'What are you saying, that Cobalt can't be trusted?' *Tell me*, Byren willed Orrade to speak, *tell me so that I can help you*. Though, in truth he did not know how he could help either of them.

'I did not say that. But I think it is odd that Utland Raiders risked the winter seas to attack Port Cobalt precisely when he was there.'

'He explained that. There were spies in Ostron Isle who knew he carried a king's ransom in jewels.'

Orrade let his breath out slowly. 'That sounds believable. But what of his bride? It's rare for raiders to kill women and girls.'

'An unlucky blow, I guess.' Byren didn't want to defend Cobalt, least of all to Orrade. He decided to throw caution to the winds. 'If you were in trouble, you'd tell me, wouldn't you, Orrie?'

'You mean apart from being disinherited and having the possibility of being accused as a Servant of Palos hanging over my head?'

'Eh!' Byren grinned, acknowledging a hit. 'But you're not a Servant of Palos, you're a...' He found he couldn't say it. The memory of Orrade in Cobalt's arms still made his blood boil.

Orrade snorted. 'A lover of men. Even you can't bring yourself to say it. And no one seems to be able to separate the two.'

Byren cleared his throat, aware that his face was flushed. He was grateful for the starlight that leeched colour from everything. 'I don't get it, Orrie. Many's the time you've gone wenching with Lence and I. What makes –'

Orrade turned to him. 'Many's the time you've bedded girls gifted by grateful villages, what made that last girl different?'

'I told you. Elina.'

'What about Elina?'

'I've given my heart and my body goes with it.' As the words fell from Byren's lips, he realised they were true.

Orrade said nothing with great eloquence.

Byren made the connection. Orrade loved him like that? He wanted to argue that Orrade's feelings for him were different, but honesty forced him to ask who was he to say? They had faced death together and lived. He had not shared that with Elina.

While Byren brooded over this, several shooting stars speared across the sky towards the pass. Star-rocks were highly prized by renegade Power-workers.

'What will you do when we get to Unistag Stronghold?' Orrade asked.

He had no idea. It all depended on how he found things. He gave himself a mental shake and checked the wandering stars. 'Almost time for the next watch. I'll go back and wake them.'

He would also check on the sentries on the other side of the camp. The path was narrow here with a big drop on one side. Jagged rocks poked through the powdery snow. The soft squeak of something heavy compressing the snow made him hesitate.

Whumpa.

Something collided with him, but because he'd hesitated he took a glancing blow to the shoulder and not the full impact. The foetid stench of a carnivore filled his nostrils.

Chapter Sixteen

As BYREN REGAINED his balance he found his sword was already drawn. Ideal for warriors, not so good for the predators. He didn't want to get that close. With a yell, Byren threw himself back. A dark head with blazing eyes speared into the place where he had been a moment before, jaws slashing. A second blazing-eyed head lunged. Two of them.

He yelled again.

His boot snagged on a rock as he tried to back up. His legs went out from under him. *Thump*. He hit the ground, almost losing his grip on his sword. Two sets of blazing eyes reared over him. He saw long necks, vestigial wings.

Still, he could not make sense of what he saw.

'Over here!' Garzik yelled to distract it, charging in from behind.

'Freezing Sylion!' Byren muttered. They didn't even know what they were fighting and Garzik was going to tackle it alone. Byren struggled to his feet and felt Orrade almost collide with him.

Against the starry sky Byren saw Garzik wrestling with a man-high snake. No, it had small forearms and vestigial wings. Where its tail should have been a second head reared up, eyes blazing like lamps.

'Amfina,' he warned. Both heads had to be removed before the beast died. If only the primary head was removed the secondary would become primary by growing horns, and the damaged end would sprout a secondary head.

Garzik screamed with pain.

Byren lunged in, attacking the secondary head which turned and went for him, jaws snapping. He jerked aside, swinging his sword, but the amfina weaved away. At least the primary head released Garzik. To attack him. It darted in before Byren could bring the sword up. He only escaped the lunge by throwing himself back on the snow, narrowly missing a large, balanced rock.

Orrade had already run around and was dragging Garzik out of reach of the Affinity beast. Garzik left an ominous dark streak on the snow.

The secondary head speared down. Byren rolled, bringing the sword up, straight into the creature's mouth. The head reared back, pulling the hilt from his hands which left him with only his hunting knife. Again.

'Help Byren, not me!' Garzik urged.

The primary head swung in an arc, going for Byren's face. He slashed, leapt and rolled. Luckily the injured secondary head was slowing the amfina down.

'Garzik, are you all right?' Captain Temor charged down the path with the others puffing behind. 'Byren?'

'Over here. Watch out. Amfina!' Now that the pressure was off him, he felt dizzy from lack of air.

Temor darted between him and the amfina, yelling to distract it. The old captain stumbled into a rock and lay still. Must have hit his head. There was little room to manoeuvre, too many rocks, narrow path, a terrible drop. The primary head swerved for Temor. Byren sprang to his feet. No point in attacking one head with a hunting knife and leaving himself open to the other head. He searched for inspiration; nothing but rocks and snow.

The other men-at-arms got in each other's way. Orrade stood over Garzik, prepared to defend him.

The secondary head writhed as it flung Byren's sword away. The weapon clattered, falling over the edge, striking rocks on the way down. Enraged, the amfina's secondary head turned on Orrade. He was the only person who did not back off, refusing to leave Garzik undefended.

Byren cursed again.

Throwing his weight behind the chest-sized, balanced rock, he thrust at it with all his might. It teetered. Muscles straining, he put his legs into it. The rock slipped off its perch, rolled and landed on the amfina's back. Pinned by the rock, the creature's two heads writhed, hissing in fury.

One of his men cheered and threw Byren a sword. He caught it, the hilt slapping into his palm. Now they could deal with the beast.

He ploughed in, distracting the primary head as he dragged Temor out of striking range. There was blood on his forehead but he was coming around.

Byren placed him next to Garzik and straightened.

'So that's why the pass was unguarded,' Orrade muttered.

Byren laughed, then took another deep breath. 'Why waste men, when a beast will do it for the price of a few tethered goats?'

The new warlord was a clever man. Byren stood back and let his men hack the amfina to pieces. With no Affinity warder to say the words, Byren whispered them hoping to settle the beast's innate Affinity. Then he and Orrade carried Garzik to the camp fire. Of course, the boy protested all the way. They peeled off his bloodied clothes.

'It's nothing,' Garzik insisted.

'You're lucky the amfina is not poisonous,' Byren told him.

Orrade and Temor caught his eye. The amfina's bite was not poisonous, but it was prone to going bad. Garzik would have to be treated by a healer, and soon.

'I'll wash the bite out with wine and pack it with herbs,' Temor announced. 'With his woolens and bearskin coat it isn't deep, but anything that breaks the skin is dangerous.' The bleeding from his head wound had slowed.

Byren nodded. 'Treat yourself, too.'

'I'll help,' Orrade offered.

'We'll ask the warlord's healer to take a look at Garzik,' Byren said.

Now there was even more reason to get down to Unistag Stronghold. Byren inspected the stars. 'Be dawn soon. We'll move out at first light. We'll need to build a litter for Garzik. Exertion will only weaken him.'

'I'm sorry,' Garzik croaked.

Byren laughed. 'You jumped in to save my life. I won't forget. It could have been me with the bite or worse.'

Garzik grinned, but already his face was flushed and his eyes too bright. Byren's spirits sank. It would break Elina's heart if anything happened to him.

Leaving Orrade and Temor to look after Garzik, Byren moved off to walk around the campsite, stopping to speak with the men and see how they had fared. He was annoyed because now he would be greeting the warlord from a position of weakness, needing a healer's help.

IN THE DARKEST time of the night, just before dawn, Fyn stood at Master Wintertide's side fighting exhaustion. They were surrounded by many abbey masters who had come to witness the starkisses bloom. Being allowed to attend was an honour, but he could barely keep his eyes open. If he could just stay awake long enough to escort Master Wintertide back to his chamber...

Sweat trickled down Fyn's face. Hot water – pumped up from the spring in the abbey's courtyard – usually kept the garden pleasantly warm, but tonight Master Sunseed had turned the heat up to encourage the flowers to open. The heat, the long sled trip and the beating all took their toll. Fyn felt so tired he caught himself drifting into a half-waking state where time slid past him.

Through the roof's glass panels he could see the night sky ablaze with stars. They were so thick in places that they formed clouds of rainbow brilliance. Blazing starlight filled the hothouse, also enticing the starkisses to bloom.

In their natural state these flowers were extremely rare and only the size of a thumbnail. The abbey's starkisses would be the size of an open hand when their petals unfurled, but in the selective breeding they had lost their hardiness and could only survive in the hothouse.

'The blooming is late this year,' Master Wintertide observed. His gaze met Fyn's and held it briefly. Fyn's heart lifted. His old teacher understood that he needed to speak with him.

'There have been years when the starkisses did not bloom at all,' the history master said heavily. 'Why, in the year of –'

'They will bloom this year,' Master Sunseed said.

'Hopefully it will be a good harvest,' Willowbark, the healers' master said. 'Our stock of dreamless-sleep is running low.' Seven of his healers waited to collect the pollen.

'Late blooming is a bad omen,' Master Catillum said. Behind him three of his mystics played an eerie melody on their silver flutes to entice the starkisses to bloom. Fyn could have sworn the petals vibrated in time to the high notes.

After that no one spoke for a while. Fyn shifted from foot to foot. He found his eyes drifting shut and forced them open. Finally, he leant closer to Master Wintertide to ask, 'Can't they peel the blooms open, then collect the pollen?'

'They could, but the pollen would not have its power. The starlight and heat trigger its potency.

Have a little patience.' Wintertide smiled. 'See, the first one is about to open.'

An expectant hush fell over the hothouse. Fyn watched the first flower's long white petals part with languid ease. As it opened an exotic scent filled the night, reminding him of oranges and musk. The scent made his groin throb and he felt himself harden. Luckily, his robe hid this. If it affected the others in the same manner, no one mentioned it. The mystics lowered their flutes and everyone pulled their cowls up over their mouths and noses, to escape the narcotic effect. Pure starkiss scent like this could cause hallucinations in those without Affinity and visions in those with it. Only mystics used the scent to induce visions and only under special circumstances.

Master Willowbark nodded to his healers. One monk stood by each starkiss waiting for the right moment to gently scrape the pollen from his flower's stamen. He had to leave just enough for the gardeners to ensure next year's crop.

The abbot sprinkled droplets of water, Halcyon's blessing from her sacred pool, on the plants and the harvesting began.

Master Wintertide let out a sigh of relief. 'I have seen many bloomings, yet I never tire of it. But now these old bones are ready for bed. If you're finished with Fyn, Sunseed, I'll have his help getting down the stairs.'

The gardens master waved them aside.

Fyn offered his arm to support Master Wintertide and they turned towards the door. At last he could unburden himself. Wintertide would know what to do. But he found the top of the stairs barred.

'That's the one,' Monk Galestorm said, pointing at Fyn. He was with the acolytes master, who Fyn now realised had missed the blooming.

'Fyn Kingson tortured the grucranes,' Galestorm accused.

A wave of outrage rolled over Fyn.

All the masters turned.

'So he's the reason our sentries have abandoned us,' Master Firefox said. 'His cruelty drove them off!'

'That's a very serious accusation.' The abbot looked from the acolytes master to the Fyn.

Galestorm nodded. 'My friends and I stopped him before he could injure more than one.'

'But it was one too many, for we are without our faithful sentries,' Master Firefox said, sounding rehearsed. Fyn marvelled that no one else noticed.

'It's not true,' he protested. 'I was trying to save the grucrane!'

Galestorm rolled his eyes and appealed to Masters Hotpool and Firefox. 'Of course he'd say that. But I have witnesses.'

'Who? Your friends?' Fyn countered.

'Three fellow monks, and Master Oakstand and Healer Sandbank –'

'Wait,' Oakstand objected. 'I didn't see Fyn hurt the grucrane –'

'But we did, my friends and I,' Galestorm insisted.

'Silence!' the abbot snapped, then beckoned Master Firefox. 'Acolytes master, isolate this youth until we can call the witnesses tomorrow.'

As Firefox turned towards him, Fyn appealed to the boys master. 'You know I would never hurt a person or an animal, Master Wintertide. Tell them.'

'I can tell them this, but I was not there so I cannot be your witness,' he explained regretfully.

Galestorm's gloating gaze fixed on Fyn. It would come down to the word of four monks against Fyn and there was nothing his old master could do. But why had Hotpool and Firefox put Galestorm up to this? Fyn's head swam.

BYREN WALKED BEHIND Garzik's stretcher, carrying the ends of the poles himself. If it had been flat ground, they could have dragged the stretcher behind the pony, or if they had been near a farm they could have borrowed a wagon. Instead, Byren carried the poles. The lad winced at every bump but did not complain.

They had been walking since dawn and now Byren's back and shoulders ached but all he could think of was getting Garzik to a healer.

Orrade led the pony. When it stopped and did not move, Byren took the chance to ease his grip on the poles.

'What is it?' Byren whispered. 'Trouble?'

'Can't see from here,' Orrade muttered.

Byren waited a moment, put the stretcher down gently and climbed up onto a rock beside the narrow path, shading his eyes. He couldn't see Temor who was leading them, because there was a bend in the path, but from his vantage point he could see the spar, a long ridge of rocky land with small valleys and narrow inlets, spreading out below him. Steep islands shot out of the jewel-bright sea. Even on the small ones terraced fields had been tilled and houses sprouted from the rocks. From each chimney a trickle of blue smoke rose on the still air. How many people lived on Unistag Spar? It was hard to know. He doubted if even the old warlord knew, if he still lived.

Byren jumped down. The pony behind him nuzzled his pocket, looking for oats. He chuckled. 'Not yet. We've a long way still to go before we camp tonight.'

He debated whether to walk to the front of the column.

Thwang.

The unmistakable sound of an arrow cutting the air made everyone duck instinctively. There was a clatter as the arrow skittered off the rocks ahead. The pony behind him whinnied, reacting to their fear.

'That's far enough,' a voice called. It sounded like a girl, or a boy whose voice hadn't broken. 'The next one won't miss.'

The man behind Byren muttered, 'Impudent whelp. Let me teach him a lesson, kingson.'

That was how things started, threats and counter-threats, and soon someone was dead.

Byren found a laugh. 'No. This one is mine.' He picked his way around the stretcher and horse, passing Orrade.

'Don't get yourself killed, Byren. Who'll carry the stretcher?'

He grinned as he edged along the path, past the men and pack ponies, until he came to Temor, who was stood with his hand on his sword hilt, back pressed to a rock wall.

'Up there,' Temor whispered, nodding to a ledge on the right which overlooked this part of the path.

'How many?'

'Don't know.'

'Turn around and go back,' the youngster ordered. 'Unistag Spar is closed to all merchants.'

'Do we look like merchants?' Byren asked, then laughed. 'Is this any way to greet King Rolen's delegate?'

There was silence. Good, he had them on the back foot.

'Well, where's my escort?' Byren demanded. 'I am Byren Rolen Kingson and I am here to meet the warlord of Unistag Spar.'

There were muffled mutters, then a boy of about twelve stepped out from behind a bend on the path to their left. They had them pinned.

'Are you the Byren who killed the leogryf with a hunting knife?' he asked.

Temor grinned. 'Everyone's heard of your leogryf slaying.'

'I told you it was true!' the boy yelled back to the person on the ledge.

A girl jumped down to join him. Byren was a little surprised to find two youngsters watching the pass. Still, it was midwinter, not generally a time for raids, and the warlord had left the amfina to guard the pass, so these two were only backup.

'You did not,' the girl countered. 'You said –'

'Enough!' Byren barked. The youngsters fell silent, responding to the voice of authority. 'Does the old warlord still live?'

'He died ten days ago.'

'Take me to the new warlord.'

The children exchanged glances. They were alike enough to be brother and sister.

'We'll take you to Lady Unace,' the girl announced. She was probably older by a year.

'Does she have a healer?' Byren asked.

They nodded.

'Good. The sooner we get there the better.'

Byren sent a man back to carry the stretcher, then continued on with the children. Happy to oblige, the youngsters fell into step with him, chattering away. According to them, when the old warlord died his nephew, Steerden, had taken the Stronghold, murdered all his rivals and claimed the spar.

This left only Lady Unace, and her infant son who had been smuggled out to safety.

'She's camped outside the stronghold now,' the boy explained.

'With all the warriors who served her brothers. The ones who escaped the castle,' the girl added. 'Lord Steerden can't get out and she can't get in.'

Great, Byren thought. *I'm walking into a stalemate with two dozen men, an injured youth and no real authority.*

If he was killed, his father and brother would seek revenge. But revenge did him no good if he was dead.

FYN WAS GIVEN some bread and watered wine at around mid-morning. He tried to make it last, but he had been smelling the buttered mushrooms, eggs and beans cooking on the floor below since dawn and his stomach rumbled in protest.

That had been hours ago. Now only a thin arrow of natural light filtered through to this inner chamber. He could tell by the colour and the way it was creeping up the wall, soon to disappear altogether, that it was past midday and still no one had come for him.

No. He mustn't think like that. He was innocent and he would prove it, somehow. His head ached because, try as he might, he couldn't see how Masters Hotpool and Firefox benefited from his disgrace. Galestorm's motivation was easy to see. For some reason this youth had always hated him.

If the ruling went against Fyn, the abbot would have two choices, cast him out or make him serve some sort of penance. If he was banished from the abbey he would be exiled from Rolencia because of his Affinity. The injustice of it made him pace from one end of his prison to the other. He was innocent, but how could he prove it?

When they came for him it was just before the evening prayer bell and he'd given up pacing, choosing instead to sit and meditate. The time elapsed made him wonder what had been going on behind the scenes. Had the history master made some sort of deal with the abbot?

The accusation must have undermined his chances of being accepted into any branch of the abbey. Before this, he had been worried which one to choose. Now he would be lucky if any of the masters accepted him.

His cell door swung open to reveal Feldspar and Lonepine. Feldspar looked worried, but then he always did.

Lonepine gave Fyn a wry grin. 'We're your escorts. We've offered to vouch for your character.'

But they were only acolytes and he'd been accused by four monks.

'Thanks.' Fyn's voice cracked from lack of use. He stood up and stretched. He was still wearing the same clothes he'd been in last night and he felt strangely distanced.

'Don't worry, Fyn. The abbot is a fair man,' Feldspar assured him.

Fyn nodded once. He just wanted to get this over with.

The walk to the abbot's chamber seemed to take forever. His knees felt weak. He hoped he wouldn't disgrace himself and fall flat on his face when he went down the steps.

The official greeting chamber was where the abbot met representatives when he wanted to impress them. Before today, Fyn had only been inside to polish the brass work and mop the floor mosaics. In niches around the room were statues of Halcyon, some dating from the earliest times. They ranged from crude stone effigies which showed her big with child, to a recent gold statuette from Ostron Isle which portrayed her as a young woman on the verge of womanhood, for Halcyon was the child-woman, the pregnant mother and the crone.

Under the greeting chamber's central dome was a flat circle then a series of concentric shallow steps so the chamber became a theatre in the round.

Fyn's friends escorted him to a spot opposite the abbot and then retreated to join a group of monks who had to be the other witnesses, some ready to vouch for his character, others ready to assassinate it. Galestorm sent him a stern look in keeping with the formality of the chamber, but there was a glint of malice in his eyes. It was clear he believed, with Fyn disgraced, the path to mastership and eventually the abbot's position would be open to him.

Had his future been so decided? Fyn hadn't thought so, but then perhaps he'd been naive. He caught Master Hotpool watching him and looked away quickly. What if all the other masters refused to take him and he was left with only Hotpool's offer? He'd have to serve the history master. Was that why he and Master Firefox had done this?

Panic threatened, making Fyn's stomach churn with nausea. He didn't want to be in Hotpool's power.

His gaze flew to Master Wintertide. Was there any hope? His old master's mouth remained immobile, but his deep-set eyes smiled and Fyn felt a little better. Like all the other masters, Wintertide knelt on a cushion on the fourth stone step so that Fyn faced a semicircle of masters, their heads one step above his.

The abbot nodded to the clerics master, who cleared his throat and read from a scroll. Another cleric waited with a scriber, ink and paper to take notes. A record of this hearing would go into the abbey's great archives. One day it would be dry, dusty history. Right now Fyn's heart hammered and his palms felt sweaty.

The master cleric's voice echoed in the dome above them. 'This hearing has been called to determine if Fyn Rolen Kingson did wantonly torture the abbey's grucranes and in doing so, drive them off. How do you plead?'

Fyn blinked. 'Innocent, of course!'

Then he heard himself and winced. He had sounded rude. Or perhaps his unguarded reaction would convince them of his innocence? Frustration flooded him. He didn't *know*.

First the abbot called on Galestorm to recount his version of events, which were corroborated by his three companions. Fyn watched them lie straight faced and wondered how they slept at night.

The weapons master could only confirm that he had come upon Fyn and the monks just as they had described it. 'They were running across the lake towards Fyn who had the grucrane wrapped in his cloak.'

'To protect it,' Fyn protested.

'Silence,' the clerics master warned, then dismissed Oakstand and called on healer Sandbank who confirmed what the weapons master had said.

'And then Fyn said to me "There's something wrong with his wing and I think he broke his leg when he hit the ice." Fyn was clearly concerned for the grucrane.'

'Because he realised how seriously he'd hurt it,' Galestorm insisted.

'Silence,' the clerics master snapped.

'Tell me, Sandbank, what happened to that grucrane?' the abbot asked.

'The break was a bad one. We could not save the bird. The grucranes seemed to know because they left the day he died.'

'And haven't been seen since!' Galestorm added with relish.

'One more comment from you and you'll be sent

outside,' the clerics master warned, but it was too late. The damage was done. Fyn's hopes sank as Master Hotpool exchanged looks with his crony, Firefox, then permitted himself a small, satisfied smile.

Master Wintertide came to his feet. 'Permission to speak, abbot?'

'You wish to vouch for Fyn's good character.' The abbot anticipated him. 'I know, and there are several more who would do the same.' The abbot fixed on Fyn. He was a small man of the same generation at Master Wintertide. His head was completely bald and a wispy white beard hung from his chin like summer moss from a branch. Fyn had not had much to do with the abbot, being only a lowly acolyte. The general feeling was that the abbot was fair. Fyn certainly hoped so.

'You have heard the accusations levelled against yourself, Fyn Rolen Kingson. What have you to say?'

It was his chance at last. 'I was trying to save the grucrane. It wasn't my slingshot that crippled the bird.'

'Whose slingshot was it?'

Fyn licked his lips. 'Monk Galestorm.'

'Why didn't you tell the weapons master this when he arrived?'

Fyn shrugged. 'I was worried about the bird and besides...' he heard bitterness creep into his voice. 'I knew it was my word against the word of four monks.'

The scribe scratched away diligently, while the masters muttered amongst themselves.

'This is a very serious accusation, Fyn,' the abbot said at last.

'Perhaps there is someone who can corroborate his version of events,' Firefox suggested, knowing full well there wasn't.

Fyn had never hated anyone before. The force of his emotion surprised him. He could not even look at the acolytes master.

The abbot turned to Fyn. 'Is there a witness who saw Galestorm take a shot at the birds?'

There was. The old seer had seen it all, but she was dead, killed by his brother. And who would have believed her anyway?

'No,' Fyn admitted. Yet he held his chin high, refusing to let his enemies know how he felt.

'I can vouch for Fyn,' Feldspar announced suddenly. He darted from his spot amidst the witnesses, dropping to his knees beside Fyn and bowing in apology. 'Permission to speak, abbot?'

'A character witness won't help now, acolyte Feldspar,' the abbot told him, though not unkindly.

'I have a confession to make,' Feldspar blurted, lifting a strained face to the masters. 'As much as I long to, I am not worthy of becoming a mystic. I did not find Halcyon's Fate, Fyn did. He gave it to me because he knew how much I longed to be a mystic. That is the sort of person Fyn is. He would never hurt a defenceless bird!' Feldspar turned a little so that he could bow to the mystics master. 'Forgive me, Master Catillum. I could not go into your service with a lie in my heart.'

Masters Hotpool and Firefox looked stunned. Obviously they had not planned on Feldspar's confession, though Fyn didn't see how it could help him. The other masters muttered, while the abbot consulted with the mystics master.

Finally Master Catillum turned back to Fyn. 'Is

this true, Fyn Rolen Kingson?'

Fyn dropped to his knees and prepared to lie. He had to protect Piro no matter what. 'I was not worthy. I only found it by chance and I knew Feldspar's Affinity was greater than mine, so –'

'You gave the Fate to him?' the mystics master marvelled.

Fyn nodded miserably.

Master Catillum frowned at Fyn. 'Tell me, when you touched the Fate, did you see a vision?'

Feldspar glanced to Fyn, who hesitated.

'The truth, lad,' Master Catillum urged. 'We have no seer and the abbey needs to know what the future holds.'

Fyn's face flamed. 'I saw Isolt Merofyn Kingsdaughter.'

The weapons master gave a bark of laughter, which several others echoed. A smile tugged at the mystics master's mouth. There were dismayed mutterings from several others.

'What does it mean?' Firefox asked.

'It means he's a normal young man,' Oakstand answered. 'With normal appetites.'

'It means he is not worthy of the abbey,' Hotpool snapped, 'being consumed with the hungers of the flesh.'

'And you'd be a shining example of abstinence?' Oakstand jeered.

'Silence!' the clerics master clapped his hands. 'The abbot wishes to speak.'

The abbot turned to the mystics master. 'What does Fyn's vision mean, Catillum?'

'It means there is a connection between him and the girl, not surprising since his brother is betrothed to her. His vision has no significance for the abbey. But of greater significance is the fact that he had a vision. I must have him for the mystics.'

Fyn's heart lifted. Piro might have found the Fate but the vision had been his. Then he noticed how Feldspar's shoulders sank. He wanted to argue that Feldspar's Affinity was stronger than his but he felt he was skating on thin ice. He shuffled his knees closer to his friend. 'I'm sorry.'

'It's all right,' Feldspar whispered. 'I shouldn't have agreed to take the Fate. It was weak of me.'

Guilt twisted in Fyn's gut like a thief turning the knife. He'd almost been just as weak. Piro had meant well, but look how her interference had complicated things.

'This hearing comes down to the word of an acolyte against the word of four monks,' the abbot began.

'Not just that,' the mystics master said. 'I could skim Galestorm's mind, see if I can find the truth.' Catillum's penetrating black eyes settled on the young monk who cast a look of panic to Masters Firefox and Hotpool.

'Tell the truth, lad,' Firefox urged, when Fyn was reasonably certain the master had coached the monk to lie for him. 'If the mystics master must plumb your mind it will be painful.'

And more might be revealed than whose slingshot hurt the bird? The acolytes' and history master's plans? Fyn fixed on Firefox, who cultivated a benign expression and tapped his chin once.

As if this was a signal, Galestorm fell to his knees. 'Forgive me, abbot. I was trying to protect Beartooth. Sometimes, he acts without thinking. He never meant to hit the grucrane, just give them a fright.'

Behind him, Beartooth, Whisperingpine and Onetree fell to their knees, foreheads pressed to the floor.

'It appears the hearing is over,' the abbot muttered and signalled the clerics master. 'See that these four are contained until we decide their punishment.'

The masters came to their feet, many of them in deep discussion. The abbot beckoned the clerics master and nodded in Fyn's direction. Lonepine made his way through the others to meet up with Fyn and Feldspar, who stood, massaging their knees.

'Well, that'll serve them right,' Lonepine said, the tips of his large ears red with excitement.

'Yes, justice. If only it were so simple,' Master Wintertide agreed as he joined them. He turned to Fyn. 'Why did you give Feldspar the Fate? Do you really feel so unworthy?'

Fyn wanted to reassure Wintertide but at that moment the clerics master came over and ordered Feldspar and Lonepine to escort Fyn back to his cell.

'But –' Lonepine objected.

'Fyn lied to Master Catillum,' Wintertide explained. 'This is serious, no matter how honourable his motivation. Take him to his cell and count yourselves lucky you are not staying there with him.'

'Come on.' Lonepine turned towards the door. When they left the masters behind, he whispered, 'You've certainly set the cat amongst the pigeons, Feldspar!'

'Master Catillum would have discovered it once I began training. To train your Affinity you must be open to your teacher.'

He was right. Fyn glanced back to the masters.

Hotpool and Firefox listened intently to the abbot and the mystics master. Catillum was sure to discover Piro's part in all this. How could he hide her guilt from a master who was able to skim the minds of those he trained?

'Hey!' Lonepine protested as Galestorm shouldered him aside while being escorted from the chamber.

'Ignore him. He's gone too far this time,' Fyn advised.

Feldspar nodded. They escorted Fyn back to the cell in silence, then they paused at the door. There was no lock, no guard. Honour held Fyn captive. After all, where would he go if he ran away? All of Rolencia would turn on him.

Feldspar cleared his throat. 'I may lose my place with the mystics, but I'm glad I did it. You don't deserve this, Fyn.'

'Don't worry, a seer is too valuable for the abbot to do more than give you some mild punishment.' Lonepine squeezed Fyn's shoulder. 'You'll be right.'

Fyn had to smile. If only his problems were so easily resolved. By trying to help, Feldspar had made things so much worse.

'Thanks. I guess, all we can do now is wait.' So he went into his cell and sat there stewing. If only Piro hadn't interfered. If only he had found the Fate by himself, then he would gladly accept his place with the mystics!

Chapter Seventeen

'So this is Byren Rolen Kingson, the leogryf slayer?' the woman asked. She could have been twenty-five, but her eyes looked older. Her hair hung in one battletale with seven gold links. Life on the spars was hard. Women fought alongside their men, sometimes by choice, often through necessity. 'And why are we honoured with your presence?'

'Lady Unace of Unistag Spar.' As Byren made his court bow, he decided she looked like the sort of person who liked plain speaking. 'The warlord of Unistag did not send a delegate to renew his oath of loyalty, so King Rolen sent me to ensure this happens.'

'You and twenty-five men?' Humour glinted in her black eyes.

Byren grinned, acknowledging a hit.

Her smile vanished. She strode to the canvas flap which hung in the doorway of the large snow-cave and flipped it open to reveal Unistag stronghold. Lit by the setting sun, it was built into the cliff opposite, projecting out from stone ledges. Layered and cantilevered, the whole thing looked like a strong wind would blow it down. The walled town spread down the slope to a narrow bay. The place was a rabbit warren, though Byren conceded it would be easily defended. From the stronghold's tallest tower a banner blew, a white unistag on a green field, the symbol of the spar.

'I was born there, along with my four brothers. When my father lay dying he called all his heirs into his bedside to elect a new warlord. But, before he could, my cousin Steerden had him suffocated, then he murdered my brothers, their wives and their children, my husband and little boy of six summers...' Her voice cracked, mouth twisting as she fought to hold back her grief.

After a moment she went on. 'The only reason I'm still alive is because the stronghold's healer and I were in Halcyon's chantry to have my ten-day-old baby receive his life-blessing. The monk smuggled us out.' She strode over to the cradle and lifted the infant for them to see. Startled by the move, the baby flung out both small hands, fingers spread as if to cling to life. 'If I fail to take back the castle, my son will not live to see his first birthday. If we flee Unistag Spar, my cousin will send assassins after us, for he cannot rest easy in his bed while little Uniden lives.' She hushed the infant and returned him to the cot then faced Byren. 'So I ask again, why are you here?'

He knew what she wanted to hear, that he could help her avenge her family and win back the leadership of the spar. Warlords were mostly male, but there had been some remarkable women who ruled the spars. However, he wasn't here to help. He could hardly send Temor back to Rolenhold to gather a small army, for though the warlords of the spar swore fealty to his father, they were princelings of their own kingdoms and Rolencia never interfered with their rule. If he brought in an army to make Unace warlord, he would be setting a bad precedent.

Even as he took a breath, he saw her shoulders sag. She had read his face.

'I'm sorry. It is not my place to intervene. I am here only to ensure the next warlord's fealty.'

'I thought as much.' She nodded, then glanced to an old monk. 'Monk Seagrass is our healer. I owe my life and that of my son to him.'

Byren nodded to the monk, who was small and slightly stooped because of a hump that rode his back, just to the left of centre.

'Seagrass will see to your wounded man.' Lady Unace met Byren's eyes. 'You are welcome to eat and sleep in our camp. If I become warlord I will swear fealty to King Rolen.'

Byren nodded, made uncomfortable because she was ready to give, when he could give nothing.

The healer collected his pouch of herbs. It was not customary for the monks and nuns to support aspirants vying to become warlord. Seagrass must have been motivated by his conscience.

'Garzik is this way,' Byren said and led Seagrass to a large snow-cave, which had been hastily erected for them.

Orrade watched everything the healer did, his anxiety palpable. Temor stood back but his sharp eyes missed nothing. Byren knelt by the fourteen-year-old while his wounds were cleaned and packed. Garzik did not let out a whimper.

'You're lucky the bite is only shallow,' Seagrass said as he mixed up a tisane.

Byren lifted Garzik so he could sip it. He was flushed and had been delirious earlier but was clear-headed now, if a trifle pale from the pain of the monk's ministrations.

'This will bring the fever down and fight the evil humours which had taken root in your body,' Seagrass told Garzik who nodded, wearily.

Byren wanted to ask what Garzik's chances were, but not in front of the lad. 'Watch over him, Orrie, while I walk the healer back to his snow-cave.'

'I share with the Lady Unace. I have been serving her family since before she was born,' Seagrass explained.

Byren nodded. Before he left he paused to ruffle Garzik's hair. 'As for you, hurry up and get well. I didn't bring you along so you could lie about while everyone else worked!'

Garzik managed a weak chuckle.

'I'll have him up and digging latrines in no time,' Temor announced.

Garzik gave a mock groan and Byren grinned.

But once they were outside he paused beyond hearing range of the campfires. Firelight flickered on the unfamiliar faces of Lady Unace's supporters. His own men clustered around a camp single fire, a token force unable to make a difference. It frustrated

Byren. He cleared his throat. 'Young Garzik, how –'

'Too early to say. I've seen men sicken and die from a single scratch and the amfina's bite is known to carry evil humours. But he is young and he believes he will recover. That could make all the difference.' The healer studied Byren, went to say something then hesitated.

'Speak freely,' Byren urged.

'I can see why the men follow you so willingly. King Rolen is lucky to have such a worthy son.'

Byren shrugged. He had no time for flattery.

The healer seemed to sense this and lowered his voice. 'If Steerden defeats Unace his fealty won't be worth a cockatrice's spit.'

'I know.'

'He has the townspeople and the stronghold's inhabitants terrified. Unace has their sympathy but they fear, if they support her and he wins, he will go hard on them. Anyone who can kill his own kin won't baulk at killing townspeople.'

'I know,' Byren repeated. 'But I don't have enough men to make a difference and even if I did, Rolencia can't be seen to interfere!'

'Then there's nothing you can do?'

Feeling frustrated and unjustly criticised, for he was bound to follow the law whatever his personal feelings, Byren escorted the healer back to the would-be warlord's snow-cave. It had been constructed between two outcroppings of rock and was larger and more luxurious than anything he built while out hunting. Just as well, for they were in for a long siege if the warlord could not be winkled out of his shell.

'Often it is not the truth that decides someone's fate but people's perception,' Seagrass said. 'Your young friend has a better chance of recovering because he believes you expect him to. The people of Unistag Spar already believe Unace's cause is just, they need to believe that she can win. They need a sign from the gods!'

Byren uttered a short laugh. 'And how do you propose I arrange that?'

HE WAS STILL stewing over what the monk had said when he arrived back at his snow-cave. Orrade met him at the entrance.

'How is he?' Byren asked.

A grin broke through the serious lines of Orrade's face. 'I swear he's improving already.'

'Good. Get something to eat. I'll watch over him.'

Orrade nodded and left. Byren hesitated at the entrance. From here, he could see Unistag Stronghold and the fortified township that spilled down to the valley floor but only as pinpoints of light. The emblem was visible as a flapping flag, black against the brilliance of the stars' sparkling froth. But he knew the white unistag, had known one all his life.

As an idea struck Byren, he smiled slowly. Turns out he *could* arrange a sign from the gods!

His heart rate lifted as he examined his plan looking for flaws. It would take time but they had time, five days' forced march for Temor to travel back to Rolenhold, a day to collect the tame unistag and sneak it out of Rolenhold, five or six days to bring the beast here.

The people of the spar must not know his part in this. He'd have to lure Unace back to the pass so that he could introduce her to the beast. Then, when she rode into the camp on the back of a white unistag (lucky for them Rolenhold's menagerie held a white), they'd see it as a sign from the gods.

Byren grinned and silently thanked his grandfather for establishing the menagerie. It was not as large as it once was because god-touched beasts like the unistag tended not to breed except in the wild. All the other beasties had died off and, as far as he knew, this was the last unistag in captivity. It had been fading away, only to rally recently.

And the people of Unistag Spar would not realise this was the famous Rolencian unistag for it had not ventured out of the menagerie since it had been captured as a foal. By Halcyon, it had to be nearly forty years old. He hoped it was up to the climb over the Dividing Mountains. With a shrug, he put that aside, as being out of his control.

Under his control was how events unfolded here.

It would be best if he and Unace appeared to have a fight, and then he could march off with his men. If the camp thought Rolencia had abandoned them then it would have even more impact when Unace rode in on the unistag.

Yes, he would send Temor directly to his mother. She was sure to grasp the elements of his plan immediately.

Feeling lighter of heart, Byren ducked and entered the snow-cave. 'What, still lying about, Garza? I expect you to be up and on duty by tomorrow!'

The boy chuckled, sounding stronger still.

THIS TIME IT was the acolytes master who escorted Fyn to the abbot. He had lain awake all night considering his options. The abbot would agree to the mystics master's claim on him. Come spring cusp, Master Catillum would undertake his training and then he would uncover the truth about Piro, for Fyn feared he could not hide it. There was only one thing to do. Before spring cusp, he would have to leave the abbey.

Leave Rolencia. Unthinkable.

But, once contemplated, the unthinkable became possible.

The abbey had taught him many useful skills. He would never become a sell-sword, but he could weave, cook, garden and look after animals. He would run away and earn his living somehow. His hair would grow back to hide the abbey tattoos.

Master Firefox escorted Fyn to the abbot's private chamber, overlooking the abbey's courtyard. Fyn glanced through the arched windows. Far away, across the patchwork of winter-mantled canals and fields, loomed the Dividing Mountains. Rolenhold stood on its protective pinnacle, painted in shades of lavender and blue. Piro was there right now, pretending to have no Affinity. Fyn felt heart-sick, for his parents would never understand why he'd run away from the abbey. He would be dishonoured in front of everyone, branded a coward. But he had been over and over it and he could see no other solution.

He looked around the chamber for the mystics master but Catillum was not present, only the abbot. Fyn hid his surprise.

'Thank you, Firefox,' the abbot dismissed the acolytes master. When he had gone, the abbot came out from behind his parquetry-inlaid desk and sat on a stool in front of the fire. 'Come here, lad.'

As was proper for an acolyte, Fyn knelt on the cushion at the abbot's feet. While the abbot stared into the flames, Fyn wondered what his punishment would be.

At last the leader of the monks sighed. 'Your presence in the abbey makes things very complicated, Fyn. All the masters seek to have you in their service. They believe that one day you will be abbot.'

'But I would have to earn that position,' Fyn argued.

The abbot merely looked at him. 'You are a clever young man, thoughtful beyond your years. By giving up your place in the mystics to your friend you displayed unusual humility. Or was it fear, Fyn?'

'Fear?' he repeated, thinking furiously. Had he betrayed Piro in some way already?

The abbot nodded. 'There are many who fear the power that great Affinity brings. Some even try to deny theirs. It is your destiny to serve the goddess through the mystics. You cannot deny Her, Fyn.'

He nodded. It seemed Master Wintertide had convinced the abbot his lie had been prompted by the fear he was unworthy. He would be given to the mystics and he would have to run and everyone would think him a coward, motivated by fear.

In that instant he realised it did not matter what they thought, as long as he did what he believed to be right.

'Fyn?' the abbott prodded. 'Is there anything you wish to tell me?'

Fyn licked his lips then shook his head. What could he say?

'Very well. This spring cusp you will join the mystics. You can go back to your rostered duties, Fyn. Once the gardens master has finished with you, you can serve the mystics.'

He stood up, bowed and backed out. At the door, he hesitated.

'Ask,' the abbot said.

'It was Galestorm, who shot the bird, not Beartooth.'

'I know. Sixty years in the abbey have taught me to recognise a bully and a liar. I don't have to be a mystics master to see the truth.'

Fyn blinked. 'They why...'

The abbot sighed. 'Galestorm and his companions are backed by powerful masters, who seek to cripple me through you. Do you understand?'

Fyn nodded, though he wasn't sure he did, wasn't really sure why the abbot was telling him this.

'I could not clear you of the accusation without a confession. Feldspar's revelation made it abundantly clear what sort of person you are. Anyone who gives up power because he thinks he does not deserve it would not wantonly harm a defenceless creature.'

Fyn swallowed. 'What will happen to Galestorm and the others?'

The abbot smiled. 'Their penance is to serve the livestock master. They are currently mucking out the stables.'

A laugh escaped Fyn.

The abbot grinned. 'I believe the punishment must fit the crime.'

Fyn discovered he liked the abbot. He bowed and backed out into the hall. No wonder the abbot and Master Wintertide were fast friends, they saw the world in the same way.

It was a pity he had to let them both down.

The thought made him feel heart-sick, again. If the abbot knew the true extent of Fyn's crime, what punishment would he assign him? Deeply saddened, for he had several true friends in the abbey who he would be sorry to disappoint, Fyn headed back to the acolytes' sleeping chamber.

He had until spring cusp to plan his escape.

With a start he realised he would miss his parents' Jubilee. Worse, Piro would think he'd deserted her.

PIRO TICKLED THE foenix's chest. 'How's my pretty?'

His chest scales were becoming more pronounced. Eventually they would be hard as armour to protect him in mating fights. She wasn't sure how long it took for a foenix to mature but she hoped they would be able to capture a female for him.

'Here he is, Temor,' her mother said, her voice carrying in the quiet of the menagerie.

Piro came to her feet, creeping between the hothouse plants. What was her mother doing here with the captain? Had Byren come back?

They had entered through the far door and now they stood in front of the unistag enclosure. The creature had a stall, fresh hay and space to wander but Piro had always felt sorry for him. He should have been wandering the high mountains, lithe as a mountain goat. Instead he'd spent all his life here, after being captured as a new-born by her grandfather, founder of 'Mad King Byren's menagerie.'

Temor lifted a horse's halter and stepped through the gate, advancing on the unistag making soft noises. It would have worked with a horse, but this was an Affinity beast, never meant to wear a halter.

The unistag reared, spinning on its rear legs, cantering off to the far side of the enclosure.

Her mother opened the gate and entered. 'I'll herd it towards you.'

'That will never work,' Piro told them, climbing onto the top rail of the fence. Her foenix flew up to land next to her.

Both Temor and her mother gave a guilty start, which intrigued Piro.

'You can't capture a unistag, you must woo him.' She jumped down. 'Go back and let me show you.'

It was only when they latched the gate that she realised how dangerous this was. The unistag had been one of her friends for years, but more recently it had become very fond of her because she let it absorb the excess Affinity from her skin by licking her fingers. This had helped her limit her use of dreamless-sleep. She hated the way the drug made her feel thick-headed and stupid. Since she'd begun feeding the unistag her unwanted Affinity, the beast's coat had improved and its spiral horn gleamed again.

It trotted over, intelligent silvery eyes fixed hopefully on her, velvet muzzle quivering, but she didn't want to betray her Affinity in front of the others. She gathered her will to halt the build-up, finding it harder than she'd anticipated. It had become habit, and habit was hard to break. Too late, her fingers tingled with unwanted Affinity and the unistag snuffled eagerly. She put her back to her mother and Temor in the hope that this would hide what she was doing. The exchange worked on touch, so it was very isolated. She prayed that unless someone was looking for Affinity, they would not notice.

The rasping tongue of the unistag tickled and she smiled as she stroked his muzzle.

'There, see,' she called over her shoulder. 'He's friendly really. You just have to know the way to go about it. Why do you want to put a halter on him anyway?'

When she turned to face them, the unistag nuzzled her neck giving her goose bumps.

Temor and her mother exchanged glances.

'Could Captain Temor lead the unistag across the Dividing Mountains?' her mother asked.

Piro laughed. 'He couldn't lead him out of the enclosure.'

'But the unistag will follow you?' her mother prompted.

Piro nodded.

Temor sighed. 'We'll have to tell her. It won't work without Piro.'

'She'll have to go with you,' her mother agreed, not sounding pleased at all.

'Go where?' Piro asked, consumed with curiosity.

'But that means she will have to stay with the unistag as long as it is needed,' Temor countered.

'She'll need a disguise,' her mother said. 'I'm sure I can rig something to make her look like a goatherd from Unistag Spar. We've plenty of props in our stage craft chest.'

'I'm going to meet up with Byren?' Piro pounced on this eagerly.

Temor cleared his throat. 'It will be dangerous. Warlord Steerden is a ruthless man and even if this works, Lady Unace still has to take back the stronghold.'

'I'm going to help Byren win the warlord of Unistag's loyalty?' Piro guessed.

Her mother fixed on her. 'You'll have to obey your brother implicitly.'

Piro nodded. She could do whatever she liked. Byren always forgave her.

'No running off on escapades of your own.'

She shook her head. Only ones that would help Byren.

'You'll have to keep your mouth shut,' Temor warned, 'or your accent will give you away.'

'Arrh, but you're wrong there,' Piro countered.

A surprised laugh escaped Temor.

Her mother smiled. 'You always were a quick study.'

Piro basked in her mother's approval for a change.

'Very well,' the queen said. 'Temor, get Seela to pack enough food for the journey. No one must know you've been here. You'll leave as soon as possible.'

He hurried off.

Piro couldn't stand still, could hardly believe her luck.

'Come here,' her mother beckoned.

She darted over, stepping through the gate as her mother opened it. The queen snatched Piro's hand and lifted it to her face to inhale.

Piro froze. Could her mother sense the Affinity she'd used to lure the unistag?

Queen Myrella's eyes widened and Piro's heart missed a beat.

'You reek of Affinity. Why didn't you tell me, Piro?'

'Seela said –'

'Seela knew?'

Piro nodded. 'She told me not to tell you because you would be disappointed.'

The queen let her hand drop. She looked pale and her fingers trembled visibly. 'Oh, Piro. I am so sorry. Your father will be devastated.'

'We don't have to tell him. We can hide it,' Piro insisted. 'After all, you've been hiding yours for years!'

'Seela told you about me?' Her mother went even paler.

Piro nodded. 'I've been careful, just like you.'

'You just gave yourself away!'

'But only because you knew what to look for,' Piro insisted.

'The abbey mystics know. Our Affinity warders will guess –'

'They haven't so far and my Affinity came on at autumn cusp.'

'You'll give yourself away. I know you.' Her mother sank to sit on the lower rail of the enclosure, head in her hands.

Piro rubbed her back and the foenix came over, making soft interrogative noises in his throat. Piro knelt to reassure him, as well as her mother. 'I won't slip up. I stood right next to the mystics mistress at midwinter and she sensed nothing.'

Her mother lifted her face to Piro, black eyes swimming with tears. 'You've no idea what it means to live your life as a lie. Sometimes, I... but then I look at you children and think, if I'd joined the abbey, I wouldn't have you. Only now you and Fyn are both cursed. Oh, Piro, I'm so sorry!'

And then her mother... her proud, regal mother... burst into tears.

For a moment Piro stared, stunned. Then she put her arms around the queen's shaking shoulders. Tears stung her own eyes. She laughed at herself. 'Oh, Ma. It's not so bad. It's not like anyone's died!'

Her mother pulled back. 'But don't you see? It means the seer was right. And if she was right about us being alike, what else was she right about?'

The seer had forecast death for the queen's loved ones. Piro fought a moment's panic, then rallied. 'But the mystics mistress said there are many possible future paths. We're lucky we know about this one. Now we can make sure it doesn't happen!'

Her mother smiled through her tears, visibly regaining her composure and strength of purpose. 'I'm lucky to have you, Piro. For you the cup isn't half full or half empty, you're always topping it up.'

Piro laughed and her mother joined her. It felt good.

BYREN HAD TIMED everything and planned for every contingency. He knew how long it would take Temor to trek back to Rolenhold and how long it would take to return with the unistag. If Temor arrived at the Lower Portals, the camp below the pass, before Byren did, he was to wait for him just off the track in a cave Byren had chosen.

Today was the day he had to fight with Unace and storm off with his men. She had been quick to understand his plan and embellish it, suggesting that he march off about mid-afternoon and then she could reconsider overnight and follow him the next morning, seeking reconciliation. This would explain how she happened to be in the high mountains to find the unistag.

Byren hadn't warned his men to pack. Their reaction had to look authentic. Lucky for him, the wait had given Garzik a chance to recover and he would be well enough to make the journey.

'There you are, Byren,' Unace announced as she strode into the open area in front of her snow-cave. They wanted a public place for the fight. 'I'm getting tired of this waiting game. My fighters need to be home by spring cusp to put their crops in. I need to take the stronghold and avenge the murder of my kinfolk.'

'I understand but my hands are tied,' Byren protested. 'I could support you if the warlord of another spar attacked Unistag, but not with an internal war.'

'What kind of man are you?' Unace demanded. 'Here I am, wronged, cast out, facing a ruthless kin-killer and you –'

'I can't –'

'You can't do anything. You're useless!'

There was a hushed intake of breath. The healer, who was the only other person to know of their plan, stepped in to play his part.

'Lady Unace,' he pleaded. 'Think –'

'Too late,' Byren snapped. 'Rolencia has been insulted. I cannot stay.' He glanced at the sun as if to gauge how much time he had before nightfall. 'We'll march now.'

'Lady Unace?' Seagrass repeated.

'Good riddance,' she snapped and strode into her snow-cave.

As Byren went back to his snow-cave, news travelled apace with him. Old fighters sent him worried looks, young men muttered under their breath. The scattering of women, some camp followers, the rest shield-maidens, exclaimed at the news then discussed the argument, their high voices carrying above the men's.

The healer caught up with Byren as if to try and persuade him to stay.

'We'll meet you at the Lower Portals, midday tomorrow,' he confirmed.

'All being well, Temor should be there with the unistag,' Byren whispered, then raised his voice. 'No. I won't be insulted. Tell her she can come crawling to me!'

By the time he entered his own fire circle the men knew. They were gathered uneasily, waiting for him.

'Orrie, see to the packing,' Byren ordered. 'We march as soon as we're able. I won't spend another night in this camp.'

Orrade left Garzik's side and approached him, speaking softly. 'Byren, stop and think. If Rolencia pulls out now –'

'Warlord Steerden may hear of it and open the gates to attack. So be it!' It had been a possibility he had discussed with Unace. People would think him ill-tempered and hasty. He'd thought himself ready for this but, now that he saw the disappointment in Orrade's eyes, he was surprised by how much it stung. Byren wished he could have been honest with Orrade of all people, but the fewer who knew about this trick, the more chance it had of succeeding.

He consoled himself with the thought that they would reach the Lower Portals just after dusk, where Temor and the unistag would be waiting just out of sight.

PIRO PERCHED ON the ledge, watching the track below the Lower Portals, while trying to ignore the butterflies in her stomach. Now that their meeting was imminent, she realised Byren was not going to be pleased to see her, but she had their mother's support. As far as the rest of Rolenhold knew the kingsdaughter was in bed with a sore throat, refusing to see anyone but Seela.

Above her the sky gleamed like mother-of-pearl, but here on the steep slope twilight cloaked the jagged rocks. Chilled from sitting still for so long,

Piro blew on her hands to warm them. The soft snort of a tired pony made her listen intently. Yes. They were coming.

She jumped from the ledge, running down the path to meet them and test her disguise. Would Byren and the others recognise her?

Taking up a stance, she leant against a rock, watching them come round the bend.

The first man-at-arms was tired and grumpy, obviously not looking forward to making camp in the dark.

'Out of the way, goatherd,' he muttered, brushing past her.

She stepped aside and let them pass. They hardly cast her a second glance. Out of devilment she fell into step beside Garzik's pony which Orrade was leading.

'Spare a coin for a poor goatherd, kind sor?' she whined, holding up a hand and cringing as if she expected to be kicked.

Orrade barely glanced at her, eyes on the track ahead. Garzik looked tired and his gaze went right through her. That's right. Temor said Garzik was recovering from the amfina bite, that explained Orrade's distraction. Trust Garzik to get in the way of an enraged amfina.

Piro spied Byren leading another pony.

'Spare a coin for a poor goatherd, kind sor?' she repeated, hand extended palm up. 'Please, sor.'

Byren frowned and felt in the pony's pack, pulling out a roast chicken wrapped in calico. He tore off a leg. 'Here, take this and be off with you.'

Piro contained a bubble of laughter and accepted the chicken. She was hungry after all. 'Is that all you can spare, sor?' She winked as she said it.

Byren blinked, and stepped off the path, handing the pony's lead to the man behind him. He lowered his voice. 'Piro? What are you doing here?'

'Hush. I am a simple goatherd.' She danced in front of him, just stopping herself from hugging him. 'And I'm bringing the unistag. What made you think he'd go anywhere with Captain Temor?'

Byren frowned. 'Does Mother –'

'She knows.' Piro rolled her eyes. 'I can't wait to meet this Lady Unace. Does she really have a battletale with five kills?'

'Seven,' Byren said with a smile, but his eyes held worry.

'Come on.' She danced ahead of him. 'I'll lead you to the cave where Temor's hiding the unistag.'

Byren signalled to the last man who was waiting for him to catch up and called, 'I'm going to see if this goatherd's got any decent cheese for sale.' He diverted from the path and fell into step with her saying, 'I don't know, Piro –'

'Don't worry. I can pretend to be a goatherd for a day or two. Then you can get Lady Unace to gift the unistag to Rolencia and I'll escort it home. No one but you and Temor will know.'

Byren looked grim. 'A fine plan, but things never go according to plan. I learnt that on my first raid.'

Piro ignored his gloom. She was out of the castle and having fun for a change. And she didn't intend to go back to the restrictions of her old life. Knowing

that she could get away like this would make the days
when she had to do the castle accounts bearable!

Chapter Eighteen

BYREN STRAIGHTENED UP, flexing his shoulders and looking around the camp. It was mid-afternoon and he'd told the men he was giving Lady Unace time to reconsider. He intended to stay at the Lower Portals so Unace could send him a message when she retook the stronghold. Then she would welcome him into Unistag Castle and give the oath of fealty as arranged. That meant Piro would be on her own for only a few days. He would have to let Unace into the secret of her identity. He only hoped nothing went wrong while Piro was out of his sight. He checked the angle of the sun. Unace would arrive at the cave soon. He wanted to be there when she did.

'Ho, Orrie,' Byren called. 'Think I'll go see if that goatherd's got any more cheese for sale.'

Without waiting for a reply he set off down the path then stepped off it, following an almost invisible path to the cave itself.

Piro gave him a wave and continued to groom the unistag.

'You'll spoil the beastie,' Byren told her.

'We want him looking his best,' she said.

'Where's Temor?'

'Looking out for Lacy Unace.'

'As I live and breathe I don't believe it,' Orrie muttered coming up the path to the clearing in front of the cave. He held back, turning to his brother. 'Would you look at that, Garza, a tame unistag. The only other one I've seen was in Rolenhold.'

Byren cursed softly. He had hoped to keep this from Orrade. Not that he could see a way for Cobalt to discredit him with it. 'What are you two doing here?'

'Watching your back,' Garzik said. 'We wouldn't be true honour guards if we didn't.' His gaze wandered past Byren to the unistag. 'You weren't after goat cheese at all.'

Byren was struck by the similarity between the brothers. Garzik's injury and fever had left him thinner of face, more like Orrade.

Across the far side of the clearing Piro continued to brush the unistag's coat, humming a song that Seela used to sing to them as children.

'That goatherd,' Orrie whispered, 'there's something odd... why, it's –'

'Piro!' Garzik gasped.

Piro's face fell and she crossed to join them. 'How did you guess?'

'And that is the Rolenhold unistag.' Orrade turned to Byren. 'What are you up to?'

'Lacy Unace needs to break the siege. Only a sign from the gods will do that, so I've arranged for one.' Byren smiled at their surprise, then noticed Piro's frustrated expression. 'You were humming one of Seela's songs. That's what gave you away.'

Her eyes widened. 'I'll have to be more careful.'

Byren's conscience stabbed him. He was mad to send Piro into danger. But Rolencia needed the Unistag warlord's loyalty and he needed the Unistag's support of Unace, so he needed Piro.

'What's she doing here in this disguise?' Orrade asked.

'Piro was the only one who could get the unistag to behave.' Byren heard his own voice, a mixture of pride and annoyance.

Orrade swore under his breath. 'You'd never catch Elina dressed in rags with dirt under her nails, grooming an Affinity beast!'

'That's for sure,' Garzik muttered, but he sounded admiring rather than amazed.

Temor's deep voice could be heard, answered by a higher one.

'Lady Unace is coming,' Byren warned. 'Bring the unistag over here, Depiro.' He added for Orrade and Garzik's benefit. 'That's what we're calling Piro. Don't forget. It's the spar version of her name.'

She clicked her tongue against the roof of her mouth and the unistag picked its way over to join her. When it did she wound her fingers through the unistag's mane and whispered to him.

Within a few moments Unace and the healer entered the clearing. Both of them stared at the white unistag. Nimble as a mountain goat but twice the size, fiercely shy and independent, unistags were rarely sighted. To see one calmly standing with several people was enough to make anyone stare.

'Lady Unace, Monk Seagrass,' Byren greeted them.

Unace laughed softly and approached him cautiously. 'You said you'd do it, and you did. I shall never doubt you again, Byren.'

'Indeed,' Seagrass marvelled. 'When Unace rides into camp on this unistag no one will doubt the gods are with her!'

'No.' Byren's lips twitched. 'But there is one small hitch. You'll have to take this disreputable goatherd with you.' He nodded to Piro, who beamed through her dirt.

PIRO BROUGHT THE unistag to a halt in a hollow just before the first camp lookout. She patted the beast's neck as Unace climbed onto the healer's cupped hands and gently swung onto the unistag's back. The beast shuffled, made uneasy by the sudden weight. Piro had accustomed him to carrying her on the journey to the spar. Luckily, he was sturdy despite his forty years. Piro suspected the unistag would never have lived so long in the wild.

'I feel strange with no reins to hold,' Unace muttered. Piro could tell she was still awed by the beast, which had walked beside them all afternoon on their way back to camp.

'Use your knees to guide him,' Piro explained. 'He's gentle really, but if he gets frightened he'll try to gore his attacker.'

Both the healer and Unace looked worried.

'That's why I'll be just to one side, in front of you,' Piro reassured them. 'He knows me. If he can see me he'll stay calm, and I can help if he gives you trouble.'

Unace nodded. 'Very well, Pi – Depiro.'

It was one of those sunny winter afternoons when the snow seems sprinkled with sparkling diamonds and shadows are so rich a blue it made your eyes hurt to look at them. Piro never felt happier.

Unace wore her woolen cloak of emerald-green, and carried a hastily embroidered emblem, the white unistag on the green background. She had confessed to Piro that the white material was made from Ostronite silk and had been cut from her best chemise.

'Ready?' the healer asked.

Unace met Piro's eyes. 'I am, if you are.'

Piro nodded, repressing her uneasiness, for if the unistag panicked, she would have to call on her Affinity to soothe it and she feared the healer would notice. As one of Halcyon's monks, he had been trained to recognise and deal with untamed power.

Piro pressed her forehead to the unistag's cheek, to whisper soothingly. While she spoke, she concentrated on warm, safe images. 'It is a beautiful afternoon, King Unistag, and after so many years you are coming home. Stand tall and proud. No harm will come to you.'

Then she pulled back and smiled up at Unace. 'Ready.'

Piro and the healer fell into step ahead of the unistag. As they rounded the bend a greeting cry echoed across the rocks, followed by a startled exclamation when the lookout spotted the unistag.

Piro straightened her shoulders and inhaled deeply, smelling the camp's cooking fires: roast lamb with sage tonight. Her stomach rumbled. She was hungry, but first they had to get through this.

The lookout had been waving madly and, when they breasted the crest, people already lined the path. Beyond them, she saw the camp spread across the steep slope. It was hard to pick because their shelters were snow-caves, only the smoke of cooking fires giving them away.

The healer began to hum under his breath. Piro recognised the tune, a spar song of praise for their icon, the unistag. She took up the words, thankful for her mother's tutoring.

In awe and wonder, Lady Unace's warriors dropped to their knees, some in the snow, others on the bare rocks, and a deep-throated version of the song sprang from many fighters' lips, embroidered by the high voices of the shield-maidens, who harmonised around them.

Piro glanced behind her. Unace sat astride the unistag, black hair dark against the vivid green cloak, pale skin glowing in the afternoon sun. She carried the spar's emblem so proudly, no wonder her people responded.

The sound of their voices carried across the deep valley to the castle opposite where helmeted heads bobbed and pointed. Piro nudged the healer. 'Look. They've seen her on the castle battlements.'

'They'll be sending for Steerden now.'

After that it was all a blur. When Lady Unace reached her snow-cave, an area was cleared for the unistag. Then her supporters crowded around. While Unace debated the best course of action with her supporters, Piro cared for the unistag, rubbing him down and sneaking him treats. The unistag was unsettled by the many visitors.

The healer joined her, studying the unistag with great interest. 'I find it hard to believe this is the creature King Byren the Fourth captured thirty... nearly forty years ago,' he whispered. 'The beast looks so well. I'm sure they don't live that long in the wild.'

'Good food and a safe life,' Piro said, growing uncomfortable.

'We should all be so lucky,' he said, with a grin.

She smiled. She liked him, couldn't help it. With his crooked back, he was only a little taller than her and he reminded her of a fragile but clever bird.

'The unistag is an Affinity beast. I suspect that he needs more than food and a warm stall.' Seagrass stepped closer, offering his palm to the unistag who snuffled hopefully. 'I've read of rare people who could share Affinity with the god-touched beasts.'

Pretending she did not understand what he was hinting at, Piro yawned and stretched. 'I'm tired. Where do I sleep?'

The healer glanced down to the carpet-covered ground. 'Here, beside the unistag would be best.' He lowered his voice. 'Don't worry, your secret is safe with me.'

Her guilty gaze flew to his face, then she realised she had given herself away.

'In Rolencia all those with Affinity must serve the abbey or choose between death or banishment,' she whispered. 'The warlords all agreed to follow father's law on this. Why risk yourself to keep my secret?'

'I have seen Unace and her brothers grow into adults, seen their children born.' Tears glistened in his old eyes and his chin trembled. 'I never thought I'd see the day they were all murdered by a kin-slayer!'

Tears of empathy blurred Piro's vision.

He managed a sad smile. 'Sleep, little goatherd. You can trust me.'

Piro nodded. It would kill her to lose her family.

'Sleep,' he repeated.

Piro made herself comfortable with a rolled-up blanket for a pillow. The unistag knelt beside her and dozed. The drone of the adults' strategy discussion echoed in her ears but Piro did not mind. She was finally living out an adventure as she had always longed for.

It felt as if she had only just fallen asleep when there was a distant but ferocious clashing of metal and yelling.

Piro rolled to her knees, calming the unistag reflexively. Unace opened the canvas flap. The healer lit a lamp and joined her at the entrance. Piro went over to peer into the night.

'An uprising in Unistag Stronghold,' Seagrass said.

Around the camp, people came out of their snow-caves, trying to see what was going on. But, though the stars were bright enough to cast shadows, events in the Stronghold remained obscure.

'I can't tell what's going on,' Piro whispered in frustration.

'They deal in death,' Unace replied with a shiver. 'I've known the Stronghold men-at-arms and servants all my life. I'm guessing they've turned on Steerden and his warriors.'

'Will they succeed?' Piro asked, then cursed herself. How would Unace know the answer?

'We'll know tomorrow,' Seagrass said softly as he draped a blanket over both their shoulders.

'Thank you,' Unace whispered.

'It is cold, you haven't had much sleep, Unace,' he said.

'I can't sleep, not while my supporters are fighting for their lives,' she replied.

Like Unace, Piro felt she couldn't sleep. So they huddled under the blanket, watching the Stronghold. Light gleamed in a row of high windows.

'Those are the warlord's private chambers,' Unace whispered. Her small son woke and cried. She fed him.

Piro let his tiny fingers curl around her little finger. He was a marvel. 'So small but strong.'

'He will have to be, with his father and brother dead,' Unace muttered.

'Byren told me,' Piro whispered. 'I'm so sorry.'

'I can grieve later. Right now I must avenge them.'

Piro couldn't bear to think of anything happening to her family.

A fire broke out, sending sparks showering up through one of the stronghold's slate roofs.

'The armoury,' Unace whispered.

Eventually the stars faded and the world took on grey form as dawn crept across the hillside. By the time the sun had come up, the fire was under control and only a smudge of dirty grey smoke hung over the Stronghold in the still morning air.

Unace stood up, returning her son to his cradle and stretching. 'Better get ready, Pi – Depiro. I plan to ride right up to the gates and demand entry.'

Piro nodded. She had listened to them debate all possible alternatives last night and it seemed the night's uprising would not change their plans. Flanked by her best fighters, decked in their finest, Lady Unace would approach the town. She hoped the townspeople would open the gate and take their chances.

If Unace and her people got that far, they would march right up to the Stronghold gates, backed by their most experienced warriors. If the usurper Steerden had not been overthrown last night, he might just be tempted to make a sally, hoping to wipe her out for good. This would entice him out of the Stronghold, which made him vulnerable.

Even if Steerden didn't venture out, someone inside the Stronghold might be convinced that the gods favoured her. They just might open the gates. If Unace and her supporters got inside, after the night's fighting Steerden's defenders might have been weakened enough for them to retake the Stronghold.

There were a lot of 'mights,' but it was their best chance. Who knew, perhaps Unace's people had already retaken the stronghold. It was hard to tell with the spar's emblem flying undisturbed.

Unace kissed her sleeping son, all bundled in his woolen blankets, and looked over at Piro. 'Ready?'

For today's assault Unace wore the green cloak again, but this time she wore chain mail and carried her weapons.

'Ready,' Piro agreed, mouth dry, heart racing.

'Remember, if the fighting starts, don't stay by me, run and hide,' Unace warned. She held Piro's eyes. 'Promise me this, if I am killed run back here, rescue my son and take him to Rolencia. He can grow up as a stable hand in your castle. As long as he has a chance to grow up!'

Emotion closed Piro's throat. She could only nod.

It was enough for Unace, who put her hand on Piro's shoulder. 'Thank you. I am lucky to have met you and your brother.'

Piro managed to swallow.

Seagrass returned. 'We are ready, Unace.'

Piro walked the unistag out of the snow-cave into the crisp first light. It was a clear morning, so sharp and bright the air was cold enough to make her chest ache. She glanced up at Unace, who had taken her position on the unistag's back. It was hard to believe that this woman, who only moments before had been breastfeeding her infant son, could soon be dead. Everything was so sharp, so beautiful.

Is this what Byren and Lence experienced every time they led a raiding party, this amazing clarity of perception?

Then suddenly they were moving, with Piro trotting along beside the healer. Apart from Seagrass and Unace, no one knew who she was, or cared. Back in Rolencia there would have been explanations if a goatherd turned up in the royal party, but here, with the chaos of the camp and the excitement, she was overlooked.

Unace's people cheered as they passed. Piro thought the spar warriors looked very fine. Not as good as her father's honour guard, when they turned out for a special event, but good in a more ferocious way. She could sense their common purpose. The intensity of their feelings called to her Affinity.

She glanced quickly to Seagrass. If he had noticed anything he did not reveal it.

Down the steep zigzag path they strode. Someone had crept out early and shovelled the snow. Uneven cobbles filled the gaps between exposed rocks, that was about all there was in the way of a road. The lower they marched, the higher and more imposing the Stronghold and its fortified town appeared.

As they rounded the second-to-last bend, Piro caught a glimpse of a bridge over a frozen stream. The bridge was only wide enough for a cart, but sturdy. The spring melt would make the stream a raging torrent.

The bridge was lost to sight as they made the last turn. Then they faced it and the entrance to the town's gate. Piro heard Unace's unconscious sigh of relief, for the people had seen their old warlord's daughter approaching and made up their minds.

The gates were open.

Anxious but hopeful faces lined the streets.

The unistag gave a nervous snort. Piro soothed it with a touch and they crossed the bridge. There was no cheering.

One voice called, 'Welcome home, Lady Unace.'

'Welcome me after I've rid my stronghold of vermin!'

There was laughter and several cheers. The healer began to sing and Piro joined him in the unistag song of praise again. Soon a full choir of voices carried the tune as they wove up the steep main road to the Stronghold gates.

Piro craned her head up and, in a gap between the teetering second storeys of houses, she saw the tall stone battlements of the stronghold. It still did not compare to Rolenhold – too many wooden protrusions – but it was an amazing sight. Several heads watched them from the crenellations, but there was no way to tell if they were Steerden's supporters.

'Can you tell if the stronghold had been retaken?' Piro asked.

'What news from the stronghold?' Unace called to the crowd as they rode by.

A man ran up to walk at her side. 'No news, Warlord Unace. There was shouting and fighting last night. But none of us dared approach.'

Piro didn't blame him as he fell back.

'Not far now,' Unace muttered. 'We'll know soon enough.'

Piro licked dry lips.

They rounded the bend to see the stronghold's portcullis being raised. The ropes creaked on the winches. A dark tunnel no deeper than a cart's length stretched before them, ideal for pouring hot oil and flaming torches on an enemy. And beyond that was the first courtyard, the killing ground. If this place was anything like Rolenhold it would have numerous slits in the buildings for archers to fire down on the invaders. But a clever invader could form a tortoise by wedging their shields together and proceed under cover.

At the sight of the opening portcullis, a cheer broke from the ranks of their supporters.

Piro's heart lifted.

'Let's go,' Unace urged, but the unistag balked.

Piro touched his muzzle, letting him sense the build-up of her Affinity, yet holding back so that he would follow her. Seagrass caught her eye, giving a small nod of approval.

Entering the dark tunnel made Piro shiver. She fixed on the paved courtyard, swept free of snow. They were so close to victory. Byren's ploy had worked. She was proud of him and proud to be here with Lady Unace.

The courtyard was empty.

Unace urged the unistag into the centre, twisting from the waist to look around.

'Where is everyone?' she muttered, then raised her voice. 'I'm Lady Unace, daughter of warlord Uniden and I claim this castle in my own right!'

Her people cheered.

Still no one appeared.

'Open the doors to the great hall so we may celebrate!' Unace swung her leg over the unistag's back and dropped to the ground lightly. She strode towards some steps.

'No!' Seagrass leapt forwards, shoving Unace in the back so that she sprawled on her hands and knees on the bottom step.

The arrow caught the healer in the hump. A murmur of horror and cries of protest filled the courtyard.

'Seagrass?' Unace scrambled to him as he collapsed, gathering him in her arms.

Piro was close enough to hear him whisper, '...knew it was too easy.'

Then the doors of the great hall swung open and a man swaggered down the steps, flanked and followed by heavily armed men. He carried the symbol of Unistag Spar, a white unistag horn set on top of a staff.

'Steerden!' Unace swore under her breath. Releasing the monk, she sprang to her feet. 'Kin-slayer!'

'*Warlord* Steerden!' he corrected. Then he used the unistag-horned staff to gesture to the walls which overlooked the courtyard. 'I have two dozen of my best archers in position. You are dead where you stand. All of you.'

Piro glanced behind her. There was nowhere to run. No way to get back to save Unace's infant son.

It wasn't supposed to end this way.

This wasn't a fireside song. There were no guarantees. And she was powerless to help herself, let alone anyone else, as blood seeped from under the healer's torso, dripping down the steps.

The unistag reared, startled by the smell of blood and the sudden rise in fear which emanated from those around them. Piro could feel it too. She caught his neck and soothed him, concentrating on her hands, so that the overflow of her Affinity came through her skin, calming him as she stroked his muzzle.

'But first I must have that unistag,' warlord Steerden announced. 'Then everyone will know that the gods favour my rule.'

What manner of man could murder his own kin, many of them children? Piro stared at Steerden, trying to understand. A strange buzzing filled her head. The world shifted.

Her knees went weak and she had to lean into the unistag to keep her balance. Nausea roiled in her stomach as her vision blurred.

Feeling strangely detached, she realised she was seeing the Unseen World. When she looked at Seagrass, kneeling on the ground, a warmth pulsed from him, brightest where he bled. The same warmth pulsed from the unistag, glowing around her hands.

But around warlord Steerden the waves pulsed differently, distorting everything, blighting it. This made no sense, unless...

...he had Affinity and it had made him a channel for evil.

'He has untamed Affinity,' Piro whispered.

Steerden's eyes widened. He fixed on her.

Panic swamped her. With his Unseen sight had he seen her, recognising her own Affinity?

She could see him gathering his power, focusing it. And she knew, he'd corrupt her with his taint, just as he would corrupt everything he touched. He had to be stopped.

The unistag responded to her terror. Leaping forwards, it lowered its head. Horn as long as a short sword, it charged Steerden, shouldering Unace aside.

Time stretched for Piro. The warriors at the warlord's side reached for their weapons, but they were too slow. The unistag mounted the steps and speared the warlord through the chest, just under the ribs. The horned staff flew from Steerden's hand, clattering on the stones.

With a wrench, the unistag lifted Steerden off his feet and swung its head, knocking the warlord's supporters off the steps. Then the unistag staggered under the man's weight and fell to its knees.

Piro sprang forwards, afraid her beast had been shot by one of the archers. But, as the warlord slid off the unistag's horn, the creature regained its feet, snorting and shaking so that it nearly fell on the shallow stairs.

She caught its muzzle and wiped the foul blood from its beautiful horn with her own hands. Tears steamed down her cheeks. It horrified her to see the unistag's purity sullied by Steerden's evil taint.

'There. It's over, King Unistag,' she whispered. And in that heartbeat everything returned to normal. Her Unseen vision faded, leaving her weak-kneed and bleary eyed. She staggered, falling to her knees on the steps near the dying warlord.

Steerden clutched her arm, fingers biting into her flesh, dragging her close to him. Bright blood bubbled on his lips as he fought to speak. 'Who are you?'

She stared at him, no longer able to see the taint of his Affinity.

He grimaced with pain. 'Who –'

'Are you all right?' Unace demanded, catching hold of Piro and hauling her upright.

She nodded.

Unace stood over Steerden, staring down at him. 'I wanted to see you suffer for killing all my kin. This is better. I'm not stained by your death.'

Seagrass gasped with pain as he reached for the horned staff. His hand closed on it and he struggled to lift it. 'Warlord Unace, take this.'

She blinked and accepted it from him with a smile of acknowledgement. Then she straightened up and raised her voice, turning to the others with the horned staff held above her head. 'The gods have spoken!'

There was a cheer. It startled the unistag, which reared, backing down the steps. Piro ran after the beast and went to rub its muzzle, but sensed the taint on her hands and stumbled, stiff-legged, to the well, where she hauled up a bucket and thrust her hands into its cold, cold water... rubbing, rubbing and whimpering.

From a distance, she heard someone sobbing. It took her a moment to realise it was her. She felt as if she could never get clean, yet there was nothing to see, just a feeling of sick miasma which clung to her.

The unistag nudged her, snuffling her neck. Its breath was hot and fresh with clean Affinity. It was trying to reassure her. She laughed with relief. Arms around the unistag's neck, she cried and laughed the evil away.

Chapter Nineteen

WHEN PIRO FINALLY lifted her head to look around she felt drained, but refreshed. Everything was sharp and clear.

And everything had changed.

The evil warlord's body had been removed, leaving only a bloody patch on the steps. Unace was trying to convince Seagrass to go into the hall with the help of some of her supporters, but he refused to leave her side.

Unace's people must have rushed up into the towers and buildings that opened onto the courtyard, for now they escorted the warlord's supporters, who had all surrendered. Shoving them to their knees in front of Unace, the spar warriors stood back waiting to see justice done.

'Do you want us to kill them?' one of Unace's men asked.

'Spare us, warlord Unace,' they moaned. 'Spare us.'

The new warlord stared at them, her mouth set in a hard line.

Piro held her breath, sensing this was a significant moment. Her stomach turned at the thought of seeing thirty unarmed warriors slaughtered without mercy.

Leaning heavily on a shield-maiden, Seagrass spoke up. 'I know you, Bearclaw. I healed your wife when she nearly died birthing your son.' He nodded to another. 'I know you, Whiplash, I treated your toothache.'

'Yes,' Unace whispered, voice growing in strength. 'I know you all. Many's the time we dined at my father's feasting table. Why did you do it? Why did you follow Steerden? How could you kill innocent children?'

It was a cry from the heart. Some of the men and women dropped to the cobbles, heads on the stones, moaning.

'Kill me! I am unworthy,' one cried.

'I cannot live with what I've done,' another pleaded.

'Then why did you follow Steerden?' Unace demanded.

All shook their heads, unable to explain it.

Piro understood. They had been swayed by the warlord's tainted Affinity. The same might have happened to her and she hadn't even thought to use the wards Fyn had taught her. The heat of shame flooded her, then drained away, leaving her light-headed.

A moment before, Unace's supporters had been ready to slay their captives, now some wept openly, many looked confused but a few were still angry.

'What happened to my kin is too great a crime to let pass unpunished,' Unace said, her voice hard. 'By the laws of Unistag Spar your lives are forfeited!'

Piro shuddered. She did not want to see the paving stones run red with blood. Too much had been spilt already. The unistag nudged her as if sensing her distress.

'Wait.' She ran to Unace, tugging on her arm to whisper. 'Let the unistag decide the fate of these warriors.'

Unace fixed on her and Piro held her breath as the new warlord debated.

'Yes.' Unace glanced once to the bloody stain on the steps, where Steerden had died. 'Let the goddess decide.' She raised her voice. 'Bare your chests to the unistag's horn. If you are truly remorseful, the unistag will spare you.'

Eagerly, Bearclaw undid his sword belt so he could take off his chain mail. 'I cannot go back to my wife and child, after what I've done. Let the gods decide my fate.' And, with that, he pulled off his chain mail and padded vest.

His chest was broad, covered with slabs of hard muscle, the pale skin scarred from old wounds. Piro could see the pulse beating madly in his throat, but he did not falter.

Though Steerden's death was still fresh in their minds, the rest of them eagerly tore off their chain mail and opened their padded vests to reveal their hearts.

Piro became an instrument of the goddess, as she walked slowly between the kneeling warriors, with the unistag at her side. Too tired and stunned to try to use her Affinity, she had no idea what the unistag thought they were doing as it followed her, keeping close enough to touch. Each time she passed a warrior they stared up into the unistag's eyes, baring their souls, searching for something.

It took her a moment to realise they needed forgiveness.

Like her, they had been tainted by Steerden's Affinity. She had washed his blood off her hands, but he had turned them to an evil purpose and they needed to be cleansed. So this was why the abbeys feared untamed Affinity.

When every last one of them had confronted the unistag and lived, Piro looked up at Unace expectantly.

'You are all forgiven,' the new warlord announced. 'Go home to your families, plant your crops, build, don't destroy.'

Bearclaw placed his hand on his heart. 'I beg a boon, warlord Unace. I beg to serve you if you are ever in need.'

'And I,' echoed the others.

'I am honoured to accept your service,' Unace said.

In sparing their lives, she had won their loyalty. If Warlord Unace had begun her rule with the slaughter of these warriors she would have begun it in blood and so stained her leadership. Piro felt relieved that they had all come through this test, but now that it was over she was so tired she could hardly keep her eyes open.

Unace took Seagrass's free arm. 'I am blessed by good-hearted supporters. Come into the great hall, everyone! Time to forgive and feast!'

They cheered.

Once inside, Piro discovered she was hungry. She took her seat at the high table, hardly able to think straight. Unace ordered someone to fetch her baby and another to recall Byren Rolen Kingson. There was so much to think of when you were a ruler. Piro was glad she was not a warlord.

Servants came up from the kitchen with platters of cold meat, sliced preserves and day-old bread. Piro could just imagine the poor cook madly scrambling to serve up a breakfast feast without warning. Still, there was enough for everyone. While the others ate and talked, Piro slipped treats to the unistag. Having eaten her fill, she just wanted to curl up and sleep. The spot in front of the big fireplace looked good.

THAT EVENING BYREN strode into the great hall of unistag Stronghold to see Lady Unace in her place as the new warlord. Clearly unhurt, she sat at the high table with her infant son in her arms. The healer still looked pale from his wound. Byren had been given a full description of how they won the day and, as soon as he had formally greeted the new warlord, he looked around for Piro.

'Are you hungry, Byren? You must be!' Unace decided. 'Today has been one long feast but I'm sure the cook can find enough to feed you and your men. I owe you a debt, kingson, and I won't forget it!'

'Where's Piro?' he whispered.

She smiled. 'Our goatherd is by the fireplace.'

Byren spotted Piro, asleep like so many other exhausted supporters. And not far from her, in pride of place, was the unistag. Someone had taken down the large emblem from above the fireplace and spread it on the floor. The Affinity beast knelt on its namesake, dozing in the heat.

'After what happened today, the unistag must stay,' Unace told Byren.

He nodded.

Unace frowned. 'But when your sister leaves...'

He understood. How were they to resolve this? Much as he liked Unace, he didn't want to leave his sister here. 'I must speak with Piro.'

He weaved his way through the tables and sleeping bodies to kneel at Piro's side. Curled into a ball, hand near her mouth, she looked absurdly young. He touched her gently on the shoulder.

Like a warrior on a raid, she woke instantly. He saw fear and horror in her eyes, making his heart lurch with guilt. Then she recognised him and beamed. 'Byren!'

'Yes, little goatherd. I hear you have been busy. Come up to the high table.' He stood, pulling her to her feet.

She laughed and went to hug him, then remembered that she was meant to be a goatherd and gestured to the busy hall. 'Did you ever think your ploy would be so successful?'

He smiled slowly. 'It is everything I hoped.' Then he sobered. 'But we have a problem. The unistag must stay here, Piro. I know you're fond of –'

'Oh, I agree. He must stay to validate Unace's rule.'

'Validate Unace's rule?' Byren teased, then rubbed his jaw thoughtfully. 'I don't see how it can be done since he is so attached to you.'

Unace's infant son gave a lusty squall. Byren glanced towards the high table to see the new warlord feeding her baby. It was an odd sight, but considering how warlord Steerden maintained his power through fear, having a warlord who personified the goddess Halcyon would reassure the people of Unistag Spar. Seagrass poured Unace a drink and adjusted the cushion behind her.

'Don't fret, Byren,' Piro announced. 'I know how we can keep the unistag happy.'

She darted away towards the high table just as servants arrived with platters of hot food, beef and sage stew, freshly baked bread and cinnamon apples for his men. Byren's stomach rumbled appreciatively and he headed towards his place at the table.

He only hoped Piro was right. But for now he concentrated on eating while noting that she was speaking very seriously to the healer, who seemed to agree with her. Strange, before today he would have said Piro was hardly more than a wilful child. Now, he felt inclined to trust her judgement.

TWO DAYS LATER, still in her disguise as a lowly goatherd, Piro waited to leave Unistag Castle. The rest of Byren's men had loaded their pack ponies, ready to leave. She scratched at a flea bite and wished the formalities finished. It had been fun to sleep on the floor with the servants, and go where she wanted with no one to question her. But there were disadvantages. How she longed to get home so she could have a bath, rid herself of fleas and change into clean clothes!

Warlord Unace cleared her throat and the crowd in the courtyard fell silent. 'As a symbol of the loyalty of Unistag Spar I present Byren Rolen Kingson with the horned staff.'

Her people cheered. They did not begrudge him

the staff, not when they had a live unistag in their hall. Piro grinned.

'I accept this staff on behalf of Rolencia. May there always be friendship between our people,' Byren said, giving a courtly bow that would have made their mother proud. 'We will see you at the Jubilee celebrations this spring cusp, warlord Unace.'

Byren wrapped the unistag staff in a cloak and strapped it onto the nearest pack pony, then turned to leave. As Piro went to take her place in the line, Seagrass caught her arm.

'Little goatherd, listen to the advice of someone much older than yourself,' he whispered. 'I sense no evil in you but you saw what became of Steerden. As a boy there was no evil in him either. When you go home, tell King Rolen and Queen Myrella the truth. Go to the abbey and serve Sylion. The mystics mistress will teach you how to keep evil at bay. And you will have the satisfaction of knowing that you serve Rolencia to the best of your ability.'

Piro gritted her teeth, staring at the pony's rump in front of her nose. She liked the healer but she didn't want go to the abbey and she didn't want to lie to him.

He touched her arm softly. 'I will be coming to Rolencia for the Jubilee. If you have not revealed your secret by then, I am honour-bound to reveal it.' His voice dropped. 'Please don't make me do that.'

'I understand,' Piro said and, as the line moved off, she moved with it. She understood but she didn't want to serve Sylion. She didn't know what she was going to do.

She had until spring cusp to work something out.

'QUICK, OFF YOU GO,' Byren told Piro as they entered Rolenhold's main gates. His sister had to sneak into her bed chamber, where she would make a miraculous recovery from her sore throat and be present to greet him in the great hall, when he officially returned.

While they travelled back she had played his servant. With only Garzik, Orrade and Temor any the wiser, the rest of the men had thought nothing of her caring for the ponies, cleaning his boots and cooking his dinner. Funny thing was, Piro had thought nothing of it either, never complaining.

'See you inside,' Piro whispered, then blended into the busy stable yard, just another servant.

Garzik slid his pack off his shoulders, passing it to Orrade. 'Think I'll go after her, make sure she gets in safely.'

'Don't.' Byren caught his arm. 'She won't thank you.' He grinned. 'In fact, she'd probably say you were in the way.'

Orrade nodded. 'Piro isn't in need of your protection, little brother.'

Garzik grinned sheepishly. He seemed unable to make up his mind whether to be outraged by her unorthodox behaviour or impressed. Byren suspected he was veering towards impressed.

Temor came over. 'We're ready.'

Byren nodded.

The grizzled old captain put a hand on his shoulder. 'It was nigh on impossible, but you did well.'

Byren felt the heat race up his cheeks. 'With your help.'

Temor nodded. 'A good leader knows the strengths of his men and how to use them.'

Byren cleared his throat and unstrapped the unistag horned staff then turned to face the others. 'Ready?'

Orrade and Garzik nodded.

It was good to return successful. What would his mother and father say? And Lence?

Would Orrade run straight to Cobalt and reveal the ruse Byren had used? And if he did, how would Cobalt turn this knowledge to his advantage? The only sour note in the whole campaign was the fact that Orrade hadn't trusted him enough to reveal Cobalt's threats.

SINCE SHE WAS supposed to be recovering from her sickbed, Piro put up with wearing a shawl. There had been no time to speak with her mother. As soon as word of Byren and his party's return reached them, everyone had gravitated to the great hall, eager to hear his news. Now Piro stood on one side of her mother, with Lence and her father on the other.

Her heart lifted as Byren strode into the hall with Temor and the others at his back. He held the staff, its horn gleaming. With each step he took, its base struck the stones, the sound echoing off the ceiling above.

People muttered, pointing and marvelling.

'By the look of things, Byren has been successful,' her mother whispered approvingly.

'King Rolen, Queen Myrella.' Since he had been on a mission for Rolencia, Byren greeted them formally. With a flourish, he flicked the staff's end up so that it lay horizontally across his open palms. 'I present the horned staff of Unistag Spar as a symbol of Warlord Unace's loyalty.'

King Rolen accepted the staff and the crowd cheered. Lence shifted impatiently.

'Well done, Byren.' Their father handed the staff to the queen and marched down the two steps to congratulate him and his men.

Piro would have run down but her mother took her arm firmly, saying, 'You must not make yourself ill again, daughter.'

Piro flushed and nodded. Her mother's keys of office chinked elegantly with each step as they descended from the dais. Ever since Piro could remember, they had been a symbol of the queen's power. She was the hub of the castle and the hub of King Rolen's world.

Piro now knew that she could never be the kind of woman her mother was.

What was she thinking? If she did not confess her Affinity and retreat to the abbey, monk Seagrass would reveal her deception. She glanced swiftly to her mother, who was smiling at Byren, and her heart faltered. By failing to hide her Affinity she had let her mother down. She would have to confess her failure, but not yet.

'Byren.' The queen hugged him. Their father had moved along to congratulate Captain Temor. Young Garzik was telling him about the amfina attack and offering to show off his new scar. Her mother smiled and met Byren's eyes. 'I'm sure you have some interesting stories to tell.'

Piro could hear the teasing laughter in the queen's voice, because no one else would ever know the ploy

Byren had devised. His trusted men were sworn to silence and, as far as the menagerie keepers knew, the unistag had died of old age and been buried. Her mother had only had to take Halcyon's Affinity warder into her confidence because Autumnwind had to hold a mock ceremony to be sure the beast's Affinity returned to the goddess's breast.

'And no more scars, thank Halcyon!' Byren grinned.

Just then King Rolen called for his finest Rolencian red and the men moved off to celebrate. Their father put an arm around Lence and Byren. 'Now nothing can spoil our Jubilee Celebrations. When we line up with all our warlords to greet King Merofyn and his daughter, he'll –'

'That reminds me, father,' Byren said, gesturing to the staff in his mother's hands. 'Lence was saying he wished he had a unistag horn to give King Merofyn to replace the one that was stolen... well, here it is!'

King Rolen glanced to the queen. 'Give it away? What do you think, Myrella?'

She studied the horn on the end of the staff. 'The greater the gift, the greater the giver. Lence would –'

'Excellent!' King Rolen beamed and retrieved the staff from the queen, thrusting it into Lence's hands. 'A handsome betrothal gift from the future son-in-law to King Merofyn, eh?'

Lence studied the horned staff.

'Handsome indeed,' Cobalt said. 'Your twin does you great honour, Lence.'

'I don't know what to say,' Lence muttered.

'No thanks needed,' Byren told him, then hesitated as if he would say more, but didn't.

'Well...' Their father filled the silence. 'Come, let's hear how it went.' And he led Byren off, leaving Lence with the horned staff.

Lence and Cobalt strode after Byren and their father.

'Now tell me the true story,' the queen whispered, linking her arm through Piro's. 'The one that your brother and father won't hear!'

'Can we go to your chamber?' Piro asked softly.

Her mother took one look at her face and agreed.

Three floors up, they sat in the queen's private solarium, alone but for Seela who seemed to have a nose for trouble. The outer room, usually filled with chattering ladies, was oddly silent as Seela stirred up the coals in the ornately tiled warming stove.

Piro held out her hands, but no heat reached her. She was cold from the inside out. Aware of her mother and old nurse waiting for her to begin, she took a deep breath. Best get it over with. 'The warlord's healer, Monk Seagrass, sensed my Affinity. I must go to Sylion Abbey voluntarily or he will reveal everything, when Warlord Unace comes for the Jubilee.'

'But how –' Seela began.

'He saw me quieten the unistag with my Affinity.'

Her mother's shoulders sagged. 'Only a monk could have sensed this. The chances of one being present... but I should have –'

'Don't blame yourself,' Seela insisted. 'It's bad luck, Sylion's luck.'

Her mother just shook her head.

'I'll have to go to the abbey,' Piro finally admitted, then turned to her mother. 'Can I stay for the Jubilee? Please? I don't want to miss it.'

The queen nodded and swallowed. 'We can tell the mystics mistress and the abbess the "good" news when they come for the celebration. Make a formal announcement.' She met Piro's eyes, her own shimmering with tears. 'I'm so sorry –'

Piro dropped to her knees and threw her arms around her mother's waist. 'It's not your fault. Who would have thought you'd have two children with the Affinity?'

Seela rubbed the queen's back. 'A curse on unwanted Affinity.'

Piro's mother lifted her head, brushing tears from her cheeks. 'It's not so surprising, really. I never met him, but I suspect Rolen's father had it, too.'

'King Byren the Fourth?' Piro sat back on her heels.

'Why else do you think he collected god-touched beasts? In fact, I think Rolen's older brother, Piren, also had Affinity.' She hesitated, then seemed to make up her mind, holding Piro's gaze intently. 'Rolen once described how they died –'

'On the battlefield, killed by a Merofynian renegade Power-worker,' Piro supplied.

Her mother nodded. 'There's more to it than that. They were in the tent with Rolen planning the dawn battle. Suddenly, the Affinity warders rushed in and began a chant to ward off evil power, but before they could finish it, they fell to their knees vomiting blood. Without their protection, King Byren and Piren clutched their heads, went into convulsions and died. There was nothing Rolen could do. At barely eighteen, their deaths left him king of a country at war. Don't you see? If Rolen'd had the same Affinity, he would have died along with them. His father and brother were susceptible –'

'To evil,' Piro whispered. 'But why didn't it affect father? On Unistag Spar, Steerden's evil Affinity tainted everyone around him.'

'Over time, Affinity can seep into those who would normally be unaffected by it,' her mother said. 'It wears down their natural resistance.'

'Oh.' Seagrass was right. Piro had to go to the abbey, where her life would be spent amidst hundreds of women, serving the cruel god of winter when she loved summer and growing things. Somehow she summoned up a smile. 'At least I won't have to marry warlord Rejulas.'

Her mother and Seela exchanged looks.

'What?'

'He will be furious. He'll think Piro has chosen abbey life rather than marry him,' Seela predicted.

'We should tell him before the Jubilee,' her mother decided. 'It would be rude to have him ride in and find out when we announce it. Lence can go. He gets on well with Rejulas.'

'When will he leave?' Seela asked.

'The sooner the better. Give the warlord of Cockatrice Spar plenty of time to get used to the idea.'

Piro felt awful. This time, through no fault of her own, she had complicated things for her family.

Her mother leant forward, to catch her hand and pull her to her feet. 'Come downstairs. Whatever we feel inside, we must present a united front for the celebrations tonight. Byren has done well and Lence is no longer trying to talk your father into war. The king can be pleased with his two eldest sons.'

Even this felt like a condemnation to Piro, because King Rolen's only daughter had failed him.

BYREN HELD THE matching lincurium rings, studying the way a star of light appeared in each of the stones' centres. He'd arrived in his bedchamber, only to receive word from the jeweller that his gifts were ready.

'A beautiful matched pair of winter-crystallines,' the silversmith agreed with Byren's unspoken thoughts. 'But nothing compares to this one.' He withdrew the pendant from its bed of azure velvet. 'Your brother's betrothed is a lucky woman. He will be honoured by your gift for her.'

'I hope so,' Byren said. The pendant was remarkable but he suspected it would take more than pretty jewels to mend things with his twin. He returned the pendant, becoming aware of the silversmith, who waited for his approval. 'Impressive. You've done the stone justice.'

The silversmith beamed and replaced the pendant to its carved wooden box.

Byren paid him for his services and thanked him, sending him on his way. If only he could give this pendant to Elina, but the kingson's wife must not outshine the kingsheir's. The thought made Byren pull up short. As yet, he had not even spoken with Elina, let alone won her forgiveness. If he could not give her the pendant, he could at least give her something that let her know how he felt.

Drawing a sheet of writing paper from his desk, Byren began composing a poem to his Dove. After many attempts on several sheets, he felt it was almost ready and tucked the drafts away in his top drawer, along with the rings and pendant. He'd come back and read the poem again, then write a clean copy for her. But he was in two minds whether he should send it to her and ask for a meeting, or meet with her, apologise and give it to her in person.

Still debating this, Byren went down to the great hall to rejoin the celebrations. Two tankards later, he turned at the sound of his name.

Winterfall, Chandler and the others who had been on the ill-fated expedition to find the lincis waited, grinning expectantly.

Byren felt the same happy grin tug at his lips. 'Chandler, how's the shoulder?'

'Stiff, but getting better.'

'Winterfall, how did Blackwing go, tracking the ulfr pack?'

He shook his head. 'We followed their trail high into the Dividing Mountains. By then the village had a new Affinity warder. He and the wardess contained the seep. They each sent a large pair of sorbt stones to their abbeys, so it was a bad one.'

Byren nodded. The stones would remain dormant unless separated, then the Affinity trapped in the stones would leak out, or it could be drained by a renegade Power-worker. Rogue mages would pay a small fortune for stones like that. Luckily, the abbeys kept the sorbt stones securely guarded in their Inner Sanctums. 'And the Royal Ingeniator?'

'Safe. He has already reported to King Rolen.'

'And what of that complaining monk... Hedgerow, wasn't it?'

Winterfall grimaced. 'Lucky for us, he was recalled to the abbey.'

Byren chuckled.

Winterfall grinned and nodded to his five young companions. As one, they all dropped to their knees. The men nearest stepped back to watch and the silence spread until Lence and Cobalt also turned. Byren felt them watching. Knowing what he did about Cobalt, he found it impossible to meet the man's eyes. He feared Cobalt would be able to read the contempt Byren felt for him, and he was too cunning not to realise Byren had seen through him. If only Lence could!

For a heartbeat Byren considered taking his twin aside and revealing all...

'We want to offer our service to your honour guard, Byren Kingson,' Winterfall said formally.

Byren felt heat race up his cheeks. He'd led them into danger, which had caused Chandler's injury. He did not feel worthy of their service.

'Will you have us?' Winterfall asked.

What could he say? 'I'm honoured.'

Ten minutes later they were on their second bottle of Rolencian red, while Winterfall and Chandler tried to outdo each other, describing the near misses they'd had with the ulfr pack.

'...and Blackwing said he's never known such a cunning pack leader,' Winterfall said.

'Did you set traps?' Garzik asked eagerly.

'Aye.' Chandler nodded.

'All useless,' Winterfall added.

'How about...'

Byren was aware of a gentle tug on his arm and turned to see the castle scribe waiting patiently with a roll of vellum. Amongst his tasks were making a record of the hearings, transcribing any new poems and sagas that took King Rolen's fancy and keeping track of the tithes for the queen. He could also draw a good likeness, or embellish a shield with the royal foenix. But Byren hadn't asked him to do any of these things.

Despite the large meal, Byren's head was spinning and all he really wanted to do was go to his bed and sleep. 'What's this?'

'The emblem for Byren Kingson's honour guard,' the scribe said and unrolled it with a flourish. There was a moment's stunned silence as Byren took in the illustration – a foenix on defence against a leogryf with its wings raised.

'Do you like it?' Garzik tugged on Byren's arm. 'I asked Piro to do the original design to commemorate your leogryf kill. The scribe has embellished her work.'

Byren did not know what to say. The drawing itself was excellent... but he wasn't ready to formalise his honour guard with an emblem.

'Excellent idea,' Cobalt agreed. 'Lence Kingsheir should have an emblem for his honour guard.' As he turned to Lence, Byren noticed that all his twin's honour guard wore their hair loose on their shoulders, Ostron Isle style. 'If you will give me the honour, I will design one and have the scribe embellish it. Now... what will it be? As heir, Lence should be represented by the foenix.'

Everyone nodded and turned back to the emblem the scribe held. Suddenly, Byren saw it in the worst possible context. If Lence was the foenix – and he had more right to that symbol than Byren – then that meant Byren was the leogryf, doing battle with the foenix. He was dismayed.

'But it's not meant to be taken that way,' Garzik protested, following the same train of thought.

'Lence, your foenix's feathers could be picked out in gold thread,' Cobalt suggested, as though unaware of the connotations his last comments had triggered. Byren believed otherwise.

'Lence? I...' Byren began, then hesitated, not sure how to go on.

Lence tossed back his wine, ignoring Byren. 'Red and gold... I like that, Illien.' He beckoned the scribe. 'Meet me in my chambers first thing tomorrow. We'll have a design ready for you. I want surcoats for my men and shields. When can they be ready?'

'Soon.' The scribe was eager to please. 'Once you approve the design, I can have the pattern transcribed, ready to be embroidered. As for the shields, you'll have to speak with the weapons-master. But they could be completed for the Jubilee.' He glanced to Byren. 'The material has been purchased. And the seamstress is waiting to measure your honour guard for your surcoats. You'll want shields as well.'

Byren went to tell him not to bother but he didn't get a chance.

'My honour guards' shields and surcoats must be finished first,' Lence insisted, belligerent with wine.

'Of course,' Byren snapped. 'It's your wedding.'

The moment he said it, he wished it unsaid. It rubbed salt in the wound.

Sensing trouble, the scribe bowed then hurried off. Byren wanted to apologise but Lence did not give him the chance.

'Come, Illien.' Lence shoved between Winterfall and Chandler and marched off, followed by his honour guard, all eager to advise him on the design of their emblem.

Byren's honour guard began filling goblets to celebrate with a toast. Was he the only one who sensed the widening rift?

Isolated in a sea of celebration, Byren caught Orrade's gaze on him. His friend's eyes held a kernel of worry, so Byren wasn't imagining things.

Garzik tugged on his arm. 'I didn't mean for it to be taken that way, Byren. I was only trying to please you.'

'I know, lad,' he said softly.

'I suspect Lence would take anything Byren does as a challenge,' Orrade muttered.

'But why?' Byren turned to him, frustration welling up.

'Because you'd make a better king and he knows it.'

Byren starred at Orrade.

A goblet full of rich Rolencian red was thrust into his hand, as happy faces crowded his vision.

'A toast,' Winterfall cried. 'A toast to Byren, the leogryf slayer!'

For Byren the wine had no taste. He could think only of the old seer and her seemingly impossible prophecy.

It took the better part of the evening, but he finally managed to escape his honour guard. He headed up the stairs to the family's wing of private chambers, deep in wine-befuddled thought. How could he stand by and watch Cobalt insinuate himself into Lence's trust? He had to act before it was too late.

The clink of keys made him look up to see his mother coming down the stairs.

'You can't trust Cobalt,' he blurted.

She blinked, her preoccupied expression clearing as she focused on him. She sniffed, disapproval tightening her mouth. 'You're drunk.'

'A little,' he admitted. 'But that's not the problem. It's Cobalt. He's turned Lence against me.'

'You did that yourself, Byren. I warned you not to outshine him. Even giving him the unistag staff was an insult of sorts.'

This was so unfair that Byren gaped, then tried to focus on what was important. 'Cobalt's –'

'I'll not hear a word against Illien. Many years ago, when you were a child, he was kind to a lonely young woman, who could do him no favours.'

He stiffened, not liking the implications. 'But –'

'Oh, Byren. Sleep it off. I have real problems to deal with. Your father's offended both Halcyon and Sylion's healers by refusing to let them treat him!'

Byren recalled the time he'd walked in on his father receiving treatment from the manservant. 'Valens was Cobalt's manservant, he –'

'He's helped Rolen walk without a limp. That's good enough for me. Let it go, Byren.' His mother stepped past him, keys clinking as she hurried down the steps.

Chapter Twenty

PIRO HAD ALWAYS wanted to take her place at the war table, but not like this. She sat across from her family, isolated by her Affinity, as her mother explained the unwelcome discovery. Byren looked dismayed, Lence and her father stunned, while Captain Temor shook his head sadly.

'...so Piro must join the abbey of Sylion,' her mother finished.

'Ah, Piro.' Her father came to his feet, eyes gleaming with unshed tears. 'My pretty little Pirola... who would have thought?'

Her own eyes stung.

'I'm sorry,' the queen whispered. 'I'm so sorry, Rolen.'

'Why? It's not your fault,' he told her.

She covered her mouth. He opened his arms and the queen went to him, sobbing softly on his chest.

'Can't we hide Piro's Affinity?' Lence demanded, casting her an annoyed look.

She bristled. It wasn't as if she chose to have Affinity.

'Break the law? My own law?' King Rolen shook his head.

'But this means Piro will turn Rejulas down. Again. After I patched it up and promised she would have him.' Lence sprang to his feet, thumping his fist on the table. 'I'll look a fool!'

'You couldn't know that Piro had Affinity,' Byren pointed out, calmly.

Lence swore like a stable hand.

'Lence!' Their mother turned a voice of steel on him. 'That doesn't help.'

'No. And what will?'

She straightened, wiping the tears from her cheeks. 'You'll have to go to Cockatrice Spar and make our apologies. Any sensible person can see that we have no control over whether Piro has Affinity or not. Go before the Jubilee celebration to give Rejulas time to come to terms with it. Make him see it from our point of view. We have lost two of our four children to Affinity.'

Piro felt this as if it was a personal failing.

'People will say the royal family's cursed,' Lence muttered. 'Very well. I'll go. I'll ride out this very day.'

Byren rose. 'Do you want me to come with you?'

'Why?' Lence rounded on him. 'Do you think I can't manage?'

Byren took a step back. Piro flinched with him.

'Lence!' King Rolen's voice cracked like a whip.

Lence glared at their father. 'We wouldn't be struggling to control our warlords if you'd just listen to me. If we'd declared war on Merofynia they'd be right behind us, eager for their share of the bounty. And I wouldn't have to marry Isolt. Illien says –'

'I know what Illien says, I've...' King Rolen ran down, looking tired. He grimaced as if something tasted bad. When had her father grown old? 'The cut and thrust of political manoeuvring is never a simple as the cut and thrust of real battle. I've given my word and I won't break it.'

Lence glowered. Without a word, he turned on his heel and strode out, slamming the door after him. The reverberation echoed through Piro like a physical blow.

'Should I follow him?' Captain Temor asked softly.

The king considered.

'Father, I don't trust Cobalt,' Byren said. 'I know he is our cousin by blood but what if he is feeding us a pack of lies?'

'What lies?' her father countered. 'Palatyne has been named overlord of the spars. King Merofyn's health is failing daily. Cobalt has the elector's trust. What Ostron Isle knows, Cobalt knows. No, Byren. It is too easy to destroy a man's good name. I won't stand by and see it done.' He shook his head grimly. 'My own father refused to acknowledge his bastard son. That left us vulnerable to the wiles of the Servants of Palos. They would have used Spurnan as their puppet king, but my half-brother refused to play their game. He went to father and proved his loyalty by revealing the plot. I owe Spurnan's son a debt. I won't hear a word against Illien!'

Byren compressed his lips, obviously holding back things he wanted to say. Piro was pleased. At least Byren could see through Cobalt. If only the others could.

'Do you want me to go to Cockatrice Spar with Lence?' Temor asked.

Her father debated.

'Yes,' her mother said.

'No,' the king said, hard on her heels. 'Let Lence handle this.'

'You sent Temor with Byren,' the queen pointed out.

'That was different. The warlord of Cockatrice Spar has already sworn fealty to the crown.'

'Temor could –'

'No, Myrella.' The king was firm.

Piro watched her mother's lips compress in the same thin line as Byren's. What was happening to her family? Worry sat like an indigestible lump in Piro's stomach.

As Byren made his way to the stables, his mind returned to his cousin. Maybe Cobalt's Merofynian reports were based on truth, but what of his conclusions? From what Lence was saying, he'd been urging war, which happened to suit his twin. What had possessed Lence to confront their father like that?

Byren went to his hunter's stall. Speaking softly, he checked the horse's foreleg to see if the poultices had healed its shin. Satisfied, he let the beast's hoof drop and straightened up. It paid to look after their mounts. There weren't many horses he and Lence could ride.

This time of year, the quickest path to Cockatrice Spar would be to skate via the canals and hire ponies to take them over the pass but, knowing his twin, Lence would choose to ride, it did not suit a kingsheir to travel on foot. So Byren was not surprised to see Lence stride in with his travelling kit and call for his horse to be saddled.

He cast a glance at his twin's companions. Cobalt, well that was no surprise... but Brookfield and Dellton? Both were seventeen and had only recently come into their titles. They would be out of their depth amidst spar politics.

Byren managed to nod casually to Cobalt, who returned the nod as though he had not threatened to reveal him as Orrade's lover. Byren found his hands curling into fists. Since they'd returned to Rolenhold, Byren had been wondering what Orrade had reported to Cobalt. Illien of Cobalt had stolen his place at his twin's side, his father's confidence in his decisions and now, it seemed, Byren's trust in his best friend.

'You're riding to Cockatrice Spar, Lence?' Byren made it a question.

'Yes.' His twin slung travelling gear over the rail and stepped back to let the stable boys saddle his mount. Lence folded his arms and eyed Byren. 'I suppose you'll be escorting Garzik back to Dovecote Estate? Knowing you, you won't pass up the chance to see Elina.'

Byren struggled with the complexities of this. He could hardly reveal that he had been banned from the estate. This would raise too many questions. Lence was right, he should escort Garzik back to his home to honour the lad's bravery facing down the amfina.

Had everything been right between them, it would have delighted old Lord Dovecote. Byren was very tempted to slip onto the estate and find Elina, but she'd be just as likely to order the stable lads to throw him out. Maybe he should send the poem first then approach her, but what if the poem was intercepted?

Lence shifted impatiently and Byren glanced at him. His twin was being a dog in the manger. If Lence couldn't have Elina then he didn't want Byren to have her either. He fixed on Lence. 'Elina can never be yours, so what is it to you?'

Lence glared. 'Nothing, and don't you dare pity me. My decisions are all made for me. Who I'll marry, whether I claim my birthright or not!'

'What birthright?'

'Merofynia!'

Byren blinked. The stable lads went about their tasks, pretending not to hear. Brookfield and Dellton kept their heads down as they checked their horses' saddle girths. Only Cobalt glanced their way. Byren ignored him.

'I'm mother's first born,' Lence said, 'and she is the rightful heir to Merofynia, not her cousin. That makes me kingsheir, not this brat that they've betrothed me to. I should be ruler of Merofynia in my own right, able to choose who I marry!'

'But –'

'Don't bother. I know all their arguments. But no one asked me. Mother and father just gave up the rights to my inheritance!'

Byren did not know what to say. They'd been not quite thirteen when King Sefon was killed. Too young to understand the significance of their parents' decisions. He'd never given it another thought. 'But –'

'Forget it.' Lence strode over to his horse. 'Come on, Illien.'

Byren stood aside, while Lence led his horse outside into the stable courtyard to mount up. Byren followed, watching as the rest of Lence's party took to their mounts.

His twin headed towards the archway first, with Brookfield and Dellton next, then Cobalt. Not by so much as a quirk of his lips did Illien betray his feelings as he urged his horse past Byren. But Byren could stand it no longer. He grabbed the saddle's pommel. The stable boys had retreated, they were alone. 'You've been putting ideas in Lence's head.'

Cobalt's lips pulled back from his teeth in a smile that did not reach his eyes. 'Nothing that isn't justified, kingson.' His clever black gaze fixed on Byren. 'Ask yourself this, if Lence claimed Merofynia, who would rule Rolencia?'

It took Byren a moment to grasp the implications. 'But I don't want to rule Rolencia!'

Cobalt snorted. 'Then why do you try to outshine Lence at every opportunity?'

He kicked the horse's ribs and the beast plunged past Byren, through the archway into the next courtyard. Byren watched them go, stunned by what he had learnt, but also oddly relieved, for he had begun to understand what had driven him and Lence apart. It wasn't anything he had done but, conversely, it wasn't anything he could fix. Lence had finally found a grievance he felt was justified.

As for Byren, he could avoid Elina – had no choice but to avoid her – but that would hardly satisfy Lence. Briefly, he considered asking their mother's advice, but Cobalt seemed to be her blind spot.

Everything came back to Illien, son of the King's bastard.

Byren had to handle this himself.

FYN AND FELDSPAR knelt to scrub the floor of the mystics' inner sanctum where Halcyon's sacred lamp burned eternally. Actually it had burnt for the last three hundred years, ever since King Rolence the First gave thanks for his victory and gifted the mountain to the abbey. Other equally precious relics stood in niches around the walls. One row consisted entirely of sorbt stones. The mystics had shaped them so that they sat linked, one on the other, in pairs. Their pearly surfaces glistened as if alive. Communing; it was whispered by mystics in training.

Fyn and Feldspar would not begin training until after spring cusp. For now they had been assigned to serve the mystics branch, which meant they were given all the dirtiest tasks. But it was better than serving the livestock master. Galestorm and his friends were still reporting to him each morning as part of their penance. No one liked the bullies and their past victims made no secret of the fact that they were glad to see them mucking out stables and shovelling chicken manure for the gardens. Personally, Fyn saw nothing wrong with caring for animals. He would count himself lucky if he was able to get work as a stableboy, when he ran away from the abbey. Still, he was careful never to go anywhere alone.

'...looking for Fyn Kingson,' a voice said.

Fyn glanced up as Joff came to the sanctum's

entrance.

Farmer Overhill's son now wore the ochre boys' robe and his hair was pulled back in a single plait. He gave the proper bow of a boy to an acolyte. 'Master Wintertide sent me to fetch you, Fyn. He wants to speak with you.'

So far, Fyn had avoided his old master, but he couldn't avoid a direct summons. The boys master was sure to quiz him about finding the Fate and he didn't want to lie. Tension coiled through him as he stood up. 'I'll have to clean up. I can't go to the master covered in dirt and suds.'

'Lucky you,' Feldspar muttered and went back to scrubbing, with a suffering expression on his long, narrow face.

Fyn grinned and glanced to the other youth, who was still waiting.

'Master Wintertide said I was to escort you,' Joff explained diffidently.

Fyn shrugged, heading up the central stairs to the acolytes' chambers, where he had a quick wash and put on a fresh saffron robe and brown knitted leggings, tying off the straps on his ankle boots.

'How are you settling in?' he asked Joff.

'It's not so bad. Wintertide's fair.'

'Yes, there's not many like him,' Fyn agreed. That was why he felt he owed his old master nothing less than the truth. But to save Piro he would lie to the man, who had been like a father to him.

'Ready?' Joff asked.

Fyn nodded, sick at heart, and came to his feet.

They entered the corridor, almost colliding with

Lonepine, who had been assigned to laundry duties. He side stepped them, spilling an armload of clean saffron robes.

'Sorry,' Fyn said. Joff echoed him. They both knelt to pick up the robes, returning them to the basket.

Lonepine thanked them. 'Don't know why the acolytes master doesn't assign me to serve Oakstand. I'd rather sharpen swords than sort clothes.'

Fyn snorted. 'Be grateful you're not mucking out the stables!'

Lonepine grinned.

Fyn straightened up, sure the acolytes master was aware of Lonepine's preference and was punishing him because he was Fyn's friend. Guilt seared Fyn. 'See you later.'

He and Joff headed down the corridor towards the stairs to the boys' wing. Two landings below they had to step aside to let a monk past – Beartooth carrying a bucket of kitchen swill for the pigs.

Not wanting to rub salt in the wound, Fyn quickly looked away. But not before he registered Beartooth's glare of pure hatred.

When they were out of hearing range, Joff muttered, 'I'm glad I'm not a kingson.'

As they stepped into the boys' corridor Fyn wondered if Galestorm and his friends hated him because of what he was, not who he was. It had never occurred to him before and was, oddly enough, a relief.

Joff bowed at the door to Master Wintertide's chamber, and backed off. 'See you later, Fyn.'

I must not weaken, Fyn told himself. *I must not betray Piro's Affinity, even if it means losing Master*

Wintertide's trust and friendship.

He knocked on the door.

'Come in,' the boys master called.

'Master Wintertide.' Fyn gave him the bow of an acolyte to his master, even though Wintertide no longer held that position over him.

The old monk smiled and nodded to the little boy who was sharpening a quill, his tongue peeping between his teeth in concentration. 'You can go, Lenny.'

So it was to be a private talk. Fyn steeled his resolve.

Master Wintertide met Fyn's eyes. 'It does not seem that long since you were sharpening quills for me.'

Fyn glanced at the desk, nostalgic for happier, simpler times. 'May I?'

Wintertide nodded and Fyn sat down at the desk. Picking up the tools, his hands resumed the familiar task. It felt good.

'Most of the servants I've had over the years have been thoughtful, clever boys, but you were special, Fyn.' Wintertide spoke slowly. Fyn sensed he was choosing his words with care. 'You would have been special, even if you hadn't been born a kingson. Whatever happens in the future, do not doubt yourself, Fyn. I know you will serve Master Catillum well. I have faith in you.'

Fyn knew he did not deserve Master Wintertide's trust – he was lying by omission right now – and it stung him to the quick. He desperately wanted to confess the truth and ask Wintertide's advice. If only there was a way he could stay at the abbey without betraying Piro.

A boy shouted, his high voice echoing in the stairwell at the end of the corridor.

'Noisy things, boys,' Wintertide said, his deep-set eyes twinkling. 'Why walk, when they can run? Why talk, when they can shout? Eh, Fyn?'

He couldn't answer. His throat was too tight to speak.

Another voice joined the first, laced with fear. Running steps sounded on the stairs.

Fyn glanced to Master Wintertide, who came to his feet, features tight with worry.

'Some silly boy has probably hit another and knocked a tooth out,' the master muttered. 'They'll be on their way to the healers.'

The steps continued on past their floor and Master Wintertide sat down. Fyn had been willing the messenger to interrupt them so he could escape. He resumed sharpening the quill.

'Is something troubling you, Fyn?'

He looked up. How he longed to unburden himself, but...

The abbey bells began their mournful death dirge, sending another soul to Halcyon's warm heart.

'Who...?' Master Wintertide went out into the corridor, with Fyn at his heels. They hurried towards the stairwell, where the voices echoed. On the landing, they came to an abrupt stop as they spied three monks carrying a limp body up the steps towards them, a saffron-robed acolyte's body.

When they came level, Fyn recognised the acolyte.

Lonepine.

He gasped.

Sandbank met Fyn's eyes, his full of sympathy. 'He fell, broke his neck –'

'No. I was speaking with him only moments ago!'

Fyn protested, pushing between them to touch his friend's face. He touched dead meat. Lonepine wasn't there any more.

It shocked him so deeply he staggered back a step and would have fallen if Master Wintertide hadn't steadied him.

'I'm sorry, Fyn,' Sandbank said. 'He was carrying a laundry basket, must have missed his step on the stairs.'

'Rubbish!' Fyn wrenched free of Wintertide's hands. 'Lonepine wouldn't do that.'

'Anyone can trip,' Sandbank told him gently.

Those words... Fyn's skin went cold with shock. He stared at Lonepine's body. Mouth suddenly dry, his heart hammered as he recalled Beartooth's glare. A quiet corridor, an empty stair well, a monk meets an acolyte and...

Fyn's stomach heaved.

'Here, you look pale. Sit down.' Master Wintertide urged him to sit on the stairs.

Sandbank and the other monks moved on, carrying the body to be prepared to rejoin Halcyon's fiery heart.

Fyn recalled Galestorm's smirk. How could they do this? How could they kill Lonepine? Fyn stared at his old master as the ramifications hit him. Anyone who cared for him was in danger.

He pulled away from Wintertide.

'Fyn?'

But he was running down the stairs, running to see if Feldspar was all right. He found him emptying the mop bucket.

'Back, are you?' Feldspar muttered. 'That was well timed. I just finished.' Then he saw Fyn's face.

'What's wrong?'

'Lonepine's dead. Beartooth killed him.'

Feldspar dropped the bucket. 'He can't –'

'He did. He pushed him down the stairs or perhaps he broke his neck, then pushed him down the stairs.' Fyn heard his voice from far away sounding so calm and reasonable, but inside his head he was screaming. 'No one saw it happen.'

'Fyn?'

'We can't prove a thing. Don't you see? They waited until Lonepine was alone and did what Galestorm threatened to do to me!'

'And what was that?' Catillum asked, coming out of his private chamber behind Fyn.

He jumped with fright, then turned slowly to face the mystics master. It was time to speak the truth. 'Last midwinter, Galestorm told me accidents happen, people fall down stairs –'

'And you think your friend was pushed?' Catillum asked.

'I know so!'

'Did you see it happen?'

'No.' Frustration ate at him. 'But I spoke with Lonepine, Joff can confirm it, just before we passed Beartooth on the landing, and he sent me such a look of hatred...' Fyn shuddered with the sudden realisation that if he had been alone, it would have been him for whom the bells were tolling now. Grey spots flowered in his vision, spreading across Master Catillum's face.

'Catch him. He's going to faint,' Catillum said.

Which was rubbish. Fyn had no intention of

fainting.

He came around to discover he was being carried by the mystics master and Feldspar. Catillum struggled to hold his legs with his one good arm.

'I can walk,' Fyn muttered, trying to wriggle free.

'Hold still. You're only making it harder,' Catillum told him. They placed him on the bunk in the mystics master's private chamber. Fyn caught a glimpse of scattered scrolls piled high on a desk and robes flung over chair backs.

'Go to the kitchens, bring back warmed honey-wine. It's good for shock,' Catillum told Feldspar. 'You look like you should have some too.'

Feldspar nodded, but he didn't go. Fyn tried to sit up, swinging his legs off the bunk.

'Slow down.' Catillum put a hand on his chest.

Fyn brushed his hand aside and sat up. His best friend had been murdered and he was next. Surely the mystics master could see that.

Fyn froze. Was Catillum trying to protect someone?

'We must go to the abbot,' Feldspar said, his voice gaining strength. 'We must report this. Master Catillum can skim Beartooth's mind, get the truth –'

'Wait. There's more at stake than you realise.' Catillum's eyes narrowed thoughtfully, as if debating something, then he seemed to come to a decision. 'The abbot holds power by a narrow majority. Galestorm and his friends are the history master's tools and he supports the acolytes master. The abbot can't risk moving against either master, not when he's just rebuffed the history master by assigning Fyn Kingson to the mystics.'

They digested this in silence.

'You want us to let Lonepine's murderer walk free?' Feldspar whispered, his voice growing louder with indignation. 'You want us to see Galestorm and his friends every day? To eat in the same hall as them? To fear walking the corridors alone because we could be next?'

'I don't want you to do anything rash,' Catillum temporised.

Feldspar snorted. 'Lonepine's dead. I think it's a bit late for caution!'

'On the contrary, now is when we must be most careful.' The mystics master glanced from Fyn to Feldspar, then back to Fyn. 'If a feud starts it could divide the abbey. Last time the masters took sides, they used their monks and acolytes as weapons. Hundreds died.'

'I don't remember that from the history lessons,' Feldspar objected.

'That's because it's not in the official histories. It is our darkest shame. Remember the Black Summer of 182?' Catillum asked.

'The Summer of the Black Spot Fever?' Fyn whispered, sure he was not going to like what he was about to hear.

'It wasn't a fever that killed a third of us, but another kind of evil... the lust for power.'

Feldspar sat down abruptly, making the tripod stool creak.

Fyn shook his head. 'How can the balance of power be that fragile?'

'Some people crave power and the craving consumes them. All it takes is something to upset the balance –'

'And I'm that trigger?' Fyn asked.

Catillum nodded. 'Generally the abbot is voted into power by a meeting of the masters. If the abbot proves to be a despot, poison is the preferred method to remove him. Our abbot is no despot but there are some who can't wait for him to die. He is an old man after all. It wouldn't be the first time an old man's stomach played up. Then Master Firefox's supporters would back him for abbot.'

'And who do you back?' Fyn dared to ask.

'I back the abbey and the best abbot is now ruling it, but there are some who would back me when he dies.'

Feldspar swore softly, something he rarely did. 'Then everything we have been taught about the goodness of Halcyon and her monks is a lie.'

'Not a lie.' Catillum smiled painfully. 'We are only men. We make mistakes. Some of us are motivated by greed and ambition. Sylion Abbey is the same.'

Fyn rubbed his face and tried to make sense of this. 'So we're caught in the middle of a battle for succession?'

'That sums it up.' The mystics master came to his feet, one shoulder higher than the other, his withered arm tucked against his body. 'Now, do you want to go to the abbot and force a confrontation that I fear we cannot win, or are you willing to be guided by me? Well, Feldspar?'

Fyn glanced to his friend.

Feldspar sent him an agonised look. 'Lonepine did not deserve to die. It's not fair!'

'Many things are not fair.' The mystics master

indicated his arm. 'I was mauled by a leogryf when I was nineteen. I lost the use of my arm and gained access to my Affinity, which meant I had to leave my pregnant wife to join the abbey.'

'You could have left Rolencia,' Fyn ventured.

Catillum shook his head. 'She is safe with her family and my son has grown into a fine young man, about your age, Fyn. I've never seen him.'

They were silent for a moment.

Feldspar shifted impatiently. 'Lonepine is dead because –'

'Lonepine is dead because he was my friend,' Fyn whispered, soul sick.

'He died because several ambitious, impatient men don't value life,' Catillum corrected.

Fyn looked down at his hands which clutched his knees, the knuckles white with tension. He cleared his throat. In the whole abbey there was one person whose opinion he valued above all else. 'I'd like to speak with Master Wintertide.'

'Wintertide could have been abbot but he chose not to force the issue. He's the abbot's strongest supporter,' Catillum told him. 'What do you think he will say?'

Fyn looked up at the crippled mystics master and the fight went out of him. 'But what of Feldspar and I? How can we sleep at night knowing Lonepine's murderers have got away with it and we could be next?'

Catillum pulled over the other stool and sat down. 'I am almost certain Lonepine's death was an accident. No.' He held up a hand. 'I don't mean to insult you by telling you that he tripped. There's a good chance Beartooth did push him. He's hot-headed and doesn't think about the consequences of his actions. I'm as certain as I can be that he was not acting on orders from Masters Hotpool or Firefox. They are not so rash. They'll punish him in their own way. As for you two... come spring cusp you will be sleeping in the mystics' chambers, safe under my protection. Until then I will keep you close by me.' Catillum held their eyes. 'I am truly sorry. Lonepine would have made a fine monk.'

Tears stung Fyn's eyes. He tried, but he could not speak past the lump in his throat. To his horror great wracking sobs tore from him. Feldspar threw his arms around Fyn and they both sobbed unashamedly, partly for Lonepine and partly for what they had lost.

They cried until they could cry no more.

At some point the mystics master must have left them because, when Fyn sat back to wipe his face on his sleeve, they were alone.

'I'm sorry I got you into this, Feldspar,' he said, voice raw from weeping.

'Master Catillum means well, but I don't think anyone can protect us all the time.' His friend cleared his throat, fixing serious red-rimmed eyes on him. 'Do you think we should kill Galestorm?'

For a heartbeat it seemed entirely logical for Feldspar to suggest murder. Then sanity reasserted itself and Fyn shuddered, shaking his head.

Feldspar went to argue, then thought better of it and looked relieved. He shook his head. 'All my life I've admired the monks and looked up to them. Now, this. It's clear we must protect ourselves. Even if the plotters punish Beartooth there's still Galestorm. Think of a lifetime trapped inside these walls, never knowing when he might move against us. We might baulk at murder, but they won't.'

Fyn looked down. He did not face a lifetime in the abbey. He was going to run away and all the people he loved and respected would think him a coward. But what could he do? He couldn't betray Piro.

'Fyn?' Feldspar pressed.

He shook his head. 'I can't think straight.' At least that was true.

Feldspar came to his feet, his face ravaged. He seemed ten years older. Fyn and Feldspar had lost more than Lonepine's friendship with his murder.

'You're right,' Feldspar said. 'It would be foolish to make a decision now. We should go wash our faces and put on our formal robes for the farewell.' He shivered. 'Lonepine's empty bunk will be next to mine.'

Fyn felt raw and bruised, as if one more blow would shatter him. It could so easily have been he who met Beartooth on the stairs. Even now, a solemn monk would have been skating across the valley to his parents to tell them of his accidental death.

BYREN SLID OPEN the drawer where he kept the lincurium jewellery and the notes for Elina's poem. He was going to escort Garzik to Dovecote and he wanted to make a clean copy to take with him. When the moment was right he'd give the poem to her. He gathered the scraps of half-finished verse, thinking surely there were more of them. No matter, the best version was on the top so he began to write it out on a clean sheet.

'Byren?'

He looked up to see his mother at the door to his chamber. Quickly, he slid the paper under an innocuous book of pre-Merofynian myths.

'I've been thinking.' His mother swept gracefully into the room, accompanied by the soft chink of her keys of office. 'You should take Piro with you, when you go to Dovecote estate. Time with Elina would do her good.' Seeing his expression she added, 'You do mean to escort Garzik back to their estate before the Jubilee, don't you?'

He licked his lips, not wanting to lie.

'Byren?' Her brows gathered together in a straight line.

'I've been delaying leaving in the hope that Lence would return from Cockatrice Spar so I could invite him with us to Dovecote,' Byren revealed. Actually he had considered asking Lence to escort Garzik. Now he wondered if it would make Lence feel better or worse to see Elina.

He ached to see her, but to see her and have her reject him again would devastate him.

'We don't know when Lence will be back. He might stay on Cockatrice Spar until he's ready to escort Rejulas to the Jubilee.' His mother tilted her head watching him and he felt the beginning of a headache. 'Is there something you're not telling me, Byren?'

He frowned, concentrating despite the thumping in his temples. 'Do you ever regret relinquishing your claim on Merofynia?'

She looked surprised and the headache lifted. The queen fiddled with the keys on her waist ring, then laughed softly. 'How could I rule Merofynia? I would have had to leave your father and live there, for an absentee ruler would never be able to contain the warlords. I could not leave your father.'

She was right, an absentee king wouldn't be able to hold Merofynia. Byren cleared his throat. 'But Lence could have ruled Merofynia. He is next in line after you.'

'And you could have ruled Rolencia.' She frowned, releasing the keys. 'Is that what's troubling you? You two are twins after all. Only seven minutes stand between you and the throne –'

'No.' Byren sprang to his feet. 'I don't crave the kingship. I was thinking of Lence.'

'But he is the heir to Rolencia.'

'And Merofynia, if he chose to assert his rights.'

'And he will one day rule Merofynia with Isolt as his queen,' his mother said. 'Though I don't know how he'll divide his time between the two countries.' She paused, obviously mulling over the practicalities.

It was clear to Byren that Lence did not want Merofynia on those terms. 'But he does not love the Merofynian kingsdaughter.'

She laughed. 'Since when does love decide royal marriages? Lence must give poor Isolt a chance. The ambassador assures me she is nothing like her father.' His mother smiled winningly. It was the smile his sister used when she was trying to winkle her way out of trouble. 'So, will you take Piro with you to Dovecote?'

He was trapped. To refuse would lead to embarrassing questions. Besides, the request was not really a request, not coming from his mother. 'Yes, I'll take Piro to see Elina.'

Since he would not actually venture onto Dovecote estate without dishonouring the Old Dove, he would ask Piro to arrange a meeting for him with Elina, so he could give her the poem and plead his case.

Elina had been furious with him but surely, if she did not feel strongly for him, she would not have been so angry. It gave him hope.

Chapter Twenty-One

BYREN CAUGHT ORRADE'S arm as they passed on the stairs. They had hardly seen each other since they had returned from Unistag Spar. Byren was still not sure how far he could trust his old friend.

Here, on the stair landing, there was no one to overhear them, still he lowered his voice. 'I'm in a fix, Orrie. I have to escort Garza back to Dovecote estate to acknowledge his bravery, and mother wants me to take Piro to visit Elina.'

Orrade frowned, then one corner of his mouth lifted. 'Yes, that's what I'd call a fix.'

Byren's spirits lightened. He'd missed Orrade, who'd seemed withdrawn since Cobalt asked him to spy.

'You'll have to camp on the edge of the estate and send Piro on with Garzik. That'll make her wonder... I guess there's only one thing for it.' Orrade was serious now. 'You'll have to tell Piro the truth about me.'

'You don't mind?'

'A kingsdaughter, who can do what she did on Unistag Spar, is not going to worry about my preference for men.' Orrade hesitated. 'Do you want me to come too?'

'Of course,' Byren replied. 'If I'm to camp in a chilly snow-cave, while Garzik and Piro sleep in warm beds and eat hot dinners, I want you to suffer with me!'

Orrade laughed. 'You know I'd suffer far worse for you.'

Byren dropped his friend's arm. If he truly had Orrade's loyalty, why hadn't he warned him about Cobalt?

Orrade went to say something, but Byren turned and left him there on the stair. Alone.

Orrade would misinterpret his reaction, thinking Byren was uncomfortable with him. Which he was, whenever he stopped and thought about it.

Byren tried to put himself in Orrade's position. How would he feel, spending every day with Elina, unable to show that he cared? Was it even right for him to presume on Orrade's friendship? His head spun. He wished Orrade had kept his mouth shut.

BYREN LET HIS horse stand. They had ridden rather than skating so they could bring enough stores to make a comfortable camp. This camp had to be near enough to Dovecote's keep for Byren to slip over and meet up with Elina, but far enough to avoid detection.

He shaded his eyes to look across the valley. The setting sun's silvery rays picked out Dovecote's warning tower. Each great estate had warning beacons, just as they had a force of trained warriors…

once. Thirty years of peace had made everyone grow fat and prosperous. But not the Old Dove. He still drilled his honour guard himself. Mind you, he'd outlived the veterans of Byren the Fourth's War of 246 and nearly all the veterans of the Merofynian War of 269 that put King Rolen on the throne.

Byren blinked. The Dove was nearly eighty. How strange it must be to live so long, to see others who were born when you were an adult grow old and die before you.

The grey stone of the warning tower gleamed like polished pewter. It was close to spring cusp but the thaw had not yet begun. Soon the land would be madly sprouting, dormant seeds battling each other to accept Halcyon's blessing. Strange to think that this snow-shrouded valley would be a steaming jungle by summer's cusp.

'Not far.' Piro spurred her horse on.

'We'll camp here,' Byren announced. Now that it was time to reveal his banishment from Dovecote estate and the reason for it, he was worried about Piro's reaction.

His sister twisted in the saddle to stare at him. 'But we're nearly there.'

He nodded to the setting sun. 'Nearly night.'

'There's no cloud cover. We could ride by starlight,' she protested.

'We're camping here.' Byren swung his leg over the horse's back, dropping to the snowy ground.

'I don't –'

'For once, will you do as I say? There's something I have to tell you, Piro. Something important.'

This piqued her curiosity and she swung her leg over

the saddle, landing lightly on the snow. 'All right. I'm listening.'

He nodded to Garzik who collected her mount's reins, then moved off to unsaddle the horses and rub them down. Without a word to Orrade, Byren began to dig the snow out of a gully to make a snow-cave. A big one, since he planned on being here for more than a day or two.

He hoped that while they were alone Orrade would confide in him and together they could think of a way to outwit Cobalt.

Piro watched him for a few moments then asked, 'Why bother with such a big snow-cave, when we'll be in beds tomorrow night? Why camp at all, when we could ride on?'

'Orrade and I are not going to Dovecote,' Byren told her.

'I must confess, I wondered why Orrade was coming with us. But you... why aren't you coming to Dovecote?' A teasing sparkle lit her dark eyes and it struck Byren that his sister was a remarkably pretty girl... when she wasn't being irritating. 'Elina will miss you, Byren.'

That stung. 'No, she won't. She said she never wanted to see me again and Lord Dovecote's banned me from his estate.'

Piro's mouth dropped open. 'But why? That's ridiculous!'

Byren smiled because she bristled so beautifully on his behalf. He forced himself to go on. 'The Old Dove thinks I'm like Palos, a lover of men.'

Piro's laughter rang like a bell. Seeing his expression,

she sobered abruptly. 'What made him think that?'

'I told him.'

She gaped.

'He was trying to protect me,' Orrade revealed with painful honesty. 'But I've been disinherited anyway.'

Piro sat down in the snow, stunned. 'So that's why your father disinherited you, Orrie. No wonder you didn't want to tell anyone.'

'Yes. And that's why neither of us can set foot on the estate. Elina thinks I prefer Orrade to her.' Byren heard the resentment in his voice and turned away to resume digging, using his anger to fuel the work. Sometimes he wished he had sent Orrade away instead of keeping him close by, a constant reminder of what he had lost. 'Orrie and I will camp here and wait for you. We've enough food to last seven days, more if we get lucky with our snares.'

Byren concentrated on working, waiting for her reaction. He didn't know which would be worse, pity or sympathy. Then he wondered if she would ask if it was true and that would be worst of all.

Garzik came back, having overheard everything, and began to help with the snow-cave.

'You knew all along, Garza?' Piro asked.

He nodded. More silence.

'Oh, Orrie,' Piro whispered. 'Here I was, feeling sorry for myself because I have to join Sylion Abbey when you've lost everything.'

Orrade looked up, startled. 'You have to join the abbey? But that would mean... you have Affinity?'

Garzik stopped work, his heart in his face. He loved Piro. Byren had not guessed and he doubted if the boy even realised it himself.

He was equally sure that Piro hadn't noticed, as she nodded to Orrade. 'I do. How do you think I controlled the unistag?'

The brothers exchanged looks, then turned to Byren.

'We only just found out,' he explained. 'It seems everyone has secrets.'

'Some more deadly than others,' Orrade muttered. Byren felt sure he was referring to Cobalt and his threats.

'What do you mean?' Piro asked, then wrinkled her nose. 'Oh, being a lover of men.' She paused as a thought struck her. 'But I've often heard Lence boast of the times you three have gone wenching. He claimed Orrie could –'

'Piro!' Byren cut her off, shocked.

'What?' Seeing his expression she flushed, then looked frustrated. 'I have ears, Byren. I know what you males get up to.'

'Maybe, but you don't hear mother talking about it,' Byren snapped.

'Oh really?' She rolled her eyes. 'You haven't heard the women when they are alone.'

Made uncomfortable by the idea that gossip of their exploits had reached his mother, Byren fell silent.

Orrade straightened up, dusting snow off his gloves. 'Several of the lords executed for being Servants of Palos were married, Piro.'

'So they were.' She stood up and brushed snow off her riding breeches. 'Well, you learn something new every day. What's for dinner?'

A surprised laugh escaped Byren. Orrade caught

his eye, sharing his amusement in a moment of perfect understanding. No, he didn't regret their friendship and he didn't want to give it up.

So they cooked dinner and, afterwards, he beckoned Piro, leading her to the lookout where he turned to face her. Starlight illuminated her face, making her dark, tilted eyes mysterious.

'Eh, Piro, there's something you can do for me, but only if you've a mind to,' he began, reaching into his jerkin pocket to withdraw the poem.

'Does it concern Elina?'

'How did you know?'

She laughed. 'Last autumn cusp Elina told me she felt something special for you.'

'Then why'd she go off for a roll in the hay with Lence?' he demanded, surprised by the force of his anger, when he didn't really believe Elina had lain with his twin.

'She did not go off with Lence, not once!'

Byren said nothing, mouth grim.

'Oh, I'm sure Lence was swiving some girl in the hay –'

'Piro,' Byren protested.

She snorted in exasperation. 'I know what Lence gets up to. Mother's afraid she'll end up with half a dozen bastard grandchildren.'

'Piro!'

'Her words, not mine.'

'I'm sure she never told you that.'

Piro had the grace to look guilty. 'I happened to overhear her telling Seela,' she said primly. 'But that's neither here nor there. Do you want me to give

Elina a message?'

Byren nodded. 'See if she'll meet me. Give her this.' He held out the poem which he'd folded over and sealed with a drop of wax, impressed with his foenix emblem.

Piro accepted it. Showing tact for once, she did not ask what it was.

'Remember the water-wheel, where the stream feeds into the lake?' Byren asked. 'I'll be there every day around midday, waiting for her.'

'What if one of Lord Dovecote's men finds you?'

'I can take care of myself, Piro.'

'I'm sure you can, but you can't kill his servants.'

He laughed. 'That's not what I meant. I can avoid being seen if I must. I'm trained in woodcraft. I just want to explain things to Elina.'

Piro nodded.

'Do you think she'll forgive me?' He couldn't help asking.

'I don't know... what girl would like to hear that the man she loves prefers her brother to her?'

Elina loved him? Byren's spirits soared, then plummeted. Somehow, knowing she loved him only made it worse.

'Oh, Byren, don't worry.' Piro hugged him. 'Elina's got a good heart.'

'True. But she's proud and I've hurt her.'

PIRO WINCED AS Lord Dovecote greeted his youngest son grimly and led him away. Even the horses, which were being led off by the stable lads, looked happier to be home than Garzik. At least they were headed for a warm stall, a feed and a rub down.

'I fear Garza's in trouble,' Piro whispered to Elina.

She nodded. 'He'll have to sit through an hour's lecture and promise to mend his ways before father will let the matter rest. Da's proud. When Garza ran away, it hurt him.'

Byren's words returned to Piro. She could tell her friend was hurting, too.

'Oh, but I'm so glad to see you!' Elina hugged her.

'Me too.' Piro returned the hug. She needed to get Elina alone where they could talk. 'I heard Regal had her pups. Father was saying he'd like one. They're sure to be great trackers.'

Elina nodded. 'Come see. They're adorable.'

They skirted New Dovecote and entered the stable yard which had been swept clean of snow.

'They're in here.' Elina led her into the stable, into a tack room near the entrance. 'Come and look. Aren't they darlings?' She scooped up a puppy, thrusting it into Piro's arms. 'Hold him.'

They knelt on the straw, shoulder to shoulder to admire the pups. The stable was warm and cosy, redolent with the familiar smells of horse and hay, friendly with the soft singing of the lads at work on the horses. Piro felt seven years old and wished life was this simple once more.

'I'm glad Garza's come back,' Elina confessed. 'Father's been impossible to live with.'

'I'm sure everything's going to be all right now,' Piro said and tipped the puppy over to tickle his tummy. Byren's message felt incredibly important in her jerkin pocket. She needed to choose the right moment or Elina might reject it. 'You haven't asked after Byren.'

Elina became very interested in her puppy. 'Do you know why?' she asked carefully.

'I know Byren loves you,' Piro insisted. 'And you once told me you loved him, so...'

Elina said nothing, staring at the puppy unseeing.

Piro stole a look. She was in time to see a large tear slide down Elina's cheek. 'Oh, Lina!'

Piro reached out to console her, but Elina pulled away. 'You don't understand, Piro. This isn't the sort of thing that can be mended by saying I'm sorry.'

'Maybe it can be mended by listening to what he has to say. Here.' Piro thrust the message into Elina's hands. 'It's from him. He'll be waiting for you by the water-wheel tomorrow at midday. Promise me you'll read it and hear him out?'

'Oh, Piro...' Elina glance down at the message then fixed tearful eyes on her.

The horses stirred, whickering. Piro and Elina both turned their heads to listen. The jingle of harness and the stamp of hooves told her they had company.

'Who could that be?' Elina muttered. Wiping her cheeks, she tucked the message in her apron pocket and went to look through the stable door, staying in its shadow.

Piro had to stand on tip toe to peer over her shoulder. 'Why, it's Lence!' Elina whispered fondly. She pulled the apron off over her head and folded it across her arm. 'Lence and friends. Two of them are mere boys.'

'Don't let them hear you say that!' Piro warned.

'They're Lords Brookfield and Dellton now, having come into their titles since you last saw them. And they've joined Lence's honour guard. They think themselves men.' She frowned. Trust Cobalt to travel with a servant. 'The fancy one is the new Lord Cobalt.'

'Spurnan's son, Illien? The one who's been in Ostron Isle these last thirteen years?'

Piro nodded. 'Father's acknowledged him as our blood kin.'

'Really? My father will be pleased to see the breach mended. He'll be sorry to hear that Spurnan's dead.' Elina hurriedly smoothed down her hair, then threw the door open. 'Lence Kingsheir, always welcome at Dovecote.'

Piro watched her brother's face lighten with delight, then tighten hungrily. She could not imagine a man ever looking at her like that.

Lence swung his leg over the horse's back and dropped to the swept stable yard. 'Elina, lovely as always. Don't you have stable lads to take our horses?'

'I was playing with the puppies.' Her words were prim but her voice held laughter. 'We have more of King Rolen's kin visiting. Come, Piro.'

She stepped from behind the door. 'Hello, Lence.'

'Piro!' Lence looked surprised, then forced a smile. 'What are you doing here?'

Elina laughed and rolled her eyes. 'Brothers!'

Piro noticed both Brookfield and Dellton could not take their eyes off her friend and even Cobalt straightened unconsciously in the saddle. Why did Elina have this effect on men?

Lence seemed to recollect his manners. Keeping

a firm hold on Elina's hand, he turned towards the youths. 'Elina, you know Arturo and Moran, now Lords Brookfield and Dellton. And this is Lord Cobalt. Illien, this is Elina Dovecotesdaughter, the prettiest girl in Rolencia.'

Both youths dismounted and bowed formally as if they were in court, insisting that Elina use their personal names, as they made free with hers. Piro had to look away and bite her bottom lip.

Cobalt swung down from the saddle, handed the reins to his servant and made the Ostronite bow, which should have looked ostentatious but he carried off with great style. He kissed Elina's hand as was the Ostronite custom then held on to it, saying, 'In the court of the Elector of Ostron Isle there are poets who claim Ostronite women are the most beautiful in the world. I believed them... until I met you.'

Elina blushed but Piro laughed outright.

Cobalt flicked an annoyed glance in her direction. 'Little Piro, so good to see you again.' He dropped Elina's hand to reach up to Piro's head. 'Hold still, you have hay in your hair, child.'

He threw something away with a practised flick. Resentment filled Piro. She was not a child.

While the stable boys ran out to take their horses, Elina smiled and accepted clumsy compliments from Brookfield and Dellton. She was all kind forbearance as they tried to outdo Lord Cobalt. Lence let them flounder for a few moments, then took over. His line of compliments was much more polished.

Compliments usually bored Piro. Today they

annoyed her.

'Well, Piro.' Cobalt turned to her. 'I did not think to see you here. Where's Byren?'

The truth would not do. Piro searched for inspiration. 'He's gone hunting with Orrade.'

'Really? There won't be much game along the canal, too many travellers.'

'Then it's just as well they're on horseback,' Piro told him. 'Hunting's good up near the lookout.'

'I wish them luck,' Cobalt said. 'Though I'm sure they won't need it. They tell me Byren is a remarkable hunter.'

The conversation between Elina and Lence faltered to a stop.

Cobalt turned to Elina. 'Lence has been singing the praises of your cook. He says Queen Myrella has offered her a place in the king's castle but she wouldn't leave Dovecote.'

'Yes, father would never part with her. Shall we go inside?' Elina offered her free arm.

Brookfield and Dellton both tried to take it. There was almost a scuffle. Lence saved them from themselves by walking off with Elina. Piro smirked. Silly boys.

'Father will be so pleased to see you, Lence,' Elina told him. 'He was sorry to miss the Midwinter's Day celebrations.'

As Piro watched Brookfield and Dellton hurry after them, she caught herself wishing Lence hadn't arrived. She still didn't know if Elina was going to meet Byren.

Elina paused and looked back over her shoulder. 'Come on, Piro.'

Piro caught Lence's impatient glance. It seemed

she was a nuisance and it occurred to her that maybe Lence hadn't come out of his way just to see Elina, maybe he was also here to discover why Orrade had been disinherited.

'Cousin Piro?' Cobalt offered his arm.

The last thing she wanted to do was take it. She'd much rather go back and play with the puppies. Dredging up a smile, she accepted Cobalt's arm and tried to do her mother proud by making polite conversation. 'How did negotiations go with the warlord of Cockatrice Spar?'

'That's not for me to discuss,' Cobalt told her.

Piro flushed and ground her teeth. He was acting as if she was too young to be involved in strategy discussions, but they'd thought her old enough to marry the Cockatrice warlord.

Brooding over this, Piro hardly paid any attention when Lord Dovecote greeted the new arrivals. Once again, Lence introduced Cobalt as their cousin, making it clear that King Rolen had acknowledged the blood tie, and Piro had to listen to the sad tale of the Utland raid all over again. It would have touched her, if she hadn't known that Cobalt felt nothing.

While Elina played the perfect hostess and called for wine, arranging to have bed chambers opened and aired, Piro watched Cobalt set out to charm Lord Dovecote. He was up to something and she didn't like it. Suddenly she knew what Seela meant, when she said her nurslings had all grown up and had to play the game of Duelling Kingdoms for real.

Old Lord Dovecote proudly showed off his latest dove crossbreed. This one had fancy feathers down its legs. Piro thought it pretty enough, but she had seen them all before.

'Play with me, Piro?' Garzik suggested, beckoning her over to where he was opening the carved box that held the Dovecote's Duelling Kingdoms game.

'Of course.' Piro joined him, relieved one male wasn't behaving like a besotted idiot, but then, Elina was his sister. As she helped Garzik lay out the board she leant close enough to whisper. 'Do you think Lence is here to find out why Orrie was disinherited?'

After casting a quick glance to their visitors, Garzik caught her hand, placing her piece in her palm and squeezed her fingers. 'Don't worry, none of the servants know, only the family. And we're not going to tell.'

So she settled down to play.

Later, when they went upstairs to clean up for the evening meal, Piro finished dressing quickly and darted down the hall to the room Lence always used. She tapped on his door and thrust it open to find Cobalt with him.

Both turned towards her, startled by the interruption.

'Sorry,' Piro said, perfunctorily. She'd been marshalling her arguments since Cobalt refused to discuss the Cockatrice warlord negotiations and was determined to hear what Rejulas had said. 'Did you manage to patch things up with Rejulas, Lence? Is he coming to the Jubilee? Is he mad about –'

'Quiet, Piro.' Grimly, Lence pulled the strings of a small velvet bag closed and handed it to Cobalt.

'Well?' Cobalt asked.

'You've convinced me,' Lence said, with reluctance. 'Go. Do what's got to be done.'

'As you wish, kingsheir.' Cobalt tucked the bag

inside his vest, cast Piro a swift glance then left.

'Well?' Piro pressed as the door closed.

Lence focused on her with a distracted frown. 'What?'

She rolled her eyes. 'What did Rejulas say? You can't put me off. I want to know.'

'It's none of your business and besides –'

'I was there, at the war table, when father sent you. I was the one Rejulas was going to marry.' Piro relished saying this, certain she was on solid ground. 'I think that makes it my business. After all, I *am* a kingsdaughter.'

'You're a spoilt brat, Piro. And, after spring cusp you won't be a kingsdaughter bred to serve Rolencia, you'll be a lowly nun serving Sylion Abbey!'

She gasped, taking a step back. It was true and she hated him for it.

'Now get out,' Lence told her, voice rising. 'And knock next time!'

A year ago she would have told him just what she thought of him. But not now, for he was wrong – she was no longer a child. Collecting her dignity, Piro gave Lence a stiff little bow and backed out. It was only later that she wondered what had been in the bag Lence gave Cobalt and what it was he'd sent Cobalt to do.

BYREN PACKED THE entrance to the snow-cave to seal it and crawled back to his side. Orrade knelt on his haunches as he stirred their food, a small pot of stew, prepared back at Rolenhold and preserved with spices. The glowing coals of the brazier made his pale skin ruddy.

It was time. 'Why didn't you tell me Cobalt blackmailed you to be his spy?'

Orrade went utterly still for a heartbeat, then continued stirring the stew. 'How did you know?'

'I was there in the devotional box.'

Colour crept up Orrade's cheeks. 'Then you know I was not a willing party to this deception.' He glanced at Byren. 'Why didn't you bring it up before?'

'Why didn't you tell me before?'

Orrade made a helpless gesture. 'I didn't want to worry you. I've cost you too much already.'

In all honesty, Byren couldn't deny this.

'If you knew, why didn't you say something?' Orrade asked. When Byren didn't answer, the slow burn of anger made his black eyes gleam. 'I'd never betray you, Byren.'

'No?' His chest felt so tight it was hard to speak. 'What did you tell him, when we got back from Unistag Spar? He would have been expecting a report.'

'He was.' Orrade met his eyes. 'I told him only what he needed to hear –'

'Piro?'

'Nothing of Piro. When your men spoke of Lady Unace's unistag, he put two and two together, but I claimed I knew nothing. I told him we hardly speak any more, that you blame me for losing Elina's love.'

'I don't,' Byren muttered, frustrated. 'She should have known how I felt.'

'Why?' One side of Orrade's mouth lifted in a rueful smile. 'Because you feel so strongly?'

Byren nodded.

'It doesn't work that way,' Orrade told him.

Byren heard the painful self-knowledge in his voice and winced. 'Orrie, I –'

'Stew's ready.' Orrade began ladling it out, then grabbed a roll that had been heating on the brazier's edge and tossed it over to Byren. It was several days old but the heat had made it crispy.

He caught the bread and accepted his bowl. 'I owe you an apology.'

'Forget it. I've been thinking of a way we can turn Cobalt's cunning to our advantage.'

'Oh?' Byren paused, as he dipped the bread in the stew.

'I'll tell him what we want him to hear. It must be believable but it doesn't have to be the truth.'

Byren snorted. 'He won't believe the truth. I've already told him I don't want to rule Rolencia. Twice.' Even as he said this, he realised it was true. This was what that first conversation back on the Divide had been about, when Cobalt had approached him outside the council hall.

Byren caught Orrade watching him with a look that was hard to read. 'What?'

'Nothing.'

'Once Lence marries Isolt, he'll see she's not so bad,' Byren said. 'The alliance will be secure and Lence will settle down.'

Orrade dipped his roll in the stew and tore off a chunk, saying nothing.

'You don't think so?' Byren prodded.

'Ask yourself why Cobalt's mischief has fallen on fertile ground with Lence,' Orrade said, then gave the answer. 'Cobalt's telling Lence what he wants to hear.'

Byren found the stew had lost all taste. For the first time he understood that everything might not turn out for the best. What if the breach between himself and Lence deepened?

'Have you ever thought of travelling?' Orrade asked. 'Why not go to Ostron Isle as Rolencia's ambassador? I could come with you. We'd –'

'Leave?' Byren was torn between anger and laughter. As if he could leave home when Rolencia needed him.

MUCH LATER, PIRO snuggled into bed, grateful for the warming stone. Except for trouncing Garzik at Duelling Kingdoms, the evening had been an interminable bore. Brookfield and Dellton had been either tongue-tied in front of Elina, or too voluble. And Lence had discussed the Utland reprisal raid with Lord Dovecote. Piro had heard it all before. The only new thing she had learnt was that Lence had sent Cobalt to Rolenhold to let them know Lence had decided to stay at Dovecote for now.

Piro rolled over and thumped the pillow. She'd hated the way Lence watched Elina all night. He'd even saved the crackling off the top of his caramel toffee-pear for her because it was her favourite treat. Piro knew Elina was secretly heartbroken over Byren but she had seemed inclined to look more favourably on Lence, even though he was betrothed.

Piro sat up in bed. Did Elina know about Lence's betrothal? The Dovecotes hadn't come to the midwinter feast where it was announced and Piro hadn't had a chance to mention it yet. They may not have heard because news didn't travel fast in winter.

Elina needed to know that Lence was betrothed in case she contemplated opening her heart to him. She'd always been fond of Lence.

Slipping out of the bed, Piro reached for her shawl. Her toes curled on the cold rug and she quickly tucked them into her slippers and padded to the door. Elina's chamber was next to hers. She'd tell Elina now, warn her not to believe Lence's compliments and maybe take the chance to plead Byren's case.

But when she came to the door it was slightly ajar and the room was empty. Where was Elina?

Piro crept down the hall until she heard muffled voices from the balcony which overlooked the great hall. There was a rustling then a male chuckle.

'One kiss is never enough,' Lence cajoled. 'Let's see what you have under this – ow!'

Piro smiled, pleased. The wooing wasn't going all his way for once.

'I said one kiss and that's all I meant. I'm not one of your rolls in the hay, Lence,' Elina snapped. 'Now, what did you want to see me about?'

'They've betrothed me to a Merofynian prize cow!'

'What?'

'And all the while I've been dreaming of you. Dreaming of your smooth, milky skin, your sparkling obsidian eyes, your –'

'You're betrothed, Lence? When did this happen?'

'Midwinter. They betrothed me to Isolt, that usurper Merofyn's daughter. I am the true heir, not him or his daughter.'

'We had not heard about your betrothal.' Elina spoke slowly, clearly shocked. 'I –'

'It doesn't matter. I'll be coming for you.'

'But what about your betrothed?'

Yes, Piro thought. *What about her?*

'Don't worry. That marriage will never come to pass. I'll be back to claim you, Elina. You understand?'

'I don't see how you can agree to a betrothal then –'

'I'm going to be king and, when I am, I'll choose my own bride and it will be you. So promise you'll wait for me.'

She gave a bitter laugh. 'I'm not about to marry anyone else.'

'Not even Byren?' Lence countered, as if he couldn't help himself.

'Byren? He preferred my brother to me!' It was a cry from the heart.

Piro jumped, thumping her elbow on the wainscoting.

'What was that?' Elina sounded alarmed.

'Nothing. Rats –'

'We don't have rats at Dovecote. I had the best ratters in only last week –'

'Forget the rats, Elina.' Lence didn't sound surprised by Elina's revelation about his twin. 'What makes you think Byren's a Servant of Palos?'

'He told father that he and Orrie are lovers. That's why father disinherited Orrade. Da's devastated. He made us promise to tell no one.'

Then why had she told Lence? Piro frowned.

'And now Byren wants to meet me at the water-wheel

tomorrow afternoon,' Elina muttered. 'But I don't see how anything he says could change the situation. He's a lover of men and I won't be second best!'

Piro cursed under her breath.

'Did you hear something?' Elina whispered.

'There's someone in the hall.' Lence's voice grew alarmingly loud as he strode along the balcony towards the corridor.

Piro fled.

Chapter Twenty-Two

THE NEXT MORNING, Piro woke late. She'd spent another night with bad dreams, only these hadn't been about wyverns hunting her, but manticores. What next? As she finished dressing, there was a knock at the door, and she answered it, feeling tired and grumpy.

Elina stood there, flushed with anger. 'Why didn't you tell me that Lence was betrothed?'

'I thought you knew. Everyone knew,' Piro replied, then said the first thing that came into her head. 'Besides, I thought you only had eyes for Byren –'

'Byren?' Elina's laugh held fury. 'There's something you should know about your precious brother, he's a lover of men!'

'He is not!'

'He is and he used me, whispering sweet words in my ear so he could spend time with my brother!'

'That's ridiculous.'

'He made me look ridiculous. An excuse, that's all I was.' Elina's voice rose dangerously. 'How they must have laughed at me, the two of them!'

'Quiet, Elina. Think of the servants,' Garzik warned, as he came out of his chamber. 'Think of father.'

'What about my feelings?' Elina implored.

'What about Orrade?' Piro countered. Out of the corner of her eye, she noticed a servant standing open-mouthed. 'Think how he must feel. He's your own brother. How could you turn your back on him? He has no family now, nothing!'

'He has Byren Kingson for his –'

'Lina!' Piro slapped the older girl.

Elina staggered back two steps, stunned, her hand going to her cheek.

More doors opened. Brookfield and Dellton came out of their room. Lence looked up the hall to see what the shouting was all about and strode towards them.

Distracted by their appearance, Piro was not prepared for Elina's shove. The door knob hit her between the shoulder blades and a yelp of pain escaped her.

More doors opened.

'That hurt!' Piro gasped. 'You –'

'You deserved it.' Elina leapt for her. Piro defended herself, giving as good as she got. It was a flurry of hands and stinging cheeks, flying hair.

A strong arm swept Piro off her feet. She writhed and twisted, trying to get free. Then she gasped as the arm squeezed until she saw stars.

'Enough?' Lence demanded.

Unable to speak, she could only nod. He eased up

but did not release her, so that she hung from his grasp like a kitten, panting for breath.

When her vision cleared she saw Elina shrug off Garzik's restraining arms. Lord Dovecote stepped between them, his crippled face expressing concern and annoyance. Beyond him, Brookfield and Dellton looked astounded. Piro fought an urge to giggle. They were shocked to see the kingsdaughter in a scrap, but she'd grown up scrapping with Elina.

'Ho, Garza,' Lence laughed. 'Remember the time it took four stable lads to pull them apart?'

'What's this all about?' Lord Dovecote demanded. 'Elina?'

Bleeding from a scratch down one cheek, Elina assumed her dignity like a cloak. 'Piro has decided to cut short her visit, father.'

His good eye widened. 'Here, there's no need for that.' He turned to Piro. 'My apologies, kingsdaughter.'

'Put me down, Lence,' Piro ordered, cheeks flaming. She could still feel him chuckling. As soon as her feet touched the parquetry floor, she straightened her bodice and pushed her hair from her face. She had been about to apologise but this was too much. She could out-dignify Elina any day. 'I thank you, Lord Dovecote, but I must be leaving.'

Turning on her heel she went to enter her chamber, but Lence was in the way and he was enjoying this far too much to let her pass.

'Let her go, Lence,' Elina said. 'It's for the best.'

'Don't listen to Elina, father,' Garzik insisted.

'What would you know? You're just a silly little boy who thinks he's a warrior,' Elina rounded on him. 'I wouldn't be surprised if you went the same way as Orrade!'

Garzik stiffened. His cheeks grew very pale and he pulled himself up to his full height. 'Father.' He inclined his head in a short bow. 'I see I am not wanted here. I'll go. I'll serve in Byren Kingson's honour guard!'

He shoved past Brookfield and Dellton, striding off down the hall.

'Garzik,' Lord Dovecote called after him. 'I insist you stay. You are my heir.'

'Make Elina your heir. I know where my true friends are,' Garzik replied over his shoulder.

'Leave this house and you will never be welcome here again!' Lord Dovecote shouted.

Garzik spun to face his father. For a heartbeat Piro thought there was going to be a shouting match and dreaded what would come out. Then Garzik gave the old lord a short, stiff bow. 'So be it. Good bye, Father, Elina.'

Elina whimpered then spun to face Piro. 'Now look what you've done!'

Piro stared at her. Her sight shimmered and she saw invisible doors slamming shut between them. She didn't say the things that boiled for release, but pushed past Lence and ran into her chamber to pack her things.

The door opened right behind her.

'What is it now?' she spun around, fighting the tears.

'Oh, Piro,' Lence muttered, crossing the room to hug her. 'Why do you always do things the hard way?'

Her tears erupted and she wiped them away furiously, wriggling out of his embrace. She rinsed her face in the water bowl, dried her cheeks and turned to him. 'I'm fine now, Lence.'

'Good. Get Garza to take you back to Rolenhold by the canal. We saw the tracks of a manticore pride on the horse trail,' Lence warned. He frowned at her. 'Did you hear me, Piro?'

She nodded once, stiffly. Satisfied, Lence left her alone.

Throwing her travelling bag on the bed, she stripped off her good gown and dragged on her travelling clothes. It didn't take long to pack. The cook sent up a sumptuous breakfast, which she thought she'd never finished. But after the first mouthful she discovered she was hungry and polished off the lot.

By late morning, she was out in the stables helping the lad saddle her horse.

'Better prepare Garzik's as well,' she warned him.

Sure enough, ten minutes later Garzik strode into the stable and she was ready to meet him, with his mount's reins in her hands.

He gave her a short nod of thanks and swung up into the saddle.

It did not seem the right time to say she was sorry, so Piro kept her silence as they rode out of the stables, out of the yard and turned their mounts towards the trail off the estate.

How had things gone so wrong, Piro wondered, when she had set out with the best of intentions to help Byren reconcile with Elina?

'Slow down, Garzik,' she said suddenly. 'We must tell Byren. He'll be waiting for Elina at the water-wheel.'

'Then he's going to be disappointed,' Garzik muttered. They turned their horses across country.

BYREN TENSED AND untensed his muscles as he lay along the tree's broad branch. He was half frozen even in his thick winter woolens. There'd been another cold snap last night, making him glad he'd built a sturdy snow-cave.

It was only as he was riding down here that he realised Orrade's preference for men would be accepted in Ostron Isle. Was this why his friend had suggested they go there? Maybe he was being selfish by asking Orrade to stay. Ambassadors tended to be older people with years of experience at court, but Byren could suggest that Orrade go to Ostron Isle as assistant to Rolencia's current ambassador. At least then Orrade would have a respected position. Yes, he would speak to his mother about it.

Byren heard the soft clump of a horse walking through snow and the gentle snort as it blew through its nostrils. His spirits lifted. All was right with the world. Elina had come to see him, which could only mean she must be ready to forgive him.

He swung down from the tree branch, dropping to the snow.

When he straightened up, it was not Elina who rode towards him, but Lence. For a moment he thought his eyes must be deceiving him. 'Lence, I thought you were –'

'I was, but I'm back. Elina sent me to give you a message, brother.'

Byren tensed.

'She wants you to leave her alone.'

'I don't believe it. I won't. Not until I hear it from her own lips.'

'She's already told you once. How many times must she tell you? You sicken her, you and your lover...'

Byren swayed, sounds spiralling away until a roaring filled his ears. When it cleared, Lence was still sitting astride his horse about a body length from him, hands resting lightly on the pommel of the saddle. He got the impression his twin was waiting for an answer but he'd no idea what the question was.

'Lence, you've gone wenching with me enough times to know that –'

'I admit I found it hard to believe, but you were condemned by your own words.'

'I was protecting Orrie.'

'Why protect him if it's not true?' Lence countered. He shook his head, repressing a shudder. 'It all falls into place. Illien was right, but I refused to believe him. The Servants of Palos are moving again, and this time the alternative heir is not a bastard!'

Byren snorted, torn between laughter and outrage. Then he remembered Cobalt's words... the truth is highly overrated. He took a step closer. 'It's a lie –'

His brother jerked on the reins making the horse rear in protest. Byren had to dart back to avoid slashing hooves. Lence kept pulling on the reins so that the horse pivoted and sidled away.

'Lence, wait,' Byren called. 'Don't trust Cobalt. Think. How long have you known him? What do we know of his life on Ostron Isle?'

'Illien has already confessed his past to me. An older woman lured him on, a furious husband tried to blacken his name, all else is lies and slander. At least he possessed the honour to admit his past indiscretion. What of Orrade?' Again, Lence shuddered. 'I always wondered why you were closer to him than me. Now I know. How long have you two been lovers?'

Byren did not know what to say.

'You don't dare answer me.'

'I don't answer because you've already refused to believe the truth.'

'To think I was so blind...' Lence shook his head. 'Swear to me you'll give up this madness?'

'What madness? I told you, I'm not involved in a conspiracy –'

'Please, Byren!'

He lifted his hands helplessly. How could Lence believe this of him?

'Very well,' Lence said. 'Lord Dovecote's in a rage. If you are captured and dragged before him now, I don't know what he'll do. Get off the estate. And Byren? We saw the tracks of a manticore pride on the canal, don't go that way.'

A dozen birds took to the air from behind a copse of white-cloaked evergreens. The birds' raucous cries echoed in the sudden silence. Lence glanced that way. 'Someone's coming. Go home by the horse trail.'

With that he turned his mount and galloped off.

Byren ran to the trees, seeking cover. The soft rhythm of the horse's hooves faded as he peered around a snow-crusted branch. Picking their way along the bank of the frozen stream, Piro and Garzik rode towards him. He came out of hiding, signalling to them.

Piro waved and cantered her mount around to meet him.

'Was that Lence?' she asked as she arrived.

He nodded.

'What did he want?'

'Elina sent him.'

'Oh.' Piro sat back in her saddle.

Garzik looked away, not wanting to share his disappointment.

Byren noticed their travelling bags tied to the saddles. 'Leaving already?'

'Elina threw me out.' Piro gave an unsteady laugh.

'And I've been disinherited,' Garzik said.

'What?'

'Well, I told father to make Elina his heir, so it amounts to the same thing,' Garzik admitted.

'Why?'

'He was belittling you and Orrade. I... I lost my temper.'

'Lence knows, Byren,' Piro warned.

'I know he knows.' Byren turned towards his hidden horse.

'Will he tell father?' Piro asked.

In the midst of mounting up, Byren paused, then continued to swing his leg over the horse's back. 'He'll tell father all right. Tell him the Servants of Palos are planning to put me on the throne!'

'But there are no Servants of Palos, just Orrade –'

'And his attachment to a romantic myth,' Byren muttered. And suddenly he was able to forgive Orrade his foolish faith in Palos. Everyone needed a hero. A weight he hadn't really been aware of lifted from him as he spurred his horse towards their camp.

Piro took a few moments to catch up. 'Don't worry, Byren, father won't believe it.'

He pulled on the reins, slowing his horse, and twisted in the saddle to face her. 'Thirty years ago father purged Rolencia of the Servants of Palos. Noble and servant alike, they all went under the axe or dangled from the hangman's noose. Do you think he'll be any more lenient this time?'

'But Byren, there is no secret society. So you're safe.'

He thought of Lence's refusal to believe him. 'If it isn't there, how can I prove it doesn't exist?'

Piro's eyes widened and she fell silent.

Byren rode on, frustration and anger warring within him. When Lence returned to Rolenhold, Byren would lose his family and his place in the world, based on an accusation he could not disprove.

What could he do?

PIRO WATCHED DISTRACTEDLY as Byren and Orrade broke camp. When they were done, Orrade swung his leg over his mount and waited to bring up the rear, while Byren led them towards the trail to Rolenton.

That reminded her. 'Wait, Byren. Lence said he saw the spoor of a manticore pride on the horse trail. We should travel by canal.'

'Eh, you've got it wrong, Piro. He said the manticores were on the canal.'

She frowned. 'No. I'm sure –'

'You must have misheard him, Piro, because you'd expect manticores to be in the forest, not the canals.'

'Either way. We don't want to run into a manticore pride,' Orrade muttered, pinching the bridge of his nose as if his head ached. 'They'll be ravenous from their winter sleep and each female is sure to have two or more cubs. They'll be hunting to feed them as well.'

Piro nodded. 'But I'm sure Lence said the horse trail wasn't safe.'

'Slip of the tongue,' Byren decided. 'I know what he told me.'

With that, he turned his horse towards the trail.

Piro debated arguing further but now she was beginning to doubt her own memory. They were much more likely to find the manticores on the horse trail, fresh from their den in the Divide, rather than down along the canal. So she fell into place riding behind Garzik, with Orrade bringing up the rear.

FYN STIFFENED, DRAWING closer to Feldspar as Galestorm and Beartooth rounded the corner. His friend's soft gasp of fear sounded loud in his ear. They were in the hall to the mystics' store room, a place rarely visited by anyone but mystics, so Galestorm and Beartooth must have deliberately sought them out. Fyn cursed under his breath, for the monk who was supposed to watch over them had delayed to gossip with a friend. He would catch up in a moment, but by then it might be too late.

'Fyn, Feldspar,' Galestorm greeted them, malicious eyes bright with an excitement that filled Fyn with foreboding. 'I was so sorry to hear about the loss of your friend. I have been meaning to offer my personal condolences.'

Fury filled Fyn's chest, nearly choking him.

'It is a very sad loss,' he managed to say, then couldn't help adding, 'one that could have been avoided.'

Beartooth smirked. Fyn wanted to punch him.

'A misstep on the stairs. A simple accident,' Galestorm shrugged. 'So unfortunate.'

'We must all take care.' Fyn heard himself as if someone else was speaking. 'None of us are above taking a careless step.'

Galestorm's eyes widened, then narrowed.

'Even kingsons can –' Beartooth growled.

But Galestorm cut him off, stepping closer, his voice dropping. 'You think you're safe, Fyn Kingson. Sure, you've got friends in high places. But friends come and go.'

'Not these friends. They will remain true,' Fyn said.

'Ah, but some of them are old and the old must make way for the young. One day Master Firefox will be abbot and then, who will you turn –'

'Not if Master Catillum is made abbot,' Feldspar protested.

Galestorm sent him a pitying look. 'Other than Master Oakstand, Catillum's supporters are all from the abbot's generation. When they die and take their place in Halcyon's Sacred Heart, who will back a crippled mystic?'

Feldspar swallowed audibly.

Galestorm smiled and nudged Beartooth. They passed by, Beartooth deliberately thumping his shoulder into Fyn's. When they rounded the bend, Fyn felt Feldspar sag against him. He discovered he'd been holding his breath and let it out in a rush. Sparks danced in front of his eyes and he had to take several breaths to clear his vision.

Feldspar sent him a worried look.

'Don't fret,' Fyn said. 'If Galestorm could strike at us, he would have by now. He's just blustering.'

'I hope you're right.'

Fyn hoped so too.

BYREN FINISHED HIS lunch and stood up, dusting crumbs from his hands. Piro and Garzik moved off to remount. He noticed Orrade rubbing his eyes, a frown drawing his straight black brows together. 'What's wrong, Orrie?'

'Oh, nothing,' he muttered, then seemed to think better of it. 'It's just these grey spots are coming back.' He blinked several times as if trying to clear his vision.

'Headache?' Byren asked, dreading the answer.

Orrade went as if to deny it, then admitted, 'It's been coming on since last night.'

'Ready?' Piro asked, having mounted up and urged her horse over to join them.

'Garza, you lead,' Byren called. 'I'll bring up the rear.'

Orrade opened his mouth to object, then shrugged.

'Not far to the first campsite, Garza knows the way,' Byren said.

They headed off. Riding in the rear meant Byren could watch Orrade's back. Was his friend suffering a relapse of the blindness or was his newly aroused

Affinity trying to surface? Last time, Orrade had warned them about the raiders. What would it be this time? Manticores? Maybe Affinity beasts triggered his gift? No... the amfina hadn't.

'Eh, Orrie,' Byren called softly. 'Why didn't you warn me about the amfina before it attacked?'

Orrade glanced over his shoulder, his face pale, expression distracted. 'How could I, when I hadn't seen its tracks?'

And it obviously hadn't aroused his Affinity. So, Byren wondered, why was Orrade suffering similar symptoms to the ones that brought on his warning about the raiders? According to the tales, some people with Affinity could look into a person's heart and see if they were of evil intent. Certainly the amfina intended no evil. It was merely doing what beasts do, while the raiders knew they were crossing Rolencia to attack a peaceful village.

'Any trouble up ahead, Orrie?' Byren asked softly.

'See any trouble? I can't even see past my horse's ears,' Orrade muttered.

Byren chewed over this answer. It was clear Orrade's sight was fading again, and either he was unaware of his new-found Affinity or he was denying it to himself. Best to be on the lookout. The sooner they returned to Rolenhold the better.

Garzik was a brave lad but inexperienced. Like Piro, he could get himself into trouble. And if Orrade became worse Byren would have to lead his horse. Even now his friend swayed in the saddle, shoulders hunched in pain.

'Not far now, Orrie,' Byren said gently.

He didn't answer.

From then on Byren remained alert, watching for an attack or any deterioration in Orrade's state.

By the time they reached their usual camp, however, Orrade's colour was better and he helped to build the snow-cave. Garzik saw to the horses, with Piro's help. Soon they were snug in their snow-cave heating dinner over the brazier.

While Garzik and Piro bickered over the best kind of food to pack for winter travelling, Byren passed the reheated meat to Orrade. 'How's the headache, Orrie?'

'Nearly gone.'

'Spots?'

'Fading, thank the goddess.' Orrade tucked into his stew.

Byren decided it must have been a physical problem, after all.

'Eh, no visions, then?' he prodded, just to be sure.

Orrade cast him a swift, slightly startled look.

'Just kidding,' Byren muttered. If his guess was wrong, then there was no point in worrying Orrade. Still, he vowed to sleep lightly.

Chapter Twenty-Three

BYREN WOKE TO screaming horses. Forgetting where he was, he rolled to his feet, driving his head and shoulders through the roof of their snow-cave. It collapsed on the others. Snow muffled their confused cries and the brazier hissed like a trapped beast.

He leapt over Piro's snow-shrouded form, ploughing towards the horses. It was a cloudy night and the stars were hidden, but he knew the layout around their camp. A horse shrilled, then went ominously quiet. The others squealed, their hooves drumming on the ground as they tore at their pickets. He could imagine the scene from the sounds. As for the predator, he guessed it was a big one or a pack desperate and bold enough to attack their camp.

Manticores? He dreaded finding out.

He shouldn't charge in alone.

Behind him he could hear Orrade organising Garzik and Piro to protect each other. A glow of flames illuminated the night as Orrade lit torches.

'What is it?' Orrade asked, coming up behind Byren and handing him a burning brand.

'Watch my back.' Byren forged through the branches they'd stacked to form a windbreak for the horses. None of their mounts remained, only the churned snow where they had reared and fought for their lives.

Byren sniffed the air, recognising the scent. 'God-touched beasts.'

'Manticores,' Orrade confirmed.

Byren's stomach clenched. Had Piro been right? Had he misheard Lence's warning and led them into trouble?

He scouted the clearing, studying the tracks in the snow, confirming that it was a pride of manticores. 'One large male. Two females and at least five half-grown cubs from last spring.' A large pride. He indicated blood-smeared trails in the compressed snow. 'This is where they dragged the unlucky horse off. The wind has dropped. Our mounts must have caught their scent and been able to avoid their first strike.' Manticores preferred not to expend too much energy hunting. Ideally, they liked to creep up on their prey, paralyse it with the poison barb on the end of their chitinous tails then drag the body somewhere to devour it in safety.

'Let's get back. We've a long walk ahead of us tomorrow,' Orrade said.

Byren nodded. The other three horses would be running through the forest, safe enough since the manticores would glut themselves on their prey. But one kill between three adults and five juveniles was not enough to sustain the pride.

'They'll come back for us,' Byren whispered.

'Tomorrow night,' Orrade agreed.

'Are you all right?' Piro called as she ran up to join them. 'What happened?'

'Fine,' Byren told her, seeing Garzik in the clearing behind her. The boy lifted his hands helplessly as if to say, I couldn't stop her. 'Orrie told you to stay with Garzik, Piro. Next time do what you're told. We've lost the horses. Manticores –'

'The pride Lence warned us about?'

He shrugged. There were plenty of them up on the Divide, more on the other side on the spars than on Rolencia's borders. It was rare for them to come down this far into the valley. 'They must have woken early this spring. I wonder if there's another new seep. That could've disturbed their winter sleep. At any rate, they're here and they're hungry.'

Byren waited, but no one accused him of nearly killing them by mistaking Lence's warning. For once Piro held her tongue. The thing was, he hadn't misremembered it. Had he?

'What'll we do?' Garzik asked, eyes searching the circling trunks as if expecting further trouble.

'Sleep up a tree for tonight –'

'They can climb,' Garzik insisted.

'True, but they'll be gorging themselves on that poor horse.'

'And tomorrow?' Garzik asked.

Byren glanced to Orrade.

'We'll need shelter,' his cousin muttered. 'They'll pick up our tracks and follow us. If we climb a tree we'll be trapped. They could out-wait us, pick us off one by one –'

'Eh, it's not that bad,' Byren interrupted, seeing Piro's pinched face. She turned to him hopefully. 'If we leave the horse trail and march across country to Lake Sapphire –'

'But we don't have skates,' Garzik pointed out.

'They do at Narrowneck tradepost.'

'Good idea,' Garzik agreed. 'We'll be safe there and we can borrow skates.'

'See, Piro, there's nothing to worry about.' Byren squeezed her cold little hands. 'Now, gather your things and we'll sleep up a tree just to be sure.'

She nodded. Trusting him, she began sifting through their collapsed snow-cave to find her belongings and repack her travelling kit. Orrade caught Byren's eye, his expression grim. It was not as cut-and-dried and Byren made out. It was debatable whether they'd make it as far as the tradepost before the manticores attacked.

'We'll be defenceless, easy prey while we're walking.' Garzik frowned. 'If only I'd brought my hunting bow.'

Byren forced a hearty laugh. 'Planning on killing yourself a manticore, Garza? You trying to outdo me?'

The boy grinned and relaxed, but Orrade held Byren's eye. They both knew the dangers.

'Sylion's curse,' Byren muttered, 'I should have listened to Piro.'

'Why should you have listened to me?' Piro asked as she rejoined them.

'You said Lence warned –'

'A slip of the tongue. That's all it was. Horse trail, canal.' She shrugged this aside. 'What do I do with my pack?'

'Garza can climb up, toss a rope down and haul it up,' Orrade told her.

Had it been a simple slip of the tongue on Lence's part? Byren cleared his throat. 'Piro, are you sure Lence said he and Cobalt saw the manticore spoor on the horse trail?'

She frowned, thinking back. 'Cobalt didn't mention it. He arrived at Dovecote with Lence but he went on ahead to Rolenhold to let them know about Lence staying at Dovecote. When I was about to leave, Lence told me to take the canal.'

And Byren was certain Lence had told him to take the horse trail. He felt sick at heart.

'What?' Piro asked, reading his expression.

But he shook his head and cupped his hands. 'Step up. Climb as high as you can.'

For a moment it looked as if she would argue with him, then she sprang into the branches, climbing like a monkey, dislodging snow on his upturned face.

'Here, watch it!' he called.

She giggled, sounding so young and unaware of the danger that he vowed he would get her safely back to Rolenton, even if he had to kill the whole the manticore pride to do it.

But then what would he do? Sit at Rolenhold waiting for Lence to find another way to kill him? His whole body revolted at the thought. He could not accept that Lence had sent him into the path of danger. Lence didn't need to kill him. All he had to do was accuse him of being a Servant of Palos.

'Do you mean to stand there all night?' Orrade called down. Byren hadn't even noticed him climb the trunk.

'What? Here, catch.' He tossed his pack up to Orrade and climbed up, settling in the crook of the tree on a horizontal branch, three body lengths from the ground. This tree had branches like the spokes of a wheel. His was twice as thick as his waist and Orrade settled onto the corresponding branch beside him.

'Tie yourself in, Piro. You don't want to fall,' Byren called up to her, suiting his actions to his words.

'I'm not afraid of heights.'

'Tie yourself in anyway,' Orrade told her. 'You too, Garza.'

'I'm not a child!' Garzik insisted from a body length above them.

Byren could not summon up a smile, as his mind circled back. Even if Lence had deliberately sent him on the dangerous road... 'What were the chances of the pride finding us?'

He didn't realise he'd spoken aloud until Orrade answered.

'They're hungry. We crossed their path...'

'But there was a chance we'd miss –'

'I did not mention it before...' Orrade whispered reluctantly. 'But I dreamt of a manticore with Cobalt's head.'

Was it a dream or a vision? Byren didn't want to ask and it was clear Orrade didn't want to make the distinction.

'Even if Lence sent Cobalt on ahead,' Orrade continued, 'how could Cobalt ensure the manticores would attack us?'

'He couldn't,' Byren decided. Clearly, Orrade

had come to the same conclusion as him – Lence's misdirection had been deliberate.

Orrade leant closer to be sure they could not be overheard. 'At best someone could have lured the pack down into the valley with cuts of meat and tried to keep them in the vicinity of this camp. But that would be incredibly dangerous and –'

'And it would only work if Lence was sure we were going to use the horse trail back to Rolenton,' Byren admitted, forced to consider the possibility. 'I know Cobalt's cunning, but I don't see how he could have lured the manticores to this camp site. Their attack was just bad luck.'

'Can you be sure?' Orrade asked softly. 'Lence believed Piro was going back to Rolenton with Garza so he told her to take the canal. Then he deliberately directed you towards the horse trail. I think that –'

'If he planned to kill me he was taking a gamble on the manticores doing the job for him,' Byren snapped.

'True. But his plan had one advantage. No blame would ever find its way back to him.'

'Lence is not that devious.'

'Cobalt is.'

'We're arguing in circles,' Byren muttered, frustrated. 'Even Cobalt could not lure a whole pride of manticores to this camp site. Horse trail... canal... who says it wasn't a slip of the tongue on Lence's part? I can't believe my own twin would send me into danger. Back at midwinter he saved my life!'

Orrade said nothing.

The old seer's words replayed in Byren's head. She had been right so far, yet he had done everything he could to prove her wrong. He was not going to let things get to the stage where he had to kill Lence to save his own life. 'Before Cobalt –'

'Lence has always wanted Elina –'

'Yes, but before Illien came back, he was resigned to marrying the Merofynian kingsdaughter.' Byren debated telling Orrade about Lence's claim that the Merofynian throne should have been his. How many kingdoms did one man need? 'If I could just get rid of Cobalt –'

'What are you suggesting?' Orrade asked. 'Do you mean to take insult at something and force a duel on him?'

'No.' Though that wasn't a bad idea. 'I'm thinking of suggesting that he become Rolencia's ambassador to Ostron Isle.'

'But Rolencia already has an ambassador on Ostron Isle.'

'He's one of father's old honour guard. I think he's become a bit of a recluse. He didn't even tell us that Cobalt was marrying into the elector's family. Father could invite him back for Lence's wedding and Cobalt could be sent in his place.' Then Orrade would not get a chance to live where he would be accepted, but it would get rid of Cobalt. 'He knows the elector. He would be ideal.' If he actually had Rolencia's best interests at heart, that is. Byren suspected that Cobalt only had one person's best interests at heart and it wasn't Lence's. His twin was in for a nasty shock.

And he wasn't the only one. Back at midwinter his father had been certain Lence's betrothal was for the best. More recently, the king had begun to doubt his own judgement. What clever insinuations was Cobalt planting to undermine the king's confidence?

As for his mother, why couldn't she see what Cobalt was? She was usually such a good judge of character, almost as if she could look into a person's heart. Maybe, if he went to her before Lence returned home, told her of Lence's accusation and...

'Byren?' Orrade whispered. 'We can check around the camp site tomorrow, see if there are signs of one or more men, who might have lured the pride down here.'

'Manticores are intelligent god-touched beasts with wills of their own.'

'I know. But if Piro can control the unistag, then someone with Affinity could –'

'Are you suggesting Cobalt has Affinity?' Byren's heart rate picked up. That would explain much.

He heard Orrade shrug. 'We don't know why Cobalt fought with his father all those years ago or why he left Rolencia.'

Byren smiled. 'I could ask the castle's Affinity warders to test Cobalt.'

If he had Affinity he'd have to join the abbey or leave Rolencia. A load lifted from Byren. He would get rid of Illien of Cobalt, then warn his mother before Lence accused him. She would help handle his father.

Relieved, Byren tried to get more comfortable on the tree's broad branch. He was in for a long night.

PIRO DID HER best to keep up, but her legs were not as long as those of the men, and the snowdrifts were deep. Every step became an effort, making her breath burn in her chest. Plus she hadn't had much sleep last night. Byren's casual question about Cobalt and Lence had made her wonder if Cobalt had gone on ahead to lead the manticores to their camp. She'd come to the conclusion that only someone with Affinity could have lured the pride into the camp's vicinity and even then it would be a dangerous thing to attempt.

That time she'd touched Cobalt, she had thought he felt no emotion. What if he was walled? What if her mother was right and Affinity ran in their blood through King Byren the Fourth?

She would tell her mother and the queen would make the Affinity warders test Cobalt, and then he would have to leave and everything would be right again.

Or would it?

She had not been mistaken. Lence had tried to send her home by the safe road. Either he had meant to warn Byren and he'd named the wrong trail or...

Before this she would have been absolutely certain that Lence would never send Byren into the path of a manticore pride.

Now, Lence believed Byren was a Servant of Palos. What was wrong with him? She felt heartsick every time she returned to worry over the point, painful as a loose tooth. And she'd had plenty of time to think as they walked.

They ate without stopping, pausing for no more than a few minutes if one of them had to answer the call of nature. While waiting for Garzik, she surreptitiously leant against a tree trunk, pushing her pack up so that its weight didn't drag on her aching body. Byren noticed and, without a word, he took her pack off her back, shouldering it along with his. She sent him a grateful look. Garzik returned and they continued.

Today they went in single file, Orrade leading, then Piro, then Garzik and lastly Byren in the most dangerous position. It was easier without the pack, she found her second wind. But it was barely mid-morning and they had far to go.

FYN DEBATED IF he should leave the abbey now, before spring cusp. It was hard living alongside his friends, listening to them boast and tease each other about becoming monks, knowing that he would desert them soon and they would not understand why. For many of them it would be confirmation of his cowardice. He was tempted to get it over with and leave now. His travelling kit was packed, ready to go. All he had to do was slip into the abbey's kitchen and take some food. But it was still a couple of weeks until spring cusp.

Fyn shivered as a chill ran over his skin. His stomach churned. He swayed and reached for a seedling tray to steady himself.

'Fyn?' Master Sunseed asked softly. 'Is something wrong?'

'Nothing.' He made himself continue potting up the delicate seedlings. 'Like this?'

The gardens master nodded. Today all acolytes helped in the gardens. If Rolencia was to harvest two crops before next winter, the abbey had to get the hothouse seedlings started early and distributed to the farmers.

All morning Fyn had been feeling ill. But then, he had been feeling sick at heart for days now. Feldspar would never forgive him for leaving. He was tempted to reveal his plan and ask his friend to come along. Lonepine would have agreed instantly, but Feldspar loved the abbey and everything it stood for.

Fyn's vision swam and this time he almost dropped the sprout.

Through the ringing in his ears he heard the abbey's bells toll out the death dirge. There were over seven hundred monks, acolytes and young boys in the abbey so the chance that the dead person was a friend of his was slim. Yet Fyn's throat ached with loss and his eyes prickled with a presentiment of tears.

Had something happened to Feldspar?

Alarmed, he met Master Sunseed's eyes. Around him the others had ceased work and were looking at the master, with varying degrees of concern and curiosity.

'Fyn, go find out who the goddess has reclaimed,' Sunseed ordered.

Fyn nodded. He wiped his hands once on his apron, fumbling as he untied it. As soon as he was out the door, he ran down the spiral stair, only to meet the history master coming up. Fyn stepped aside to let Hotpool pass, but the master paused.

His eyes held Fyn's, glistening with something Fyn could not interpret.

'My sympathy, Fyn Kingson,' Master Hotpool said.

His friend was dead? Fyn froze. He and Feldspar should have run when they had the chance.

'I believe you were close to the boys master.'

'M-Master Wintertide?'

'Oh, hadn't you heard?' Hotpool pretended surprise. 'Wintertide was found dead at his desk. The healers say his heart gave out.'

Fyn's mouth went dry. He didn't believe it.

'Don't put your faith in the mystics master, Fyn.' Hotpool leant closer. 'Catillum's supporters are not going to be around when he needs them. You would be much better to look elsewhere for a mentor. I could be very good for you.'

Fyn looked down to hide the anger that swelled up in his throat. He could just imagine what Hotpool meant, and he would be expected to spy on Master Catillum. 'I want nothing from you.'

'Do not be so quick to spurn –'

Fyn tried to push past him.

The master caught his arm.

'Let me go.'

Hotpool's lips pulled back from his teeth. 'You might be a kingson but that does not make you better than us!'

'No, it's what's inside a man that makes him better. And Master Wintertide was twice the man you are, or will ever be. He deserves his place in Halcyon's Heart.'

'And I don't?' Hotpool bristled.

Fyn instantly regretted his outburst. 'I'm sorry, master. I did not mean –'

'You meant exactly what you said.' Hotpool's eyes narrowed, then he smiled cruelly. 'I'll see you regret this when Firefox is abbot!'

Master Hotpool turned, marching up the steps towards the hothouse gardens.

Fyn's heart raced and he felt nauseous. While bending double to catch his breath he heard the history master's voice echo down the stairwell. He was announcing that the boys master was dead, and all work was to cease in his honour. By custom the whole abbey would pray and meditate while the dead master's body was prepared to take its rightful place in Halcyon's Heart.

He desperately wanted to say a private goodbye to his old master so he ran down the stairs, heading for Wintertide's chamber. But, when he entered, he found the bunk empty. For a moment he thought Wintertide's body had been stolen. Then he remembered... Hotpool said the healers had declared it was a heart attack so they must have collected his body and done their examination already.

Stupid. He wasn't thinking clearly.

Above his own hurried breathing, Fyn heard a soft sniffling. He knelt to peer into the shadows under the bunk. Master Wintertide's servant was hiding there, weeping.

'G-go away!' the boy sobbed.

Fyn smiled despite his exasperation. 'You're being silly. Come out.'

'No.'

'You can't stay there all day.'

The six-year-old wiped his nose on his sleeve. 'Can, if I want to.'

'I was Master Wintertide's servant, once,' Fyn said.

'Really?' The boy wriggled closer to get a better look at Fyn. 'That must have been a long time ago.'

'Ten years,' Fyn agreed. 'When I was scared and all alone, he was kind to me.'

'He was kind to me, too. And they just took him away.' The boy gulped back a sob. 'Healer Springmelt didn't even let me say goodbye.'

Fyn knew how that felt. Springmelt? When Fyn was Master Wintertide's serving boy, Springmelt was one of the acolytes who'd tried to bribe him. Now the healer spied for the history master. That explained how Hotpool knew the manner of Wintertide's death. Wait a moment... 'When did you say they took his body?'

'Just now. Didn't you see them in the hall?'

Fyn's head spun. If they had only just taken the master away, the healers would not have had time to examine him and determine the cause of death. How had Hotpool known?

Catillum's words came back to him. *Poison is the preferred method to remove rivals.* The only way for Hotpool to know what had killed Wintertide was for him to have killed him with a poison that mimicked a heart attack.

When Galestorm had said the old must make way for the young, Fyn had not thought he meant the old were to be murdered. Fyn sprang to his feet, heading for the door.

'Where are you going?' The boy scrambled out and ran after him. He tugged on Fyn's arm.

Looking down into that tear-streaked face, pity stirred Fyn. 'Go to the cook and see if he has any hot soup left.'

'Hot soup won't bring back the master.'

'No. But going hungry won't bring him back, either.'

The boy smiled slowly. 'That sounds like something

Master Wintertide would say.' He slipped his hand into Fyn's. 'I'm ready.'

But Fyn wasn't. There were dangers out there that he hadn't foreseen. 'You go. I want to stay here for a bit.'

The boy nodded wisely and went to leave, then turned back. 'I'm Lenny, named after the kingsheir, Lence.'

Fyn smiled. 'Go get something to eat, Lenny.'

'I will.'

Strangely cheered by this conversation, Fyn leant his forehead against the dressed stone. It was cold and helped him think. Springmelt was Master Hotpool's tool. A healer could kill as well as heal. Fyn's eyes burned with angry tears. He could not bear to think of his old master suffering. But there was no time for grief, or anger.

The faction headed by Master Firefox wanted to undermine the abbot so they had removed his most respected supporter. Where did that leave Fyn?

He must tell the mystics master. He wouldn't even have to skim Springmelt's mind. Murder would be easy enough to prove. Poison had to leave a trace in the victim's body. All Fyn had to do was tell Master Catillum, who would tell the abbot, who would order the healers to test for poison... the healing master was loyal to the abbot. At least Fyn thought that he was.

A weight lifted from Fyn. Wintertide's body would prove how he died. This time the murderers would be punished and Lonepine's spirit would be satisfied.

But Springmelt had removed the body. What if they planned to get rid of it? Without the body, he could not prove Wintertide had been poisoned.

Quick as a thought, Fyn ran along the hall and up the steps, taking the shortest route to the healing wing. He almost ran into Feldspar on the stair.

'You've heard about Master Wintertide?' Feldspar asked, then read the answer in his face. 'Oh Fyn, I'm so sorry.'

Fyn only nodded. He found Feldspar's honest sympathy hard to bear and had to clear his throat before he could speak. 'I'm going to the preserving chamber.'

'You'll never get in. The healers won't even let the mystics see how they prepare a body for Halcyon's Heart.'

'I just want to be sure Master Wintertide's body has been delivered,' Fyn explained. Once the master's body was with the healers, Springmelt wouldn't be able to hide anything without someone knowing.

He went up two floors to the healers' chambers, meaning to slip inside and ask someone if it was too late to say good-bye to Master Wintertide's body. If it was, he would be safely in the sacred preservation chamber. But Springmelt must have been watching for him and was blocking the entrance.

'Where's the healers master?' Fyn asked.

'He is too busy to see an acolyte, even if the acolyte is Fyn Kingson.' Springmelt said, making 'Kingson' an insult.

'Has Master Wintertide's body been brought in for preservation?'

'Of course,' Springmelt snapped. Fyn glanced past him, trying to see if this was true. Springmelt moved to obscure his view. 'But you can't go in. Even *I'm* not allowed into the sacred preserving chamber.'

That was good news. Master Wintertide's body would be preserved before it was placed in Halcyon's Sacred Heart with the other dead masters.

Springmelt smirked. 'If you want to do something useful, pray Halcyon finds a place for Wintertide in her eternal garden.'

'I will.'

But Fyn planned to do something much more useful. He went straight to Master Catillum's private chamber, only to learn that he was in a meeting with all the masters. Fyn knew they would have to select a new boys master, but did they have to do it so soon? Who would they recommend to the abbot? He imagined all the masters sitting around a table putting forwards candidates from the ranks of Wintertide's assistants. The balance of power depended on who became boys master. He shivered, knees weak.

Sinking onto the step of Catillum's chamber, Fyn rested his forehead in his hands. The bell hadn't even rung for mid-morning prayers and he was already exhausted.

What should he do? He was only one acolyte, a soft-hearted coward who hated to see anyone hurt. He should leave the abbey now. Right now. It would be so easy to go down to the kitchens, steal some food then and away...

But he could not forget Wintertide's kindness. His old master deserved better. Lonepine deserved better.

'Fyn, what are you doing on my door step?' Master Catillum asked.

He stood up, his decision made. 'I have something

to tell you, something that can't be said out here.'

For a moment he thought the crippled master would send him away, then he sighed. 'I suppose I had better hear it.'

Safely inside, Fyn unburdened himself to Catillum. '...so Hotpool could only have known that Wintertide died of a heart attack if he administered the poison which caused it. Springmelt gave him the poison. I'm sure of it. All the abbot has to do is insist the healers master test Master Wintertide's body. Then you can offer to skim the minds of those who saw Wintertide in the last day and –'

Master Catillum shook his head reluctantly.

'What? Why not?'

'The masters are walled. I could not break their walls without breaking their minds.'

'Springmelt –'

'Is their one weakness. But if it looks like we are about to move on them, Springmelt will have an accident. And besides, there is another flaw in your plan to expose the poisoners.'

'And what is it?'

'The healers master supports Firefox. If we ask him to do the tests he won't find poison.'

'But... but we can't let them get away with Master Wintertide's murder!'

'No, we can't.' Catillum straightened his shoulders. 'I had hoped it would not come to this.' He saw Fyn did not understand. 'I can test for poison. But first I'll have my most trusted assistants kidnap Springmelt until we need him. If I can prove it was poison and that they stooped to poisoning a master,

I'll discredit Firefox before all the other masters. Some will change sides, weakening him. But I'll need your help to prove it was poison.'

'Anything.'

'Be careful what you promise.' He smiled sadly. 'It will take three days to prepare the body. They must do it correctly or that would raise suspicion. I must test Master Wintertide's heart. We won't be able to go near him until he is safely in Halcyon's care in her Sacred Heart...' His black eyes held Fyn. 'Only the abbot has the key. When we all go down there to commend Wintertide's soul into the goddess's care, I'll leave something wedged in the doorway so you can follow us. '

'But it is forbidden for anyone except masters to enter.' Fyn came to his feet. 'If I am caught, I'll face death.'

Catillum nodded. 'And I can't save you. I can only move against Firefox once I have proof.'

Fyn sank onto a stool.

'If you don't wish to do this, I'll understand.'

'No.' Fyn looked up, meeting the master's eyes. 'I'll do it.'

'Good. I can draw you a plan of the passages. You have three days to memorise it.'

Three days to regret he had volunteered for this. Three days to wish he'd run away before Wintertide's death.

Chapter Twenty-Four

BY MID-AFTERNOON PIRO'S strength had failed. Only determination kept her going. She wished she had taken after her father. Then she'd be at least as tall as Orrade. She had seen the armour her namesake, Queen Pirola the Fierce, had worn into battle. Now there was a woman, able to hold her own.

Exhausted, Piro caught herself slipping into a sleepwalking state and experienced a kind of double vision, as the last night's dreams came back to her. With a jolt she realised she had dreamed this right now... dreamed of stumbling through a snow-shrouded forest trying to escape manticores, with Byren bringing up the rear. She almost tripped.

'Do you need a break, Piro?' Garzik helped her up, too tired to tease.

'No.' She made herself go even faster. In her dream it had seemed they ran for ever but soon they would reach the lake, and then they would have to go either left or right and hope to find a tradepost before nightfall.

The fight with Elina had driven the dream from her thoughts but now it was clear, the dream had been a true foretelling. Did that mean that her recurring dream of wyverns stalking through Rolenhold was likely to come true? Hadn't the mystics mistress said that seers saw many possible futures, which made interpreting them difficult?

'There's one good thing about the manticore pride,' Byren muttered.

'What's that?' Orrade asked over his shoulder.

'Scare off the ulfr pack!'

'Ulfrs?' Piro echoed, happy to be distracted.

Byren nodded. 'Saw old signs of them yesterday. Probably the same pack we had a run-in with.'

'Pity,' Garzik panted. Piro was pleased to see that talking and walking at this pace was almost too much for him. 'I would have liked to get that leader's pelt!'

'Nah, that one was mine,' Byren insisted.

They laughed and Piro laughed along with them, but she did not understand how they could boast when their lives hung in the balance.

Orrade trudged on. At the top of the very next rise he stopped. 'Eh, Byren, you were right. We're just where I thought we'd be!'

Piro stopped focusing on her feet and lifted her weary head. They were high enough to see the lake, its icy surface gleaming through the tree trunks.

Byren pointed. 'And, if I'm not mistaken, Narrowneck tradepost is just around that bend.'

Now Piro knew where she was. Narrowneck was built on a finger of land that projected into Lake Sapphire. True to its name, it was narrow where it joined the land and bounded by cliffs. At one point, ladders could be lowered down to a small beach on the lake. A solid, three-storey tradepost was built there. Busy in peak times, it would be nearly empty now.

'Keeper Narrows will open his doors for us,' Byren declared. 'Though he won't be happy to hear we've drawn a pride of manticores down on him and his family!'

Narrowneck tradepost. Piro fixed this goal in her mind and kept moving, but distances were deceptive and the day dragged on.

BYREN INCREASED HIS pace. It was almost dusk. A steady wind blew into their faces, driving their scent towards the manticores. The pride could travel far in one day and were sure to be close on their trail now. He didn't want to be torn to shreds only a few bow shots from safety.

'At last!' Garzik muttered.

Byren looked up. There was the wooden palisade. Thirty years ago it had kept Narrowneck safe from the Merofynians. Now it wasn't even enough to keep the manticores out. Rolencia had grown complacent.

'We can shut the gate,' Piro said as they stepped through the opening. 'Keep them out.'

Byren reached over, grabbed a strip of wood and pulled on it. It splintered in his hand. 'Not going to keep anything out.'

'Close it anyway,' Orrade said, dragging the gate shut. It had come off one hinge; snow fell off the top and dusted his shoulders.

Byren turned to face the path up through the trees. 'Come on. Not far now.'

Piro's face was pinched with exhaustion, but she did not complain as she struggled to keep up with him. He'd do anything to keep her safe.

The thud of an axe reverberated through the woods. Byren made for it. There was safety in numbers and he had to warn the axe man about the manticores.

'This way.' He broke into a run, hearing the others puff along behind him. A deep bark was followed by more. Their approach had been detected.

Thud... thud.

The axe stopped. Suddenly, he'd arrived in a clearing on the spine of Narrowneck. Three huge wolfhounds stood in front of a boy of about nine summers and the tall youth who had been swinging the axe.

The dogs growled a warning, the noise reverberating in their deep chests.

'Get behind me, Leif,' the youth said. No, it was a girl, a handsome, very tall girl. No wonder she swung the axe like a man. Then he remembered hearing traders talk of Old Man Narrow's daughter, who believed she was any man's equal.

'You can stay right there,' she told Byren, while the boy scurried behind her.

The growling rose another pitch.

'Manticores,' Byren panted. 'A whole pride on our trail.'

'Manticores this far into the valley? Are you sure?' She sounded doubtful, almost scornful. The three wolfhounds went quiet, but remained wary.

'Took one of our horses and frightened the others off.' Byren indicated the rest of his party, who were bent double behind him, catching their breath. 'We've had to do a forced march to get here. Must warn Old Man Narrows.'

'Da's gone to see –'

'Hush, Leif.' The girl's cheeks flamed because, with that one slip, he'd revealed their vulnerability.

Byren understood her problem. It seemed she was alone with her younger brother and three wolfhounds, and his party composed of three men and Piro, who could be mistaken for a boy in her thick travelling gear.

'Then it is just the six of us to hold off the manticores,' Byren said. 'We've got to get inside and make the tradepost secure.' But he did not move, waiting for her to call off the dogs.

A thudding echoed through the trunks, followed by the splintering of wood. The boy reached for his sister's hand. 'What –'

'It's the manticores breaking down the palisade gate,' Orrade said. 'They're only a few minutes behind us.'

'This way, quickly.' The girl turned, grabbed her brother's arm and made off briskly.

Byren hurried to catch up. He could just see the tradepost's top floor peeping above the tree canopy. She easily matched his long loping stride, axe casually slung over her shoulder. 'You think they'll approach the house? Manticores usually –'

'They've come down this far into the valley and they're a large pride, with five cubs to feed,' Byren said. 'They'll need food –'

'Run ahead to the barn, Leif,' the girl interrupted him. 'Take Crusher and Queenie. Put the chickens in and bar the barn door.'

They were on the path to the tradepost now. He caught glimpses of it through the trunks, its ornate roofline silhouetted against the pearl-shell sky.

Stepping out of the trees, they approached the building. It was three storey's high. Built entirely of wood without a single nail, every join dovetailed into the next. The wood crafters had decorated every surface with intertwining floral and animal motifs. No lights burned in any of the windows. Only a thin wisp of smoke came from one of the chimneys.

'You're alone,' Byren said. 'I'm sorry I brought these manticores down on you.'

'Aye. I'm alone with little Leif. Father's gone to see his sister. Took poorly, she did. Come on.' The girl ran across the open space from the tree line to the building, diverting away from the front entrance where the tap room was, to go around to a side entrance across from the barn. There was no sign of her brother.

She flung the door open and called over her shoulder. 'Hurry up, Leif.'

'I'll help him,' Byren offered. 'Can you see to my sister? She's exhausted.'

The girl nodded and Byren sprinted into the barn, where Leif had already driven the chickens in. Crusher and Queenie came over to investigate him, so Byren offered his hand. The dogs' heads were level with his waist and their jaws could have easily crushed his hand.

'They're good dogs,' Leif said, hauling open a sack of chicken feed.

'Eh, not tonight, Leif. No time. Come on.' Byren grabbed the boy and together they barred the barn's doors. 'Is this the only way in?'

'I've barred the shutters as well.'

'Good lad.'

Byren backed across what would have been the busy stable yard, empty now of anything but their footprints in the snow. Crusher and Queenie went very still, barked twice then shivered and whimpered, slinking to their sides. Byren's mouth went dry. He scanned the tree line and the shadows between the outbuildings. He couldn't spot the manticores, but he knew they were there. Heart racing, he reached for his hunting knife. His hand felt slick on the hilt. Why was it that when he needed a bow he only had a knife?

Because he didn't want to walk around weighed down with weapons.

He heard Leif swing the tradepost door open. The boy and the dogs darted through. Byren followed, closing it behind him. The boy grinned up at him and Byren couldn't help grinning back. Even the dogs grinned.

It was dark in the hall, but a welcoming glow came from under a door further along. The smell of roast lamb and oregano made his stomach rumble. He could hear voices.

'This way,' Leif said.

Byren found the others in the kitchen, where Leif's sister was putting out plates while Piro sliced fresh bread and Garzik poured ales. Orrade had made friends with the other wolfhound, which was crunching on a bone in front of the huge oven.

'Byren, thank the goddess!' Piro greeted him. 'I wasn't sure we'd make it.'

He was glad he hadn't revealed his own doubts.

'Who says we're safe?' the girl countered.

Orrade glanced to Byren, as did Garzik and Piro.

The boy looked at his sister. 'What d'you mean, Florin? Da always says this is the best fortified of all the tradeposts.'

'Aye. And I've closed all the shutters on the ground floor, but the house wasn't meant to be defended. The Neck and the palisade should have kept us safe, only the manticores are in now. We have to come out eventually. Once the manticores have battered their way through the barn and eaten our animals, they'll be waiting for us.'

Byren knew this was true. Manticores were renowned for their intelligence. He wouldn't put it past them to figure out how to lift the bar that held the barn door closed. Then the manticores would find a way into the tradepost. He'd brought this down on Florin and Leif. It was his responsibility to keep them safe.

'We'll have to kill the manticores,' he decided.

Orrade snorted. 'Kill a whole pride? Even you can't do that, Byren!'

'No, not on my own. But the cold snap has drained all the moisture from the air. Ideal for fire, and with a little cunning...' He grinned, and they drew closer, eager to hear his plan.

* * *

PIRO TRUSTED BYREN'S judgement. If he said the flaming torches would keep the manticores away, then they would. Still, she felt vulnerable as they left the tradepost, each carrying a torch, cooking pots, several jars of pitch and more torches. She was so laden down, she couldn't have run if she'd tried. Her stomach tied itself in knots. Whatever made her think she would have enjoyed hunting the leogryf!

They were all armed with bows, courtesy of the tradepost's weapon room. But night had fallen while they planned and prepared, so it would be difficult to hit a moving target.

Byren was right, they had to kill the manticores... couldn't leave them to roam the valley, terrorising isolated farms.

The wolfhounds bayed. Piro's heart raced in response to the mournful sound. Little Leif edged closer to her. Garzik, Orrade and Florin each held a wolfhound's collar as well as their load of supplies, and the great beasts strained to be let loose. Silly things. They were outmatched. Together they could bring down one manticore perhaps, but not a pride.

She didn't catch sight of the god-touched beasts as they made their way to the palisade. Orrade and Florin dug a trench across the ruined gateway and filled it with pitch. When Florin touched her torch to the pitch, the trench filled with flames and Leif cheered. Piro was heartened, but suspected that celebrating would be premature.

'Right, you two come with me,' Florin ordered Piro and Leif. 'Orrade and Garzik go that way. Then spread out and make as much noise as possible.'

They ran down the length of the palisade, about a body length from the wood, spilling pitch and lighting it as they went. At this point, it was only a bow shot across Narrowneck. Soon the palisade's length was a line of leaping flames.

'Now that they can't get out, we'll drive them before us,' Florin urged. She began shouting, making the dogs bark madly. Piro and Leif took their cooking pots and banged them together, shouting for all they were worth. Every so often, Florin tossed a pitch-dipped flaming torch to each side, lighting up the night.

Piro could hear Orrade and Garzik, just make them out through the trunks. At its widest, Narrowneck was only two bow shots across, growing more slender until it came to the tradepost which was built just up from the cliffs that led down to the beach. Narrowneck tradepost even boasted a weighted lever that could lift the heaviest load up from the beach and lower it down again.

The shouting and the leaping flames made Piro feel safer. She only hoped Byren was as safe and that his plan worked.

BYREN SET OFF alone, heading for the platform above the cliffs to the beach. The platform was designed well, with rails and a gate the fed onto the extendible ladder. This could be raised quickly. From here, defenders could shoot down on the beach. But the platform was not defensible from the inside. When the builders had planned the tradepost they had not foreseen the need to defend the gate from this direction.

The excited barking of the hounds, then shouts and clanking told him the others had begun their part. Cutting off the manticores' last avenue of escape was his responsibility. He poured a trail of pitch in an arc around the platform which stood head high, set fire to the pitch and climbed onto the platform.

After stringing the borrowed bow, which was a little short and too light for him, he strode to the far side of the platform, avoiding the frame with its heavy weight and glanced down onto the snow-covered beach four body lengths below. It was empty of tracks. Good. None of the manticores had escaped. If all went well several would topple over the cliffs and die. The wolfhounds might account for one or two of the juveniles and, if any attacked his companions, they had their bows.

He turned to face Narrowneck and the tree line, paced to the edge of the platform and closed his eyes to adjust them to the night before opening them. Then he focused on the ground about a body length below the platform on the inland side. He had a good view of the approach to the only way off Narrowneck.

The baying of the wolfhounds changed pitch and he knew they had been let loose. They would flush out any manticores that tried to take shelter in the outbuildings.

The hunting horn sounded, high and piercing. Florin and Orrade each carried one. It meant that one of them had killed a manticore. He spotted a dark shadow with the distinctive manticore tail that curled forwards over its body, slinking through the tree trunks. He raised his bow, taking his time with the shot because he wanted to sever the spine behind the neck. The angle was good.

Thung. He let the bowstring go.

The great cat screamed, legs collapsing. It wasn't dead, but crippled like that, the wolfhounds could finish it.

Another hunting horn sounded. That accounted for three of the manticores. He hoped it was the adults. The dogs could handle the juveniles, if they got them cornered one at a time.

This was going to work.

Byren turned to survey his field, reaching for another arrow.

A manticore confronted him. It was the male, with a mane dark as old blood. While he was looking the other way, it had crept close, body low to the ground until it was about a body length from him. A short leap for a beast of its size.

'Easy... easy...' He breathed slowly, bring the arrow over his shoulder, nocking it, drawing.

Too late. The beast leapt. It was the leogryf all over, but this time there was no Lence to push him to safety.

He let the arrow fly, even though he knew it was hopeless, then threw himself back, left arm raised to fend off the jaws. He expected to hit the rail, but the manticore was already on him. It caught him on the upward arc of its leap. The impact drove him over the rail, off the platform. For an instant he and the beast hung in the air.

Then the ground called them and, with a sickening lurch, they dropped.

The world spun around Byren, icy lake gleaming

in the starlight, snowy rocks flashing past, sparkling sky. The manticore writhed, trying to right itself as it fell. With a reverberating thud they struck a rocky outcropping halfway down, with the beast under him. The impact of their fall sent them ricocheting off, out and down again.

PIRO CAUGHT LEIF and thrust him behind her, as Garzik reached for an arrow. The wolfhounds had one of the juveniles trapped in a corner of the dairy. Florin and Orrade were doing a sweep of Narrowneck to be sure they had got them all.

Garzik notched his arrow and drew, waiting for a good shot.

The side of Piro's neck prickled with warning. She turned. Another juvenile stood in the shadows, poised to attack Leif.

'Garzik!' she hissed, reaching for an arrow and nocking it.

'Quiet, Piro. I don't want to hit one of the dogs.'

She couldn't take her gaze off those gleaming orange eyes, but at the same time she was aware of the raised tail, the poisoned spike dripping with venom. Could her arrow drive through the manticore's eye into its brain before it struck Leif? She didn't think so. But she had to do something.

She thrust Leif behind her, saw a stray bucket and, quick as thought, kicked it at the beast.

The manticore struck instinctively, tail hitting the bucket with a resounding ring of chitin striking metal.

Piro loosed her arrow. It took the manticore high in

the shoulder where it met the neck. Garzik swore. A dog howled, then whimpered. The other two growled as they attacked, tearing the second manticore apart. The cornered Affinity beast screamed in pain and fury.

Piro's manticore took one step before its legs folded under it. She darted aside, dragging Leif out of the way of the falling tail. They collided with Garzik's back, driving him to safety and fell in a heap on the dairy floor.

'Whaa?' Garzik rolled to his feet. He gaped as he took in the second manticore.

Piro climbed to her feet. Odd, her legs didn't work properly.

'You all right?' Garzik asked.

She tried to say *of course*, but no words came.

Garzik hauled young Leif to his feet.

'Piro saved me,' Leif whispered, awed. 'She saved you, too.'

Garzik turned to her, with a look she couldn't interpret. 'Piro, I –'

She found her voice. 'That's two more down, better tell Orrie and Florin.'

Her knees felt like water as she moved towards the dairy door. Leif whistled to call off the dogs. The surviving two came readily, muzzles bloodied, coats torn in places.

'Poor Crusher.' Leif shed ready tears.

Garzik rubbed his back. 'You can be proud of them. They've earned their keep tonight.'

They'd only just stepped from between the outbuildings when Orrade came running towards them.

'Byren's missing,' he called.

Piro's heart lurched sickeningly.

'Are all the manticores accounted for?' Florin asked, coming in from the other direction with a flaming torch.

'We just killed two juveniles,' Garzik said.

'Then there's only the large male –'

'Are you deaf?' Orrade rounded on her. 'Byren's missing.'

'If we don't know where the pride leader is, more of us could go missing,' she told him.

Orrade blinked and nodded once. 'You're right. Leif, fetch some more torches.'

The lad ran across to the wood pile. Piro opened her jar of pitch, dipping the new torches in it and setting them alight.

Orrade took a torch, leading the way. Piro identified the platform and the machinery of the great lever, stark against the froth of stars, then the stain on the snow where the pitch had burned away. But the platform was empty.

'Gate's still barred,' Florin said. She turned towards the tradepost, peering into the night. 'Where could –'

Orrade groaned and dropped to his knees in the snow. Piro could not stop herself imagining the male manticore dragging Byren's body away to devour him. Her head reeled.

Florin walked around the base of the platform. 'No drag marks, so –'

'How am I going to tell King Rolen his son is dead?' Orrade whispered, devastated.

'King Rolen?' Leif repeated. 'You mean that was Byren the leogryf slayer?'

'Byren Rolen Kingson?' Florin rounded on them.

'And this,' Garzik gave a mock bow, 'is Pirola Rolen Kingsdaughter, manticore slayer.'

Despite her fear for Byren, a smile tugged at Piro's lips.

'Hey,' Byren's voice floated up to them. 'When you're done talking can you help me?'

Orrade sprang to his feet but Piro beat him to the rail. Fumbling in their haste, they peered between the rails, over the platform edge.

'Careful,' Byren warned, from the snow-covered beach below.

Piro laughed, then sat down abruptly, resting her forehead on the icy wood of the railing.

The others joined them. Garzik tossed his torch down, so that it landed near Byren's feet, illuminating the broken body of the great cat with Byren standing unhurt beside it.

'I swear you have more lives than a cat, Byren!' Orrade called down. 'What happened?'

'Affinity beastie leaped up and knocked me off the platform. We crashed into the cliffs halfway down. The manticore took the impact of that before hitting the rocky beach beneath me. Killed it outright. Lucky for me.'

'And you're not hurt?' Florin asked, clearly astounded.

He laughed then slapped his arms and thighs. 'The beastie broke my fall both times.'

'Of all the luck.' Florin shook her head. 'Halcyon favours you!'

'Are the manticores all dead?' Byren asked. Orrade stood and tried to get the ladder's mechanism working.

'Aye. All dead,' Florin said.

'We lost Crusher.' Leif's voice quavered.

'I'm sorry, lad. He was a fine dog,' Byren said and Piro could tell he meant it. That's why people loved her brother.

'I can't get the ladder to drop,' Orrade announced. 'The ropes are missing.'

'If the cliff wasn't covered in snow I could try to climb it,' Byren said.

Florin stepped in front of Orrade. 'We take the ropes and pulleys off for winter.' Then she leant out to call down to Byren. 'You'd never make it up the cliff, I tried last summer.'

'Ho, that's a challenge if I ever heard one,' Garzik muttered to Piro, as he pulled her to her feet.

She smiled. She was beginning to understand why they teased each other. It wasn't that they weren't afraid. They were, but the best way to meet fear was to laugh at it.

'Could you make it, if I threw down a rope?' Florin asked Byren.

'Of course he could,' Orrade said, even as Byren said much the same thing.

Florin turned to Leif. 'Run back to the store room and bring a coil of rope.'

'I'll go with him,' Garzik offered. 'Make sure it's strong enough.'

Piro found she was suddenly so tired she couldn't stand up straight, and her limbs trembled.

'Better take Piro – I mean, the kingsdaughter,' Florin advised.

'Piro will do,' she insisted. 'And I don't know

what's wrong with me –'

'Don't worry,' Florin told her. 'I feel a bit shaky myself.'

Piro laughed. She couldn't imagine Florin giving in to weakness.

'We'll be ready soon, Byren,' Orrade called down to him. 'Trust you to take on a manticore bare handed!'

'Actually, it was the fall down the cliff that killed it,' Byren corrected. 'That and me landing on it!'

The others roared with laughter. Piro found she laughed so much she cried. Florin gave her a hug and sent her off with Garzik and Leif.

BYREN HAD BEEN torn between heading straight back to Rolenhold or taking the time to remove the manticore chitin so he could present it to their father. The memory of Warlord Corvel of Manticore in his fabulous chitin breast plate decided him. Removing the chitin and loading it on the sled had taken the better part of the day. But it was a fine gift, more than enough for a full suit of armour and worth as much as a small estate.

He'd had Piro say the words over the beasts' bodies to safely release their Affinity. It was the best he could do without an Affinity warder and it meant that Florin and Leif could take the pelts and sell them, a windfall for their family.

'Ready?' Orrade asked.

Byren nodded and skated over to the snowy beach where Florin and Leif waited to say goodbye. 'We'll be off. Thanks for the loan of the sled and skates.'

Leif surprised Byren by throwing his arms around his waist.

'Next litter Queenie has, I'm going to call the biggest one Byren,' he said.

'A wolfhound named after you, now that's an honour!' Orrade said with only the merest suggestion of a twinkle in his black eyes.

Piro laughed and hugged Florin, then disentangled Leif from Byren to hug the boy.

Byren faced Florin. Standing on the beach which was higher than the ice, she was as tall as him. It was a funny feeling, looking her straight in the eye. The pink glow of the setting sun illuminated her skin and he realised what a striking young woman she was. He cleared his throat. 'We owe you our lives –'

'And we owe you ours,' she said, meeting his gaze.

He was used to girls who blushed and cast him shy glances, or ones who sent him bold looks that left nothing to the imagination. He didn't know how to take a girl who held his eyes like an equal, like a man.

It made no sense unless... Florin was like Orrade. Of course. It was whispered that the nuns of Sylion turned to each other for comfort. Not that he could see anything wrong with that. In fact, it seemed only natural. Women were so lovely, after all. Heat raced through his body. He felt himself harden and was grateful for the thigh-length coat.

'Why are you looking at me like that?' Florin asked. 'Do I have dirt on my face?'

Startled, Byren's gaze slid past her as his heart thumped uncomfortably. He took in the steep cliff behind her and said the first thing that came into his head. 'Reckon I'll have to come back this summer and see if I can climb that cliff without a rope.'

Florin snorted. 'If I can't, no man can.'

'Ah,' he grinned. 'But I'm no ordinary man.'

Orrade and Garzik laughed outright and, after a moment, Florin joined them.

Byren set off with laughter ringing in his ears. He strained against the sled's harness to get the load moving. The metal blades groaned on the ice and began to shift. Orrade and Garzik wore the other two harnesses. Only Piro skated free, gliding ahead of them and circling back, graceful as a bird on the wing.

By full dark they'd made good time and were already out of the bend of Sapphire Lake.

Even though the ache in his shoulders told him it would be hard to get the sled moving when they started up again, Byren called for a break.

'We'll eat and skate by starlight until we have to rest,' he announced.

No one complained. No one asked why they were in a rush. He wondered if Orrade had discussed things with his brother.

While they undid the harnesses, Piro unpacked the food Florin had given them. Fresh-baked bread, preserves and smoked ham. They perched on the sled frame to give their thigh muscles a rest.

'I've been thinking, Byren,' Piro announced, finishing her food and slipping off the frame to glide around to face him. Enough starlight reflected from the ice to illuminate her serious face in shades of silver.

Byren swallowed. 'And?'

'The only way Cobalt could've lured the manticore pride close enough to turn them loose on us, was if he had Affinity.'

Byren felt the smile slip from his face. Though he'd come to the same conclusion, he hadn't expected Piro to put all the pieces together. He'd underestimated her.

Orrade sent him a wry look. Byren acknowledged it and indicated Piro was to go on.

'As I see it, you have to get back to Rolenhold and discredit Cobalt before Lence can accuse you.' She paused, watching to see if he'd object.

'Keep talking.'

'The manticore chitin is to put Father in a good mood, right?'

'It's worth a small fortune and not even the warlord of Manticore Spar has a whole suit of armour. So, yes, it should impress Father.'

She nodded. 'You'll give it to him, then accuse Cobalt of –'

'Setting the manticores on us? There's no proof.'

'No, of having Affinity. Father will send for the warder and wardess. They'll test him and Father will have to banish him, or send him to the abbey. Either way, he won't be able to cause any more trouble.'

'And what of Lence's accusation?'

Piro tilted her head. Byren waited for her to go on.

'Lence doesn't have a shred of proof and all you've ever done is serve Rolencia loyally. If he arrives to find Cobalt discredited, he may not even accuse you.'

'He could have proof,' Orrade objected. 'Fabricated by Cobalt.'

Of course. Why hadn't he thought of that? No

wonder Lence had believed the worst. Relief made Byren laugh.

'What?' Orrade demanded.

He grabbed Orrade and planted a kiss on his cheek. 'Thank you!'

Orrade blinked, stunned.

Byren laughed again, stood up and turned on his skate blades to face his friend. 'I've been walking around feeling sick to my stomach because I couldn't believe Lence would turn on me. Now you've just explained it. Cobalt must have convinced him with a forgery of some kind, or with a servant paid to lie. All I have to do is discredit Cobalt and Lence will see reason!'

Piro clapped her hands in delight. Byren hugged her, lifting her off the ground, spinning her around. She giggled and clung to him.

He set her down and turned to Orrade and Garzik. 'Come on. The sooner we get back, the sooner I clear my name.'

And save his family from Cobalt's machinations. Byren couldn't wait to wipe that satisfied smile off Illien's face.

Chapter Twenty-Five

'THIS WAY, MOTHER, Byren's waiting,' Piro urged, hardly able to stand still. Excitement thrummed through her body like a drawn bowstring. She wanted to see Cobalt discredited and Byren safe.

It was mid-afternoon and, as her brother had anticipated, King Rolen was in the great hall. The decorative friezes glinted in the many candles as Piro and her mother weaved through the forest of columns towards the fireside table, where the king sat drinking and talking with his close friends. Like Captain Temor, these lords were the survivors of his generation who had stood by him during the great battle, all that remained of his original noble honour guard. All but Cobalt, who even now was leaning forwards speaking. He looked so confident, so sincere as he described the sea-hounds, a fleet of warriors, which Ostron Isle sanctioned to contain the Utland menace. Piro was not surprised the older men trusted him. Only her Affinity allowed her to see into his hollow soul.

'Piro?' her mother prodded and she realised she had come to a dead stop.

'Myrella?' The king noticed them. His weather-beaten face creased into a smile of pleasure. 'And little Piro. Back already? Where's Byren?'

Piro turned to the main entrance. Garzik must have been watching because, at that moment, the doors parted and Byren entered, dragging a low-wheeled wagon. Canvas covered the fabulous manticore chitin which was piled high as a man. Garzik and Orrade followed.

'What's this?' Captain Temor muttered.

The king's old honour guard fell silent as they waited for Byren to reach them. The few servants stopped their work and watched curiously. Was Cobalt surprised to see Byren? Piro stole a quick look. He had gone very still and his expression was blank, as she watched his features settle into a look of mildly amused surprise. It would have appeared charming, if she hadn't watched him deliberately assume the expression. It was as though he'd selected it, as you might select an outfit for a special occasion.

She shivered.

'King Rolen, Queen Myrella.' Byren greeted their parents formally. He nodded to the others present, his face unusually grim. 'A gift for King Rolen, from your second son.' With a flourish he pulled off the canvas cover. 'Enough manticore chitin to fashion a complete set of armour.'

Everyone gasped.

'Looks like you've killed a whole pride,' Captain Temor marvelled.

Byren nodded. 'A male, two females and five juveniles.'

'Amazing. And you not only live to tell of it, you bring me their chitin!' King Rolen marched over to join him. 'But how is this? I thought you were visiting Dovecote estate, not hunting manticores.'

'The manticores were hunting us.' Byren did not so much as glance at Cobalt. Piro didn't know how he managed it. 'I was unlucky enough to come across a pride, but the goddess smiled on me and, with help...' he nodded to Garzik and Orrade, 'the hunters became the hunted. So here I am.'

Their father beamed. 'You must tell me how you three lads killed a whole pride.'

'We had help,' Byren said.

'And Piro killed one on her own!' Garzik announced.

King Rolen's eyes widened. His honour guard muttered, astounded.

'Eh, my little Piro.' King Rolen chuckled. 'Your mother was right to name you after Pirola the Fierce!'

Piro glanced to her mother, who was looking at her as if she hadn't really seen her before.

'Did you set traps, Byren?' Temor asked.

'In a way. But first, I must bring something important to your attention, Father.' Byren waited until they all fell silent. 'King Rolen, I have reason to believe one of your trusted advisors has been hiding untamed Affinity.'

'What?' the king stiffened. Their father had known these men since they were boys, fought beside them thirty years ago. The only new advisor was... 'Illien? You're accusing your cousin Illien, Byren?'

Her brother nodded.

'Byren!' their mother whispered, shocked.

'Why, Byren?' Illien said sadly. 'What have I ever done to you?'

Piro had to bite her tongue.

'I'm only doing my duty, Illien,' Byren said. 'If you do not have Affinity, then you have nothing to fear.'

'Exactly,' Cobalt agreed. 'Send for the warders, Uncle. I insist!'

Cobalt was not acting like a man about to be exposed. Either he had nerves of steel or... was it possible to fool the warders? A nasty feeling settled in Piro's stomach. Had Illien learnt some technique in Ostron Isle, where Affinity was accepted and put to use? No, that wasn't possible. In her studies she had read of instances when warders exposed foreigners who were renegade Power-workers, disguised as simple merchants.

Both Halcyon and Sylion warders were sent for and there was general muttering while everyone waited. Though the old honour guard moved away from Cobalt, isolating him, the king stayed at his side. The queen edged closer to Piro to whisper, 'What's going on?'

'Does Cobalt have Affinity?'

'Not that I've sensed. He's –'

'Walled. I know. Perhaps that's because he's been cloaking it all this time.'

The queen shook her head. 'I'd know. I can't believe he could hide this from me. Why is Byren attacking him?'

'If you can't look into Cobalt's heart, look into Byren's,' Piro urged.

Her mother crossed to Byren. Taking his hand in hers she asked something softly. Piro followed, curious. As Byren went to answer, he frowned and rubbed the bridge of his nose. The queen made a soft noise of pain in her throat. She swayed.

'What's wrong, mother?' Byren asked.

She shook her head and reached out to steady herself. Piro caught her hand, helping as Byren led her to a chair.

'Do you need a drink, mother? Is it one of your Turns?' Byren asked gently. 'Should I send for Seela?'

The queen shook her head. Byren squeezed her shoulder then rejoined the others.

'Well, mother?' Piro whispered.

The queen looked up, eyes swimming with dread. 'I have always sensed Lence's shadow beside Byren. It's missing. I fear Lence –'

'He's fine. Or he was when we left him at Dovecote,' Piro said. They were a good body length from the men and it seemed the right time to explain about the manticore attack, but just then Byren spoke up.

'Why don't you ask why I accuse you, Illien?'

'I imagine you have your reasons. When I am cleared of this ridiculous accusation, I will –'

Nun Springdawn arrived, with Monk Autumnwind on her heels. They crossed the great hall, their slippers making no sound on the flag stones, then dropped to one knee in front of her father.

'You sent for us, King Rolen,' they spoke in unison, one voice high and clear, the other deep and aged.

'Yes, Warder Autumnwind, Wardess Springdawn,' the king greeted them formally. 'Byren Kingson has made a serious accusation. I want you to test Illien of Cobalt for Affinity.'

The two warders exchanged startled looks.

The queen rose and rejoined the group. Piro followed, certain whatever her mother might feel for Cobalt, this would be outweighed by her feelings for Byren.

'As you wish, King Rolen,' the monk said. They both came to their feet and turned to Cobalt.

'Beware,' Piro spoke up.

All eyes turned to her.

'He may be hiding his Affinity. I've heard it can be hidden behind walls.' She kept her voice firm while inside she quailed, wary of revealing knowledge which might lead to her own exposure.

'It is good to know my many hours of tutoring have not been wasted,' Springdawn said proudly and Piro had the grace to blush. When she had been the nun's pupil Springdawn was more often frustrated than pleased with her diligence. 'But it takes years of training to develop a wall. He may have some natural shielding. Some minds are born with it.'

'I am ready,' Cobalt announced, stepping forwards. 'What would you have me do?'

Springdawn took a slight step backs indicating Autumnwind should speak.

'Normally one of us would lay our hands on a child's head and skim the surface of their mind,' the Affinity warder said. 'With children it is very simple, they have no defences.'

'And with adults?' King Rolen asked.

Springdawn leant closer to Autumnwind to whisper.

'Speak up. I would know everything,' King Rolen urged.

Springdawn bobbed her head in apology. 'I was suggesting my colleague is better suited to this task. Affinity affects men differently from women.'

Piro hadn't known that, though she supposed it made sense. She watched as Springdawn stepped back. Why did the nun look pleased?

'King Rolen, I am honour-bound to speak the truth,' Autumnwind warned.

'Of course, of course.' Her father waved him on. Piro realised if the Affinity warder had to condemn Cobalt, he would do it, even though it would not please the king. No wonder Springdawn looked satisfied.

'Proceed,' the king said.

'Very well. Will someone restrain the candidate?'

'You do not need to hold me.' Cobalt lifted his hands palm up. With his handsome features, he looked noble and wronged. 'I will not struggle.'

Autumnwind grimaced. 'You may collapse. It can be –'

'Then I'll sit.' Cobalt beckoned a servant who hurried over with a straight-backed chair.

After this was adjusted to Autumnwind's satisfaction Cobalt sat, hands resting on his thighs. 'I'm ready.'

Everyone else seemed more uncomfortable with the proceedings than he.

'Will it hurt?' Piro asked the question that seemed to be on everyone's mind.

'Only if he resists,' Autumnwind explained.

Cobalt blinked once and inhaled deeply, as though preparing for the worst. Despite herself, Piro felt a tug of admiration and sympathy.

She gave herself a mental shake. If this hurt Cobalt – and she was certain it would – it was his own fault for using Affinity to manipulate her family.

Springdawn stepped closer to Piro, hemming her in, so that the nun was on one side and the queen on the other.

'This natural shielding, Piro,' Springdawn's soft voice fell into the rhythm of lecture, 'you have it too.'

Piro went very still.

Unaware of her reaction, Springdawn raised her voice. 'I am here if you need support, warder.'

The monk sent her a sharp look that held an undercurrent of dislike.

Then Autumnwind, Halcyon Affinity warder, stepped around behind Cobalt, placed both hands on the larger man's temples and closed his eyes.

Piro desperately wanted to observe Autumnwind's technique. She longed to open her senses so that she could see with her Unseen sight but she didn't dare, not with the wardess at her side.

'Do not fear, Piro.' Springdawn took her hand and squeezed it. 'Affinity rarely turns nasty. Though I did read of one occasion when the warder died before they could disengage his senses from the candidate, who turned out to be a renegade Power-worker in disguise.'

Autumnwind's eyes flew open and the look he sent her this time was definitely unfriendly. Then he lowered his lids again and spoke the words to clear his mind and open his senses.

Piro looked away, controlling her instinct to observe. She felt Springdawn do the same thing, distancing herself from the procedure. Why would she do that? Was the Sylion nun leaving her colleague to sink or swim?

At least a dozen people were present, but no one fidgeted or spoke as the silence stretched. Piro heard servants going about their tasks. Voices echoed down the halls, distorted by distance, while, in the great hall, there was only the sound of the fire crackling in the hearth, which was big enough to burn a trunk as thick as a man was tall.

Despite her best intentions, Piro's gaze was drawn back to Autumnwind and Cobalt. The monk frowned and Cobalt grimaced, lips white as if in pain. Sweat beads collected on the monk's forehead. Cobalt groaned and ground his teeth.

Piro had to fight the instinct to reach for her Affinity. The effort made her sway.

Springdawn noticed. 'Are you unwell, Piro?'

'She's upset,' her mother said and gently led her away from the others over to the table where their wine sat forgotten. She pressed Piro into a chair and put her head forwards. The nun followed them.

'Breath deeply, Piro. It will pass,' her mother said.

'I know it is not a pretty sight, this Affinity seeking,' Springdawn said softly. 'The smell of blood affects me the same way.'

'I'm all right now,' Piro whispered. She lifted her head, feeling her cheeks grow warm as the colour returned. 'What... what happens if he can't get past Cobalt's natural shielding?'

'Then sorbt stones are the final proof. We strap a stone to the Candidate's naked skin and leave it there. At some point his concentration must falter, he has to let down his guard to sleep, you see. The moment his walls drop the stone will sense the Affinity and naturally try to absorb it. Any trained warder can detect if the stone is activated. The danger is, that once activated the stone can drain an untrained person to death within heartbeats. Sorbt stones are very powerful.'

Piro shuddered and glanced towards Cobalt and Byren. Despite her fear of detection she wanted to see what was happening. 'How long will this take?'

'As long as it needs to,' Springdawn said.

'Are you feeling better now, Piro?' her mother asked.

She nodded and stood up. They headed towards the others but had not even reached Garzik and Orrade, who were on the outer circle, when the smell hit Piro. Sweat and vomit.

'Ugh.' Her nose wrinkled then she froze, afraid that this smell was something only those with Affinity would be aware of.

'Yes.' Springdawn shuddered. 'It's a bad one. Trust Autumnwind to force his way through.'

'What is that smell?' Piro whispered.

'It's the smell of battle,' Orrade muttered. 'Only battle's worse.'

'How could it be worse?'

He just looked at her. She glimpsed a window to horror before he shielded his mind. And she thought she knew Orrade. He was a blade, sharp and merciless. She shuddered. Damn her Affinity. Had Springdawn noticed?

'Catch them!' King Rolen yelled.

The queen thrust through the others, with Piro on her heels. They were in time to see Cobalt sway and tumble forwards off the chair. Her father caught Cobalt's arm before he could hit the ground. Autumnwind struggled to a seat, visibly shaken. No one had actually thrown up, the smell came through their skin.

Piro had never come across anything like it. The smell hit her at a primal level. *Fear*, it said. *Danger*.

Instinct triggered her Affinity and her sight shifted to the Unseen. The monk pulsed, his outline hazy as if he was only partly there. She could tell he had exhausted himself.

'Wine!' The king's words reached her as if they came down a deep tunnel, reverberating oddly. He held out his hand and a goblet was refilled then placed in his grasp. He handed it to Cobalt, who drained it in one go, hands trembling.

He hardly registered on Piro's vision. No power radiated from him. But then no power radiated from her mother either as she poured Autumnwind a drink and gave it to him.

Springdawn shifted and Piro glanced to her, not surprised to see that she also pulsed like the monk, but much more strongly. The nun had not exhausted her store of Affinity.

Made aware that she was exposing herself needlessly, Piro tried to rein in her Affinity, backing up until she hit someone.

'Piro, you're trembling.' Garzik steadied her.

'Don't feel so good.'

'I know. The smell's almost too much for me too.' He tried to lead her back to the chair but she planted her feet. She didn't want to miss a thing.

'And what did you learn, Warder Autumnwind?' King Rolen asked formally.

The monk moved off the chair, sinking to one knee before his king. 'I could detect no Affinity.'

It was as Piro had feared.

'What?' Byren unfolded his arms. 'You jest!'

'If the warder could detect no Affinity that's good enough for me,' the king said. He put a hand on Cobalt's shoulder and squeezed. The younger man reached up to return the pressure.

Piro waited for Springdawn to tell them about the sorbt stones but she didn't.

Piro thrust free of Garzik's supporting hand and darted through the others until she was in the ranks of the inner circle, where she could see the nun. Springdawn met her eyes, but didn't seem to get her message. Why didn't the nun speak up?

Piro glanced to her mother, who seemed to hesitate. Did she still harbour feelings for Cobalt?

'It's settled then,' the king said.

'No, it isn't.' Piro insisted. 'There is still the sorbt stone test.'

The monk looked startled.

'What's Piro talking about, Autumnwind?' her father asked.

He used the sleeve of his monk's robe to wipe his forehead. 'Your daughter is remarkably well educated, King Rolen. She's speaking of the final test which will either kill or clear the accused.'

Springdawn stepped forwards. 'I will send to Sylion Abbey for a pair of sorbt stones. Once we have them we can conduct the test. If that is your wish, my king.'

'I want my name cleared.' Cobalt lurched upright. He swayed and let the king press him back into his chair. 'I must clear my name.'

The old honour guard nodded sympathetically. Piro wanted to shake them but she wasn't surprised they were taken in, when Cobalt played the injured party so well.

'A man has a right to clear his name,' the king agreed. 'Send for the stones, Springdawn.'

'I must know, Uncle, am I a prisoner?' Cobalt asked.

'Of course not.' The king looked uncomfortable.

Byren muttered under his breath, radiating impatience and Piro winced for him. Instead of discrediting Cobalt before everyone, his ploy had won Cobalt their sympathy.

'I'm sorry it has come to this, Illien,' King Rolen said. 'I don't know why Byren –'

'I do.' Cobalt paused and everyone waited for him to go on. 'When I was at Dovecote estate he wasn't there. Ask him why he didn't go to Dovecote.'

The silence stretched.

'Byren?' Queen Myrella asked. 'What is he talking about?'

Byren let his breath out slowly, then lifted his hands. 'Lord Dovecote told me never again to set foot on his estate.'

There was a hushed intake of breath. Byren's cheeks flushed but Piro couldn't tell whether it was with anger or discomfort.

'Why would the Old Dove do such a thing?' the king demanded.

Byren drew breath to explain.

'Why, Uncle?' Cobalt said softly. 'Because your son and his friend are Servants of Palos. And, like all loyal Rolencians, Lord Dovecote despises them. Discrediting me was part of their plan to usurp the throne.'

Their father took a step back, visibly shaken.

Their mother lifted a hand to her chest as if in pain, her black eyes going to Byren's face. 'That's why Lence –'

'It's not true,' Piro cried. 'It's –'

'A wicked lie!' Garzik insisted, his voice cracking so he sounded like a boy and not a man.

Cobalt gestured to Orrade. 'Do you deny you two are lovers?'

'I do,' Orrade said stoutly. 'And may I face the Trial of Truth to prove it.'

The king looked impressed. The Trial of Truth was not invoked lightly.

'Answer me this if you can, Orrade the Nameless,' Cobalt countered. 'Why were you disinherited?'

'Because my father leapt to the wrong conclusion.'

'And what conclusion was that?' Cobalt persisted.

Orrade hesitated, glancing to Byren.

'What is this? What does he mean?' King Rolen demanded of Byren.

'Orrade is a true and loyal friend, who has saved

my life on more than one occasion,' Byren said. 'He is not my lover, never has been. But he is –'

'...a Servant of Palos,' Cobalt finished for him.

'There is no secret society serving Palos.' Byren rounded on Cobalt, glaring. But with Cobalt slumped exhausted in the chair and Byren towering over him, Byren appeared the aggressor.

Her brother seemed to realise this and took a step back, looking around the group. 'It is all wicked rumour spread by an evil schemer for his own advancement.'

Cobalt shook his head sadly. 'You accuse me of what you are doing. It is ever the way.'

Byren's mouth dropped open, then he turned to their father in a silent plea for understanding. But King Rolen's usually bluff, good-natured face had grown hard with suspicion.

Piro glanced to their mother who looked from Cobalt to Byren, obviously horrified by what was unfolding. If only Piro hadn't asked her mother to look into Byren's heart. Instead of convincing her of his honesty, it had convicted him in her eyes. It was Lence who had, unconsciously, severed the twin-link, not Byren.

'Byren?' the queen whispered.

He dropped to his knees in front of the king. 'I swear by the love I have for Rolencia, I have never sought to be more than your second son, Father. I have served the kingsheir –'

'As long as it suited you,' Cobalt inserted.

There was a low murmur from the old guard.

Byren shifted with annoyance. 'Out of love, I have served my twin and will always do so.'

But Piro noticed even Captain Temor had averted his face from Byren. There was only one way to prove Byren spoke the truth.

She darted in front of the queen. 'Please, mother, tell them Byren speaks the truth. You know he does. You can –'

'No. I can only see with a mother's heart,' the queen whispered, denying her Affinity.

Piro's gaze flew to Byren, who had resumed his feet. She turned back to the queen and, in a flash of insight, Piro realised that if her mother revealed her Affinity now her marriage would be annulled and her children declared bastards. Cobalt would have as much right to the throne as Lence.

Piro fixed on Springdawn. 'You are an Affinity wardess, you can look into people's hearts and tell if they speak the truth. Look into Byren's.'

But Springdawn was already shaking her head. 'I don't have that skill. It is a very specialised talent.'

'Autumnwind?' Piro pleaded.

'I can't and even if I could, I'm exhausted,' he apologised.

'Then send for someone who can,' Piro insisted.

'Enough, Pirola!' the king snapped, using the voice he reserved for hearings. 'These are very serious accusations.'

'But Father –'

He silenced her with a look. 'The Servants of Palos caused the civil war that weakened Rolencia and this was the reason Merofynia attacked us thirty years ago. It might seem like history to you, but I was there. I saw the destruction –'

'But Father, Byren is innocent!' Piro ran to him and clutched his arm. 'If anyone is guilty of deceit it is Cobalt.' She rounded on him. 'Why did you leave Dovecote before we did? It was to lead the manticore pride to our camp site, wasn't it?'

Seated, Cobalt was almost as tall as her. His handsome lips twitched. 'You must think I am a wondrous person, little Piro, if you think I could lead a pride of manticores anywhere. Why, it would take a renegade Power-worker...' his eyes widened. 'So that is why you thought I had Affinity!'

He turned an astounded face towards Byren. But Piro was close enough to see past his expression, into his heart and it was as hard as stone. She faltered. Her sight shifted to the Unseen and she recognised a predator in Cobalt's eyes, a predator in human form.

She gasped, backing up until she reached Byren, who steadied her. It seemed to take forever, but by the time her vision returned to normal Cobalt had only just drawn his next breath. Startled by her slip, she glanced quickly to Autumnwind. He was rubbing his face wearily. Then she glanced over her shoulder. Springdawn was whispering to her mother. No one had noticed her use of Affinity.

'Byren.' Cobalt shook his head sadly. 'Don't blame your misfortune on me. There is a perfectly simple explanation for my presence here at court. Lence sent me to tell the king and queen that he will be staying at Dovecote for a few days on the way home.' His face hardened. 'I am not the one who has been lying.'

Frustration welled up in Piro. Cobalt managed

to turn everything to his advantage. She glanced to her father. Surely he did not believe Byren meant to depose his brother?

But King Rolen sagged as if from a blow. 'That my own son should turn out to be a –'

'He should be disinherited,' old Lord Steadfast muttered.

'Banished,' another insisted.

Byren undid the shoulder clasp of his cloak and flung it aside, lifting his hands palm up. 'I demand the right to a Trial of Truth to clear my name.'

'He has the right,' Captain Temor began. 'He –'

'How can he even suggest a Trial by Truth when no man of ordinary size can stand against him?' Cobalt demanded, astounded. 'None but his twin, the kingsheir, can match him for size and strength!'

The truth of it made everyone draw back.

'Freezing Sylion, I don't want to fight Lence. You would twist the very goddess's words, Cobalt!' Byren hissed with frustration. 'You were the one I wanted to stand against to prove my innocence. You have accused me of treason, I challenge you!'

'Me?' Cobalt repeated, pale and frightened, for once not quick enough to hide his honest reaction. Piro smiled.

'The Trial of Truth is a barbarous custom and proves nothing but that one man is a better killer than the other,' Queen Myrella snapped.

Cobalt cleared his throat. 'I'll meet you, Byren. But I must warn you, I have been tutored by the best swordmaster in Ostron Isle.' He went to rise, still shaky. 'Send for my sword.'

'No. This is ridiculous,' the king muttered. 'Illien can hardly stand. This will prove nothing!'

'Father!' Byren appealed, searching the king's grey face.

'I can show no favour,' he whispered as he took a step back from Byren.

Piro gasped. He couldn't mean it.

'Wait.' Captain Temor leant closer to the king. 'Little Piro had the right idea, Rolen. Send for the mystics, they —'

'Yes,' Byren insisted. He cast Cobalt a furious glance. 'I do not hide behind walls and half-truths. I will bare my soul to both the mystics. Let the master and the mistress look into my heart. They will see I bear my twin no malice!'

That impressed the old warriors, who had an instinctive fear of the great mystics. Piro waited for her father to agree.

'Rolen.' The queen took the king's arm. 'Byren deserves a chance to prove his honesty.'

'I have proof of his deceit,' Cobalt announced with a heavy sigh. 'I did not want to do this...' He felt inside his vest to pull out a small velvet bag with a drawstring top. Piro recognised it as the one Lence had given him, back at Dovecote.

Cobalt held it out to the queen. 'I'm sorry, Myrella.'

Piro sent a questioning look to Byren. Her brother gave a slight shake of his head. He had no idea.

The queen opened the bag, tipping two rings into her hand and a small roll of paper tied with ribbon.

'Matching lincurium rings,' King Rolen whispered. 'Worth a small fortune.'

'They are mine!' Byren bristled. 'I found the lincurium and had them set onto rings.'

Piro frowned. Then how did Lence get them and why had he given them to Cobalt?

'Read the note,' Cobalt suggested.

The queen unrolled the scrap, read it, blanched then handed it to King Rolen. 'Byren!'

'I don't know what that paper says, mother. But I had the rings made up for you and father, for your Jubilee.'

'What does the paper say?' Captain Temor asked.

The king shook his head, unable to bring himself to read it aloud.

'It is a love poem from Byren to Orrade, asking him to share his life,' Cobalt said. 'He calls Orrade his Dove.'

'That's not –' Byren began.

'It is your writing.' The king turned the paper over so that everyone could see it.

'It is,' the queen agreed.

'Show me.' Byren held out his hand.

Piro waited for him to deny it.

When Byren took the piece of paper, his expression cleared. He waved it for all to see. 'This is a poem I wrote to Elina, not Orrie. It was Elina that I...' He ran down, seeing they did not believe him. Furious he scrunched up the love poem casting it aside. Byren fixed on Cobalt, fury choking his voice. 'You twist everything. You've been into my room, into my private things!' Byren strode the two steps to Cobalt, grabbed his shoulders and pulled him upright. 'Where's the pendant? Did you steal that too?'

Cobalt made no attempt to defend himself, instead he plucked weakly at Byren's hands and trembled as if he was too exhausted to stand upright.

'Unhand him!' Old Steadfast protested. 'Can't you see he's –'

Disgusted, Byren shoved Cobalt away, so that he staggered several steps and collapsed, leaning on the table.

Piro looked around. In everyone's eyes, Cobalt was the victim of the encounter, not the perpetrator. In that instant she realised how very dangerous he was.

Lence had not been giving the velvet bag to Cobalt, he had been returning it. This was the trick Cobalt had used to convince Lence he could not trust his twin. She did not doubt that Cobalt or one of his spies had slipped into Byren's room to steal the rings. And Piro had no trouble believing Byren had written a poem to his Dove. Unfortunately for him, that poem could be interpreted two ways.

'Where is the lincurium pendant, Illien?' Byren asked. 'Did you steal that too?'

Cobalt shook his head. 'I don't know what you mean.'

Byren radiated fury.

'Here. Enough of that.' Captain Temor stepped in to prevent Byren from attacking Cobalt again. Piro was close enough to hear Temor whisper, 'You're only making it worse, lad.'

Her brother spun away from Temor, striding a couple of steps towards Orrade. She saw Orrade's anguish and winced. For a heartbeat, his feelings for Byren were written on his face, then he recollected himself. But others had seen his façade slip.

Byren pivoted on his heel to confront the king and queen. 'Father, Mother, I swear the rings are a Jubilee gift for you both. The poem was meant for Elina. I had a lincurium pendant made to give Lence for his bride. You can ask the jewel-smith. He'll vouch for the truth of my words. You can't –'

The ring of a sword being drawn silenced him. Piro spun around. No one carried a sword in King Rolen's court.

Cobalt approached, almost too weak to hold the sword tip steady. She recognised King Rolence the First's ceremonial sword, which had hung on display above the family's coat of arms.

'Let me defend you, Uncle,' Illien offered.

Byren swore softly. 'Get your hands off that. You dishonour King Rolence's memory.'

'Only the king should wield that sword,' Rolen said, and Cobalt handed it over, feeling for the table to support himself.

King Rolen faced Byren, lifting the sword between them.

Piro turned to the queen. 'Mother!'

She went white, closed her eyes and seemed to reach a decision. Stepping between Byren and the king she said, 'Rolen, you can't.'

'Out of the way, Myrella,' the king warned.

The queen caught his sword arm. 'Rolen, listen to me. You can't believe Illien over your own son –'

'Why not? I've seen the evidence. I should have listened to Illien back at midwinter. If I had, Lence wouldn't be betrothed to a cunning vixen whose father laughs at me behind my back!' He pushed the queen aside, not roughly, but without remorse. 'Instead I listened to you. I insisted Lence marry the girl and lost his love and respect. Well, now it's time to mend my mistakes.'

'Oh, Rolen. You haven't –'

'Enough!' he snapped. 'My second son is a traitor, but I will not kill him. Too many of my kinsmen have died on the altar of power.' The king lowered the sword point, his massive fist shaking. 'I cannot order my own son's execution, but I can banish a traitor. Before everyone here today, Byren formerly known as Rolen Kingson, I disinherit you, I disinherit you –'

The hall's great doors swung back on their hinges, reverberating as they hit the walls. A single pair of boots sounded on the polished wood.

'Where's Byren Kingson?' a rough contralto demanded.

Chapter Twenty-Six

PIRO PIVOTED TO see Florin stride through the forest of columns wearing her strained travelling clothes, a pair of skates slung over her shoulder. The image made no sense. For an instant Piro thought she had slipped into the Unseen sight, but Orrade gasped Florin's name so she knew the trader's daughter had really arrived.

Florin recognised Byren and made for him.

'Bad news, Byren Kingson,' she called even as she approached. 'Da sighted Merofynian soldiers –'

'Rubbish,' Cobalt snapped. 'Who is this rough female, dressed as a man?'

Florin cast him one swift glance then focused on Byren. She was close enough now not to have to shout. 'You know how Da was off visiting his sister? Well, he come back yesterday lunchtime, with the news. I've been skating ever since.'

'If there were Merofynians in Rolencia our warning beacons would be burning,' Captain Temor said.

'And our spies would have sent word of a build-up of soldiers at Port Merofyn even before they sailed, so –'

'I don't know anything about spies or why the beacons aren't alight,' Florin admitted. She turned back to Byren. 'But Da's awful worried.'

'No one makes war in winter,' old Lord Steadfast objected.

'It's almost spring cusp,' Piro pointed out

No one listened to her.

'Girl, I am your king,' her father said.

Florin made a deep bow. 'I beg your –'

The king waved this aside. 'Now, where are these soldiers?'

Florin's cheeks were bright pink when she straightened up, but she answered the question. 'Da said they were camped below the Cockatrice Pass.'

'Highly unlikely,' Captain Temor whispered to the king. 'Lence has just been to see warlord Rejulas.'

Rolen nodded, casting a sharp glance in Florin's direction. 'How many men, girl?'

'Florin. This is Florin Narrowsdaughter,' Byren said. 'She helped us kill the manticore pride. I can vouch for her.'

'You have been disinherited,' Cobalt interjected. 'You can't vouch for anyone.'

'What?' Florin muttered, looking to Byren for an explanation.

'How many warriors, girl?' the king repeated, raising his voice.

She fixed on him. 'Da guessed around five hundred.'

'An advance party?' Temor suggested.

'A trader's imagination,' Cobalt countered. 'Too

much wine, a lonely crossroads. He overhears some other travellers, panics and runs home.'

'Here,' Florin rounded on him. 'Don't you say that about my Da. He's no fool.'

'Quiet, girl!' King Rolen snapped then turned to consult with Temor.

Piro glanced to her mother for help, only to realise that everyone had stepped away from the queen. It seemed that even though her mother had been married to the Rolencian king for nearly twenty-one years and had produced four heirs, she was still a Merofynian kingsdaughter in their eyes.

Voices filled the great hall as the old honour guard argued. Some refused to believe the Merofynian king would prepare an invasion while signing a betrothal pact. Others thought it all too likely.

'Byren?' Orrade approached him, lowering his voice, but Piro was close enough to overhear. 'If Florin is right, Dovecote is in danger. I must warn Father and Elina.'

'I'm going, too,' Garzik insisted.

'We've sworn service to Byren's honour guard,' Orrade told his brother. 'We can't both ride off –'

'I send you,' Byren said. 'Elina, your father and Lence are all at Dovecote. If Florin's father is right, you must save them and light the warning beacon.'

Orrade and Garzik nodded.

'You're sending them to save Lence?' Piro whispered. 'When he –'

Byren met her eyes, silencing her with a look. 'Don't you see what Cobalt did? He tricked Lence into distrusting me. I don't know how he led the manticores to us but –'

'King Rolen?' Their mother's high voice cut through the men's deep rumbling. She stood small, regal and alone. 'Husband, hear my counsel. If Old Man Narrows is right, the invaders could easily march between Rolenhold and the abbey, cutting us off from the warrior monks. We need to get word to the abbot –'

'Don't listen to her. She's Merofynian,' old Steadfast warned.

'Besides, for all we know there is no army,' Cobalt added.

'Myrella's right, Rolen.' Captain Temor turned to the king. 'If this is an advance attack, we can crush them between the abbey's fighting monks and our palace guard. We have to send someone to the abbey –'

'I'll go,' Byren offered.

'No, Byren. That would mean passing under the very noses of the Merofynians,' their mother protested. 'You could be captured and killed!'

Piro waited for her father to refuse to send Byren. He hesitated, considering.

'Let me go, Father. Let this prove my loyalty to you, to Lence and to Rolencia,' Byren urged. 'Lence is at Dovecote. Orrade and Garzik will warn him –'

'Send Lence's honour guard with them,' Captain Temor suggested. 'We need the heir safe back here.'

Piro glanced to Byren. His mouth tightened. To them, he was disposable and it tore her apart.

'We'll go alone,' Orrade said. 'A small party can move quickly without attracting attention, and fifteen or twenty warriors cannot hope to stand against five hundred.'

'You're right. You've a good head on your shoulders, lad,' Temor told him. Piro blinked. Had he forgotten that Orrade was a lover of men?

Byren grabbed his cloak and fixed it in place. 'I'll go now.'

'Take –' her mother began.

'I'll take no one else into danger. Besides, like Orrie said, I'll travel faster alone.' Byren glanced to their father, but King Rolen deliberately turned away to speak with his honour guard.

Byren looked stunned, then cleared his throat and spoke to Piro. 'Tell my honour guard I absolve them of their vows. They must not suffer dishonour because of me.'

She stared at him, horrified.

He turned on his heel and strode off.

Piro ran after him. She had to take two steps for every one of his. 'Wait, Byren. You'll be captured and killed –'

'I must prove my loyalty,' he said.

'Wait, Byren,' Orrade called as he and Garzik caught up with him.

'Kingson.' Florin hurried to join them, matching her stride to his. 'I don't know why you have to prove your loyalty but I do know that if your mother's right you'll be passing under the Merofynian army's nose. You should take –'

'Since when does a tradepost's daughter know better than a kingson?' Byren demanded. 'I go alone.'

Florin's mouth dropped open.

'Byren!' Piro protested, even though she couldn't blame him.

Byren caught Piro's face between his hands and pressed his lips to her forehead. 'Goodbye, little sister.'

She couldn't see him stride away for the tears.

'I fear you will have to be strong, Piro,' Orrade muttered, and hugged her.

'Be brave, Piro,' Garzik whispered as he planted the gentlest of kisses on her cheek. Then he and Orrade followed Byren out.

Echoing down the hall, she heard King Rolen order his honour guard to the war table. Still talking, the old warriors marched out. Cobalt issued orders to a wizened little man, some new servant of his, before following her father.

Piro ran after the queen, catching her arm. 'Mother.'

'Yes?' But she was watching the men leave.

'It's Lence who has cut himself off from Byren, not the other way around.'

'I worked that out.'

'Don't let Cobalt advise Father.'

Her mother gave a short, bitter laugh. 'I fear it is too late. I will be lucky if they let me join them. I must go, Piro.'

She hurried after the others, leaving Piro alone with Florin in the great hall. All the servants had run off to spread the terrible news.

'Do you want me to follow Byren?' Florin offered. 'Look after him?'

Yes, she did. But it wasn't fair on Florin and Byren wouldn't thank her. 'No. You've done so much already.' Piro tried to think straight. 'Are you hungry or tired?'

'Both, but I can't stay. Da reckons Narrowneck is in the path of the Merofynian army. With our palisade falling down and no defenders, we can't stand against them. He's going to take Leif into the Divide. I'm to meet him there.'

Piro nodded. 'Then let's go to the kitchen and make sure you have enough to eat. Do you want to borrow a horse?'

She grinned. 'Eh, me on a king's horse, now that'd be a sight!'

Piro smiled, but her heart was cold.

BYREN LOOKED UP as Captain Temor slipped into his chamber.

'There you are, lad.' His earnest eyes held Byren's. 'You know the canals better than our enemies. Go as far as Narrowneck tradepost with Orrade and Garzik, then separate.'

It was a decision he had come to, but the grizzled captain wasn't really here to advise him. He was here because he believed Byren.

'Thanks.' His voice caught and he could not go on.

The old warrior nodded. 'Good luck, lad.'

Temor left as Garzik and Orrade arrived with food for the journey.

'What did Captain Temor want?' Orrade asked.

Byren shook his head, unable to speak. He should be grateful to Cobalt. Now he knew who his true friends were.

EARLY THE NEXT morning, Piro waited by the door to her father's private chamber. Her stomach rumbled, demanding breakfast, but she was determined to catch him alone. He hadn't let her mother into the war table room yesterday, and all evening he had been surrounded by his advisors. The day her father trusted Cobalt ahead of her mother was a black day for Rolencia.

A muffled noise made her stiffen. Her father was awake at last. Giving a soft knock she entered, marshalling her arguments.

'Piro? What are you doing here?' The king drained a goblet, hands shaking as he returned it to the manservant.

'Are you all right, father?' she asked, shocked to see him so fragile. With his back to her, he stood naked on the far side of the bed. Surely his body hadn't been so wasted? She remembered great slabs of muscle on his shoulders.

'No, I'm not all right. Valens hasn't worked on me yet, that's all.' He moved like an old, old man as he lowered himself onto the bed, belly down. 'I'll be fine soon. This winter has been hard on my old injuries, Piro. Some days, if it weren't for Valens, I wouldn't be able to get out of bed.'

Piro glanced to the manservant, who waited with his jars of unguents. When he did not meet Piro's eyes, she decided she did not like him. His black hair was pulled back in a severe plait, his only concession to Rolencian custom.

'Now, what is so important that you must barge into my chamber before I've dressed?' her father asked, sounding more resigned than annoyed.

'I'll come back later.'

'I'm riding out to check on Rolenton's defences as

soon as I'm dressed. So speak now. And... a little privacy, if you don't mind!'

She turned away to face the door. This was not the way she had foreseen holding this conversation. If the manservant was Cobalt's own, likely everything she said would make its way back to him.

'Well?' her father prodded. His voice was muffled, his face in the bed clothes.

'You're breaking Mother's heart. How can you refuse to see her?'

'I haven't refused to see her.'

'You shut the war table door on her.'

She heard the king sigh and then the gentle slap, slap as Valens worked on him. A strange smell, the cream Valens rubbed into her father's sore joints, filled the air. It made Piro's head buzz. She could hear the manservant muttering something softly under his breath as he worked. It reminded her of the sing-song ward that Fyn had taught her to keep out untamed Affinity.

The back of her neck tingled uncomfortably.

She turned around, slipping easily into Unseen sight. Energy vibrated from Valens hands, moving over her father's body. She bit back a gasp. The taste of untamed Affinity sat sharp and bitter on her tongue. At first she thought it was sinking into her father, then she realised Valens was drawing it out of her father. But the king didn't have Affinity, so what was Valens stealing?

Fyn's warning came back to her. Never let a renegade Power-worker touch you.

'You wouldn't understand why I had to shut your mother out,' King Rolen told her in a weary voice. 'These things are too complex for you, little Piro.'

But she did understand, only too well.

Cobalt had planted a renegade Power-worker on her father and, since midwinter, Valens had been working on the king to weaken his body and will.

'I... I'm sorry.' She hardly knew what she was saying. 'I was just worried.'

'Let me do the worrying.'

'Yes, Father.' All she wanted to do was get out of there before the Power-worker realised she knew what he was. 'I hope you're feeling better soon.'

The king made some muffled reply as she fled.

She ran straight to her mother's private solarium, where she found the queen bent over her writing desk.

'There you are, Mother, I –'

'Quiet, Piro,' Seela said. 'Your mother's writing to Rolencia's ambassador to Merofynia. He'll know what King Merofyn is doing.'

'But it will take too –'

'Quiet!'

Piro hopped from foot to foot as her mother finished the letter, sealed it with wax and pressed her foenix sigil into the red blob as it set. She handed it to Seela, who bustled towards the door. The message would be sent on the next ship to Merofynia, but it would be too late to help them now.

'Don't go, Seela, this is important,' Piro warned.

The queen looked over to her. 'What's so important?'

'Father's new servant, the Ostronite Valens, is a renegade Power-worker!'

'A healer, with new ideas from Ostron Isle?' Her mother frowned. 'That would explain why Rolen prefers him over our abbey healers. I wonder if they suspect he has Affinity? He's been able to do more for Rolen than they –'

'If Valens was a healer Cobalt would have said so. Have you seen Father before Valens works on him? He looks like an old man. He can hardly move!'

The queen blanched. 'Rolen hasn't let me into his private chamber since midwinter. He's been acting so strangely I can't get near him –'

'We must expose Valens,' Seela decided. 'Send for the warders, Myrella.'

'What will I tell them?' she countered. 'They'll want to know why I suspect him of Affinity.'

'Tell them that I noticed Valens' Affinity,' Piro said. 'I'm going to have to confess my Affinity to them by spring cusp anyway.'

'You're right, Piro. I've crippled myself by hiding my true abilities for so long that I'm not thinking straight,' her mother admitted.

'You did what you had to do, Myrella.' Seela told her firmly, mouth grim. 'I'll send this message to Merofynia. Piro, you tell the warders what we suspect and send them to this chamber. Then you can fetch Valens. When he gets here Autumnwind and Springdawn will be waiting for him.'

The queen nodded. 'I fear he won't go quietly.'

'If it comes to it, we'll have to kill him,' Seela agreed, without a qualm. Piro blinked. Seela noticed and added, 'We're justified. According to the King's Law no renegade –'

'He will not thank us. Poor Rolen.' The queen shook her head. 'He's always feared Power-workers, to think –'

'And rightly so. One day he'll understand,' Seela insisted. 'Come, Piro.' She bustled towards the door and Piro hurried after her.

They parted on the main stair case. Piro went to Sylion's oratory first because, though she disliked Springdawn, she knew the nun best. She found her old tutor lighting devotional candles. Their sweet, citrus scent filled the air.

'Ah, Piro. You're worried too? Don't be. I lit a dozen candles this morning. It's past midwinter but Sylion's hold on our land is still strong. One good blizzard would cripple the advance army, then the king's men will be able to mop them up. A blizzard is all we need from Sylion.'

'I have Affinity,' Piro said. 'Father's new manservant –'

'Affinity? Nonsense,' Springdawn snapped. 'I would have sensed it.'

'I've been hiding it,' Piro explained. 'Valens –'

Springdawn caught Piro's face between her hands, fingers pressed to her temples. Pressure, worse than the worst migraine, pressed in on Piro's mind. Instinct made her retaliate, thrusting out the intrusion.

Springdawn gasped and fell back two steps. Gingerly, she lifted her fingers to her lips, blowing on them as though she'd been burnt. Her frightened eyes fixed on Piro.

'I was just in Father's chamber.' Piro would not be diverted. 'I saw Valens drawing power off him –'

'Nonsense. Your father has no power. He must have been pouring power into him,' Springdawn corrected automatically, then frowned. 'You're sure Valens was manipulating Affinity?'

Piro nodded. 'Mother wants you and Autumnwind to come to her solarium. She'll send for Valens. When he gets there you are to contain him, execute him if you have to.'

'The king –'

'Is under Valen's influence. This must be done to save him. You and Autumnwind –'

'He's useless. He exhausted himself on Cobalt. I can handle this.' Springdawn's eyes gleamed. 'Executing a renegade would bring me to the mystics mistress's notice. It would mark me as her possible successor!'

Piro wasn't interested in the nun's career. 'Go up to the solarium. Mother's waiting. I'll bring Valens.'

Springdawn bustled off and Piro headed for her father's chamber. She'd tell Valens her mother's Turns were getting worse. He'd probably leap at the chance to get the queen under his power. Ambition was a useful tool.

Ten minutes later Piro walked down the corridor towards her mother's solarium with Valens at her side.

'So what happens when the queen has one of her Turns?' Valens asked, his leather case swinging between them as they walked.

'I don't know exactly,' Piro confessed. 'I only know she can't sleep and Seela's been giving her dreamless-sleep but it isn't working –'

'Because it's addictive and you need higher doses for the same effect,' he revealed. 'I'm sure I can mix up something more powerful.'

Piro nodded and opened the door, entering the room. Her mother sat at the writing desk. There was no sign of Springdawn. Piro sent the queen a searching look.

Her mother put her pen down and greeted them. 'Thank you, Pirola. Come in, Valens.'

'I explained how your Turns were getting worse, mother,' Piro said, gesturing to the manservant. 'And he thinks he can help.'

'Thank you, Piro.' Her mother did not miss a beat. 'Valens, I understand you use a special cream on Rolen to help his joints? Could I see it?'

'I do, but it won't help with your problem, Queen Myrella.' He put his leather case on the desk and opened the straps with a practised flick of his wrists. Before he could open the lid, the queen grabbed the case and shoved it under her desk.

Startled, he took a step back.

Springdawn came out from behind the tapestry that covered the servants' stair.

Piro darted out of the way, but did not leave. She did not want to miss this for anything.

'Valens of Ostron Isle, you have been accused of practising unauthorised Power-working on the king,' Springdawn announced with relish.

'Send for King Rolen,' Valens insisted. 'I have been nothing but a faithful servant –'

'Then you won't mind if I search your mind for untamed Affinity,' Springdawn countered.

Valens lifted his hands palm up. 'Do it, if you must.'

Springdawn stepped forwards.

Something was wrong here. Piro went to protest, but Springdawn, eager to make a name for herself, reached for Valens. The moment her fingers touched his temples he pressed his hands over hers.

She gasped.

Piro's nostrils stung and she tasted power on her tongue as her sight shifted to the Unseen. Valens pulsed with radiant Affinity. With each pulse, he drew off more of Springdawn's power, just as he had been drawing off her father's... only the king didn't have power. No, but his innate life force animated him and, recently, he had been only a shade of his former self.

The nun dropped to her knees. Valens bent over her. Piro sprang forwards.

'Don't touch,' her mother cried, the words echoing hollowly down the long tunnel of Piro's altered perception.

Piro grabbed a foot stool and slammed it down on Valens' shoulders. The timber joints squeaked in protest. The stool rebounded from her fingers, gone numb from the impact. But Valens did not fall. Instead Springdawn collapsed at his feet.

Valens released the nun and caught Piro's arm, swinging her around. Before she could react, he had her back pressed to his chest, a small dagger digging into her throat just under her right ear.

Piro clenched her fist and drove it into his ribs. She heard him grunt with pain, but his grip didn't slacken as he backed towards the door to the corridor.

His panting and her ragged breathing were the only sounds in the solarium.

Her mother stood absolutely still. 'Let Piro go. I won't call for the guards. Just let her go.'

But Piro knew he wouldn't. He'd touched her, tasted her Affinity. When she was no longer any use to him as a hostage he'd drain her too.

Piro felt him tense as he went to reach for the door. Then he made an odd strangled sound and hot fluid ran over her shoulder, down her arm. She stared at the bright red blood.

Valens released her.

Piro stepped away, turning around to see a gaping tear in his throat under his right ear. Even with one hand clasping the wound, blood pumped between his fingers.

Valens pitched forwards. Piro only just slipped out of the way in time.

Seela came in, shut the door and wiped her dainty little knife on his back, then crossed and pushed it into the coals of the brazier for a moment.

'Fire purifies evil Affinity, remember that, Piro.' This was said in the same tone her nurse had used to remind her to wear her woolen under garments.

Piro couldn't find her voice.

'Thank you, Seela,' her mother whispered.

'Power-workers always forget a knife is just as deadly to them,' Seela remarked. She withdrew the knife, tested the blade for heat, then tucked it into her belt sheath where it had always been kept, ready to peel fresh apples and pears for hungry children.

Piro blinked. The world contracted to a single, bright spot of light reflecting off the knife hilt. She felt the floor come up towards her.

When the mists cleared her hearing returned first.

'There, love,' Seela was saying. 'Just lift your shoulder.'

Her bodice peeled off down both arms and Piro opened her eyes to find she was lying on the day bed near the tiled warming stove.

'This is ready,' her mother said, bringing a bowl of

steaming water to the low table.

Seela handed the bloodied bodice to the queen and dipped a cloth in the warm, scented water. She began to sponge Piro's arm and shoulder. 'There, you don't want his nasty blood on you. You're lucky it didn't go through to your chemise.'

Piro bit back the urge to giggle, then struggled to sit up. Valens still lay in a puddle of blood on the floor and... 'Springdawn?'

'Dead. She underestimated him.' The queen held up Piro's bodice. 'Do you think we can save this, Seela?'

'Burn it,' the old nurse advised. 'Burn anything touched by his blood.'

'Of course. What was I thinking?'

'You've had a shock, dear. Send for Autumnwind. He'll have to settle the Affinity released by their deaths and ensure their bodies are properly disposed of.'

'Springdawn's death will have to be reported to the abbess,' the queen said, as she tossed Piro's bodice into the brazier and stirred it until the material caught. 'As for Valens, I don't –'

'Now we can banish Cobalt.' Piro made the connection.

'We can't confront him.' Seela put aside the wet cloth and dried Piro's shoulder. 'He's grown too powerful. Your father has named him Protector of the Castle.'

'But Valens was Cobalt's servant.'

'Cobalt will say he did not know,' the queen pointed out. 'He'll be horrified and terribly sorry.'

Her mother was right, Piro could just imagine Cobalt's reaction. 'But Valens is dead. How do we explain that?'

'I'll remove his belongings. We can say he ran

away, back to Ostron Isle because he feared the Merofynians.' Seela winked at Piro. 'You know what cowards, Ostronites are. They never fight, not if they can wheedle their way out of trouble.'

'Cobalt will suspect, but what can he do?' The queen took off her woolen over-wrap and passed it to Piro. 'You'll have to run down to your chamber and put on another bodice.'

Piro tied the wrap. It smelt of her mother's favourite perfume and made her feel warm to the core. She came to her feet. 'Very well. Is there anything I can do to help?'

Seela and her mother exchanged looks.

'Wait down by the stables,' Seela said. 'Rolen still trusts you. If he comes back too soon, distract him until we can get rid of Valens.'

Piro nodded. She didn't ask what they were going to do with the renegade's remains. He would have to be burnt and the ashes sprinkled over water.

'Go by the servants' stairs,' Seela suggested.

Piro stepped over Springdawn's body and through the tapestry.

Back in the solarium she heard someone tap on the door and enter without waiting for a reply. 'Queen Myrella, I –'

Old Lord Steadfast? What did he want?

Piro peered through the chink in the tapestry.

Steadfast had stopped in the doorway, his path blocked by Valens' body. He raised stunned eyes to the queen.

'What's going on, Myrella?' Cobalt asked, his ashen face peering over the old warrior lord's shoulder.

'Thank Halcyon you've come. I was just about to

send for help.' Piro's mother did not miss a beat. She crossed the room, having to avoid Springdawn's body to reach them.

'What happened?' Steadfast asked, stepping around Valens' body so that Cobalt could enter the room.

'It's terrible.' The queen wrung her hands. 'I sent for Springdawn because I'd discovered she'd taken a lover. She denied it but Valens admitted it. She took poison and he cut his throat.'

'Who would have thought?' Steadfast muttered.

Cobalt stared at the two bodies, one without a mark, the other lying in a pool of blood. Piro was impressed with her mother's ability to think on her feet.

'I...' The queen reached for Cobalt. 'I don't feel...'

He had to catch her as she fainted.

'The shock,' Steadfast explained knowledgeably, shaking his head in sympathy.

'That's right, poor dear,' Seela agreed. 'It happened so quickly there was nothing we could do. Bring the queen over here, Cobalt.'

As she indicated the day bed, Piro noticed that the bowl which had been used to wash the blood from her shoulder and arm had been returned to the stove. Would Cobalt or Steadfast notice the pink water?

'On second thoughts, Myrella won't want to be near the bodies when she wakes,' Seela muttered. 'Better bring her through to the far chamber.'

And she herded both men out the door into the larger solarium.

Piro leant against the wall, weak-kneed.

Why had Cobalt and Steadfast arrived just when they did? Cobalt's spies must have reported that the queen had sent for his manservant. Whatever Cobalt might suspect, he could not disprove her mother's explanation.

She darted back inside to grab the bowl and slipped out, heading for her bed chamber. It was the work of a moment to tip the bloodied water down the drain at the end of the corridor and leave the bowl with the others waiting to be washed.

Fifteen minutes later, dressed in a completely different outfit – she couldn't stand the thought of wearing anything that Valens had touched – Piro crossed the stable courtyard. Several of Byren's honour guard were strapping travelling kits to their saddles and mounting up.

'Chandler, Winterfall. What are you doing?' Piro asked. Yesterday, when she had delivered the news of Byren's banishment, they had seemed relieved to hear that their vows of service had been annulled.

'We're going after him,' Chandler replied, swinging up into the saddle. His tired but determined eyes met Piro's. 'Byren's loyal to the core. We refuse to believe he's a traitor and we're going to help him.'

Relief made Piro feel light. She touched his boot top, level with her face. 'I'm glad. Watch over him.'

Chandler nodded and the eight of them rode out.

Piro couldn't remember how many honour guards Byren had sworn in but only eight had stood by him. Perhaps it was for the best. Where Byren was going he needed followers who were completely committed.

PIRO STAYED IN the stables until lunch time, by which time she was too hungry to think straight. She hadn't eaten breakfast and was going to miss lunch, and still there was no sign of her father. Knowing him, he was probably treating himself to roast beef and potatoes in one of Rolenton's rich merchant's homes. There was time for her to snatch some food. When the king came back, she wanted to be sure he saw her mother and Seela first, not Cobalt. She headed for the kitchen, begging some extra scraps for her foenix.

Settling in with him she shared her lunch. Glad of the foenix's uncritical company, she whispered her fears to him. 'So I don't know what Father's going to say when he hears Valens has killed himself.'

The foenix made a soft, sympathetic noise in his throat as though he understood.

'Piro, are you there?' Seela scurried into the menagerie.

Piro came to her feet.

Seela looked relieved. 'Your mother wants you.'

Piro dropped the last of the crumbs for the foenix and hurried over to her old nurse.

'Is everything all right? Did Cobalt suspect? I overheard him arrive,' she explained. 'Mother was so quick to invent that lovers' story.'

'It was not invention.' Seela looked grim. 'Something very like that happened not forty years ago in the Merofynian court. Still, Cobalt was suspicious.'

Piro smiled. 'Even if he is, what can he do?'

'Cause trouble. He has a gift for it,' the old nurse muttered as she hurried down a corridor. 'You've been taking your dreamless-sleep, haven't you?'

'Yes.' Piro only half-lied. 'Why?'

Seela didn't answer. Piro went to take the quickest route to her mother's solarium but Seela caught her arm, urging her to the left.

'Why are we –'

'Nightmares?' Seela asked, panting a little.

'Some,' Piro admitted. With the unistag gone the only surviving Affinity beast in the menagerie was the foenix, and he was too small to absorb much of her power, so it had been building up again. Too much dreamless-sleep made her feel listless and groggy the next day, and too little could not keep the nightmares at bay. She preferred nightmares to feeling half-alive.

'We're going to write down your dreams so Autumnwind can try to interpret them,' Seela explained. 'You were right about the threat to Rolen, even if you had the wrong source.'

Piro felt relieved to be taken seriously at last. They hurried up the servants' stairs to the rear entrance of the solarium. Male voices sounded muffled through the tapestry-covered opening. Seela froze. Piro almost collided with her.

Seela signalled for silence.

Piro recognised Cobalt's voice and her stomach knotted. Other voices joined him.

Seela peered through the gap in the tapestry. 'Cobalt, and he's with several of Lence's honour guard, boys who have more ambition than sense, if I'm not mistaken,' she whispered. 'You stay here.'

Before Piro could protest, Seela bustled through the tapestry hanging, entering the room beyond.

'Here, what's this all about, young Illien?' the nurse demanded.

'He has come to arrest me, Seela,' Queen Myrella said, her voice rich with scorn.

Chapter Twenty-Seven

'How could you, Illien?' the queen demanded. 'You, of all people, should know I'm faithful!'

'I am only following orders, Queen Myrella. Lord Steadfast thinks –'

'That I've been working treason against Rolencia? As if I would!'

'We have proof, madam queen. Written in your own hand,' old Lord Steadfast announced, stepping forwards. He glanced to Cobalt, who reached into his vest and handed something over.

There was a rustle of something being unrolled.

Steadfast cleared his throat. 'This is a description of the steps King Rolen has taken to ensure the safety of his kingdom. I intercepted it being smuggled out of the castle.'

Lence's honour guards murmured disgustedly.

'Let me see that,' the queen demanded. As she studied the paper Piro caught sight of the wax seal her mother had used on her message to the ambassador only this morning. 'A clever forgery. Nothing more. Rolen knows I would never –'

'The king is not here and Lord Cobalt has been appointed Protector of the Castle,' Steadfast said. 'When I intercepted this, I took it straight to him and insisted he act upon it. In good conscience I could not let a traitor wander loose in Rolenhold.'

'I am sorry, Queen Myrella,' Cobalt said, sounding genuine.

But Piro knew what he was capable of. His spies had intercepted her mother's message and he'd used it to forge this message, then arranged for Steadfast to discover it, knowing that the old man would insist he arrest the queen. Her mother had neat, elegant script. One corner of Piro's mouth lifted. It would be much harder to forge her own handwriting which, despite her mother's best efforts, was barely legible.

Cobalt bowed to her mother. 'The honour guard will escort you to the mourning tower, Queen Myrella. You may take anything you need.'

There was a moment's silence, then the queen spoke. 'Very well. Come, Seela. No… we will not need anything. King Rolen will set me free the moment he hears of this!'

There was some shuffling and then the sound of boots marching from the room. Piro leant against the wall, feeling weak-kneed.

The hide of him! Rage surged through her. How dare Cobalt frame her mother!

'Now, we must find the kingsdaughter,' Cobalt said. 'The message was discovered in her drawing satchel.'

Piro peered through the gap. The four young honour guards stared at Piro's satchel, which contained the sketches she had planned to turn into paintings. How had that got into Cobalt's hands?

'Piro Kingsdaughter?' one of the guards whispered. 'But she's Rolencian-born.'

'You doubt me?' Cobalt countered, rolling up his sleeve to reveal something Piro couldn't see because the men were in the way. 'This is where she scratched me when I tried to question her. She's as wild as a wyvern and as cunning, for all that she looks so sweet. Don't listen to a word she says.'

'They say the apple never falls far from the tree,' the first voice marvelled. 'Who woulda thought it of little –'

'Exactly. Find her. Bring her to me.'

'Not to her mother? I thought you'd want her in the Tower with the queen.'

'What, and give them time to concoct their lies?' Cobalt demanded. 'No. I want to find out who she was meeting and if there are other spies within Rolenhold.'

'Very good, my lord. Come on, lads.'

They marched off.

Piro sank to her knees, dizzy with dismay. She had underestimated Cobalt badly. But even so, how could Lord Steadfast and the others believe this ridiculous concoction?

They say the apple never falls far from the tree, the guard's words returned to her, triggering another memory. The old seer had been right. Cobalt was the bad apple and he was turning the others against them.

She had to get to her father before Cobalt did. Heart thudding in her ears, she scrambled to her feet and backed up until she came to the top of the landing. But she must have made some small noise because Cobalt flung the tapestry open. He stood a mere body length from her.

His eyes widened, then narrowed. 'You heard?'

She nodded.

His lips pulled back from his teeth in a snarl as he lunged.

Piro fled down the stairs with him not far behind. She could not outrun a grown man. What should she do? Already she could hear him gaining on her.

Rounding a bend, she came to the top of the next flight of stairs. No side passages. He'd catch her for sure. Only one thing to do.

She pressed her back to the wall, judged how close he was and, at the last moment, stuck her leg out. The impact jarred her whole body, but he was worse off. His stride broken, he missed the top step and fell heavily, thudding into the wall, bouncing off and rolling down the steps.

Piro grinned fiercely. With any luck he would break his neck!

Then she was off, running back upstairs to the solarium. She had only a few moments before Cobalt recovered and came after her. Where should she hide until King Rolen came back? And how could she prove her mother's innocence, when the seeds of doubt had already been sewn? She glanced to her mother's writing desk. If only her mother hadn't written to the ambassador. But Cobalt would have thought of some other way to implicate her in treason. If only she had proof of Cobalt's machinations.

Perhaps she did!

Valens' case of tools and creams. Maybe there was something in it to implicate Cobalt. She dragged it out from under the desk but there was no time to look through it now. Her first priority was to get to her father before Steadfast or Cobalt could. Where could she hide Valens' case?

The last place they'd look.

Piro marched down the stairs into the servants' quarters. Spotting a scullery maid, who was no taller than her with long dark hair bound in a plait, Piro beckoned the girl. 'My mother needs this. Please take it to her.'

The maid did not ask where the queen was, so the news must have travelled all over the castle. Someone was sure to get to her father if she didn't meet him at the stables. Piro hurried through the connecting courtyard. And she was only just in time for she heard the clatter of returning horses.

'Father?' She ran out into the stable yard.

There he was, riding in with Captain Temor and several of his old honour guard.

'The town has outgrown its walls these last thirty years,' Temor was saying, as he swung down from the saddle and handed his reins to a stable boy. 'But, even if it hadn't, the people are better off coming up here to take shelter. Rolenhold will never fall.'

'And if the townspeople are safe within these walls, they cannot be used as hostages to force us to open the gates,' King Rolen agreed, also dismounting. He grimaced when his boots landed on the cobbles, jarring his body.

'Father?' Piro darted through the stable boys, who led the horses away, past the old honour guard. She caught the king's arm. 'Something terrible has happened. Cobalt locked mother in the mourning tower. He says she's a traitor but it's a forgery!'

'Hold on, Piro.' King Rolen patted her arm. 'What are you talking about?'

'Cobalt has framed mother for treason,' she cried.

Her father froze, his gaze going to Captain Temor, who looked stunned.

'Cobalt did warn us that only time would show the queen's true colours,' Lord Steadfast stated, as he crossed the stable yard to join them, with Cobalt at his side. 'Looks like they're Merofynian azure.'

Piro's heart sank. Cobalt looked none the worse for his fall down the steps. Perhaps he was part cat. Snake, more like. She squeezed her father's arm. 'Don't you believe him. The letter's a forgery!'

'Naturally, the queen would say that,' Cobalt agreed. 'And it pains me to have to arrest her.'

Piro searched her father's face. Surely he would not be taken in?

Cobalt bowed to the king. 'You left me in charge of the castle's safety, Uncle. I have only been following your orders.'

'Take a look for yourself, Rolen,' Lord Steadfast nodded to Cobalt, who offered the message which her father accepted and unrolled. Captain Temor and others peered over his shoulders.

'Looks like the queen's writing,' Temor agreed reluctantly.

'It is a forgery made to look like mother's writing,' Piro insisted. 'He's trying to turn everyone against her!'

Cobalt shook his head sadly. 'Uncle, I fear you are in for a double heartbreak because it was your very own daughter who had hidden this treacherous message –'

'That's a lie!' Piro could have wept with frustration.

Cobalt shrugged. 'Say what you like, kingsdaughter. I bear the marks you left on my body, when I tried to question you.' He rolled up his sleeve to reveal two long scratches that had beaded with blood. 'You know what a wyvern whelp she is, when her temper is roused.'

Piro gasped. Everyone looked at her as if she'd sprouted horns.

Her hands curled into fists. She wanted to claw out Cobalt's sorrowful lying eyes. Then she realised something.

'Look!' She opened both hands, holding them out for all to see her finger tips. 'My nails are bitten down to the quick!' These last few weeks she had fallen back into her childhood habit of chewing her nails.

Her father's eyes widened as he took in her ragged nails, which were clearly incapable of scratching anyone.

'They weren't like that when she scratched me,' Cobalt insisted.

The king's mouth settled into a grim, sad line. 'I'm going to see Myrella.'

When he strode off, the others followed. Piro hurried to stay by his side. Captain Temor fell into place on his other side.

'Rolen, if there is any doubt we can't risk freeing the queen,' Temor whispered. 'Only betrayal from within could cause Rolenhold to fall.'

'I know.' Her father sounded bleak.

'Mother is not a traitor,' Piro protested, having to take an extra skipping step to keep up with the men.

'Can you prove that?' Cobalt asked, from just behind them.

She spun to face him. 'Can you prove she is?'

He pointed to the forgery in her father's hands.

'One of you is lying,' King Rolen said. 'Once, I would have said nothing could make me doubt Myrella. But she was the one who encouraged me to betroth Lence to Isolt, and King Merofyn has used this to lull us into a false sense of security.'

Piro's heart sank. Nearly thirty years of peace and twenty-one years of marriage to Myrella were not enough to erase the ancestral mistrust of Merofynia.

They had to mount the stairs of the mourning tower in pairs. The tower had been built one hundred and thirty years ago by Queen Pirola the Fierce to celebrate her wedding but, when her betrothed was murdered, she locked the murderer, her own sister, in its topmost room. Her sister leapt from the top rather than face trial. It had been used ever since to contain royal prisoners.

A guard stood at the door.

'Unbar the door.' King Rolen waited while the door swung open.

Piro watched her mother come to her feet, small, regal and very angry.

Queen Myrella's black eyes flashed as she took in

the crowd on the tower landing. 'So, you have come with a court, King Rolen?'

'I have come to find the truth,' he said, growing stiff and formal but, underneath, Piro heard defeat. He had already given up on the queen. This man was a pale shadow of her father.

Piro glanced to Cobalt, who was watching their faces. She remembered how he had turned everything to his advantage when Byren confronted him, and she had a bad feeling.

'Only one person is lying here and it is not me, Rolen,' the queen's voice quavered ever so slightly. 'You've known me since I was a child of eight summers. Have I ever lied to you?'

Piro froze. Her mother had lied by omission since the day she discovered she had Affinity. Thank the goddess Cobalt did not know that!

'We are at war with your homeland, Myrella.' He sighed. 'I would be a fool not to protect my castle and my people.'

'You don't believe me.' The queen blanched and turned away from him, going to the window. After a moment she recovered and faced her accusers. 'There is a traitor in our midst and it is not me. Someone forged that letter. I think...'

She stiffened, head tilting back. Piro smelt the tang of Affinity on the air. Piro glanced to Seela to see if she realised what was happening but no one else could read the signs. If her mother's Affinity came out now her father would be forced to execute her.

Her mother's eyes rolled back in her head. One

hand lifted. Piro glanced to Seela. For once the old nurse was stunned into immobility.

A voice that was not hers came from the queen's lips. 'Rolen Byren Kingson, heed this warning. Listen to false counsel and your castle will fall. A man who is half snake, half wyvern is coming. He will tear out your heart, he will –'

'No!' Piro screamed and ran across the room, shoving her mother off her feet so that she staggered, hitting her head on the stone lintel of the window.

Nimble despite her age and girth, Seela darted forwards to catch the queen as she crumpled to the floor.

Inspired by what Valens had done to her father, Piro spun to face the men. 'You must send for the mystics. Mother's been under the influence of a Merofynian renegade Power-worker. Only a mystic can counter the renegade's influence and save her!'

The men all nodded wisely. The bigger the lie, they more they believed it. Fools. No wonder Cobalt could play them like fish on a line.

'Perhaps one of the ambassador's servants was a renegade Power-worker in disguise. It's happened before,' Captain Temor muttered.

'So that is why she has been acting strangely,' King Rolen muttered. Piro wanted to kick him.

He crossed the room and knelt, lifting his wife's small body in his arms. Gently he placed her on the bed, brushing the dark curls from her forehead. 'My poor Myrella.'

The old honour guard muttered sympathetically under their breath. Only one person, other than Seela, knew what was going on. Piro allowed her gaze to meet Cobalt's. He gave her a look that could cut glass and she was glad they were not alone.

'Eh, Piro, come here,' King Rolen said.

She approached him and he took her hand in his large callused one. 'I'm sorry I doubted you, lass. You were only obeying your mother when you carried the note.'

Tears stung Piro's eyes. She wanted to howl like a baby. Even now, her father believed Cobalt rather than her.

'Here, don't cry.' He patted her back, pressing her to his shoulder. He smelt of horse sweat and leather and she just wanted to be six years old again, when he was the strongest, most powerful thing in her world and he could protect them all.

The king pulled away from Piro, so he could look into her face. 'I'll send for both mystics and they'll cast the renegade out of your mother. Never fear.' He glanced to the bed where the queen lay so still. 'But, until then, I must keep her locked up for her own good. You understand, Piro?'

'Yes, father.'

And she had to be content with that. Her mother was innocent in the king's eyes so she was salvageable. But the real traitor was Cobalt and, next to Temor, he was her father's most trusted advisor.

Then her stomach gave a sickening lurch for, when the mystics arrived, they would discover her mother had Affinity. Why hadn't she thought before she acted?

King Rolen straightened, an angry gleam in his deep-set eyes. 'Send for Autumnwind and

Springdawn. This has been going on under their noses and they didn't warn me!'

Piro cast a swift glance to Seela. The old nurse went to speak but Cobalt was too quick.

'Springdawn is dead. She took a lover and when it was discovered, killed herself and the lover.'

King Rolen blinked then frowned. 'I always thought she had too much to say for herself. Who was he?'

'Your manservant, Valens.'

The king sagged as if he'd been struck. Piro couldn't bear to see her father suffer. She helped him sit on the bed. His hands trembled as they had done this morning before Valens worked on him.

She sprang between him and the others. 'Get out. Go on. Father's had a shock. He needs time to think.'

When the king did not object they backed out, all but Cobalt.

'I would be failing in my duty as Protector of the Castle if I left before the warder arrived,' he said.

'Then you can leave now, in good conscience,' Autumnwind said, entering the room. He bowed to Piro's father. 'I came as soon as I heard, my king.'

King Rolen nodded distractedly.

Cobalt bowed. 'Call me if you need me, Uncle.'

He backed out and Piro heard him telling one of the honour guard to remain at the door. She turned back to her father, covering both of his large hands with her small ones and pressing down on them to prevent the tremor.

'We'll call the healers, father,' she said. 'We have Valens' case. We'll find out what he was using on you. They'll be able to help –'

'What's wrong?' Autumnwind asked.

Piro glanced to Seela. How much should they reveal? Autumnwind had relished sending Cobalt away, but where did his loyalty lie?

'What's wrong, King Rolen?' the warder repeated.

Rolen's glazed eyes cleared and fixed on him with growing anger. 'The queen's been under the influence of a renegade Power-worker all this time and my castle warders did nothing. You've failed Rolencia, failed me!'

Autumnwind paled then licked his lips. 'Springdawn served the queen's mystical needs. If there is any failure it is hers.'

'Since she's dead that does me no good,' King Rolen snapped. 'I want you to watch over the queen. If she shows signs of possession, ward her.'

'It is my duty and an honour,' Autumnwind said with a formal bow.

But Piro knew her father was the one who needed Autumnwind's help. 'Sit by the fire, father. We'll send for the healers and they can look at you too.'

'There's nothing they can do for me. I'm a cripple without Valens,' he muttered. 'Just when I need –'

'Nonsense, Rolen.' Seela pulled Valens' case out from under the bed. 'We have –'

The king pounced on the case. Flinging it open, he rummaged through the contents. Hands shaking, he withdrew a dark bottle with a glass stopper. 'At least I can still have my tonic.'

'Tonic?' Autumnwind repeated. He opened the bottle, sniffing their contents. 'I am not a healer, but I can recognised dreamless-sleep when I smell it, that and willweakener. No tonic I ever heard of combined those two ingredients.'

Piro and Seela exchanged looks as the king shook his head.

'No, Valens helped me,' he insisted. 'He's done wonders for me.'

Autumnwind glanced to Seela, who shook her head slightly.

'Why don't we get the healers to look at these bottles?' Autumnwind suggested.

'Good idea,' Seela agreed. 'Piro, have the guard fetch the healers.'

Even though she knew what they would find, Piro did this. Would it be enough to convince her father of Cobalt's treachery? Unless there was something that showed Valens was following his old master's order, Cobalt would not be implicated and she was convinced Cobalt was too clever to make that mistake.

BYREN SKATED ON, eyes bleary from the glare of sun on ice all day and the sting of the wind. His face felt tight with windburn. But the sun had set now and they were only around the bend from Narrowneck tradepost. He smiled to himself. He should have accepted Florin's offer to go with him, at least then he'd be sure she got this far safely.

The silver light of the stars illuminated the small beach and its cliff. The rope he'd used had been put away.

'Don't fancy trying to climb that cliff,' Orrade muttered.

'We'll have to go around,' Byren agreed. 'Any more headaches, Orrie?'

'No. No time for headaches. I'd skate all night if I had to.'

'Me too,' Garzik muttered, then yawned so widely his jaw cracked.

They laughed and he grinned. They'd skated for the better part of the previous night.

'Let's find a warm bed. Florin will have locked up but I'm sure we can get into the barn.' Byren led the way. As long as Orrade didn't suffer from headaches and blackouts they were free from pursuit. At least, that was what Byren hoped.

His body was tiring as they strode past the palisade and up the winding track between the tall trees.

Garzik gave a theatrical shiver. 'Last time we were here the manticores were stalking us and we were fleeing for our lives.'

'This time we're running towards danger to save lives,' Byren said. 'I wish I could go with you two tomorrow –'

'Don't worry, we'll get there in time to warn Elina and Lence,' Garzik assured him.

Orrade snorted. 'The hard part will be convincing father to come to Rolenhold. He won't want to leave the estate.'

'I can understand that,' Byren said. An idea occurred to him. 'Tell your father, King Rolen needs him.'

Orrade smiled. 'You know the Old Dove well!'

Byren came to a halt. The three-storey tradepost reared up before them, a dark silhouette against the froth of stars, no light burned and no smoke came from the chimney. 'Old Man Narrows won't mind if we sleep in his barn tonight.'

'I'm so tired I could sleep standing up,' Garzik confessed. 'Wonder if he took his animals with him?'

'Would have killed the chickens for travelling meat and walked the cows to the nearest farm,' Orrade hazarded a guess. 'Sylion's luck, I could have enjoyed a roast chicken!'

Byren smiled. Again he wished he could go with them to be sure Elina was safe, but duty took him elsewhere. To restore his father's faith in him he had to get word to the abbey. Elina would never believe he was innocent if his own father didn't.

BYREN WOKE TO a muffled noise. It was still dark and no birds called, so it was not yet dawn. He lifted his head to sniff the air. Something was wrong. He inhaled again. Smoke?

Orrade's face was a pale blur against his blanket and cloak. Byren nudged him with his boot. 'Wake up.'

'What is it, Byren?' Garzik asked.

'Shhh. Something –' Then he heard it, the soft crackle of fire. The smell of smoke came through the chinks in the barn walls. Byren rolled to his feet, creeping towards the shuttered window. He prised it open a fraction. Fire, horses, armed men.

'Byren Kingson, we know you're in there,' a man yelled, striding forwards, lit by the flames.

'Rejulas!' Byren muttered.

'Warlord Rejulas from Cockatrice Spar? What's he doing here?' Garzik whispered.

'Hush!'

'You've got two choices,' Rejulas yelled. 'Come out and surrender, or stay and burn!'

Garzik wasted no time, scrambling over to where his brother slept on, oblivious. 'Orrie, what's wrong with you? Wake up!'

'According to Lence, Rejulas is loyal. I don't know what's going on here,' Byren muttered. His mouth went dry. Maybe Lence had Rejulas's loyalty, maybe he was going to prove it by delivering Byren, bound and gagged.

The warlord of Cockatrice Spar must have come down over his pass into Rolencia, creeping past all the villages and fortified farmhouses. Old Man Narrows had been mistaken. It wasn't Merofynians he'd seen but Cockatrice warriors on the warpath. In one way it was good news. Byren knew his father could deal with Cockatrice raiders.

Then a sick lurch of fear ripped through him. Dovecote lay between here and Cockatrice Spar. What if they had Elina?

'Byren,' Garzik tugged on his arm. 'Orrade's unconscious. We have to get him out of here.'

'We can't run carrying Orrie and we can't fight two dozen men,' Byren told Garzik.

By the starlight filtering in the small barn window the lad stared at him, horrified.

'Byren Kingson, surrender now,' Rejulas urged. 'One man cannot stand against thirty.'

They thought he was alone... Possibilities flashed through Byren's mind. 'I'll surrender.'

'No!'

Byren caught Garzik's shoulders. 'Think. If we fight we all die. By surrendering, I get captured then you and Orrade can save me.'

'What if they kill you?'

'They could have done that already. They want me alive for some reason and this way you two stay free.'

He felt the fight go out of Garzik.

Byren coughed. Smoke stung his eyes now. 'Look after Orrie.'

For a heartbeat, he wondered if this was a side-effect of the Affinity affecting Orrade, then he dismissed it. He had his own problems.

'Stay out of sight, Garza.' Byren thrust the shutter open and shouted, 'I'm coming out. Hold your archers.'

He brought his head back inside, turning to Garzik. 'Pull your vest up over your mouth, breathe through it.' Feeling around, he found his pack and he slung it over his shoulder. 'Hide. They won't be looking for you.'

'What about the fire?'

'Bluff. They'll put it out –'

'Byren Kingson?' Rejulas shouted.

'I hear you.' He squeezed Garzik's shoulder and, with a heavy heart, opened one barn door a fraction. They were raking the burning brands away from the entrance. Red coals winked on the frozen earth.

'Get his weapons,' Rejulas ordered. 'And put out the fires. We don't want to set off a warning beacon now!'

His men laughed, hastening to obey.

Byren didn't resist as Rejulas's warriors divested him of his weapons, both his knives, his sword, his bow and his arrows. He'd armed himself properly for once and it had done no good.

'Right,' Rejulas said. 'Restrain him.'

They moved efficiently in the pale predawn. His hands were tied behind his back and a pole slid under his arms along his back, and he was lowered by pulley to the beach.

After herding him into the centre of the group, they slung a rope around his neck and handed it to a grizzled campaigner. Then they set off in the chill predawn.

'Where are we going?' Byren asked.

'Dovecote,' a youth near him muttered.

The old campaigner cuffed him, then cuffed Byren for good measure, jerking on the rope.

Head still buzzing, Byren managed to keep skating.

One piece of the puzzle didn't fit. Only Captain Temor and those who had joined him at the war table knew Byren planned to sleep here last night. He knew Cobalt was sitting at the war table advising his father, privy to his secrets. But that didn't explain how Cobalt could get word to Rejulas so fast.

Before long they had moved off Sapphire Lake. Tall, snow-capped pines flashed past him, dark against the gradually lightening sky.

They'd be at Dovecote by late tonight and then his questions would be answered. Byren dreaded what those answers would reveal.

Chapter Twenty-Eight

FYN REMAINED STILL, trusting to the shadows to hide him. His heart hammered uncomfortably. The dim glow of the abbot's lantern illuminated a halo of light around the masters as they followed the abbot down the corridor. Master Catillum came last, glancing casually into the corridor where he knew Fyn hid.

Fyn swallowed, licking dry lips.

The scuffing of the monks' soft leather slippers ceased, signalling that the abbot and masters had arrived at the secret entrance to the catacombs. Fyn waited. The secret passage lay behind an ordinary stretch of wall decorated with the same carved frieze that enlivened even the simplest abbey vessel.

There were too many masters clustered around the abbot for him to see which key the old man selected from the ones on the chain around his waist. Fyn strained to see which carving the abbot slid the key into, but this was also impossible. With a soft grinding noise the stone slid away to reveal a dark passage. The abbot and masters entered, taking the lantern with them, and the stone slid back into place. But not before Master Catillum left a small wedge of wood in the doorway.

Eyes still blinded by the passing of the lantern light, Fyn stepped out of the cross passage and ran to the secret entrance. A dark sliver was all that remained. He glanced up and down the corridor. Only the faintest of lights came down the stairwell from the floor above. By this feeble illumination, he could see no one.

Slipping his fingers in the narrow slit, he forced the panel wide enough to slide through. Bending down, he scooped up the wedge and tucked it in his pocket. The stone panel slid closed after him, leaving him in total darkness.

A wave of oppression rolled over Fyn, making his heart labour. Usually being below ground did not bother him. In the abbey you could always see reflected sunlight or look out a window. But here, he felt the whole weight of Mount Halcyon pressing down on him.

Nausea roiled in his belly, urging him to retreat. He refused. He had to prove the death of the boys master had been murder and the only way to do that was to retrieve the sacred vessel that held Wintertide's heart.

Fyn visualised the map he'd memorised and stepped into the darkness. After rounding two bends he could just hear the soft shuffle of the monks' shoes on the stone, echoing back to him.

Silent as a winter hare, Fyn scurried after them down the stairs. It grew steadily colder. Strange, he had expected it to be hot in the very heart of Mount Halcyon. After all, the goddess's blessing was heat.

He shivered and turned a bend, then stopped.

A glow came through a tall doorway with smooth stone lintels. The pool of light seemed glaringly bright to Fyn's dark-adjusted eyes. He crept closer, listening intently. He could tell by the echo of the monks' steps that they were walking across a cavern. As yet no one had spoken.

Pressing his cheek to the cold stone, Fyn peered around the entrance. His breath caught in his throat.

Halcyon's Sacred Heart opened before him, a great cavern filled with the glow of many candles... more were lit every moment as the masters performed their task. Each candle sat on the cupped hands of a long-dead master. Each mummified master knelt on a flat-topped stone, his face serene. They seemed to be scattered at random across the floor. Then Fyn noticed that above every master there was a finger of glistening stone extending down from the cavern ceiling.

The masters' skins glistened like glazed pottery. Stone had dripped down from above, encasing the long-dead monks in columns of stone. So this was what meant by the words *embraced by the goddess*.

Abbot Halcyon and the masters had gathered around a flat-topped column, which stood beneath a glistening spike of rock. When the abbot stepped away Fyn recognised Master Wintertide. Bound in fine cloth, Wintertide's body had been placed in the kneeling position, hands folded left on right, palms up in his lap. A newly lit candle flickered in his upturned hands. Fyn searched for and found the sacred jars with his master's internal organs ranged in front of his knees. All he had to do was wait out the ceremony, take the heart jar and return to Master Catillum's private chamber.

'Who brings this worthy master to join the goddess?' a woman asked, her voice echoing across the cavern.

Fyn blinked. For a heartbeat he believed it was the goddess Halcyon herself. Then the woman turned and he recognised the abbess of Sylion.

He bit back a gasp of surprise, for females were not allowed past the courtyard of the sacred pool, yet here she was. How had the abbess slipped into Halcyon's Sacred Heart unseen? There must be another way into the cavern, a passage just as secret as the one the abbot had used. It appeared Sylion and Halcyon had a much closer bond than he had been taught.

Fyn wrestled with this while the abbot and masters chanted Halcyon's psalm of praise and the abbess gave Sylion's formal responses.

Once the ceremony was over, the abbot spoke briefly with the abbess and headed towards Fyn, who stumbled backwards. He found a niche and stood pressed against the stone, hardly daring to breathe.

One by one the masters passed him. This time Master Catillum did not look for him. The abbess did not come this way.

'So, abbot, have you considered our list of possible boys masters?' Hotpool asked, his voice carrying back to Fyn. 'It will have to be someone well versed in the history of our order. The boys must respect the past.'

The abbot sighed. 'Tonight, Master Hotpool. You'll know tonight.'

As soon as their footsteps faded, Fyn resumed his place near the cavern entrance. He waited, listening to the soft tone of the female voices on the cold air as the abbess discussed something with a companion. Their voices faded, then he heard the grate of stone as a passage closed.

Believing the cavern deserted, Fyn stepped into Halcyon's Heart. His nostrils stung in reaction to intense Affinity. The intermittent seep below Mount Halcyon must be releasing power again. Not surprising, since other seeps had risen recently. The masters would have to bring down sorbt stones to absorb the Affinity.

As it was, he had to blink tears from his eyes. Since he meant no harm, he trusted the goddess would not hurt him. Still, his blood roared in his ears as he crossed to Master Wintertide's resting place.

Kneeling reverently, he looked up into his old teacher's face. Wintertide's pale skin had been painted with a clear glaze so that it resembled the finest porcelain. His expression was calm.

'I will miss you, Master Wintertide, more than I can say,' Fyn whispered and bent forwards, bowing from the waist, pressing his forehead to his hands on the floor. His royal emblem rode up, sliding out of the front of his robe to dangle in front of his eyes.

He straightened up, fingering it, feeling the familiar pattern of the embossed foenix. The metal was warm from his skin. The day he put this aside was the day he put aside his claim to his father's throne. He had thought he would be putting it aside to take up his place in the abbey, but now he knew that, after he did this last service for his old master, he would be without allegiance. The emblem must not fall into the wrong hands.

'Master Wintertide, I ask you to watch over this, as you watched over me in the abbey.' Fyn stood and undid the royal emblem's chain. It felt heavy in the palm of his hand. In the candlelight the foenix gleamed. He placed the pendant in the hollow behind his master's hands. The wax would burn down, hiding it. One day, many years in the future, Halcyon's stone would encase it.

'I promise you this, Master Wintertide, I will not rest until your killer has been punished.' He studied the four jars, comparing each one to Master Catillum's sketch. His hand moved even before he consciously recognised the jar that contained Master Wintertide's heart. 'Forgive me, master. This will be returned as soon as possible.'

He tucked the jar inside his belt pouch. All he had to do was take it to Master Catillum.

Feeling lighter, Fyn left the cavern. It was completely dark in the secret passage. He should have taken one of the candles but he recalled the way, counting the steps and making the turns until he came to a dead end, the sealed exit. No light seeped around the hidden door. Fyn's blind fingers brushed the stone wall, seeking the device which Master Catillum had told him would trip the opening.

Twice he searched where it should have been and found nothing.

What if he could not find it?

His mouth went dry with fear. Panic threatened. If he

did not find the trigger to open the panel he would starve alone in the dark. The great weight of the mountain pressed down on him, making it hard to breathe.

He struggled to clear his mind.

Think. There had to be a way out.

Then it came to him... If he could not open this door he would return to Halcyon's Heart and try to find the passage the Abbess had used – it had to come out somewhere on Mount Halcyon – then he would double back to the abbey.

Having thought it through, Fyn calmed down and widened his search. As his fingers dipped into a depression in the stone, he realised the mystics master was taller than him. Catillum hadn't taken this into account when describing where to find the catch. The device sank at his touch and the panel slid open.

Blinking in the dim light and relieved beyond words, Fyn stepped into the hall.

Now, to take the jar to Master Catillum. He hurried up the steps, pressing the jar to his chest so it would not be jolted.

As Fyn rounded the corner, relieved he had got away with it, a large hand descended on his shoulder, squeezing painfully.

'What do we have here, Beartooth, a little mouse stealing about in the dark?'

'And what has it been stealing?' Galestorm asked.

Fyn tried to pull away from Beartooth.

'Grab him, Onetree,' Galestorm ordered.

Arms pinned him. Fingers prised at his, forcing them away from the jar. Fyn stopped fighting, fearful the jar would fall and shatter.

Whisperingpine whistled. 'That looks like –'

'A jar from Halcyon's Sacred Heart.' Galestorm's eyes narrowed, then he smiled with malicious glee. 'Fyn Kingson, you have just signed your own death decree!'

'Huh?' Beartooth muttered.

Galestorm held up the jar. The semi-precious stones set on the lid glinted. 'All we have to do is show the abbot this and he'll have to order the king's brat executed for profaning the goddess. Come on.'

As they dragged Fyn upstairs his heart sank. Master Catillum had made it clear he could not help him if he was caught. To have come so close!

EVEN SO, FYN did not struggle. Since he had nothing to lose, he would reveal his suspicions to the abbot. As they had the jar, all the abbot had to do was ask the mystics master to do the tests on Wintertide's heart. Firefox and his supporters might still be proven murderers.

'What I don't understand is why he wanted the jar,' Whisperingpine muttered.

Fyn tensed, but Galestorm was too busy gloating over his downfall to listen.

They drove him up the spiral staircase, through the passages, past the young boys headed into the dining hall to eat their first meal of the day, past the acolytes who were already leaving to learn their crafts. Behind many curious faces, Fyn recognised Feldspar's worried face. Without a word his friend took off, running towards the mystics' level.

'Should I stop him?' Whisperingpine asked Galestorm.

'Don't bother. No one can save the king's brat now.'

Fyn did not say a word as they herded him along the busy corridor towards the stairwell at the far end.

Master Firefox stepped out of his chamber, accompanied by Hotpool.

'What's this?' Firefox demanded. 'Where are you taking Fyn Kingson?'

'To the abbot,' Galestorm announced loudly, holding up the jar. 'We caught him stealing from the goddess's Sacred Heart!'

The nearest acolytes gasped and stared at Fyn, horrified.

When Firefox recognised the jar his eyes widened. Master Hotpool took a step back, going pale. He went to speak, but Firefox touched his arm.

'Well done, Galestorm.' Firefox recovered quickly. 'Give me the jar. We will take him to the abbot.'

No, Fyn thought. If Firefox and Hotpool took over he would never get to the abbot. They would kill him, hide his body and replace the jar.

Galestorm hesitated, obviously torn because he wanted to see Fyn suffer, but obedience won out and he handed over the jar.

Fyn's head filled with a roaring noise.

'Yes, let's take Fyn Kingson straight to the abbot,' Master Catillum said, joining them.

A firm hand descended on Fyn's shoulder, urging him forwards. As Fyn strode towards the stairs, followed by Masters Firefox and Hotpool, the acolytes parted for them, whispering intently.

On the abbot's level they marched down the main

corridor, past the archways that looked out over Rolencia.

Master Catillum thrust the doors to the ante-chamber open.

The clerics master leapt to his feet. 'You can't go in –'

'We must!' The mystics master insisted and strode right past him.

He thrust the doors open and marched in.

The abbot and weapons master looked up. The desk between them was littered with notes, paper weights, ink wells and maps.

'There you are. That was quick,' the abbot said. 'But you didn't need to bring Fyn Kingson.'

'Oh, but we did,' Master Catillum insisted. 'He's –'

'He's stolen something from Halcyon's Sacred Heart,' Master Firefox asserted.

Fyn realised the master was going to try to bluster his way out of trouble.

'He's been in the sacred passages. Sacrilege!' Master Hotpool announced.

'It's sacrilege to murder a master,' Fyn cried. 'I took Master Wintertide's jar to prove that he was poisoned!'

'The healers said he had a heart attack,' Firefox countered. 'Surely they would know better than a mere acolyte?'

'A simple test will prove one way or the other,' Catillum said softly. Everyone went still. 'A test I can do before everyone here, now. Shall I send for my equipment?'

'To prove what?' Firefox countered. 'Even if you prove Wintertide was poisoned, how will you find out who poisoned him? Search the mind of every monk?'

'I won't have to search every monk, will I, Fyn?' Catillum prodded.

Fyn swallowed. 'Master Hotpool told me that the boys master died of a heart attack, but this was before the healers had even examined him. Hotpool could only have known what the healers would say if he knew which poison killed Wintertide. And he would have got that poison from the healer, Springmelt.'

'And Springmelt is safe in the mystics' chamber, waiting to be called,' Catillum explained.

They all turned to Hotpool including Firefox, who took several steps back from him. Hotpool opened his mouth, appealing wordlessly to his partner.

Firefox shook his head sadly. 'I always knew you hated Wintertide, but poison?'

Hotpool looked so shocked by this betrayal that Fyn almost felt sorry for him.

But he recovered quickly, gesturing dismissively to the mystics master. 'Catillum may swear Springmelt was working under my orders but it is his word against mine. He'll lie to implicate me.'

Crack!

The weapons master slammed a paper weight on the desk top. 'Enough of this. Rolencia has been invaded!'

Fyn gasped.

The masters turned in stunned silence.

'A rider just delivered this.' The abbot pointed to a message cylinder which lay on his busy desk. Beside it was a roll of vellum which had been sealed with a red wax impressed with the royal foenix.

'Father's royal symbol,' Fyn whispered.

'King Rolen has called on us to defend Rolencia from the Merofynians,' the weapons master explained, then glared at Firefox and Hotpool. 'So your petty politics can wait!'

'But King Merofyn betrothed his daughter to my brother,' Fyn protested.

'What better way to buy time to prepare for an invasion?' Master Oakstand countered. 'Remember your tactics lessons, lad. Force wins battles, but so does guile and it costs less lives.'

Fyn shook his head. He'd had a vision of the king's daughter in Halcyon's Fate. If she was not going to become his brother's queen, why had he seen her? 'I –'

'I know what you're going to say. I must refuse, Fyn,' the abbot told him. 'Acolytes cannot take up arms.'

Fyn gulped.

'According to King Rolen,' the abbot continued, 'the Merofynians are commanded by an ambitious warlord, who has been named overlord of the army.'

'How did they get into the valley undetected?' Fyn asked.

'The traitorous warlord from Cockatrice Spar let them use his pass,' the abbot said. 'King Rolen is going to march out to deal with Rejulas. This will leave his castle defended only by a few old men and untrained boys.'

Fyn froze. His mother, old Seela and Piro were in danger. For a moment he heard nothing but the rushing of a stream running fast with spring melt.

'We must stop this overlord from marching across the valley and laying siege to Rolenhold.' Master Oakstand unhooked one hand from his belt to tap the map. 'We must hold him until King Rolen's dealt with Rejulas and can bring his warriors back.'

Fyn remembered convincing Piro not to go to the abbess. If he hadn't interfered she would be safe in Sylion Abbey now. What if the Merofynian overlord reached Rolenhold before the monks could stop him? 'Please, Abbot Halcyon, I must go home!'

'Well spoken, lad. But what can one acolyte do against a whole army?' the abbot asked. 'No, your place is here.'

Annoyance flooded Fyn, then relief. It was true, he was useless. Hot on the heels of this came shame.

He was a coward.

Even as he thought this, he could not stop himself imagining Piro in danger. 'My mother and sister need me, I have to –'

'Master Oakstand,' the abbot overrode him. 'Take every able-bodied monk. Only those over seventy will remain here. Overlord Palatyne must be stopped!'

The weapons master grinned. 'Six hundred abbey warriors should hold this Merofynian overlord long enough for King Rolen to return. Quality against quantity!'

Master Catillum rubbed his jaw with his good hand. 'The canals are still frozen. If we leave by mid-morning and skate all night we'll make good time. Time to find the best defensive spots, time to plan.'

'Good.' The abbot rolled up the king's message, nodding to the weapons master. 'Gather your warriors and supplies.'

As Fyn struggled to take this all in, Master Oakstand hurried out, closely followed by Firefox and Hotpool.

The room went very quiet and the door latch clicked behind them.

'If they are ready to murder Wintertide then they are ready to move against us, abbot,' Catillum said softly. 'You can't let them get away with this.'

'They won't,' the abbot assured him. 'But for now we have a common enemy. Until the overlord is defeated we need not fear them.' As the abbot studied Fyn, his warm brown eyes gleaming from a nest of wrinkles. 'You've made a bad enemy there, kingson. And you profaned the catacombs.'

Fyn flushed but held the abbot's eyes. 'I know. But Master Wintertide was murdered and I believe the goddess would want to see his murderer brought to justice.'

'Will Hotpool's disgrace bring back your old master?'

'No, but...' Fyn swallowed, thinking of Lonepine. Then his mind did a mental shift and his real motivations became clear. 'I didn't want to see Firefox become abbot. I think his rule would be bad for the abbey.'

The abbot's eyes widened. 'You are a deep thinker, Fyn. It is a pity you are not the kingsheir.'

Fyn blinked. He'd never given this a thought.

The abbot smiled and caught the mystics master's eye. 'If you are to be abbot one day, Catillum, you must watch your back. Many a warrior has been killed by his "friends" in the heat of battle.'

'Then why risk sending...' Fyn fell silent. It was not his place to question the abbot's decisions.

'D'you think me helpless because of this?' The

mystics master lifted his withered arm with his good one. Fyn went to protest, but Catillum didn't wait for an answer. 'There will be renegade Power-workers with the Merofynian army, each with their own basket of nasty tricks. I must protect our people.' He frowned. 'I admit, I'd hoped never to see this day…'

Turning on his heel, he left Fyn alone with the abbot.

'As for you,' the abbot smiled at Fyn, 'I know your fellow acolytes will be chafing at the bit to go, but we don't send boys to war. You can rest assured Master Oakstand will stop those Merofynians.'

A wave of relief rolled over Fyn. Piro would be safe.

FOR FYN THE early morning passed in a blur of preparation as the whole abbey was turned upside down. Despite this, he was troubled by a niggling worry that he couldn't pinpoint. By mid-morning the monks were ready. The musicians played as the warrior monks of Halcyon assembled in the square around the sacred pool.

'Dreaming of battle, Fyn?' Feldspar asked, coming up behind him as he hesitated on the stair. 'Come on. Master Oakstand's ready to leave. We can watch from the gallery.'

Others had the same idea. The long corridor with its arched windows was crowded with boys, acolytes and the oldest of the monks. Fyn chose a window embrasure where he could look down into the abbey courtyard. It held the finest of Halcyon's warrior monks. They wore white cloaks so that they would blend in with the snow and each man carried his weapons strapped to his back, along with his food, his bedroll and skates. Every tenth man carried a small pot for cooking and a small medical kit, while every hundredth had a small forge. His task was to repair weapons. Halcyon's warrior monks were a highly disciplined fighting force, and ready to die for King Rolen.

Fyn's heart swelled with pride as he imagined the monks skating down the canals, racing faster than a horse could run through snow, racing to defend Rolencia.

And Fyn thought of the people who relied on his father and the monks to keep them safe. The farmers would be repairing their fences, getting ready to put their cows and goats out to pasture, and sharpening their plough shares. On the mountain slopes they would be repairing winter's damage to the terraces, eager to sow their crops. This was no time for war. The truth of an old saying hit him: *A summer spent warring meant a winter spent starving.*

'They do look fine,' Feldspar whispered, wistfully. His hands rested on the window sill, knuckles white with tension.

Hawkwing leant closer, his four-fingered hand resting on the ledge next to Fyn. When Hawkwing spoke, his voice was too loud, and his eyes were bright with excitement. 'The best we can hope for is that the fighting lasts past spring cusp. Then we can prove ourselves!'

Fyn nodded, but in truth the thought of war sickened him. If he was lucky the warrior monks would hold Overlord Palatyne until his father could defeat Rejulas. Then King Rolen would march on the Merofynian army, who would surrender and their king would sign a new peace treaty.

He caught a glimpse of Galestorm and his friends, down amongst the warriors, along with Firefox and Hotpool. Although he felt relieved to see them leave, he had to wonder how many of them would be coming back. Hopefully, Halcyon would protect the mystics master and Oakstand. It would be too much to ask that only his enemies fell under Merofynian swords. But he could hope for Feldspar's sake. Then it hit him, if he ran away from the abbey now it would confirm the whispers. Even his friends would believe him a coward.

But what could he do?

'The mystics master took a sliver of the sacred flame with him. Halcyon will protect them,' Feldspar said.

'A sharp sword and keen wits are a man's best protection,' Hawkwing insisted. 'Halcyon helps those who help themselves.'

Foxtail pointed. 'There they go!'

The monks marched out the gate and Fyn took comfort from the thought that at least Rolenhold was not under siege, so Piro was safe.

'YOUR TURN, MOTHER,' Piro said. They had begun a game of Duelling Kingdoms, Piro playing the King Rolen piece and her mother King Merofyn. 'None of my warning beacons have been lit.'

Aware that both the guard and the Affinity warder could hear every word, Piro was careful how she phrased things. Her father had decided it would be safer, when she visited her mother, if Autumnwind waited by the open door. His reasoning was that if the Merofynian Power-worker took over her mother again, the warder could save Piro. And he had forbidden her to discuss the situation in Rolencia, fearing the Power-worker might gain knowledge of their preparations for war and use it against them.

Piro wished she'd never used that ploy to hide her mother's Affinity, but even now she couldn't think of another.

While they played, Seela sat by the fireplace, tutting and humming softly. The rhythmic creak of the rocking chair soothed Piro's fluttering stomach.

Her mother studied the game board. 'Since your soldiers have not lit the beacons in time, my warriors can advance, but where –'

'Dovecote is in your path,' Piro said. The longer this went on, the greater the danger for Dovecote in reality. Her gaze flew to her mother.

Queen Myrella nodded once.

Piro wanted to ask if she believed Orrade and Garzik were captives or worse, but she dared not. Frustration and fear welled up in her.

Seela began humming a jolly midwintering song. The main character was a roistering warrior who was popular with the ladies, reminding Piro of Byren.

'I know.' Piro smiled. 'I'll send my faithful captain of the honour guard to alert Halcyon Abbey.' She moved the captain. There was no kingson in the game.

'A difficult journey with my warriors deployed across the valley,' the queen whispered.

'He is clever and brave. He'll get through,' Piro

assured her mother. 'Your turn.'

'I have three Power-workers. I choose to deploy them with each commander. They will be on the alert for your warriors on their missions.'

Piro nodded. Merofynian commanders always travelled with renegade Power-workers. But Byren and the Dovecote brothers had no Affinity so their own Affinity could not be turned against them.

'My go.' Piro turned over a wild card. 'Ah.' Swiftly she read the card and found a way to use it to warn her mother. She moved a warlord off his spar and put him on Rolenhold, saying, 'Ostron Isle is always sending surprises with its wild cards. And this one is much more dangerous than I thought. It gives my player the ability to shield himself from those with Affinity and so hide his true nature.'

Would her mother understand the implication? Cobalt had hidden his true nature.

'I fear you are right. How will I warn my king?' her mother whispered. 'He must beware false advisors...'

Piro nodded. But what could she do? She was only a child. Her father would never listen to her.

And so the game of Duelling Kingdoms went on. If there hadn't been so much at stake, Piro would have enjoyed tricking the guard. As it was, she finished up the game, assured only that her mother knew how serious things were.

They hugged at the door holding back tears, while the guard and Autumnwind looked the other way.

'Take care, Piro, I fear you may have to be as fierce and brave and your namesake,' her mother whispered.

'I'm not brave at all,' Piro admitted. 'I thought I

was, but I'm not.'

Her mother placed one finger under her chin, tilting her face to look into her eyes. 'We are all as brave as we have to be. Have you any idea how many times I cried myself to sleep when I first came here, a captive of war, surety for my father's honourable intentions?' She smiled through her tears. 'And look what came of us? Rolen and I have been happier than anyone thought possible.'

Until now, Piro thought. Her unspoken words hung in the air. She would burst into tears if she wasn't careful. 'I must go.'

Her mother released her and Seela gave her a quick hug. 'Take care, Piro. Your mother wants you to have these. Remember, a queen always carries her keys of office.'

Seela pressed a ring with a bundle of keys into her hands. The guard glanced swiftly at the heavy key ring but did not intervene since the key to their tower room had been removed.

'But these are yours.' Piro tried to give them back.

Her mother caught her hand and firmly closed her fingers over the keys. 'Until I am restored to the king's trust you must watch over him for me.'

Piro nodded, tears slipping down her cheeks. Her father was under the care of both the castle's healers, but Valens had done a great deal of damage. After consulting with Autumnwind the healers had not accused Valens of having Affinity, only of being misguided. Piro suspected they were protecting themselves and Autumnwind from the king's ire. They declared Valens guilty of using dangerous

Ostronite techniques, which did more harm than good. The healers had become quite powerful in that they now said what the king could and could not do to restore his health.

Piro brushed tears from her eyes and headed down the stairs. She undid her belt, slipping the key ring through it. With each step she took she heard the chink of her mother's symbols of power and felt their weight, both literal and figurative.

It was still weighing on her mind when she went up the servants' stairs to the family wing.

'Piro Kingsdaughter?' a small, wizened servant asked.

'Yes?'

Someone grabbed her from behind, holding her against their body, lifting her off her feet.

'Cobalt!'

'How did you know?'

'I smelt you!' The scent of Ostronite myrrh clung to his skin.

Cobalt laughed. 'I'll hold her. See what you think.'

Cobalt's servant approached, his black eyes malicious and bright. She knew him from somewhere.

Piro's nostrils stung and her vision quivered as she slipped into Unseen sight. The servant pulsed with Affinity. Another renegade Power-worker. Clearly, Cobalt had no qualms about dealing with them. She tried to rear back but he held her firmly.

The Power-worker raised one hand, fingers spread. Behind the darkness in his eyes she saw the flash of a manticore tail lifting to strike.

Piro clenched her fists, brought both her arms forwards and drove the sharp point of her elbows back into each side of Cobalt's midriff. Air escaped him in a grunt of pain and his grasp slackened enough for her to duck under his arm. She sprang behind him and shoved, sending him staggering forwards to collide with the renegade Power-worker who cursed, knocked off his feet by the bigger man.

Then she was running up the stairs, running towards the solarium, but there was no protection there, so she changed direction, heading for her bedchamber. But before she got there she skidded to a halt as realisation hit her.

The Power-worker had cursed in Merofynian.

She'd claimed a Merofynian Power-worker was loose in the castle to save her mother, but it really was true!

The implications made her head spin. A door opened along the hallway. Before anyone could see her she darted down the passage, heading for the stairs. She had to warn her father. King Rolen was spending more and more time at the war table, as if staring at the map would tell him the true extent of the Merofynian army and its whereabouts.

Hand on her keys to stop them jingling, she slowed to a hasty walk in the passages where others could see her, and sped up in private.

'Kingsdaughter,' the guard at the bottom of the steps to the war table chamber acknowledged her. 'I don't –'

'I do!' She thrust past his half-hearted attempt to stop her. At least she knew Cobalt would not be with her father right now.

With a quick knock, she thrust the door to the war

table chamber open.

The king sat on the far side, alone for once. Relief flooded her and she felt tears sting her eyes. 'Father?'

'Eh, Piro. What's the matter?' He stood up stiffly and opened his arms to her.

She headed around the table towards him. 'Cobalt's new servant is a Merofynian Power-worker!'

He drew back before she could reach him, shaking his head. 'Cobalt warned me of this. He said you'd try to discredit him again. Oh, Piro –'

She stamped her foot. 'I tell you it's true. I heard the man curse in Merofynian.'

Still, her father shook his head. 'You chose the one thing you knew I hated most. It's a wonder you didn't try to tell me Cobalt was a Merofynian Power-worker. But then you couldn't, not when we've already proven he has no Affinity.'

'Not without the sorbt stones test,' she countered, however she could see her father had already made up his mind. Frustration flashed through Piro. 'Cobalt's the true Servant of Palos, not Byren!'

As it left her lips, she realised it was true even if Cobalt wasn't a lover of men. Then, she wished it unsaid.

Radiating fury, the king strode towards the door. She ran alongside him. 'Where are you going, father?'

He flung the door open. 'Guard, come here. Escort my daughter to her chamber and see that she does not leave.'

The guard at the bottom of the steps gaped.

'Move, damn it!' King Rolen roared.

Piro lifted her chin. 'I do not need an escort, Father.'

'But you'll have one. I won't have this kind of vicious gossip-mongering undermining the reputation of an honourable man.'

'Honourable man?' Piro bristled. 'If you cannot see how he had undermined Byren's honour you are —'

'Byren?' The king's hands lifted as if he had only just restrained himself from shaking her.

Piro's sight shifted to the Unseen. She saw the face of a youth of eighteen, a youth who had watched helplessly as his father and elder brother were murdered by a renegade Power-worker. As the horror and sorrow faded, they were replaced with implacable anger. This was the expression the young King Rolen had worn when he ordered the execution of the Servants of Palos. And she realised that he did not truly see her or Byren, he saw only a threat that he did not know how to fight. This was his one blindness and Cobalt had used it, just as he had used her mother's blind spot, her kindness.

Piro backed up. Her heel missed the top step and she teetered, vertigo snatching at the base of her stomach.

'Kingsdaughter!' The guard only just caught her. She clung to him, disoriented. 'This way.'

Gently, he guided her down the stairs. Stunned, she followed him along the hall.

'Are you all right, Piro Kingsdaughter?'

As the guard lifted his arm, the flash of manticore tail returned to her. She ducked.

The guard took a step back, horrified. 'Eh, I wouldn't hit you!'

Even as he spoke, she recalled where she had seen the manticore tail – inside the Power-worker's mind. And she recalled where she had seen the servant before – at Dovecote, riding in with Lence and Cobalt.

So that was how Cobalt had lured the pride down to attack Byren. He'd worked with the renegade Power-worker, a Merofynian who was helping Cobalt weave his subtle poison. And now Cobalt and his servant knew that she knew, her life would be forfeit.

She had to hide.

The guard was saying something, Piro could not understand him. Her world tipped then spun.

He caught her for a second time.

She was vaguely aware of him staggering under her weight, not that she was heavy but her collapse was unexpected. Regaining his balance, he lifted her, carrying her towards her bedchamber. Her first impulse was to throw off his help but she made herself go limp as a plan formed.

She was still feigning a faint when he placed her gently on the bed.

'Poor little thing,' he muttered. 'Out cold.'

He stood there helplessly for a moment then ran off to get someone.

The moment he left the chamber, Piro rolled off the bed, grabbing her cloak. For a heartbeat she saw stars pinwheeling across her vision. But she refused to give in to weakness.

Where should she go?

Sure only that she had to remain free, she realised she had become the hunted in her own home and Cobalt and his Merofynian Power-worker were the hunters. Her recurring nightmare of being stalked by wyverns had come true.

Chapter Twenty-Nine

BYREN SKATED, HIS body following a mindless rhythm. Having travelled all day the warriors were tired, but Rejulas had ordered the torches lit. Privately, Byren thought they would have been better off skating by starlight, after giving their eyes time to adjust, but perhaps it was a good idea, when you considered it was almost spring cusp. The winter-dormant creatures would be stirring, hungry after their long sleep.

Skating with bound hands interfered with his balance and he couldn't save himself if he fell. But he dare not stumble deliberately. He already had rope burns on his neck from the last time he'd slipped. When the right moment came, he would drive the pole from behind his arms, wriggle his legs through his arms and chew at the knot until he was free. But the moment had not come yet.

Hopefully, Orrade had recovered quickly. He hadn't been unconscious for long the last time. With any luck, Garzik and Orrade were watching him right now, waiting to make their move. Two men against twenty or more – three men once he was free – the odds were not good.

'Not far now, kingson,' Rejulas told him.

They rounded the bend in the canal to see Doveton, across the small lake. There were lights in every window and Byren guessed warriors had taken over the villagers' homes. New Dovecote was also aglow, every window gleaming yellow, while behind it stood the sturdy old keep, lights burning there too. So many warriors, Byren would not have guessed Rejulas could muster such a large force.

His gaze flew to the high tower. Had Lord Dovecote kept the warning beacon readied with oil to hasten its burning? Byren trusted to his thoroughness.

Too late to try anything now. Better to wait until he saw how things were inside Dovecote. Maybe they could free Elina and the old lord. And there was still Lence. Though all the evidence pointed to Lence's betrayal, Byren was convinced his twin had been tricked by Cobalt.

They slowed as they reached the village wharf. Someone shoved Byren backwards until he sat on the wharf step. His skates were unstrapped while his hands remained tied. Then they trudged up the road through the village. It was filled with Rejulas's men. Warriors stood in doorways, tankards in hand as they yelled congratulations and toasted to their warlord's success.

Beyond the village, they wound their way up to the terrace, where light poured from the large indefensible windows. On the terrace, in front of the great double doors, stood the two huge foenixes. Cast in bronze, they had been given to Lord Dovecote by King Byren the Fourth as a reward for his loyalty. Their backs were hollow, forming braziers, and flames leapt from them, casting crazy shadows across the front of New Dovecote.

The big double doors stood closed. Byren frowned. There was something strange about the doors. From where he stood on the terrace below he could see someone was waiting, standing pressed against the door. By the flickering flames Byren suddenly understood what he was seeing. 'Lord Dovecote!'

He staggered.

They'd run the Old Dove through with a lance, pinning him to one of the doors. But why leave him there?

Rejulas laughed. 'How do you like our little welcoming gift?'

Rage surged through Byren. Rejulas was a typical spar warlord, a leader only because he was crueler and more vicious than his barbarous warriors. He did not deserve Piro. Byren was glad she was safe back at Rolenhold. His stomach knotted with fear. If only the same could be said for Elina!

If he could get her to safety he would die happy.

The double doors creaked and swung open, carrying their grisly symbol.

Word of their arrival must have gone on ahead because a tall man in armour strode out, the torchlight glinting on the embossed metal on his chest plate. For a moment Byren could not make sense of what he saw, he had been expecting... hoping to meet Lence and convince him this was all a terrible misunderstanding.

The pattern on the stranger's breast plate was that of a two-headed snake, the amfina.

'Overlord Palatyne.' Rejulas bowed.

Byren felt this revelation like a body blow. It knocked the air from his chest and patches of grey swam in his vision. So Old Man Narrows had not been mistaken. There were Merofynian warriors in Rolencia, making Rejulas a traitor. This explained how the Merofynian army had penetrated the valley without triggering the warning beacons. The warlord of Cockatrice Spar had let them use his pass.

Where was Lence in all this? Captive, Byren fervently hoped. Captive and cursing his naivety.

'I bring you Byren Kingson, overlord,' Rejulas said with a flourish. 'Never question my loyalty.'

'Do you think me a fool, Rejulas?' Palatyne countered.

At his signal two warriors wearing helms bearing horse-hair plumes dyed the royal azure of Merofynia dragged Elina out from the ranks behind Palatyne. Her hands were bound at the wrists in front of her. She almost stumbled. Byren's wanted to help her but he dared not move.

'There, my pretty,' Palatyne gestured to Byren. 'I said we'd bring you a playmate.'

Elina stared at Byren, her dark eyes blazing.

Byren's stomach turned over. Seeing her a captive of the Merofynian overlord had made him a coward. He was ready to fall on his knees and promise them anything, as long as they let Elina go free.

'Why did you come here, Byren?' she demanded. 'Why?'

Palatyne caught her chin in one hand and said something softly that made her shoot Byren an agonised glance.

'Don't listen to him,' Byren yelled. 'I'm a dead man anyway.' Then the back of his head imploded and the ground came up to hit him in the face.

Consciousness returned as they dragged him, none too gently, up the steps.

'He weighs as much as a full-grown wyvern,' one warrior complained.

'And smells almost as bad. Quit your griping!'

Byren let his body stay limp, pretending to be worse than he was, as they hauled him across the terrace. They shoved him through the double doors, dragged him past the great fireplace, and came to a halt.

He sagged between them.

Someone grabbed his head by the hair and threw a tankard of wine in his face. He spluttered, pretending to be groggy. It gave him time to look around Dovecote's great hall.

This was not an ancient hall with huge columns decorated with ancestral friezes like Rolenhold, but a well-proportioned long chamber with polished wood panelling, and exquisite hangings depicting famous scenes from Rolencia's history. He pushed away the memory of Lord Dovecote walking them around the hall as children, telling them the stories of their shared history.

Directly in front of him, a balcony looked down from the floor above, where the family's bed chambers were. From this railing, a great embroidered banner hung to the ground depicting the estate's emblem, the feather and the sword.

Byren looked at the elegant brass aviary which housed Lord Dovecote's fancy birds. No birds fluttered from perch to perch, no soft cooing came from the cage.

He knew that if he went closer he would find the doves lying dead and this told him more about his captor than anything else. Harmless, beautiful creatures killed for effect.

Byren glanced away, trying to think. To each side of the fireplace stood stone pedestals on which rested the family's treasured firestones. They were just close enough so that they glowed with a fiery inner radiance, yearning for each other like lovers.

Byren focused on Overlord Palatyne, who stood in front of a high table laden with gold ornaments, personal items of great beauty like tortoiseshell combs and mother-of-pearl jewellery. These things sat oddly amidst steaming dishes of roast mutton, goose and fresh-baked bread. A dozen lordlings roistered drunkenly, waited on by curled and perfumed servants. Byren suspected this was the cream of Merofynian aristocracy, who had come along to see Rolencia conquered. But where were the real warriors?

Two of Dovecote's servants hurried out with a huge chair, which they set up in front of the high table like a throne for Palatyne. Then Byren noticed silent warriors standing in the background, alert but relaxed, their hands resting lightly on their sword hilts. They wore the amfina crest on their surcoats and they watched everything. Palatyne's honour guard, Byren guessed, veteran spar warriors who had come up with their warlord as he rose in rank.

As for the overlord himself, he was perhaps as tall as King Rolen. No longer a young man, by the grey in his beard he looked to be in his mid-to late thirties. His nose had been broken and set badly so that it was flat from the bridge down, giving him a pugnacious aspect.

Palatyne grabbed a sword from the laden table and lounged in the great chair, the weapon resting casually on his lap. For a heartbeat Byren wondered why he bothered, until he recognised the Old Dove's sword, the one that should have been Orrade's.

Just behind him stood an old renegade Power-worker. He wore a necklace of wyvern teeth and, on the tip of his staff, a stone wyvern's head sat. His hair was completely silver and hung in a single thin plait from the crown of his head. His waist-length beard was loose and threaded with bones and things Byren didn't want to identify. Everything about him proclaimed his barbaric Utland origins.

'Your foretelling was right, Utlander,' Palatyne told him.

'Of course,' he countered. 'If you would only trust –'

'You sent for me, overlord?' A tall, iron-haired man, who wore the indigo robes of a noble scholar, entered from under the mezzanine floor and strode around the table to stand on the left of Palatyne's chair. Byren had expected to see barbaric Power-workers serving the overlord but not a cultured man like this.

'There he is.' Palatyne indicated Byren.

The noble Power-worker shifted his weight, causing the globe on the end of his staff to flare briefly, attracting Byren gaze. Penetrating black eyes searched Byren's face.

Byren returned the stare, refusing to back down. His head thumped and his vision blurred. The noble blinked first but Byren's stomach lurched with the knowledge that these were renegade Power-workers like the ones who had murdered his grandfather and uncle from afar on the battlefield. He was grateful he had no Affinity to make him vulnerable.

Unlike this Merofynian noble, a Rolencian noble with Affinity would have been sent to Halcyon Abbey as a child and taught to serve Rolencia, not a wicked overlord and his corrupt king.

Byren shuddered, licking dry lips. He had really fallen into the fire this time.

Palatyne snapped his fingers and the two honour guards behind the laden table bent down. When they straightened up, they dragged Elina to her feet. Blood trickled brightly from her swollen bottom lip, running down her throat, into the delicate shadow above her low-cut bodice. They marched her around the table to stand on Palatyne's right. Her gaze flew to Byren for one desperate heartbeat, then she looked down at her bound hands, apparently defeated.

Byren steeled himself to give nothing away, not even if they threatened Elina, but the overlord ignored him.

Turning to Elina, he said, 'There he is, my pretty Dove, the second kingson. I already have the heir to use against King Rolen, so I'm going to execute this kingson at dawn. How he dies is up to you. A swift axe or burnt alive? You'll watch whatever happens.'

She wrung her roped hands.

'Well? Are you going to welcome me to your bed tonight?' Palatyne prodded. 'If you please me I may let him live another day –'

Throwing aside the ropes, Elina sprang towards Palatyne, plucked the knife from his belt, and stabbed for his throat. He only just managed to divert the blow so that it wedged in the wood of the chair next to his neck. His great arm swung in an arc, sending Elina flying like a rag doll. He lurched to his feet and the sword fell forgotten to the ground, clattering on the tiles.

Elina hit the floor a body length from Byren, skidding. She lay there stunned.

Byren kicked one guard, shouldered the other and ran to her side, dropping to his knees. His arms pinned behind his back, he leant over her. 'Elina, can you hear me?'

Her eyes fluttered open as she struggled to drag in a breath. He was only vaguely aware that Palatyne had called off his warriors and was watching them.

'Byren,' she gasped, lifting her hands to touch his face. 'Why did you come?'

'I had to,' he whispered. 'I've always loved you, Lina. Always will.'

'I know.' She blinked away tears. 'But I was so angry, so hurt –'

'I'm sorry. I wanted to explain.'

'I read your poem. But, when I went to the water-wheel, you weren't there.'

'You didn't tell Lence to send me away?'

She shook her head.

Byren was aware of Palatyne bearing down on them.

'Ask for quarter,' Byren whispered. 'Go to Sylion Abbey. You'll be safe there –'

'You little bitch.' Palatyne pulled Elina upright by her hair. She cried out as he swung her around, sending her staggering away. 'You two are lovers!'

She kept her feet and straightened up, tears of pain glittering in her fierce eyes. 'No. But I wish we were!'

With a roar he leapt on her, his hands closing on her throat.

Byren lurched, trying to rise, but two of the honour guard held him down. He could only watch as Palatyne throttled her.

The noble Power-worker strode over to Palatyne, slamming his staff on the floor so that the tip glowed, illuminating Palatyne's rage-engorged face.

'Think, overlord!' his voice rang out. 'Think how much more satisfying it will be to bed this wench while her lover is your captive. Think how he will feel going to his death, knowing you have taken what he prized!'

Palatyne grimaced with annoyance but released Elina. She dropped to her knees, gasping for breath. She was only a body length from Byren, yet he was powerless to help her.

'Yes,' Palatyne agreed. 'His suffering will add to my enjoyment.'

He strode towards Byren, a boot swinging for his head. Though Byren threw himself to one side, the tip caught him a glancing blow, sending him sprawling on the floor.

When his vision cleared, Palatyne had Elina's bodice in his hands. With one heave he tore it open and swung her around so that Byren could see her naked breasts. 'Look what I will be enjoying tonight!'

Though every man present stared at her she lifted her chin, staring past them all, her gaze defiant.

Byren's heart swelled with pride.

Palatyne fixed on Byren, triumphant. 'Take him away and lock him up.' He turned to the noble Power-worker. 'See, Lord Dunstany, your prophecy will not come true. I'll kill every last one of King Rolen's kin. They will not be my downfall. I make my own destiny!'

Lord Dunstany's reply was lost to Byren as they dragged him out of the hall, past the sullen, subdued kitchen staff and into the stable yard. Behind the stables, the road rose to the old keep with its warning tower, every window lit. As it loomed over Byren, despair welled up in him. How would Orrade reach him now? How would he light the beacon and save Elina?

He would never get to Halcyon Abbey to deliver his father's message and no one would ever know that he had died loyal to Rolencia.

'Drink, my lord?' a throaty female voice piped up.

The Merofynians stopped and turned around to see a pretty serving girl standing in the kitchen doorway. She held a tray laden with tankards and a steaming jug of mead.

'This is for them in the keep, but they've been guzzling all evening.' She nodded towards the warning tower, where men could be heard singing loudly off key. 'Want a sup?'

'Don't mind if I do.' The leader of their group strode back towards her, followed by the other four guards with Byren in the middle.

Byren noticed a familiar face peering out from behind the serving girl's skirt. Rifkin, the kitchen boy. As the honour guards grabbed themselves a tankard, the lad caught Byren's eye, holding his gaze with desperate but impenetrable meaning.

A body barrelled into Byren's back, driving him to his knees. The Merofynian groaned and collapsed beside him, blood dark as night, pooling on the churned up snow.

'Hold still,' Orrade whispered, grabbing Byren's arms.

His shoulders protested. Then he felt the blessed release as the pole was pulled out and the ropes fell off his hands. 'What took you so long?'

Orrade laughed and hauled him to his feet. Two bodies shot past them, locked in desperate combat.

Byren blinked recognising one of them. 'Winterfall?'

Orrade nodded. 'Eight of your honour guard. Chandler and Winterfall convinced them that you were wrongfully accused.'

Crack. Mead showered Byren's left leg as the serving maid smashed the jug over the last struggling Merofynian. Young Chandler cut his throat, then cleaned his knife.

'We couldn't let you down,' he said.

Byren grinned and tried to massage feeling back into his hands.

'We're in luck,' Orrade whispered. 'Only Palatyne and his lordlings are housed in New Dovecote.

His honour guard refused to sleep under the same roof as Rejulas's honour guard. Couldn't stomach traitors. So they've taken the old Keep and Rejulas's men have the town.'

Byren grinned. 'You've been busy.'

'Servants hear everything.'

'What of the townspeople?'

'Turned out of their own beds. They're sleeping in the servants' quarters in New Dovecote. Here's your hunting knife. It was all Rifkin could steal.'

'I'm obliged,' Byren said, slipping the knife into its customary place. If he were Palatyne, he would have Rejulas and his warriors killed the moment they were no longer useful. Anyone who could betray their sworn oath of allegiance was a worthless ally. 'Where's the healer and Affinity warder?'

'Willowtea's dead. The Affinity warder took a blow from one of Palatyne's Power-workers. They thought it had killed him but he was just knocked out. The cook hid him. Unfortunately he's too weak to help us.'

'Too bad.'

By the time Byren could use his fingers, they'd dragged the bodies away to hide them and Rifkin was raking the snow to disguise all sign of the skirmish.

Winterfall returned with a broken nose and a sheepish grin. 'I neber doubted you.'

Throat tight, Byren hugged him. 'Pack snow on that nose.'

As the maid took Winterfall off to apply the snow, Chandler said, 'You've eight more swords at your back.'

Eight honour guards, some of them mere callow youths, townspeople and servants... Byren ran his hand through his hair. They were vastly outnumbered; subterfuge was their only hope. 'We need a plan.'

'This way.' Orrade led them back into the new wing, through the kitchen and down a long hall where the able-bodied townspeople huddled. They touched Byren as he passed and whispered a welcome to Orrade and Garzik. Byren's bloodied honour guard impressed them.

Orrade led Byren into the cold-cellar. Great blocks of ice lined the walls to preserve food all year round. Amidst the frozen meat and stores, about two dozen men and half as many women waited, their breath steaming. Byren surveyed them by the light of the single lamp. He recognised stable lads, household servants and gardeners; most of the males were under sixteen or over sixty. At ten, Rifkin was the youngest.

Orrade gestured. 'This is all that remains of Dovecote's defenders.'

'Captain Blackwing?' Byren asked.

'Amongst the first to fall.'

'I'm sorry –'

'What should we do first, Byren?' Garzik asked. The boys of thirteen and fourteen had gravitated to him, eager to follow his lead.

Byren's heart sank. They were all going to die. He glanced to the old gaffer who used to look after the chickens. From his expression, it was clear he knew it too but he still clutched the garden scythe in his gnarled hands and waited for orders.

'Byren?' Orrade prodded.

'Right,' Byren muttered. 'We need to light the warning beacon. Is it prepared?'

'The Old Dove always keeps it ready,' the chicken keeper said.

'But the tower was the first place the Merofynians took over,' a stable lad piped up. 'It's full of them!'

'They're nearly all drunk,' the serving maid announced, eyes sparkling.

'We've been keeping them well supplied,' the cook explained. 'They think they're safe because no one knows the Merofynians are here except for Rejulas and his men.'

'Good.' With everyone watching him, Byren felt the weight of their expectation.

'We need to get Elina away from Palatyne,' Orrade said. 'He's taken the Royal Chamber.'

'I'll go save her,' Garzik offered, 'then kill Palatyne!'

'Let me go,' Winterfall offered.

Orrade caught Byren's eye. Garzik wouldn't stand a chance against a warrior of Palatyne's experience and Winterfall was not much better.

'No, I need you two to lead the youths. Dress as servants and sneak up to the top of the warning tower to light the beacon,' Byren told him. 'But don't do it until you get my signal. Once the beacon is alight the Merofynians will know we've risen.' He caught the cook's eye. 'I want to get the household servants and townspeople out into the forest and hidden before then.' He was thinking aloud. Seeing the fate of Lord Dovecote and his birds had convinced Byren that Palatyne would not hesitate to take his anger out on the servants, women and children alike. 'I want everyone hidden before we light that beacon. Just as well the tower guards are drunk.' He smiled at the cook and she blushed as if she was fifteen, not fifty. 'This will make it easier for Garzik and my honour guard to get past them to the top of the tower.'

But how would they get down again? And what about Rejulas's men in the town?

'Set fire to the town. It's wooden, it'll go up like tinder,' Orrade suggested, following the same train of thought. A dismayed mutter arose from the townspeople.

'While the town burns Rejulas's warriors will be too busy escaping with their lives to hunt down the townspeople,' Byren assured them.

Orrade nodded. 'I'll send some men into Doveton to prepare the fires. They can light them the moment the beacon is lit.'

'I'll go,' the chicken keeper offered. 'Take the stable boys with me.'

'What of Lence Kingsheir?' Rifkin piped up. 'He's being kept in the blue chamber.'

Byren felt his first surge of hope. Everyone looked to him. Did they suspect that his twin was a traitor? Why should they?

'I'll deal with Lence,' Byren muttered. If it came to the worst and Lence had betrayed them, he was anxious to save his family shame.

'We can deal with the Merofynian servants,' the cook volunteered. Half a dozen serving girls nodded eagerly. 'Not a warrior amongst them!'

'Good, but quietly,' Byren warned. 'I don't want

Palatyne slitting Elina's throat.'

'Goddess forbid!' the cook cried, echoed by others.

Byren smiled. 'Mistress cook, you organise the household staff. Deal with the Merofynian servants then as soon as Palatyne and his lordlings fall asleep, grab food and blankets and lead the townspeople out. Hide in the forest tonight and tomorrow...' Where would they go? '...head into the Divide. That goes for all of you. Don't waste your lives trying to fight the Merofynians. Hide until it is safe to come down.'

They all nodded.

'What of Rejulas?' Garzik asked, rubbing his arms to keep warm. 'He betrayed King Rolen. His life is forfeit. Let me go after him. Winterfall can light the beacon.'

'Rejulas is in the Green Chamber,' the cook volunteered.

'I'll deal with Rejulas,' Byren decided. The last thing he wanted to do was place Elina at risk but his duty was to Rolencia. He fixed on Garzik. 'The beacon is most important. We must alert my father so he can muster Rolencia's defences.'

'What of Elina?' Orrade caught his arm. 'Let me go. I'll slip into Palatyne's chamber, cut his throat and –'

Byren nodded. 'When I give the signal. Once you have her, take her to Sylion Abbey. They'll protect –'

'Not the Divide?' Garzik asked.

Byren shook his head. He didn't know how many of them would reach the dubious safety of the Divide or how long they would be living like savages in the high country.

'If you think Elina will run from a fight you don't

know her,' Garzik muttered.

He knew her. The problem was he loved her. 'Time to get moving.'

'Right.' The cook gathered her people and left.

As the last of the women filed out Byren caught Winterfall's shoulder. 'Watch over the young ones.' He didn't mention Garzik by name, didn't want to shame him. 'This won't be like weapons drill. Afterwards meet me at the water-wheel.'

Winterfall nodded then led the youths and the honour guard away. Byren watched them leave with their makeshift weapons, wishing he did not have to send them on this task.

As soon as they were alone Orrade turned to Byren, face grim. 'I'm coming with you when you confront Lence.'

Chapter Thirty

BYREN GRIMACED. 'You think I'm too soft, Orrie?'

'I think you're too good-hearted. And I'm not convinced Lence is Rejulas's captive.'

This was what Byren feared. 'You saw the trick Cobalt pulled, presenting those rings and the poem to blacken my name –'

'I saw. But ask yourself this, why is Lence so ready to believe what Cobalt tells him?'

Byren shook his head. 'If I can just explain –'

'Here.' Orrade radiated an intensity of purpose as he unfastened the borrowed sword. His breath plumed in the cold-cellar's chilly air.

'No.' Byren didn't want to leave Orrade unarmed. 'What will you –'

Orrade held up the Old Dove's sword, the one Byren had seen fall on the floor near Palatyne's chair. 'Rifkin retrieved it for me. Come on, I want to get this over with so we can save Elina before...'

He did not bother to finish but headed for the door. Byren caught his arm.

'What?'

In that instant Byren saw the consequences of going for Elina now. Palatyne would put up a fight which would alert his warriors. In no time at all the place would be swarming with armed men. The townspeople and Dovecote's servants would not get away. Winterfall wouldn't have time to light the warning beacon. His followers would be captured. They'd all be executed. There was no alternative. 'We can't save Elina yet. We don't want to trigger the alarm.'

'But Palatyne will...' Orrade shuddered. 'I can't let that happen.'

Byren couldn't stop the thought of Elina's slender body trapped under Palatyne's. A flash of rage ignited him. He repressed it, driving it down deep inside. 'No, Orrie, we –'

'What of Elina?'

Yes, Elina... Byren's stomach churned. He forced himself to ignore it and go on. 'Elina's the Old Dove's daughter. As long as we get her out of here, she will understand.'

Orrade cursed, tore his arm free and shoved past.

Byren caught him by the jerkin, swung him up against the door and pressed his forearm to his throat. Orrade gasped, fingers prying at Byren's arm.

'She's m'sister!' he ground out.

'And I love her!'

'It's not right!'

Frustration swept through Byren. The gods knew, he would give his own life for Elina's if he had to.

'Would you let your own people down to save Elina? She wouldn't thank you.'

He gave Orrade a moment to digest this.

'I don't like it any better than you,' Byren admitted. 'But this is the right thing to do. I know it is.'

Even as the words left his mouth, he recalled the old seer's seemingly senseless babble about right being a matter of perception. Shocked, he released Orrade and stepped back. Who was he to say what was right? He shivered.

Orrade stared, as if he had never seen him before.

'Very well,' Byren told him. 'Do what you think is right.'

Orrade straightened his jerkin and went to grab the door latch. He hesitated, the struggle clear on his face. He agonised until, finally, the fight went out of him. 'Sylion take you, Byren!'

'May Sylion take Palatyne into his cold embrace,' Byren whispered. 'I'll see him dead before dawn.'

'That's no comfort for what Elina's going through,' Orrade snapped and again his hand went to the latch, but he stopped himself.

Unable to sit still, Byren paced. It was too cold to sit.

Palatyne was right, this was agony. No matter what his logical mind told him, he couldn't stop his imagination.

He caught Orrade studying him. 'What?'

His friend's smile held a great deal of anger mingled with admiration. 'I was wrong. You are strong enough to make the hard decisions.'

Byren said nothing. Was he as hard as his father, Rolen the Implacable? He would not have thought it. He never wanted to have to make this kind of decision again. Elina might understand, but would she ever forgive him?

Curse Palatyne. Curse his pet Power-workers.

That reminded him of his experiences playing Duelling Kingdoms. 'Be on your guard, Orrie, Palatyne has two renegade Power-workers with him, a barbaric Utlander and a noble called Dunstany. They may sense your Affinity and try to use it against us.'

'You knew?' Orrade stared at him. 'How long –'

Byren shrugged. 'I suspected almost from the start.'

Orrade sank onto a barrel, his shoulders hunched. 'At first I thought I was imagining it. But then it began to add up. I had a vision of a manticore with Cobalt's head before we were attacked by them, but it was so bizarre I thought I must be going mad. If I hadn't refused to believe it, I could have warned you. I should have warned you about Rejulas.' He lifted a tortured face to Byren. 'While we were hiding in the barn at Narrowneck I had a nightmare... a cockatrice entered the yard and spat poison at the barn door, setting it alight. I refused to admit –'

'Forget it.' Byren shrugged.

Orrade sprang to his feet, confronting him. 'Why don't you hate me? Why don't you denounce me?'

Byren laughed. 'You're a lover of men. If that didn't worry me, why should your Affinity worry me?'

Orrade tensed as if he'd been hit, then he went strangely silent.

Just when Byren was about to demand what was wrong, Orrade retreated to sit on his barrel, contained, quiet and... seething. He said nothing while the minutes crept by. The cold settled over them. Meeting here had been a good idea. The ice slabs lining the walls stopped their voices from travelling, but now the chill crept into their bones.

Byren looked away from his friend. He didn't see why he should apologise to Orrade for speaking the truth.

A cold half-hour later the cook came to report that the Merofynian servants were locked in the wine cellar and all of their people were out of the keep, fleeing into the forest. 'There are two guards at the door of the blue chamber, one of Palatyne's men and one of Rejulas's.' Her eyes glinted. 'I don't think Palatyne trusts the Cockatrice warlord or vice versa!'

Byren grinned and slapped his thighs to get his blood moving. 'Thank you, may the goddess be with you. Give Winterfall the signal. It's time to light the beacon.'

She bustled away, as efficient in battle as she had always been in the kitchen.

'Rejulas first?' Orrade asked, coming to his feet stiffly. He stretched and stamped his boots.

Or Lence? Byren wondered. At least he could kill the Cockatrice warlord with a clean conscience. But he had to try to convince Lence. 'My brother first.'

They slipped out of the cold-cellar and took the servants' stairs up the back way to the long corridor which led to the best bedchambers. To their left was the lord's bedchamber and opposite it, the royal chamber where Byren's parents stayed when visiting. These opened onto the mezzanine balcony which overlooked the great hall. To their right were the rest of the bedchambers.

Byren peered around the lintel to the right. Lit by

a single lamp, two warriors stood at the entrance to the blue chamber, giving substance to the fiction that Lence was a captive. If it was fiction.

The cook was right, one guard wore the amfina surcoat and the other, the cockatrice cloak.

Byren made a soft noise in his throat. Both warriors stiffened. He made the same noise again. They looked at each other. Finally Rejulas's man headed towards the dark stair well, his boots making soft thuds on the polished wood.

Orrade waited, knife ready. Byren pinned the man's arms as soon as he stepped into the stair well, covering his mouth. Orrade drove the knife up under his ribs, straight into his heart. Byren eased the body to the floor, even as the life left him.

They waited. But Palatyne's man was not going to risk his life to investigate the Cockatrice warrior's fate. Instead, he moved towards the overlord's door, passing on the far side of the dark stairwell opening.

Byren lifted his knife, aimed and threw. The man had time only to register surprise before the knife took him in the throat. Though Byren darted out across the hall to catch him, he hit the floor with a soft thud.

Byren retrieved his knife, wiped it and hurried to the door of the blue chamber. Orrade did not follow.

He glanced over his shoulder to see his friend standing in the hall, torn.

'Go, save her,' Byren whispered. Elina would think he had failed her again, but he had to see Lence.

Orrade's expression cleared. 'Don't be misled by Lence's lies. I believe he's already tried to kill you once.'

Had he? Byren wondered. Or had it been a slip

of the tongue? After all, how could Cobalt have led the manticores to their camp, when it was almost certain he had no Affinity?

Byren thrust the door open.

Lence turned, shielding a flickering candle. He stood unarmed.

'Byren?' His gaze flicked to the naked sword blade and back to his face. 'You're free.'

Byren's shoulders relaxed and his sword tip dipped a fraction. 'Lence, you mustn't believe the things Cobalt said. I haven't betrayed you. The rings were for mother and father's Jubilee. The poem was for Elina, not Orrie.'

His twin shrugged. 'He said you'd say that.'

Byren closed his eyes in frustration.

A mistake. When he opened them Lence had snatched the poker from the fire place. The end glowed menacingly as he raised it between them.

'If you'd only listen, Lence,' Byren pleaded.

His twin's gaze flickered behind Byren. A floor board creaked.

Byren spun just in time to side-step Rejulas's attempt to run him through.

Something hard struck the back of Byren's head, making him stagger and drop to one knee. Lence had hit him? He couldn't believe it.

Rejulas turned his blade, swinging it for Byren's throat. Byren fumbled as he lifted his sword to deflect the strike.

'No!' Lence diverted the stroke so that the blade sang as it slid down the length of the poker.

'Why not?' Rejulas snarled.

Byren lurched to his feet, backing away until

the fireplace was behind him. His sword came up between them. Rejulas was his enemy but Lence had saved his life. Why?

'Thought better of it. Can't risk giving the alarm,' Orrade said as he padded into the chamber. On seeing Byren's predicament he froze, weapon ready.

'Shut the door,' Lence ordered. 'We don't want those Merofynian lordlings overhearing.'

Byren's heart soared with hope.

Rejulas cursed softly as Orrade closed the door.

'Byren?' Orrade whispered. 'What's going on here?'

'Yes, Lence?' Byren echoed. 'What's going on?'

'I'm claiming my birthright,' his twin explained. 'Using the Merofynian army as my tool.'

Byren blinked. 'Lence, Merofynia has invaded Rolencia. Unless we stop this overlord everything we hold dear is going to be destroyed, everyone we love is going to die. Palatyne –'

'I'm not Palatyne's captive.' Lence almost looked sorry for Byren. He nodded to the Cockatrice warlord. 'I'm Rejulas's captive, but only for as long as it suits me. We've hatched a plan, Rejulas and I.'

No one lowered their swords. Rejulas edged closer to Lence so that he confronted Orrade. 'Tell them, kingsheir.'

'I have it on good authority that the Merofynians despise their king and fear his overlord,' Lence said softly, reasonably. 'They were planning to invade Rolencia so –'

'They made overtures to me,' Rejulas laughed. 'Expected me to betray Rolencia.'

'Merofynia is ripe for invasion. I know for a fact

that the people would welcome Queen Myrella's heir,' Lence continued, his voice gathering strength. 'When Father refused to even consider invading –'

'Did you tell him they were massing an army, that they'd approached the warlord of Cockatrice Spar?' Byren demanded.

'We didn't know that at first.' Lence nodded to the warlord. 'Rejulas –'

'I was sitting in the Three Swans, having been rejected by your vixen of a sister, thinking I'd be better off accepting Palatyne's offer, when Lence came in,' Rejulas explained. 'And I was just angry enough to tell him so!'

'Luckily, Illien was with me,' Lence said. 'He saw how we could use Palatyne against his own king. We're going to let the Merofynian army wear itself down taking Rolencia. Then Rejulas will reveal his true loyalty by releasing me, and together we will crush the crippled Merofynians and take back what should have been mine,' Lence revealed, scorn threading his voice as he went on. 'And you, you came in so slobbering drunk you did not see any of this!'

Byren closed his eyes, remembering the scrap of paper with its hastily drawn map and army movements. He had thought Lence was planning how to defend Rolencia, when he had really been planning how to defeat their father!

He couldn't believe it. 'I don't –'

'That's why you will never be king,' Lence told him. 'All along, everyone thought you were the clever one and I was second best –'

'That's not true!' Byren protested.

'But you're not clever in the ways that matter,'

Lence ignored him. 'I set this up. I'll have the crowns of both Rolencia and Merofynia as their saviour and rightful ruler –'

'What of Father?' Byren protested. 'He's the rightful ruler of Rolencia.'

'Father...' Lence's voice faltered. 'He was a great king once, but he's been making bad decisions – giving up the right to rule Merofynia, refusing to invade, forcing me to marry this Merofynian cow, not seeing what you really are...'

Byren's heart faltered as Lence fell silent, staring at him, seeing things Byren could not.

'I'm not a Servant of Palos, Lence,' he whispered, mouth almost too dry to talk. 'Believe me, there is no conspiracy.'

'Of course you'd say that. Illien warned me to harden my heart against you of all people.' Lence's eyes glistened with tears but underneath anger grew. 'You –'

'What of Rejulas?' Orrade asked suddenly, gesturing with his sword to the warlord. 'What do you get out of this trickery, warlord?'

Rejulas nodded to Lence. 'My king has promised me Piro and overlordship of all the spars as a reward for loyalty.'

'Loyalty?' Byren snorted.

'That will never work,' Orrade argued, edging one step closer to Byren. 'The spars will never accept –'

'They will send their best warriors to support King Rolen. There'll be nothing but the old and children left, no one to object to me as overlord.' Rejulas smiled. 'Palatyne employed a similar ploy to become overlord of Merofynia's spars.'

'In fifteen or twenty years the spars will grow a new crop of warriors. They'll revolt,' Byren insisted. 'Lence, how can you turn on Father like this?'

'Father had his chance. He threw it away. He could have been King Rolen the Great, ruler of the known world!'

Byren shook his head.

'Illien was right.' Lence lifted the poker tip. 'He said you did not have the breadth of vision to see.'

'Illien?' Byren felt sick to his stomach. Illien had long since ceased to be the youth he admired and become Cobalt, the bane of his life. 'What's his reward for advising you?'

'He'll be my Grand Vizier. I'll need someone to govern Merofynia in my absence.'

'And what of Ostron Isle?' Orrade mocked. 'Do they figure in your plans?'

'Of course.' Lence failed to see the mockery. 'Ostron Isle will pay me homage as their High King, as will the city states of the Snow Bridge. They dare not resist. I will be King Lence the Great.' He focused on Byren. 'I'm only completing what King Rolence the First began.'

Byren swallowed. Lence and his conspirators had expanded the game of Duelling Kingdoms to carve up the world. They were mad. 'What of Mother and Fyn?'

'Fyn will be abbot and support me, if he knows what's good for him,' Lence said. 'As for Mother, she denied me Merofynia. She only ever had eyes for you. Don't deny it!' He overrode Byren's objection. 'As for you –'

'What of Elina, Lence?' Orrade asked quickly,

edging another step closer to Byren, who realised he was manoeuvering so they could protect each other's backs. 'My sister is innocent of any wrongdoing. Palatyne has her right now. You don't want him raping her. With your influence you could suggest she retire to Sylion Abbey. She'd be safe there.'

Lence tilted his head, giving this some thought. 'No... she's been too arrogant. If Palatyne swives her she'll be doubly grateful when I come to her rescue.'

Molten fury poured into the pit of Byren's stomach racing up his spine into his brain, clouding his vision, making it hard to breathe.

'I'm not a love-blinded fool like you,' Lence told him. 'She's been leading us both on, playing us off against each other for years.'

'That's not true.' Byren's hand tightened on his sword hilt.

'Enough, Lence,' Rejulas snapped. 'Kill them before the Merofynians wake.'

Suiting his actions to his words, Rejulas leapt for Orrade with a strike that should have skipped over his blade and plunged straight through his throat, but Orrade deflected and side-stepped neatly. They eyed each other warily.

Byren searched Lence's face. How had his twin grown into this stranger?

'I know I have to kill you, brother,' Lence grimaced. 'But who would have thought it would be so hard?'

'It doesn't have to be this way,' Byren whispered. He knew that as soon as Orrade and Rejulas struck out at each other the ring of steel on steel would bring the Merofynians running. 'We can still escape, return to father and defeat Merofynia.'

Lence shook his head as though Byren was a foolish child.

Meanwhile, Orrade circled Rejulas, both stepping as light as cats, deadly as manticores about to strike.

'Why do you want Piro?' Orrade taunted Rejulas. 'She's already turned you down once!'

The Cockatrice warlord grinned, a cruel smile lighting his handsome face. 'I want her because I intend to make her sorry.'

'You'll be the one who's sorry,' Orrade countered. 'Or didn't Lence tell you about her Affinity?'

Rejulas's gaze flew to Lence. 'Aff –'

In that instant, Orrade lunged, running him through. Rejulas dropped his sword. Sagging to his knees, he stared up at Orrade in disbelief.

'Piro would have been the death of you,' Orrade told him. Then he pulled his blade free and turned to Byren. 'I had to kill him quietly.'

Byren grinned and shook his head. 'You –'

Lence scooped up the blade Rejulas had dropped, lunging for Orrade's belly. Only his quick reflexes saved Orrade. On the back foot, he retreated. Byren darted around behind Lence, kicked his knee out from under him and disarmed him as he fell. Lence's sword skittered away across the floor.

Orrade stamped on it, flicked his boot under the hilt and kicked it up, catching it in mid-air. It was a trick they'd practised when they were Garzik's age.

On his knees, Lence stared up at Byren.

'Kill him,' Orrade urged. 'Now.'

'I can't.' Byren would not prove the seer right.

'Then I will.' Orrade strode forwards.

'No!' Byren reversed his sword, bringing the pommel against his twin's head. Lence slumped to the floor.

'You should cut his throat,' Orrade whispered.

'If I was the sort of person to give up on him, I would have given up on you by now,' Byren muttered.

Orrade's mouth dropped open.

A muffled shriek of despair came from the next room, the Royal Chamber.

'Elina!' Byren shoved past Orrade, running for the door.

Byren cursed himself for delaying so long. What horrible act was Palatyne committing on Elina?

He thrust the door open and stopped. Orrade barrelled into him. By the light of two tall stands holding lamps on each side of the bed, Palatyne held Elina, his knife under her chin. Naked, her pale skin gleamed through hip-length black hair and tears glittered on her cheeks, but her eyes held a fury that would never surrender.

Palatyne appeared to be naked but for the knife. 'Ah. So that was your plan, vixen!'

'My plan was to slit your throat!' she hissed. 'But you sleep like a cat.'

'Amfinas never truly sleep, one head is always awake,' Palatyne told her.

'But you are only a man,' Byren countered.

'You know nothing of Power-workers!' Palatyne spat.

Elina whimpered as he pressed the blade into her flesh. A single trickle of blood ran down her slender throat, over the rise of her breast.

Byren's mouth went dry with fear. 'You won't hurt

her.'

'Why not? I've already had her.'

'Release Elina and we may let you live,' Byren bluffed. 'My men are already lighting the warning beacon. King Rolen will be here by dawn with more than enough warriors to crush your advance party.'

'King Rolen is in Rolenhold waiting for a signal and that won't come. I destroyed the beacon fire.' Palatyne countered. 'Drop your weapons.'

Orrade cursed under his breath.

'No!' Elina cried. She elbowed Palatyne in the ribs, ducked under his arm and leapt across the bed, long hair flying. Before anyone could move she'd grabbed the lamp, tipping it so that burning oil flew in an arc across the bed. Drops hit Palatyne's naked shoulder, neck and face. He screamed, beating at the stinging spots. Flames licked up the velvet bed curtains, across the sheets and covers.

The door from the hallway swung open. Lord Dunstany stood there, his staff in one hand, a robe hastily thrown over his nakedness. Merofynian lordlings jostled behind him, frightened, fascinated. The Utland Power-worker shoved through them, cursing fluently.

'Kill them!' Palatyne roared.

Elina gave a cry of despair and flung the other doors open, running onto the mezzanine balcony.

'Elina, no,' Byren called, fearing she meant to jump to her death. With warriors blocking the corridor she would be trapped, unable to reach the stairs. He cast one glance to Palatyne, who was hastily dragging on his breeches, and ran after her.

'We'll be trapped.' Orrade ran at his side, sword

in hand.

But Elina had already swung one long leg over the balcony. As Byren watched she grabbed the embroidered emblem and lowered herself over the drop.

'Clever girl!' Orrade said, following her.

Byren heard footsteps, turned, blocked Palatyne's attack and avoided another stroke from one of three lordlings who jostled to kill him. The nearest died on the edge of Byren's blade, but even as he fell another stepped into his place.

Without looking, Byren placed his left hand on the rail and leapt over, reaching for the emblem. It screeched as it tore, falling with him. But it was enough to absorb his momentum and Orrade helped steady him as he landed on the floor below, only a body length from the dove aviary. He had a glimpse of dead birds amidst feathers and blood as Elina hugged him. Wearing Orrade's shirt, which revealed her long thighs, she looked every bit the Old Dove's warrior daughter. Byren hugged her fiercely, wondering if she would still speak to him if Orrade ever revealed how they'd delayed rescuing her.

'Hurry,' Orrade urged, pulling them towards the far doors and the terrace. 'They'll be down the stairs in a moment.'

Byren backed up with Elina at his side. 'You two get out. I'll hold them. I'll meet you at the water-wheel.'

'We still need to light a warning beacon,' Elina protested. Pulling away from him, she ran to the fireplace and stood on tiptoe to grab the firestone. Before Byren could stop her, she ran to the other stand and tossed the first firestone up to join its mate. Byren had never seen two firestones meet. They exploded in a ball of blue-white fire. The wall hangings burst into flames, hungrily racing up to the vaulted ceiling above.

The force of it flung Elina back off her feet. Byren and Orrade ran to her, dragging her to safety. Byren could feel the heat beating on him from three body lengths away.

'Elina, are you all right?' Byren turned her hands over to reveal her burnt palms. 'Oh, Lina.'

She managed a smile.

'Here they come,' Orrade warned.

Byren looked up to see Palatyne, the Utlander and his warriors race through the door under the mezzanine into the great hall. He caught Elina by the arm, hauling her to her feet and thrust her towards Orrade. 'Take her. Get out.'

But when they turned to face the great doors he saw the Merofynian servants had escaped the wine cellar and cut them off.

'The cook should have cut their throats,' Orrade whispered.

Seeing their predicament, Palatyne laughed and lowered his sword. 'Surrender and I'll let the girl live.'

'First man to come within range of my sword dies!' Byren raised the sword tip.

'Stay back. I have sent for archers, Overlord Palatyne,' Lord Dunstany called from the balcony above.

Byren cursed.

Palatyne smiled. 'Work your power on them. First one to make them suffer earns my gratitude.'

Orrade cursed under his breath. Byren gripped his

sword tighter, ready for anything.

There was a moment's tense silence as both Power-workers sent out mental probes.

'Power-working is a lot like metal working, overlord. A smithy can't fashion a sword from thin air,' Lord Dunstany said. 'These three are without Affinity so there's nothing for me to work with.'

'Not so, Dunstany, I sense something,' the Utlander insisted.

'By all means expend your power on a hopeless task. It will only make me stronger,' Dunstany urged.

The Utlander glared at him.

'Byren, I think I can bluff the perfumed parasites between us and the door,' Orrade whispered. 'Those servants'll run at the first sight of blood.'

'Well, Dunstany?' Palatyne demanded.

'The archers will be here soon.'

'Useless Power-workers,' Palatyne swore. A nasty slow smile spread across his face and he left the mezzanine calling, 'Bring me the kingsheir.'

'What's he doing?' Elina whispered as they waited.

Byren did not know. But he suspected he would not like it.

In no time at all, the overlord strode into the hall as his men marched Lence over to stand in front of Palatyne. He looked groggy. There was blood on his shirt from the blow Byren had delivered to the back of his head.

'Give him your sword.' Palatyne gestured to one of the lordlings.

Lence lifted the weapon, blinking fiercely to clear

his head.

'Now prove your worth, kingsheir. Kill them or die with them!'

'No, Lence,' Elina pleaded.

Byren's mouth went dry as his twin turned and strode towards him. He read determination in Lence's eyes.

No regret. No doubt. No last-minute signal.

Orrade swore. 'You should've killed him when you had the chance, Byren.'

'So, I'm a fool,' Byren muttered bitterly. 'The moment he attacks, charge the servants. Get Elina out of here.'

'Give me your hunting knife, Byren,' Elina ordered. 'It's long enough for me to use as a sword.'

He handed it over and wiped his palm on his thigh, sweating from the heat. Already the wooden panels were well ablaze.

Byren focused on Lence as his brother brought his sword around for a huge, two-handed swing. Lence always had preferred strength to subtlety, relying on his size to carry the encounter.

Byren ducked and deflected, but did not follow through.

'Fight me!' Lence roared. His blade leapt in an arc for Byren's throat.

Again, he deflected, staggering back two steps. He could hear Orrade yelling as he charged the servants. His sword arm throbbed with the impact of Lence's strike. Using his twin's momentum, Byren took his sword down and around in a classic deflection arc. The blades sang as they parted.

'Join me, Lence. Don't die a traitor.'

'You think you can better me?' Fast as a viper, Lence snatched a fallen chair, throwing it at Byren.

Dodging the chair, he lost his balance and went down on one knee. Lence bore down on him.

Byren knew he had waited too long. If he wanted to live he would have to prove the seer, right but he didn't want to kill his twin.

Something darted in front of him, taking the impact of Lence's strike. Fine black hair brushed his face, long legs. Blood on white linen.

'Nooo!' Lence cried.

Arms too weak to fully divert the blow, burnt palms unable to properly grasp the knife hilt, Elina dropped the hunting knife and buckled around the sword which impaled her.

Lence dropped to his knees. Byren caught Elina as she crumpled.

'Lina...' Lence whispered.

She clutched Byren's arm, eyes fierce. 'Burn Dovecote, burn them all, promise!'

He nodded. A great gout of blood burst from her lips and the life left her.

No. Not yet. Not ever. Byren lifted his face to Lence, who stared at Elina, stunned.

'I'm waiting, kingsheir,' Palatyne goaded. 'Where are those archers, Dunstany?'

'Delayed, it seems,' he said.

Lence stood stiffly, pulling his borrowed sword from Elina's body.

Byren came slowly to his feet, lifting his own sword.

The ring of metal on metal told him Orrade was occupied with the servants, as yet unaware of Elina's death.

Lence adjusted his grip on the blade. 'Down, Byren.'

The leogryf leapt all over again. Byren dropped. With a roar Lence charged past him, bearing down on the servants who battled Orrade. They took one look at him and dropped their makeshift weapons to flee.

Byren rolled to his feet, charging after Lence, who threw his weight behind the door, dragging it open.

'Go!' Lence shoved Orrade through, caught Byren's vest and shoved him as well. 'Go. I'll hold them. Seal the doors. Let the hall be our funeral pyre!'

Before Byren could protest, the door closed in his face and he heard the great bar drop.

'Elina!' Orrade tried to prise his sword in the crack between the doors, to lift the bar. 'Byren, she's still in there.'

'She's dead, Orrie. Died in my arms.' He indicated the blood down his vest. 'Her last wish was to burn the hall and everyone in it!'

'No. She can't be dead. She was right behind me.'

Byren did not answer. He ran to the first of the great bronze foenixes and judged the angle. Getting his shoulder under the bird's belly he shoved. It rocked on its base. He shoved again. The bronze was not solid, but still it was heavy. With a resounding thump it toppled, its head hitting the doors. The contents of its charcoal brazier spilled onto the ground.

'Watch it!' Orrade shouted, dodging burning coals.

Byren ran to the other bronze.

'What're you doing?' Orrade demanded.

'Wedging the doors closed so they can't escape the hall,' Byren panted.

'They can still get out the windows.'

'If they can get to them,' Byren agreed. 'Shut up and help.'

Orrade added his wiry strength. The bird toppled and hit the other door. More coals fell to the stones.

Byren jumped the bird's legs and ran to where Lord Dovecote was still impaled. Kicking the coals towards the old man's robes, he knelt and blew on them. They flared bright, greedy little flames licking up the cloth.

Orrade stared, panting. 'Father...'

'He would've wanted it this way,' Byren said.

Orrade nodded as he brushed tears from his face. 'And Lence?'

'Saved our lives. He's holding them back even now. Come on. Garzik and Winterfall will be waiting at the water-wheel.' He hoped. But he'd sent them to light a beacon which had already been destroyed, if Palatyne could be believed.

As they ran Byren glanced back over his shoulder. Flames leapt from the upper windows of the hall where the hangings had been burning strongly. Byren was not convinced everyone would burn, but the hall would and it would be their warning beacon.

Fierce tears stung his eyes.

Elina would be satisfied.

Chapter Thirty-One

BELOW THEM, DOWN around the frozen lake, Doveton burned fiercely. Rejulas's warriors ran about trying to drag friends and mounts from burning buildings. Avoiding the chaos, Byren and Orrade ran parallel to the shore towards the forest. It was a clear night. The stars formed an effervescent froth above them, strong enough to cast shadows on the snow.

They ran until the fires behind them were blotted out by the snow-covered evergreens, until they reached the dark building of the water-wheel, and there they stopped to catch their breath.

'Elina was right behind me,' Orrade panted. 'How –'

'Byren Kingson?' a voice piped up.

'Rifkin?' Byren answered softly.

'We're over here.'

They ran around the far side of the building to find a handful of people huddled near the frozen water-wheel.

'Garzik, are you there? ' Byren called. 'Winterfall?'

'He's not here,' Rifkin said. 'None of them are.'

'Didn't make it down from the tower,' the cook said. 'I waited as long as I could, but the town started burning.'

Orrade dropped to his knees in the snow, dry-retching.

'They may still get away,' little Rifkin insisted.

'Not Garzik, too,' Byren whispered.

The cook looked a question at him.

'Elina...' Byren could not go on.

Rifkin burst into the tears. The cook and her companions wailed, covering their mouths to stifle the sound.

Byren dropped down beside Orrade, one hand going to his back. 'Orrie...'

His friend pushed his hand away, rubbed clean snow on his face and straightened up. Byren stood up, suddenly tired.

The cook wiped her face and retrieved two travelling bags, the occasional sob still escaping her. 'Here's your packs. There's food for several days, some clothes and...' She could not go on.

Byren grunted his thanks, as she shoved the pack into his arms. He noticed two more and felt the loss of Garzik and Elina, sharp as a knife wound.

'We have to get out of here,' the cook said.

She was right. Byren focused. 'Orrie, listen to me. You must lead the servants and townspeople into the Divide. I still have to go the abbey.'

Orrade came to his feet with a nod. He turned to the Cook. 'Go, take the others. I'll catch up.'

She herded them away, taking the two spare packs, symbols of silent accusation. Byren felt sick to his stomach.

Orrade stepped in front of him. 'I'm not like Lence. I'd give my life for you. He betrayed you over and over. How could you compare me to him?'

Byren blinked.

'You said if you'd given up on Lence, you would have given up on me long ago. But I'm not like him. I'd never betray you!'

'He didn't betray me, not in the end.' Byren swallowed. He had proved the seer wrong about that at least. He had not killed his brother. 'Lence held the door so we could get away. He died to save us.'

Orrade said nothing.

'Orrie?' Byren whispered.

Orrade shook his head.

'Lord Dovecote?' the cook called softly as she scurried back. 'Merofynians are coming.'

'I'll be right there.'

'Yes, m'lord.'

Realisation hit Byren. Orrade was Lord of Dovecote now and, as for him, he was kingsheir. If there was anything left after this... if Rolencia survived.

He had to get to the abbey and enlist their aid. Somehow he had to convince his father that Cobalt was a traitor of the worst kind. But all he could think of was how he had alienated his best friend.

'Orrie, I –'

'Go, do what you have to do.' Orrade turned and walked off.

Byren fought the urge to go after him. Instead, he strapped on the skates the cook had provided, silently thanking her foresight.

If he skated night and day without rest, he would be at the abbey in two days and return to Rolenhold two days after that. He had to deliver terrible news. Lence was dead and he was kingsheir, whether he wanted the honour or not. Only by bringing the abbey warriors could Byren convince his father of his loyalty.

He set off.